PR 9199. T99

11013

Closer
to
the
Sun

Closer
to
the
Sun

GEORGE JOHNSTON

William Morrow & Company
New York

Contents

Book III—Fegel

It must have been observed, by many a peripatetic philosopher, that Nature has set up, by her own unquestionable authority, certain boundaries and fences to circumscribe the discontent of man; she has effected her purpose in the quietest and easiest manner by laying him under almost insuperable obligations to work out his ease, and to sustain his sufferings at home. . . . It will always follow hence that the balance of sentimental commerce is always against the expatriated adventurer; he must buy what he has little occasion for, at their own price—his conversation will seldom be taken in exchange for theirs without a large discount—and this, by the by, eternally driving him into the hands of more equitable brokers, for such conversation as he can find it requires no great spirit of divination to guess at his party.

LAURENCE STERNE
A Sentimental Journey

For
Ketty Christopoulos

BOOK I

Meredith

I

SILENOS

. . . approaching at three hours easy sail from the mainland, the aspect is forbidding, with two conical rock peaks, that to the east foreshortened, elevated above barren lava slopes and untimbered land. The northern harbour provides deep and sheltered anchorage at all seasons; and the inhabitants, although of poor and lowly situation, are of good heart and countenance.

18TH CENTURY JOURNAL

THE MOST important man on the island of Silenos was Dionysios, the public garbage collector.

In the season between Carnival and Easter the bank manager Stathis Vlikos surpassed him in importance, for it was then that he made the annual advances of money to the sponge-boat captains, to pay crews and divers and to victual their ships for the cruise to Africa. But Easter had passed and with it this temporary ascendancy of the banker's. Except to a few friends—for he was not a Sileniot, but a man from Euboea, and he had few friends—and to Captain Andreas of the *Twelve Apostles*, he had become just a more resplendent figure added to the groups around the *tavli* boards in the big Katraikis coffeehouse.

The garbage man, on the other hand, was important every day of the year to one section of the town or another. For without his high-wheeled cart and his string of basket-burdened donkeys, and, most important of all, his goodwill, how was the rubbish of the town to be carted away in conformity with the proclaimed and printed order of Lieutenant Fotis, the police commandant, that streets, walls, and courtyards should be kept clean and all houses in a state of reputable whitewash? Dionysios was a heavy drinker of resinated wine and at times unreliable, but he was nearing eighty and he worked long hours in heat or cold, and these facts were taken into account.

Dionysios then was up and spitting out phlegm well before the sun came out of the sea, as it did at this time of year just over the little satellite island of Paralia, where a tiny church of Saint Nicholas, scarcely bigger than a privy, was kept in a state of spotless whitewash by a fisherman's wife. The garbage man began the day as he always did. He sopped a crust of dark bread in well water, for there were no teeth in his tannin-dark gums, and he sucked on the sweet mush while he harnessed the big black mule to his battered cart, mumbling all the time to the animal or blubbering and whistling to the waiting donkeys. Every now and then he would interrupt this to indulge in some monotonous cursing of his still-sleeping wife, but he did this without much conviction. Leaving the house he hawked and spat a big gobbet against the lintel for the luck of the day, then led the mule slow-footed and the big wheels rumbling and the donkeys cat-treading down the dark slanting cobbles to the harbour to collect the shop garbage before it was picked over and scattered by the scavenging cats.

The port, when he came out of the side lane into its unawakened emptiness, was dark and still, with the green harbour light on the mole and the red beacon on the eastern headland behaving as they had behaved at nightfall on the day before, jabbing splintered jaggedy darts of brightness into water that looked for all the world like thick tar. Looking seaward, the only other lights visible were scattered glowing coals very far away where the mainland charcoal kilns were smouldering.

On the deserted quay the cart wheels had a disconsolate ring, hollow and sad, like the cry of a gull. It was a sound that made the surrounding emptiness seem emptier, so that there was consolation in the fitful light that touched the dew-damp flagstones outside the Constantinos bakehouse where the baker and his son were still firing the big furnace with armfuls of pine-brush; and the garbage man turned the mule towards this comforting beam, for next door to the bakehouse a tube-light hung askew and blue above the door of the Katraikis coffeehouse, which stayed open all night because of late *tavli* players and the chance of a steamer being delayed or a caïque putting in and for early fishermen, and where Nicholas the all-night waiter would generally fix for Dionysios a deep-sweet coffee and a mouthful of cognac the width of a thumb. In this lifeless and indeterminate time, the coffeehouse was deserted, and the waiter Nicholas in his long white apron slept at the third table from the door with his head buried in his arms.

The light reflected off bare boards and cold marble tabletops seemed to have a smell of aniseed and sawdust.

Hearing the wheels of the garbage cart, the waiter stirred and stretched, and when Dionysios began meaningly to clatter the rubbish cans outside he shuffled to the door and saw that the town was awakening.

He saw this, as it were, only out of the corner of his mind. He saw it perhaps as a door opening or a figure moving or somebody spitting or the arm of the garbage man scooping and swinging. It may even have been more a taste in his mouth and a stinging in his eyes than any visual image of the island dissolving and disintegrating into the individual and separate components of its awakening.

It was not until the sun rose in a sudden quick glinting flick above the ragged edge of the spur leading to the truncated peak known as the High Lady, and a tumble of light flooded through the olive groves between this landmark and the still higher summit called the Prophet's Peak, that the island of Silenos was seen to be sealed within a pearl-like globe of sea-mist, so that it appeared not to be related in any way at all to a real thing of geography. The sun, having created substance out of darkness, allowed it to dissolve into nothing at all but a bell of light.

Neither Nicholas the waiter nor Dionysios the garbage man was aware of this, of course—it would need a quick, all-encompassing eye and a mind alert to poetry to appreciate the symbolic image of the solitude and isolation of Silenos—and in any case the picture changed as the sea-mist gradually lifted and the town began to quicken, roused some of it by the rough grinding turn of the cart wheels as Dionysios pressed his menial round with the cognac warm across the tight part of his spleen, or by early coughings and urinations, or by the variant exigent demands of a day's beginning.

In almost no time at all the sea was blue as blue and jumping with dazzling little flecks of light, so that the flashing of the red and green beacons was no longer to be made out, and the distant kilns of the charcoal-burners, all evidence of which had vanished for a time behind the sea-mist, had reappeared as little woolly drifts of smoke against the mainland mountains, and a slow pausing movement had begun to develop all around the port.

Up near the post office beneath the faded *Taxydromèion* sign a group of a dozen men strolled and talked, mostly about weather and food and illness. All of them were scratching where their underwear prickled. Some were coughing also, but all were scratching. Big Andrea had taken the canvas covers off his fruit stalls and was picking over the bad loquats and the plums. It was always the first thing he did after he had coiled the lashings back—picking off the bad apples, the bad grapes, the bad pomegranates, depending on the season. The rejected fruit he always put into a big frayed basket to feed his donkey and his goats. From the Constantinos bakehouse a warm smell of bread had lifted on the air, with a tang of coffee from next door, and from the boatbuilder's shed around the corner a jack-plane had begun sweetly to chirrup.

Yet the quickening of all the town, through the narrow lanes and around the slaughterhouse above the sea and at the quay where the market boats were mooring and at the coffeehouses and barber shops, was very real and altogether different from the nightbred fantasies which had troubled David Meredith in his house by the well above the church of the Virgin.

The house was one of only five other houses on the island which were owned by foreigners, yet nothing in particular, at least from the outside, distinguished it from any other. It was square and white and uncompromising, and an accident of placement and proportion made it beautiful.

At some time in the middle of night David Meredith had been aroused by a rattling scurry of wind and rain which had banged shutters and scraped the budding branches of the peach-tree against the window-panes and set all the neighbouring cockerels crowing. He awakened, as for many nights now he had awakened, to an immediate sense of uneasiness which he found difficult to explain. His wife Kate slept beside him undisturbed. Her left arm was thrown across the pillow above her head, where it rested upon a tumble of loose spread tawny hair, and her breathing was scarcely audible. She had not stirred to the shuddering batter of the wind. Now the gusts had grown milder, but the old house still creaked a little, although not enough to provide reason for his disquiet. It was, he decided finally, the crowing of the cocks again.

For as long as he could remember, right back to his childhood, he had had an odd terror of the sound of cocks crowing in the darkness. (It was connected somehow with a night of long ago, a night that had had a queer colour and texture, as if there was something across the surface of it, like the shine of a wet slate, and something embedded in it that was rich and deep and resembled the stone in the middle of his grandmother's big brooch: a particular quality of the night that lasted only briefly, then faded and grew dull, exactly like a slate drying. . . .)

As he moved his arm stiffly to reach for cigarettes, his wife began to breathe more heavily and moved her legs beneath the blanket and turned away from him, her fingers plucking vaguely at the sheet, then falling softly against her pretty, half-exposed breast. For a long moment he looked at her. He had an impulse to waken her. It was an impulse that was strong and warm and related to the movement of her legs and the disorder of her hair as much as to the shadowed delicacy of the exposed nipple upon her small smooth breast. Yet he looked at her with an odd shyness, as if she were a woman not familiar to him, and then awkwardly he arranged the sheet across her shoulder, and rose from the bed and wrapped his dressing-gown around his long naked legs.

He went thoughtfully down the stairs to the big, stone-flagged kitchen. It had a well in the corner, and bunches of garlic and onions and herbs hung from the open beams. He lit his cigarette first and then the lamp. The square-cased old ship's chronometer on the wall ticked in rhythm to the jerky circle of the second hand. It was almost five-thirty. As he made coffee he heard from two streets away the rumbling wheels of the garbage cart trundling down to the port. The wind had dropped altogether: it was a still morning, and in its quietness he could hear the tangled tinkling of the goat bells on the hills. The cocks had stopped crowing. After a time the bells began to peal from the monastery in the hills, and then from the church of the Virgin, three bells in quick, eager clamour, and the catch of sound was flung from church to church around the little town.

From the corner window he could see part of the gulf, and the distant mainland as an almost indefinable shape—an obliteration of stars more than a true shape—and he saw it as a space of dark air and water where a sea-mist was gathering as if the combings of the night were being raked away. Nothing had any real definition except the fires of the charcoal-burners which glowed along the hidden ridges like the eyes of animals.

Sipping at his coffee, he remembered how as a small boy in Australia he used to be sent away on school summer holidays to a little mixed farm in the scraggy gully country west of Ballarat, and there he would help old Pop Chinnery stack clods of earth and turf around his charcoal kilns. In Australia it was called a "kill," and they would say, "Pop Chinnery's got a kill up there in the dry paddock behind Thornton's dam," although if it was a young man talking it was more likely he would be thinking less of Pop Chinnery's "kill" than of his daughter Suzie, who was a bold, good-looking girl—the handsomest, they used to say, between Corindhap and Rokewood Junction—who had finally run away to Melbourne with a salesman for Pelaco shirts. At that time there was still a coach drawn by four horses running between Ballarat and Rokewood Junction, and they used to let him ride it on the box with the driver. He had been very miserable when Suzie Chinnery ran away, because then her father grew surly and would never let him help with the charcoal kilns, and Suzie had always made the raspberry vinegar and wonderful lemon biscuits which were kept in a tall glass jar on a high shelf in the kitchen, and she would feed him sweet condensed milk straight out of the can. And after Suzie ran away the horse coach stopped running to Rokewood Junction and an automobile took its place. . . .

He was aware without any sense of surprise that his wife was standing in the doorway, looking in at him.

She had a golden look in the lamplight, in her yellow dressing-gown, with her chestnut hair loose about her face. Again he seemed to see her with the reticent curiosity of an awakened vision that hesitates to explore beyond a certain point, as if in some way she had become different from the woman he had grown to know and he was afraid to explore this subtle unfamiliarity lest other changes might be revealed. And so he sought for the recognisable in her—the soft flow of her hair, the faint smile touching the corners of her mouth, the face strong and compassionate, and moulded on good bones, so that it had a quite distinctive beauty, even though she had last night's make-up still on, and it was smeared a little where he had kissed her clumsily in the dark after they had gone to bed. They had stayed in a tavern until late, drinking wine and talking with Conrad Fegel, and they had got home around midnight just as the town's electric supply was switched off. On Silenos electric power for the town was provided only from dusk until twelve o'clock—the harbour lights and the beacon on Paralia and some of the waterfront shops worked on an independent system—and after that there were no lights in the town except candles and oil lamps.

"You didn't sleep again?" she said, with a touch of concern. Her eyes were large, and dark in the lamplight. She had a hair-pin against her mouth like an admonition to silence.

"I slept," he lied, smiling at her. "I woke early, that's all. Around five. There was quite a little storm. Rain. Lots of wind. You didn't hear?"

"I didn't hear anything. I didn't hear you get up." She went across to the big canopied stove to light the kerosene burner. Her feet were bare. Small and bare, and cool-looking on the grey flagstones. She yawned and pushed her hair back. "I think we drank too much wine last night," she said, but it was a statement, not a reproof.

He shrugged. "We drink too much every night," he said good-naturedly. "What else is there to do?" He knew that he did drink too much. And he sensed that perhaps Kate drank a good deal more than she really wanted to just so that she could be with him—part of her striving towards . . . towards what? Well, towards being together. What else? And in fact what else *was* there to do?

She brought her coffee across to the table and said, "I got up when I saw you weren't there. I wanted to get up early, anyway. There'll be quite a lot to do. Will you work today, or not?"

"We'll see." He said it in Greek, *tha thúme,* as he almost always did, because he liked the sound of the phrase. "Well, probably not," he said on second thought. "There doesn't seem much point if I have to be down there to meet the boat."

"Are you worried?" She looked at him directly. "About his coming? Is that why you aren't sleeping?"

"Mark?" His eyes met hers for a moment, then he shook his head slowly and took some matches from the box and began to arrange them in the shapes of Greek letters on the dark tabletop.

He thought again of the vanished snow and the fires of charcoal-burners and drops of rain on window-panes and roosters crowing in the dead of night and a sea-mist forming on the face of the gulf and dim lamps distantly burning in the silence of waiting for the day to happen. Lying awake listening to the storm, and later, it had been of these things that he had been thinking. Evocative, unsettling things that had kept forcing him to wonder how it was that he had come to be living on the island of Silenos—but nothing at all to do with Mark's coming. He had been thinking of journeys—of his journey, on the surface of it, not Mark's—and yet now he could see that it was all related in a special way to the imminence of his brother's arrival. The journey perhaps had its setting-out point on that last ride back to Ballarat behind the four bay horses with old Rudge Midgeley on the coach box, flicking his long black plaited whip around their dusty rumps, and it was a journey that had taken him since then through a good many years and a whole lot of countries and had brought him finally to this little island in the Ægean Sea. But Mark would have been there too, at the beginning of the journey, on that coach setting out from Rokewood Junction after the buggy ride from Corindhap. The funny thing was that he could not see him, nor even imagine where he would have been sitting. But he would have been inside, of course, being so much older, almost grown-up, sitting inside with the shearers and the cocky-farmers and the stock-and-station agent. . . .

"Mark?" He repeated the name again and smiled slightly. "Worried? I don't think so. A little uneasy, perhaps. After all, it's been quite a few years. There will be an awkwardness, I expect. All those questions. All those do-you-remembers. And a little homily or two, no doubt. You know Mark." His smile broadened. "I can't resist the thought that the gates of the underworld are about to open to admit the messenger from the outer world."

"Or the other way round?" she suggested. "He might be coming *from* the underworld."

"Do you think so?"

"He'll be envious of you, anyway. I'm sure of that."

A wry smile twisted his mouth. *"Tha thúme,"* he said again. "It'll be interesting at any rate trying to explain to him what we're doing here, what we've been doing these last few years. He will insist on explanations, you can depend on that."

He waited to see if she had anything to say, but she had turned away to pour more coffee. He had wanted her to say something, but he was not sure what. "During the night," he said, tentatively, "I was pondering over it myself. This question of why and how. This odd pattern of yourself that keeps merging into the patterns of other people. Sometimes the other people turn out to be yourself, of course, but you scarcely realise it because you've lost the sense of recognition. And of course it's possible that Mark is really part of the pattern too, yet——"

"Well, of course he is. He must be."

"You'd think so. Although I was thinking about when I was a kid in Australia, and he didn't come into the picture at all, although he must have been there all the time, with me. Have I ever talked to you about Suzie Chinnery? Or Rudge Midgeley and the Rokewood Junction coach?"

"You've talked to me about most things, darling."

"Yes. Yes, I have, haven't I? Are the children awake?"

"They're dressing now."

"It's Jerry's turn for the bread, but I think I'll walk down and fetch it myself." He wanted very much to talk more to her, to go on exploring what he had only begun to say. But the old difficulty had come up again—a feeling that the time for discussions of that sort had passed, had vanished into some seldom visited territory that lay between them, not necessarily a hostile territory but one that had in some way been disappointing to both of them. That lay between them? Behind them, more correctly; perhaps as far behind either of them as Pop Chinnery's charcoal kiln. It was a sad thing to know this and not to be able to talk about it. And being gentle with each other—perhaps being too gentle—didn't really make up for not being willing to talk about it. There were times when he had the feeling that their relationship was tender in a sort of compulsory way—like a set bone that has been fractured and joined again . . . not quite healed yet . . . to be touched with caution for fear of inflicting pain. There were even times when he felt that they were like people *starting again* . . . and moving with a weakened certainty down the same road where once before an accident had befallen them. Yet it was really only to Kate that he could look for reassurance. If it was reassurance he was seeking. . . .

"If you're going to Constantinos," she said, "will you get the yeast for the *pizza*? And I'll want anchovies from the grocer. Or shall I get them later?"

"I can get them. I want to find that damned Dionysios, too, and ask him to cart the garbage away. He was supposed to call yesterday."

"What do you think I should do about the Arákhova rug?" she asked. "Shouldn't it go in his room?"

"Whatever you think. The living-room will look pretty bare without it, though. We mustn't let him see too much of our seamy side." He smiled at her as he took his jacket off the hook.

"Well, never mind now. I'll see how it looks." She brought her coffee across and put the cup down and laid her fingers for a moment on the back of his hand. It was a trivial gesture, of nervousness as much as of tenderness, and yet it gave him comfort. At least he could rely on her. She would want to put up a good show for his sake.

He walked down to the port slowly, as if he was keeping step to the rhythm of the awakening town. How completely familiar he was now with it all. He could close his eyes and give a name to voices heard from beyond walls, identify footsteps heard around corners. This was Dimitri the bootblack with his box banging against his crippled knee; that was Vassos the flenser, who would appear around the wine-shops later in the day dangling the tripes and trotters thát were his perquisites; here was old Alecto, stick-tapping past the church garden to fetch down her goats. From behind the frosted glass screen of the corner barber shop came the pompous sonorities of Pavlos, the headmaster of the municipal Greek school which Meredith's two sons attended. (Jerry was now in the fifth grade and for the first time taking science and physics: "*Kyrios* Pavlos," he had told his father with questioning gravity, "has a galvanometer, but he doesn't know what it is, what it does, or where to put it!") This year Jerry would have to face up to a lot of problems like that—geometry, and geography lessons that gave at least a token recognition to a world beyond the frontiers of Greece (a world which Jerry was forgetting and which had already passed altogether from the memory of his younger brother Simon), and *Kyrios* Pavlos wrestling as well as he might with the solar system and evolution and elementary biology, in relationship to the teachings and dogma of the Greek Orthodox Church, which just made it all the harder. This year for the first time Jerry would have a lot of new things to contend with. A big year for Jerry. Every year in your life there was a this year for the first time . . . Suzie Chinnery making the lemon biscuits this year for the first time, and the grizzled head of Rudge Midgeley missing for the first time this year from the crowd on the veranda of the Diggers' Rest pub at Rokewood Junction, and Pop Chinnery chasing a frightened small boy from his charcoal kilns. And now, with Mark coming, and an audit to be taken, this year for the first time. . . .

When he reached the quay he saw that the sea-mist had lifted high above the surface of the water. He could no longer see the other islands or the mainland. Like some tiny, undiscovered planet hidden in the swollen bubble of its own atmosphere, Silenos seemed to exist beyond any point of verification. He loitered by the Katraikis coffeehouse, watching the day's beginning as a consciousness of shapes falling into allotted places to form a predesigned and familiar whole. Was it the sour, lingering taste of the hangover from the night before, or the depressing effect of insomnia, or the inconclusiveness of his attempt to talk with Kate that made him aware that in the formal pattern of the picture no shape nor allotted place had been provided for him? To be familiar with it was not necessarily to be a part of it, and there was no place in it for him. Unless, he reflected, by pressing himself into it he pressed something else out— something else of himself, probably. . . .

To have pressed much else out would have left him too spare altogether, for he was a thin man, taller than average, with slightly stooping shoulders. At the age of thirty-nine, David Meredith's appearance offered a reasonably accurate balance-sheet of his experience and all the debits and the credits were marked upon him. For all his adult life he had drunk too much, smoked too heavily, lived too nervously, and travelled too hard and too far. He had not become a permanent drunkard, nor fallen a victim to lung cancer, he had never had to seek the aid of a psychiatrist, and he had been wise enough to see that vital moment in the traveller's time when the bones on the sirens' beach are as visible to the eye as the music is captivating to the ear. Yet the score of both experience and excess were marked upon him. His dark, suntanned face was already more deeply lined than the face, say, of a businessman in his middle fifties, but the erosion seemed more by a process of weathering than of worrying. He had deep-set, grey-greenish eyes, a high wide brow topped by thick brown hair which had been cut badly and combed untidily, a well-shaped mouth that was both wry and kindly, and a nose from a Bellini painting. It was a face that was intelligent and interesting rather than good-looking, and perhaps because the marks of experience and excess were about equal it had a remarkable quality and range of mobility: in the deep, carefully appraising eyes one might see compassion as well as callousness, the pity that came from experience and the impatience that was the fruit of excess: the mouth with its curious lopsided twist might be sardonic or good-humoured at will. The man's body, one could sense, had already hardened in its mould. It had been treated too carelessly for too many years: it had gained a lean, tough, sinewy virility at the cost of grace and beauty—it had been Kate who had once said, affectionately: "Well, thank heavens you'll never have a paunch: you'll live to eighty and then you'll be just a skinny, stringy old corpse, and you'll still have all your hair and you won't ever have worn glasses!"

After he had left the bakehouse he saw Captain Andreas of the *Twelve Apostles* sitting by himself inside the blue-lit, aniseed-smelling, sawdust-scattered Katraikis coffeehouse. The captain's back, tight and broad in heavy blue serge, was as usual turned away from the door. There was a tiny coffee cup in front of him and his short blunt fingers were moving domino pieces around the marble tabletop. He remembered how in the winter in the taverns at night he had talked with this strong, lonely, taciturn man about journeys and voyages, and now the sight of the man in his solitude saddened him.

The sadness stayed with him as he turned up the lane that twisted towards the well through square white houses, with the two long brown

loaves warm beneath his arm and the yeast in a twist of newspaper and
the anchovy tins stuffed into his jacket pocket. In some queer way that
he could not quite define he had a sense of communion with the master
of the *Twelve Apostles*. He picked the sesame seeds off one of the loaves
of bread and nibbled at them as he walked back home.

*   *   *

The *Twelve Apostles* was a sponge-diving boat. She was exactly nine
metres in overall length, sloop-rigged, well-kept, painted pink and lemon-
yellow with a blue strake at the waterline, and powered by an old
Mercédes diesel engine. The boat was moored at the inner hook of the
western mole, not far from the slaughterhouse. It had a high curved prow
and a deep sheer and a white-painted diving ladder folded back and
lashed to the starboard stays. At the moment when Captain Andreas was
fingering dominoes in the Katraikis coffeehouse, Dionysios was emptying
the collected garbage of the shops down a rock chute into the sea about
midway between the *Twelve Apostles* and the slaughterhouse.

The boat was moored in that particular position, out of the way of all
the normal port activities except this disposal of waterfront garbage, for
the very reason that kept its owner and master solitary at the coffee tables
looking for double-six among a scatter of black-and-white oblongs. The
Twelve Apostles was the only sponge-boat remaining in the port—the
other caïques moored everywhere around the wide bright harbour were
market boats, or for fishing, or for moving about between the islands with
pinewood or lime or cement or wine casks or resin or olives or tomato
paste or general merchandise—and it was the only craft of its kind still
harbour-bound because the bank had refused to make an advance of
money to Captain Andreas, as a reproof for two bad seasons in succession.
Without the bank's advance, Captain Andreas could neither victual his
ship for the six-months' cruise to the Libyan sponge-beds nor recruit his
crew and divers. All the rest of the fleet had gone to Africa, most of the
boats before Easter and the last of them a week before, and Captain
Andreas sat by himself day after day in the Katraikis coffeehouse, or in
one of the taverns away from the sea, and waited. People wondered why
he waited, and what he was waiting for—and no doubt Captain Andreas
wondered this also as he moved the domino pieces back and forth across
the marble table.

When he was doing this, or when he was drinking by himself in one
of the taverns, he always sat with his back to the sea.

It was because of this that he did not observe Stathis Vlikos the bank manager when he came walking down towards the Katraikis coffeehouse an hour or so later, walking high and springy on his two-tone shoes with the shine of the morning upon him. The banker had been shaved and toileted in the corner barber shop, where he had gone over the Cyprus problem with Pavlos the headmaster, and now a smell of cologne and a dusting of talcum clung to his thick neck above the collar of his new pearl-grey nylon shirt.

Captain Andreas looked up slowly, and carefully moved the domino pieces into a pile at the side of the table when he saw that the banker intended to sit with him.

Vlikos tweaked the legs of his trousers, and clapped for the waiter to remove the ash-tray and the captain's coffee cup and the stack of dominoes before he sat down.

"Well, Andreas," he said when he had finally arranged himself, "I've got you an advance."

The captain nodded without speaking, not taking his eyes off him, still waiting.

The banker sat the way he did at the big oak desk in his office behind the lattice grille. He was a bald man and he sat turned to one side, because he imagined he had a strong profile, and when he talked he would put his right elbow on the table, or the desk, with his hand up over his head and the fingers spread. When he had made his statement he would take his hand down, and a pink, flushed stain would appear on the skin of his head where his fingers had pressed. It was always very plain to see because the rest of his skin was a sort of grey-white powdery colour.

"It was not easy to convince the head office that you would be a reasonable risk," the banker said in amplification, staring obliquely above the other man's head. "Still, they have agreed."

"Why now?" Andreas asked quietly.

Vlikos shrugged. "It has taken time. They remember things. Two divers lost on last year's cruise. Nothing but third-quality sponges the year before. Business is business, Andreas."

"Do they remember the five years before that?" the captain asked carefully. "They were good years."

"They were good years," the banker agreed, and took a cigarette from his silver case without offering one to the captain. He lit the cigarette with a Ronson lighter which he took out of a small square of dark velveteen.

"There were two Thiakos boats lost off Crete on the way down," said Andreas quietly.

"That may be the reason, I agree," said the banker, and smiled. "Very likely. But you are not in the position, Andreas, to look for reasons, are you? You are lucky. I've got you the advance, haven't I? You must not expect them to overlook another bad season, though, so you had better be careful the way you pick your divers."

"There won't be much choice, will there?" said Captain Andreas. "All the boats have gone. Anyone worthwhile has been signed on and gone."

"Yes—well, that is your problem, Andreas. You can't tell me there aren't men about, with all that tramp tonnage laid up in Piræus."

"I'm talking about divers."

"Yes. I've got you the advance, Andreas. The bank would like you away before next Friday. You will bring the crew list and the victualling accounts to my office. I suggest you see Phrontis"—Phrontis was the mayor—"to begin with. He will have some men in mind, no doubt. He is looking for votes." He rose carefully and turned to the waiter. "Here!" he called, "I am paying Captain Andreas's coffee."

The two-drachma piece tinkled on the marble as he walked slowly away.

2

POSTE RESTANTE

ALONG THE WATERFRONT the people were moving now with a careless majesty, appropriate to their individual purposes, appropriate to the awakened promise of the day.

On the breakwater the fishermen with their nets unconsciously made frieze patterns against the sky, and there were other patterns of the men lifting and passing cabbages and artichokes and oranges from the mainland boats, and of two fishermen setting out for squid and octopus sculling a blue dinghy through a harbour crust of discarded vegetables and fruit parings and rotten lemons. The *Twelve Apostles* sat within this decaying flotsam like a model ship cemented into a paste of coloured papier mâché. The fisherman in the bow of the dinghy carried a trident spear.

Yet with all the formalised rhythm of the harbour to examine, it was Beth Sinclair who held Meredith's attention. So gaunt and gnarled a figure, so starkly alien, so grey-bleached and stiff and upright, like one of the mooring piles—yet as she marked her stiff pavan upon the morning she walked like a music mistress, pointing precisely autocratic toes. Perhaps somewhere along the quay, he thought, an accompanist at a hidden piano was playing, secretly and silently, a Chopin *étude* just for her.

With nothing to do but wait for the steamer, Meredith idly, admiringly, watched her slow judicial appraisal of the cabbages and broccoli and early pears, the hidden head bent in scrutiny of the piles and pyramids and cones and baskets standing row on row along the washed stone flags before the high bright prows of the market boats. Once the long skinny pointed shoe probed forward, dislodging a cauliflower. Her walking-stick prodded at it. The imperious throwback of the stringy neck in contemptuous rejection gave Meredith a stinging feeling of gratification.

The old crone Alecto also had a stick, but it tapped rather than prodded, an appendage more sinister than proud, a thing insectine, a kind of antenna that probed in a constant suspicious questing. Her thin, black-coifed, ancient figure was hunched witch-like over the tapping stick as she herded three of her goats towards the slaughterhouse. Going to the slaughterhouse the goats had yellow eyes, unsurprised, bright with life. And they had curly sacrificial horns that cried out for garlands. Alecto tapped along with them like an implacable priestess there to see that some ancient ritual of sacrifice was observed to the letter. In fact the old woman moved on an entirely material plane. She was there to see that the killing was efficient, without any extravagance of blood-letting, that each of her animals received the meat-inspector's approval in the form of a stamp in indelible ink on the still-warm flesh, and—this most important of all—that Costas the butcher did not cheat her by so much as a dram in the final weighing.

Costas himself was returning from his second trip to the slaughterhouse, mincing dreamily, ogling the women with instinctive and unimpassioned lechery. His short-stepping, dainty walk, feminine—eunuchoid perhaps if one had ever seen a eunuch—made his belly jiggle beneath his long apron. The apron, glazed with blood, flapped around his neat white ankle-socks. Around his neck and shoulders was draped the flayed carcass of a slaughtered ram, fat-white and flaccid, still warm, the head glossy-red and dripping rubies one by one on the flagstones. The blood had blurred into the sweat-stain on the back of his shirt. Between his teeth he held a white gardenia, and his lips were parted slightly in a secret, sensuous smile.

Meredith was aware of the blood and the gardenia as sometimes he was agonisingly aware of Jumping Jack the epileptic when he staggered like a jerking puppet through the summer visitors at the coffee tables, but he was disinclined to dwell on the indigenous dignities, which after all were commonplace enough, when he could consider the awesome transplantedness of Beth Sinclair.

Although it was still only spring, she had already adopted the island summer custom of throwing a floral silk kerchief over her head, which completely covered her face and neck, mercifully concealing the craggy Scottish nose and the pink wattles working beneath the strong line of her jaw. She looked now remarkably like some exiled queen who has long since been altogether forgotten by the world at large but who was not yet prepared to relinquish the personal drama of the incognito.

It puzzled David that she was able to see the fruit and vegetables at all through the veil, lacking even the eye-slits of the woman in purdah. Not, he supposed, that it mattered all that much. She would see everything only with a vision that would be dour and practical and conditioned to a discriminating cynicism by her thirteen years of living on the island. In all that time she had resolutely refused to learn even a single word of the native language: on this point she had once said, "Shaw was perfectly right when he said that if you wished to be totally misinformed about a foreign country you must seek out an Englishman who has lived there twenty-five years and speaks the language like a native. Arthur's Greek is admirable, and he does not know the name of a single tradesman on Silenos!" Arthur was Lieutenant-Commander Arthur Sinclair, R.N. (retired), her husband.

Vlikos the banker passed Meredith with a slight nod and a greeting that was as stiffly formal as his smile. His attitude was distinctly less cordial than it had been: David wondered whether this could be attributed to the latest Balkan crisis or to the dwindling Meredith bank account.

The steamer, which for half an hour had been an emergent whiteness in the deep gulf blue, growing from a speck like a gull's dropping to an engineered sleekness of blue and white that was still somehow vaguely flippant, was yet some distance away, sliding through a milky sea with a slow, lifting curl of the wake which reminded him of some of the passages in *Moby Dick*. He could hear the sibilance of its movement in Melville's syllables; even across that expanse of water it was as if he could feel the skin of the sea heaving up and breaking and curling in just the way that Melville had written about it, as if what Melville had had to say about the sea was not related at all to the profound darkness of the terrible and beautiful allegory he had created. Yet looking at the sunlit skin of the sea how could one imagine the profundity of all that darkness and seethe and turmoil that lay within it. Once, in the Pacific to the northward of the Philippines, Meredith had seen an island born out of the sea, a black, shining, obscene thing labouring out of the steam and the water-churn and the whirl of gulls, jerking higher and higher into a pyramid of rock as the destroyer had circled it all through the day, warily, rolling to a slow, convulsive swell that was like the gasping breath of birth. . . .

When the ship finally rounded the rocky headland it came edging in past the red cliffs on a thin metallic edge of amplified radio music. "Stormy Weather." With Mark coming, he reflected, it would have to be something as improbable as that! They had cut the engines and the ship was sliding in rather slyly towards the waiting landing-boats, sneaking up on Silenos as if it planned to take it by surprise. The wake bulged into a curl of dark water and subsided into the still sea.

"Young man, you spend a great deal too much time sitting at coffee tables, brooding."

She was standing behind the chair, looking down at him sternly through the floral veil. It was more transparent than he had thought. He could see the hooked beak of her nose, and the eyes which were now very old and quick to irritation but which once must have been beautiful.

"It is my business to brood," he said, rising, and smiling at her. She was almost as tall as he.

"It's more than a business with you. It's an obsession."

"Lately, perhaps," he admitted. "In fact, Beth," he said, "I am waiting for the ship."

"For the mail, you mean," she said reprovingly, and took the other chair. "I never see you but you're waiting for the mail."

"Well, why not?" He studied her across his clasped hands. "If your living happens to depend——"

"Fiddle!" She cut him short with a dismissive gesture that was as imperious as her earlier spurning of the cauliflower. "You come to live here to escape from something, then spend every moment of your waking time clinging to that something as if it were a lifeline."

"So it is." He looked at her amusedly. "Besides, you're being sweeping again. I don't think I'm here to escape from something. To tell you the truth, my brooding, as you call it, is only because I'm trying to find out why the devil I *am* here. I haven't settled on escape as the reason . . . not yet. Beth," he said, "why did you come to Silenos?"

"Asthma," she said firmly. "That, and Arthur's wish to write his history, and my own passion for Byron."

"You still complain of your asthma. And Arthur hasn't written his history. Byron? I don't know about Byron."

She sniffed. "I am quite over Byron. I recovered from Byron at once."

"He's an easy poet to recover from, I think."

"I feel now it should have been Shelley. He might have lasted longer. But then it would have been Italy instead of here, and one would have decayed even more rapidly." She lifted the veil. The pink, crusty skin at her neck worked slightly. She was old, gaunt, raddled, worn, but there was still vitality in her eyes and discipline in the set of her mouth. Certainly she had not decayed. It was doubtful, he thought, looking at her, if she ever would decay. Perhaps corruptibility was not inherent in her —she would not rot: she would weather like a fallen oak or petrify into stone.

"You haven't really answered my question," he reminded her mildly. "My research at the moment is quite introspective, but I'm sure that what worries me isn't essentially a personal thing. I mean, I want to know what all of us are doing here on Silenos. You and Arthur, Kate and I, poor little Fegel in that shack of his around the cliffs, Erica Barrington stuck up there like an ascetic nun in that great desolate house of hers."

"She does not, at least, shuffle around the post office day in and day out, like a pauper on Maundy Thursday waiting for alms!" she said with a caustic sniff.

He smiled slightly, paying no attention to her rebuke. What *were* we all really doing here? he wondered. Obviously, since we were all non-indigenous to the island, journeys and voyages had brought us here, but when you tried to examine the journeys their reality dried on the tongue. Arthur Sinclair, for instance, had spent the better part of fifty years as a permanent naval officer, and had voyaged in grey ships all over the world; yet in reality he had gone nowhere, he had never made a journey in his life. And Fegel's journey had been forced upon him against his will, like a condemnation. And Erica Barrington? Perhaps she had made her own decision and had simply come to a day when it had seemed natural for her to walk out and take a side road and go from one way of life to another. Perhaps. He really didn't know about Erica Barrington. Nobody did know very much about her, if it came to that. . . .

"Listen to me, David," said Beth Sinclair. "When I first came here, that was just after the war ended, I was no different from you. I remained two whole years poste restante before I saw the utter absurdity of it. Now there is no point, of course. Nobody writes, and I take only the *Scottish Field*. That, I consider, is sufficient."

"Ample. Your advice then is that all my anxieties will vanish the moment I change from poste restante?"

"I never offer advice. I simply believe you will spend more time working and less time brooding about yourself. Try it. Have the man deliver. You will be surprised how completely it expatriates you."

"Must one be completely expatriated?"

She sniffed again and dismissed the subject. "How is Kate?" she asked.

"Well, thank you."

"The children?"

He nodded.

"Tell Kate I shall call on her just as soon as Arthur is over his spondilitis."

"What is spondilitis?" he asked, teasing her.

"It is what he calls whatever he gets. And, as you know, he gets most things."

"Tell him I hope he is better soon."

"Arthur is never better. However, it will comfort him to know you were solicitous. He is always more amiable if he knows somebody is still interested in his ailments." She straightened into an angular stiffness. "I must leave you," she said curtly. "All these impossible people are coming ashore."

"Yes," he said idly. "I am waiting for one of them. My brother Mark."

"Oh yes, you told me, of course. I had forgotten the day. Well, I dare say I shall meet him later. You must bring him to the house. Tomorrow evening for drinks, if you wish, when the children are down."

"Yes, he would like that."

She lifted her gnarled hands and faded into a blur behind the floral veil, and made a stately withdrawal along the waterfront with a distant nod here and there to favoured townspeople.

Perhaps she was right, he reflected. Perhaps that was what you had to do in island living—turn your back on basic activities and have the man deliver. He left the money beside the coffee cup and began to walk slowly down towards the landing steps, but Vlikos the banker came across to him from the barber shop, his round damp face fixed in a stiff, frosty smile.

"Ah, Mr. Meredith," he said in his hesitant, sing-song English, "I wished to see you a moment. Your account. It is below your reserve for credit. A thousand drachmas. You asked me to keep you informed."

"There's a cheque on its way," said David impatiently. "A remittance from London. It should have arrived. The mail service here is very difficult to understand, Mr. Vlikos. Besides, I have already explained to you that with royalties there are always ups and downs, time-lags, delays. . . ."

"I am not worried about it, Mr. Meredith," said the banker, without friendliness. "It was you who asked me to keep you informed as to the state of your account."

"Thank you. You should have the remittance any day now." They bowed stiffly to each other and Vlikos moved back to the barber shop as David angrily walked on towards the steps. The landing-boats were already coming in. The second launch was still in mid-harbour when he identified Mark. It was his stance more than his appearance, for he seemed stouter and stockier than David remembered, and he had grown a short, pointed beard. Because of the explicit character of the beard, he looked exactly like some *conquistadore* come to plunder a new land.

As the launch drew in to the steps David saw that he was wearing a well-cut suit of what appeared to be good Irish tweed, and a hand-knitted tie with horizontal stripes in Braque colours. He had sun-glasses, the usual hanging leather appurtenances, an Air France zip bag, and a stout brief case.

His first words were, "Good heavens, man, you're thin as a rake!"

"You mustn't be banal, Mark," David replied. "That's what mothers and elder brothers always say."

"Well, you are. You've hardened up, though. You look fit, I must say."

"The quiet life," said David.

It was enough to see them over the first embarrassment of meeting. David had a sense of relief, a feeling of "so far, so good," as he ushered his brother to a table on the quay in front of the coffeehouse. "We might as well have a brandy or something while we're waiting for the baggage. They'll bring it ashore in the last boat."

"Soda for me," said Mark. "Or mineral water. Whatever is available." From his jacket pocket he took a leather tobacco pouch and a thick-bowled, heavy-stemmed pipe and a thin silver tube which opened ingeniously into a set of probers and reamers and cleaning instruments.

David went across to the door to tell Taki, the day waiter. Captain Andreas, he observed, was no longer there. Walking back across the quay he had an image of all the harbour laid out behind the seated figure of his brother, with the *Twelve Apostles* riding on a crust of garbage, and a thick-set figure in the bow of the boat carefully coiling ropes.

"Picturesque, I must say," Mark observed judicially, suspending for a moment his activities with the pipe-cleaner. "Damned picturesque. I was looking at it coming in. Those two peaks give the place an extraordinary distinction."

"It has quite a character, yes."

"Not at all what I'd expected from your letters. I jotted down some notes while the ship was approaching. Damned hard to get the character, though. Very elusive."

"Very elusive, yes," David agreed.

Mark had taken off his sun-glasses and was now examining the visible aspect of the town through narrowed eyes. He seemed to have developed a habit of narrowing his eyes and setting his face very sternly at whatever he wished to appraise, a habit which David suspected had developed out of the growth of the beard. At the same time the beard did give the face a certain distinction which otherwise might have been lacking: without it the tendency to pouchiness about the eyes and the slight flabbiness of the cheeks might have been more evident. Lacking the beard, Mark Meredith might well have been taken for a well-to-do merchant or a prosperous businessman; with it it was feasible to see him as the successful playwright. The pipe too, and the silver gadgets, played a role in it.

"Nice pipe you have," said David.

Mark blew out a thin plume of blue smoke and nodded. "Italian briar," he said. "I have a chap outside Venice makes them for me."

"Italian tobacco too?"

"Heavens, no! Don't tell me you haven't smoked Italian tobacco! No, this is English. Three Nuns. Been smoking it for donkey's years. Pipe-smoking has its conventions. One has to conform." He was silent for a few moments, and then he frowned thoughtfully and said, "There is a good hotel here, I suppose?"

"Passably good." David looked at him. "But why? You will be with us."

"Well, yes . . . that is, for tonight, at any rate. Of course. But . . . well, since I wrote to you there's been some changes of plans. In fact, I have some people coming down tomorrow; and others on Sunday." He squared his shoulders and sucked on his pipe. "What it is, David, is that I'm committed to have this new play ready for autumn rehearsal, and we all thought it would be a jolly good plan to work it out here. Quiet. No distractions. Nobody to interfere and say do this, do that. It *is* a good place to work?"

"I suppose it is. I suppose it depends, really."

"Yes, well, we shall look around for a house . . . take it for two or three months, I expect. You'll be able to help with that angle?"

"If you want, yes. Kate will be rather disappointed you're not staying with us. Still, it's for you to say, of course. Am I allowed to ask what the play is about?"

"Why not? If you want to know, it's based on one of your stories. Set in Assam. You told me about it once. You'll never get round to using it."

"I suppose not. Some time you must tell me which one it is. Hallo, they're bringing off the bags now. Shall we go across? Kate will be waiting. She's made a *pizza* specially for you." He rose, stared for a long moment at the crowded landing steps, then quickly sat down again.

"What's the matter?" said Mark, looking at his brother's face. "My God! they haven't messed up my luggage?"

"No, no. It's just somebody I didn't much want to see. He was here last year."

Watching the young man pushing towards them through the crowd, David found himself wondering why he had wanted to evade the issue. His acquaintance with Achille Mouliet the previous summer had been casual enough. He had not liked him very much, but the feeling had never been pronounced enough to bother him particularly; it had been a distaste rather than a dislike—a distaste for his exhibitionism and his suspect nihilism, for his air of condescending decadence, for his careless promiscuity, for his tendency to become ill-mannered and truculent when he drank too much. No more than that—and even then it had been distaste at a distance, since each of them had moved in very different orbits of living.

The young man gave the distinct impression of having come to stay. He carried a bulging portfolio of drawings or drawing paper, a wheel of Athens bread, a good many heavily-wrapped packages, and a one-eyed tabby cat in a string bag. A small bare-footed boy followed him with a heavy brown valise.

David saw that in his right ear he still wore the small gold earring he had favoured the summer before. Beneath the yellow cap of hair that was still cut Roman fashion his brown face was the face of a faun, or of an old Greek god, a face with the pagan look of an ancient angel. In fact he was on the verge of looking almost too pagan really to be believed in, and yet there was something in his personality that enabled him to get away with it. The strange mobile quietness of the face made you forget the affectation of the earring, the harmonious proportions of the sunburnt body cancelled out the fact that he was rather short in stature and that the blue jeans he was wearing were so tight on his legs that you felt they must have been soaked overnight so they could be peeled on. His teeth, as he came to the table, were startlingly white and even. (David had a sudden odd pleasure in recollecting how two of the Frenchman's teeth had been knocked out by a fisherman in a tavern brawl the previous August, and how astonished and disturbed everyone had been at the revelation that the teeth were false.)

"Hallo," David said, his voice warmed into cordiality by the memory of the teeth. "So you've come back to Silenos."

"Oh, yes." Mouliet smiled gently, almost shyly, as he shook hands. "I like this island very much. We all come back to it. But I tell you last year I would be back this summer."

"Did you? I'm afraid I had forgotten."

"Tell me, 'ow are Katherine and the children?"

"Fine. They're all fine." It surprised him a little that the Frenchman used his wife's first name—or was that something else he had forgotten? "Where will you stay?"

"Conrad Fegel is 'ere?"

"Yes, he's still here. I was drinking with him last night."

"Ah, then I will stay with Fegel. Fegel is good for me. This year I will work very 'ard. Not like last summer." He smiled. It was a slight smile, strange and haunting, as if it came from far back in time. "It is when I am away from Silenos, it is then I am knowing 'ow much I like it." He looked across at David, sea-green eyes in a tawny skin. "Your wife is as lovely as ever?" Again the slow, far-away smile touched his mouth as his gaze moved from one brother to the other and then lifted to the sharp ridge of rocks encircling the harbour. "I remember 'er very well," he said, and paused, and then, "I am so 'appy to be back," he said quietly. "We shall get to know each other so much better. We shall 'ave a very 'appy time together."

After a little more talk he took his leave, walking away with an oddly provocative shuffling gait behind the boy with the brown valise. Mark Meredith said, "Well, now!" stroked his beard, considered the bottle of mineral water for a moment, then added, "It'll be interesting to see how Janecek reacts to *that.*"

"Janecek?"

"He's one of the group coming tomorrow. Czech by origin . . . one of those D.P.s, I dare say. Lives in Italy now. In Venice," he said with significance, "they call him the Giant Pander. At the same time, he's unquestionably the most brilliant young man on the Continent today on theatre décor. He did the sets"—he paused religiously—"for Vramantin."

"Oh," said David. He had a sudden feeling of immense depression. He had never heard of Janecek and he had never heard of Vramantin. Perhaps he had been away too long. "Shall we organise the baggage, and go up?" he suggested.

Back at the house, while his brother was washing his hands, David said to Kate, "Nature Boy is back. He came on the boat."

"Mouliet? Not really!" She looked up quickly from the big, marble-topped farm table. "Earring and all?"

"Earring and all."

"Odette?"

"Odette?" He repeated the name questioningly.

"Why, that girl he was with last summer. You can't have forgotten her, David. All that weird jewellery made from sea pebbles and drift-wood? The dog's jawbone she used as a pendant?"

"Oh, her—yes. It seems she left him in Tangier and went back to Paris, and now, I gather, she's taken up with some other character in Majorca."

"You mean he's come here *alone?*"

"This year he has a cat."

"It's difficult to imagine Mouliet without a woman, isn't it?"

"It's difficult to imagine Mouliet. This summer he'll stay with Fegel. He intends to work very hard."

Kate laughed softly and went back to the salad.

"Tell me about Mark," she said.

"Mark is Mark. Even with that beard. I'm sure he'll tell you about himself." He went across and lifted himself on to the big, eight-foot slab of marble, and reached across and fingered out some chopped lettuce. "Kate?" he said.

"Yes?"

"This is a very fine kitchen."

"This is a wonderful kitchen," she said. "I adore this kitchen. Do you know, it's exactly the sort my mother always dreamed of having, and never did."

He looked carefully about him. From the varnished beams which were almost the whole trunks of trees dangled the pale strings of garlic and the purple onions, a bunch of bay-leaves, rosemary and mint and basil, and tufts of wild thyme and *rigoni* from the mountains. A wreath of

early vine-leaves hung green as youth over the great stone water-jar in
the corner by the well. The flagged floor was damp and cool. He watched
his wife as she moved across to the arched stove with its ledge of scarlet
tiles. She looked slim and cool and very beautiful. She looked as if she
belonged. Eleven years ago, they had said the marriage would never last
six months. She had been wild then, and unpredictable.

"It's got a nice feel about it, this house," he said, munching on the
salad. "A sort of lucky feel. I think we'll be happy here."

"I am happy here," she said simply. "Happier than I've ever been in
my life, darling." She turned with a smile. There was a smut of charcoal
on her nose.

"What did you do about the Arákhova rug?" he asked.

"I left it where it was. It belongs in there."

"Yes," he said, and waited for his brother Mark to come down.

3

THE BROTHERS MEREDITH

"Yes, well, you've got a nice place here," said Mark finally. "You'd pay a packet for anything like this in England or the States. In fact, around London you wouldn't get a decent garage built for what you paid for this."

"You couldn't buy a house like this in England or the States," said David truthfully. "Or Australia," he added as an afterthought. Mark, he had observed, was reluctant to use Australia in any terms of reference. Success in London sometimes did that. "This was a sea captain's cottage," he explained. "A man named Zaraphonitis built it in 1798. He was the captain of a brig, a privateer brig. Later he made himself a lot of money running Nelson's blockade, and he built a bigger house, higher on the hill. A woman has it now. Erica Barrington. Maybe you'll meet her."

Mark nodded. "Interesting," he said, and took his coffee cup across the room to the big old map squared into its frame of yellowed wood.

"*Carte de Tartarie*," he read aloud. "*Dressée sur les Relations de plusieurs de differentes Nations et sur quelques Observations qui ont été faites dans ce pais la Par—*" he paused to make a flourish—"*Guillaume del'Isle de l'Académie Royale des Sciences. A Paris Chez l'Auteur fur le Quai de l'Horloge à la Cour de Diamas avec Privilège—1706.*" Looking across at him, David was aware that it was being done for the purpose of showing off his French. It had improved, certainly, but the Australian accent, slightly nasal, not fluid enough for the Gallic vowels, was still there. Mark, he suspected, would not like to be told of this.

"A nice map," said Mark. "Old. Quaint. Hopelessly inaccurate, of course. Just look where they've put Tibet!" He turned to his brother as he began to fill his pipe. "I notice you keep lots of maps."

"I like maps," said David.

Mark smiled, a tolerant, meaningful smile. "It would not be that you still have the old wanderlust," he said.

"It wouldn't be that, no," said David.

"Oh, come now!"

"It's true. I keep them to remind me of how wise I was to get the wanderlust out of my system. That's all. Oh yes—other things too, I suppose. When we bought this house the first thing I put up on the wall was a big map of the world. What intrigued me after it was up was that it was drawn on a projection of Van der Grinten's. When we were at school there was only one name as far as maps were concerned, and that was Mercator. I'd never heard of this Van der Grinten. Had you?"

"No."

"Well, as far as I can remember, the map looked pretty much the same as Mercator's. I remember I began to examine it to see what the difference was, but before very long I'd forgotten all about this intention. I found myself thinking not about the places I had seen, but all the places I *hadn't*. I'd been in China for two years and never got to Peking. I'd been up the Old Silk Road to Urumchi, but I hadn't gone on as far as Alma Ata. Sad, you see, Mark. Because I'll certainly never be over there again. It was easier in the days of Mercator, when we were at school. Do you remember what we'd always do when we got a new exercise-book? We'd write on the cover, 'David Meredith, *Avalon*, 11 Buxton Street, Elsternwick, Melbourne, Victoria, Australia, Southern Hemisphere, The World, The Universe.'" He smiled. "Did you do that too?"

"I don't remember," said Mark. "Did we live in a house called *Avalon*? Or are you making that up?" For a moment he looked uncomfortable, and plucked at his beard. Then he cleared his throat and said, "Look, you're not suggesting that you're content to sit on this rock here for the rest of your life?"

"I'm content for the moment."

"What does that mean?"

"I'm content for the moment. I can't go beyond that."

"David, let's get down to brass tacks." Mark moved away from the map with a resolute squaring of his broad tweeded shoulders. "Listen to me. What do you think was the primary purpose of my coming here?"

"To do your play, wasn't it?"

"Primary, I said. Doing the play fits in, that's all. No, no, I came here —let me be perfectly candid with you—I came here to fetch you back where you belong." He cupped the pipe bowl in his hands and looked across at his brother through narrowed eyes. "This . . . this visionary escapism of yours is all very well," he said, "but you've had over three years, man, and where has it got you? What has it proved? No, no!" —he raised his hand—"you listen to what I have to say. I must talk to you now, while Kate's putting the children down. And tomorrow we'll have all those people. I'm dealing with this in your best interests, understand that."

"Go on," said David passively.

"This is not entirely my view . . . Benchley, Kreuger, Tom Fairley, they all agree." He had gone back and settled himself heavily into the leather arm-chair. His face was set into an expression of earnest concern. Between the fingers of his left hand he slowly revolved the silver tube containing the pipe-cleaners. "It's time you were back in London, David," he said. "Beechcroft's magazine is there for you. He specifically requested that I should speak to you. There's a *place* for you, an enviable place. Another year's delay, though, and you'll be forgotten. It will be too late."

"The line-of-no-return," said David musingly. He stared thoughtfully around the room. At the far end, in half-darkness where the lamp had not been lit, the geometrical patterns on the Arákhova rug glowed and smouldered like strange abstract symbols, and a glint of fiery light was caught on the cupola of the old copper brazier.

Mark took a deep, controlled breath. He carefully put his fingertips together and leaned forward, his elbows resting on his thick thighs, his mouth resolutely set above the pointed beard. "You don't mind if I'm blunt?" he said.

"It's the privilege of an elder brother, surely. You don't have to ask."

"David," he said, "what are you doing here?"

"On Silenos?"

Mark nodded. "On Silenos," he repeated gravely.

"I'm trying to live."

"And are you living?"

"Learning to . . . at least I think I am."

"All right. Take it a step further." Mark stared at his impacted fingers. "What have you accomplished since you've been here? What have you done?"

"I thought you knew. I've written a book. In fact, I've very nearly written two."

"In three years. That's quite an output! And both of them, moreover, novels." He studied his brother severely.

"Well, what's wrong with that? You make it sound as if they're pornographic."

"Nothing's wrong with it, I suppose, if you can't find anything better to write about. But why the devil don't you write about your own experiences? War memoirs, personal experience stuff, travel . . . that's the line now. Look at Stonemount. And Priddon. Edition after edition. Who reads novels?"

"Search me!" David smiled. "I know that not many bothered to read mine. That's fair enough, I suppose. I don't read Stonemount or Priddon. I think they write trash. I should point out, I think, that my second novel is very much better than the first one. At least I think it is."

"Come back to the main point. You're nearly forty, aren't you? Nearly forty?"

"Until I am forty, I'd prefer to say I'm thirty-nine."

"You had the ball at your feet a good many years, didn't you? You were streets ahead of Stonemount or Priddon."

"Oh; to hell with Stonemount!" he said with sudden irritation. "And Priddon! What have they got to do with it?"

"David, as a journalist you were a considerable success," said Mark, unperturbed. "And now?" Again he examined his fingertips. "As an author?" he said meaningly.

"I'm learning."

"Of course you're learning. All of us are always learning. That's not the point, is it?"

"Well, what is the point? Stonemount and Priddon? If they're your yardstick." He had a sudden deep resentment of what his brother was implying. It was not only what he was saying now, but it involved the earlier, more casual talk over drinks in the garden—the flood of memories and reminiscences, the anticipated do-you-remembers, the reports on mutual friends and acquaintances. Who had what job now . . . who was in New Delhi . . . who had got a visa to Moscow . . . who had moved into Sara's flat in Eaton Square. . . . And so much of what it had once all meant had come back to David in a way he had not at all expected —like returning to China after his first absence from the country and finding such delight in the smell of the human nightsoil that fertilised the Yunnan fields. Because it had not been just the horror of the rat race that came back to his mind as Mark gabbled on. There had been that too, of course—a deep thankfulness to have escaped from the prostitutions and the pressures, the snide sycophancies, the wearing loyalties that were so artificial—but with it also a rekindled sense of the exhilaration of success: the taxis and mackintoshes and brief cases and expense accounts, the first nights, the parties, the dinners in Soho, the interviews in quiet rooms, the week ends in Paris and Rome, assignments abroad, the lights of airports like jewels arranged on black velvet, the continental holidays, pretty clothes for Kate, shopping in Bond Street. The good moments as well as the bad ones. "All right, they're not queueing up for my books yet," he said deliberately. "On the other hand, I'm not altogether a failure."

"Rather a negative conclusion, isn't it?" Mark said. "I mean, after three solid years of trying. Besides, you've put your finger on another thing. Coming up to the forties isn't the time to find yourself at a half-way house. Believe me, I know. It's a dangerous situation. Very dangerous."

"Christ! do you think I'm not aware of that?" David pushed himself from the chair and walked across to the sideboard, aware of the disapproval on his brother's face as he refilled his glass. It was so bloody easy for Mark to sit there, the complacent elder statesman with his fingertips together, puffing on his pipe. He was a free spirit. He didn't have a dependent in the world. He had plenty of money . . . he could have his pipes made by a chap outside Venice, his tweeds woven in Ireland, his ties crocheted in God knows where. He had his life arranged for his own comfort, as if it were the neat little silver gadget that contained his pipe-cleaners. He didn't have two kids and a wife to support . . . and to support by a gambler's life that was outside all the frames of reference, where there were no guarantees, no securities, no insurances against failure or loss or destruction. It wasn't he who was being coldly chided on the quay by Vlikos the banker for not being prosperous enough. Yet Mark himself had come to his half-way house at a pretty late age. He had been past forty and a not-very-bright advertising copy-writer when he had had his first play accepted. Now he had had quite a number. His name was known on both sides of the Atlantic—by some critics rather slightingly, it was true. Nevertheless, he was a success. Mark Meredith's *Summer Solstice*. Mark Meredith's *Once Upon a Dime*. Mark Meredith's *Calico Moon*. Whether one was successful or not was the real issue—nothing else—and there was a formula for success just as there was a formula for failure. To be *sure* of things was the important thing, and Mark was very sure of everything, including himself. He could not imagine Mark staring blankly at a whole stack of typescript which had taken him more than a year to write and wondering whether in the final analysis it was no more than a bundle of rubbish.

David went back to his chair and looked across at his brother and said quietly, "It's dangerous, yes, Mark, but it's never too late to learn. You should know that." He had his anger under control now, and he spoke with a genuine kindliness.

"But what are you learning, David? That's the point I want to get at."

"Lots of things. I told you—I'm learning to live. I'm learning to know my own children. I'm learning to know my wife." He glanced across carefully. "I don't say this maliciously at all, Mark, or with any intent to hurt, but it's quite possible you wouldn't have divorced Gwen if you'd learnt to know her better than you did. I think she was a good woman. Good for you, too, in a way."

"Yes—well, we'll keep her out of this, if you don't mind," Mark said, without warmth. "That's finished. Unfortunately, but finished. It has nothing to do with what we're discussing."

"Perhaps it hasn't. I'm sorry. All right. You want to know what I'm learning. Shall I say that I'm learning to know something about the light and shadow on rocks against the sky, the true taste of water, the rhythm of seasons, the values of simplicity, the——"

"Oh, for God's sake, David, be practical!" The reference to his wife had obviously irritated him: the change of subject provided him with the opportunity to express his irritation elsewhere. "All this pseudo-poetic Henry Miller guff!"

"It's not guff—not all of it. I know we're inclined to take things for granted, but . . . well . . ." He broke off. "It doesn't matter. This is all a waste of time, anyway. Because the real point is quite simple, Mark. I don't want to go back. That's all. As simple as that."

"You prefer living here with a lot of wops and goats and prickly-pear, alienated from your own society, out of touch with everything real that's happening, turning your back on your moral responsibilities, throwing all your ability and talent into the garbage can for the dustman to cart away! So that you can do what? Prove what? This is cowardly, David. Cowardly! It is, I tell you!"

In the pause that followed, his heavy, determined breathing filled the mellow room, and it was an appreciable time before David spoke.

"You may be right, Mark," he said quietly. "That's the one point I've never been able to work out, whether it's something brave to do or something cowardly. When I do work it out I'll let you know." It was a curious thing that he could no longer clearly assess the actual point of decision. Had it been only his remedy to the situation, or had Kate, too, been a party to it? . . . an act of individual adventure or of mutual desperation? "I'm not sure what you mean, though, about moral responsibilities. Isn't it simpler than that? Remember what you said this morning when the boat came in. You told me you wanted to get your new play ready. You thought this would be a good place to come. Why? A quiet place. No distractions. A good place to work. Nobody to interfere and say do this, do that. That's what you said, Mark. Where do moral responsibilities come into it?"

"The good professional, the trained man, has a moral obligation to——"

"Ah, I see. We're back to journalism again. Mark, you never worked as a foreign correspondent. You never edited a magazine. You never ran a newspaper bureau. But supposing you had, and supposing you'd been at it for years and years, and you were getting deathly weary of treading that same old sterile beat, feeding out those safe old formulas, thinking in the reliable, oven-tested cliché patterns, rubbing up all the familiar little dishonesties, and then one night—at three-fifteen in the morning, to be exact—when you were very tired and sour with grog and your mouth was dry and you couldn't sleep, the bedside phone rang and the man on the night-desk read over to you an urgent cable. And supposing the cable, Mark, was a request for you to file immediately and at urgent rates the vital statistics of Carmel Rosa—with a radiogram picture if one was available. Mightn't that give you pause for thought . . . to wonder what the hell you were doing with yourself, where you were going?"

"The responsibility of the good journalist is to combat that sort of cheap sensationalism," said Mark with more than a trace of pomposity.

"Nonsense! The good journalist supplies what he's told to supply."

"His responsibility to society should override that. Beechcroft's magazine is as much against this form of trashy sensationalism as you are," Mark said patiently. "It has fine critical analyses, liberal politics, an admirable——"

"I know. It offers alternatives to Carmel Rosa's breasts. Zen Buddhism. The Beatniks. The Japanese *No* plays. West African fetish carving. The poetry of urban planning. The relation of the Upanishads to abstract-expressionism. The narcotics come more expensive, that's all. And they have longer names."

"You're obstinate, David. You've always been the obstinate one. Even as a kid, you were exactly the same."

"Do you remember Pop Chinnery?" David asked wearily. "And Suzie?"

"Pop Chinnery?" Mark looked at him blankly.

"Nobody. A man I knew once. And his daughter. It's of no importance. I wondered if you remembered, that's all."

"This is another of your irrelevancies, isn't it? To dodge the issue."

"No, it's not. I'm beginning to think there's no such thing as irrelevance. Or perhaps it should be the other way round. No such thing as relevance. I'm not philosophical enough to work that out. You don't really have childhood memories, do you, Mark?" He looked across at his brother interestedly. "You don't ever try to go back, do you, to see how it began. You didn't even remember we had a house called *Avalon*. You don't remember the Chinnerys."

"I remember my childhood," Mark retorted with a touch of stiffness. "Am I supposed to remember yours too? After all, I was working in the agency when you were still playing cherry-bobs. Anyway, to hell with that! We're not discussing child psychology. Oh, the whole thing is a damned waste of time," he said in a sudden flurry of impatience. "I'm not going to push it any further at this stage. I shall have to talk to Kate." He scraped the pipe dottle into the ash-tray and methodically assembled his pouch and gadgets. He did it so fussily, and with such a comical old-maidish petulance, that David felt a sudden deep affection for him.

"Yes, you should do that, I think," he said. "Talk to Kate. Get her view." A slow smile warmed his lean brown face. "Mark," he said, "thanks for your concern about me. I appreciate it, really. But just let me work it out, will you, in my own blundering way?" And then, to change the subject, he said, "Let's talk about you now. I read your last play, of course. I enjoyed it. I'd have liked to have seen it played."

"You'll see the next," said Mark, mollified at once.

"*Tha thúme*," said David.

The discussion ended there, for at this point Kate came into the room. She was wearing a full skirt of faded blue peasant cotton and a white shirt and a broad orange-coloured cummerbund, and around her shoulders the fringed woolen shawl he had given her two birthdays ago. In her eyes as they met his was a look of faint inquiry, faint concern. Mark, he saw, was looking her up and down, very appraisingly. Suddenly he was angry again, guessing the thoughts that would be passing through his brother's mind. Another specimen beneath the slide! Another subject for contrast! Well, what did he bloody well expect to see?—the same smart, well-groomed, sophisticated woman he had known in London?—tailored suits, accounts at Harrods, new hats for garden parties, Paris umbrellas? He wouldn't be able to see that Kate was ten times more beautiful now than she had ever been . . . oh no! he wouldn't see *that*, because that wasn't the way his mind worked, that didn't fit in with the set of values he believed in. He would see Kate as a woman who hadn't been to a decent hairdresser—to any sort of hairdresser!—in three years; a woman who only wore the clothes she made herself—with a twisted bitterness that was pleasure as much as pain he saw the skirt that had faded streakily with too much washing and too bright a sun, the darn on the shoulder of her shirt, the little piece pulled out from the fringe on the shawl, the strap missing from one of her sandals; a woman who, by his ridiculous standards, had obviously begun to "let herself go" a bit.

"Kate," said Mark, with beaming gallantry, "I do declare you are the most beautiful woman I've ever seen! You are, you know!"

She made him a mock curtsy, but she looked pleased.

"I know it's supposed to be more or less compulsory for a man to fall in love with his brother's wife," he said ruefully, "but you *do* make it difficult!"

"Are the kids all right?" David asked deliberately, and she smiled at him and nodded. "Both sleeping like angels," she said. "Simon wants to grow a beard like Uncle Mark's."

"Well, let's take Mark and the beard down to a tavern for a drink," he suggested quickly.

"We've been whacking it pretty solidly here, haven't we?" Mark looked at him uncertainly. "I mean, haven't you had about enough? Or doesn't wine matter on top of all that other?"

"That's what you have to find out. Come on. It'll do you good to see how the other half of the family lives."

They went down through back streets where starlight washed the walls and the scent of jasmine was in the air. They had passed the grove of almond-trees by the church when they saw two men in altercation at the top of the steps, one low-voiced and the other loud and thickly raucous with drink. David greeted them as they went by. The drunken man responded with a hoarse, incomprehensible sally. The other man, broad-shouldered, thick-set, was silent, watching as they went away to the left and up the next flight of stairs. "Did you remember to remind him about the garbage?" Kate asked, and David frowned and said, "Oh blast! I forgot! Shall I go back now?" Kate took his arm. "Not now," she said. "Tomorrow will do. He's very drunk."

"Our garbage man," David explained to Mark. "Quite a character! Not notably efficient, but all we have."

"And the other chap?" Mark asked, looking back at the two figures in the lane below.

"A sponge-boat captain," said David. Odd that Captain Andreas had not responded to his greeting; it was a formality that everybody observed, even though acquaintance might be slight. And last winter he had drunk often enough with Captain Andreas in the taverns. . . .

*   *   *

The captain waited until they had disappeared, watching them all the time, before he turned again to Dionysios, who now, drained suddenly of all exuberance, was standing on the moon-washed cobbles with his eyes closed and his body gently swaying, and his arms hanging limp and useless as if they were fastened to his shoulders with thumb tacks.

Andreas began as if to say something, then saw that the man was past comprehension. Better just to leave him there and walk away. He would find his own way home. And going to the house of Petros he did not wish for company—certainly not the company of Dionysios, bawling out his obscenities and saying all the wrong things. It would be hard enough anyway, even though he knew that Petros would have to say yes because he was a poor man and his family was hungry. Even so . . . In the truth of it, Andreas had hoped to find Petros in one of the taverns, because there, amid the company of other men, they could have talked the thing out perhaps without too much resentment or bitterness. His search had taken him from one tavern to the next, and that was where he had picked up old drunken Dionysios. Come to think of it, Dionysios, too, had a reason for being drunk so often, or anyway he thought he had, which amounted to much the same thing. Although it was a long way back in time—forty years or more, maybe fifty—that Dionysios had stabbed his first wife to death because he'd caught her in bed with another man . . . and then the fat, sluggish wife he had now was only a slut and a shrew, and she was the one he wanted to stab to death, except that he was too old for that sort of thing now, and, in any case, he was afraid of her, and he only made threats when he was drunk or a good distance away from the house. . . .

Captain Andreas pushed his fists into the pockets of his blue jacket and turned his back on the drunken man—seated in the gutter now with his head in his hands, and weeping very softly—and set off slowly up the hill towards the little coloured cube of a house on the rock cliff above the church of Saint Stephanos.

As he climbed there was a queer almost sick feeling in his stomach, because he remembered the last time he had been to the little coloured house on the cliff, with the two women in black watching him secretly from the bed-shelf and not saying a word. Watching him from a long way off, as if they were embedded in some thick, transparent substance, like amber. And he had seemed to see a thread there, a thin red thread, running out of the house and running back all the way to that day in August more than half a year before. Off the coast of Tripoli. Even now he could see it quite clearly, burnt out of the white sun, with all of them crowding and pushing on the bleached deck-planks, and sprawled out below them in the heat was the blotched, drowned body of young Elias, and behind him the grotesque shape of the yellow rubber diving suit thrown over the bitts like a cardboard cut-out that had gone soft in the water . . . and Vassilis the engineer on his knees in the shade of the engine-house weeping and cursing and making his crosses over the broken coupling of the air-line. . . .

When he came to the house he saw there was a lamp burning, very faint through a cheap-curtained window, and they called him in after he had knocked on the green door. They could not have known who it was, and it must have been a shock to them to see him, but there was not much change of expression on their faces.

The two women were there—in the same place, as if in all those months they had never moved—the wife of Petros and the widow of Elias, and both of them were still wearing black and watching him from the bed-shelf, not saying a word, nothing at all after the *"Kaliséra"* they had murmured when he arrived. And for most of the time Petros didn't have much to say for himself either. He just sat there under the lamp, picking at the bones of a mackerel. Andreas guessed he was thinking that there was not much food in the house apart from that picked-over platter of fish, because his eyes were very sombre on the plate. Or maybe he was angry inside himself, knowing he would have to say yes in front of the two women: knowing right from the beginning that he would have to

go sailing again with the captain who had drowned his younger brother
Elias off Tripoli.

All these thoughts were in the mind of Captain Andreas as he sat
well forward on the edge of the cheap cane chair, with his knees together and his big thick hand gripping the saucer of preserved fruit
which the wife of Petros had handed to him, the ceremonial offering to
the house-caller, soon after he had come in. She had not said anything
when she had given him the saucer with the sweet syrupy *frappa* and
the glass of cold water with the spoon in it.

The room was fairly small, because the whole cottage was really only
the one room, if you did not count the roofed-over hole in the ground
built against the side wall or the brick stove outside where they did the
cooking; but it was warm enough from the hot grey dust of a charcoal
fire in the shallow *mangháli*, and the walls were limewashed a streaky
blue which made the place look tolerably cheerful. There was only one
lamp and it was turned low to save the kerosene—the only other speck of
light was in the corner where a wick burnt in a dish of oil in front of a
cheap chromo ikon of Saint Peter surrounded by angels and clouds of
glory—so most of the room was in deep shadow although it was small.
Still, he could see the two silent women staring out at him, and he could
make out the old photographs on the wall, with the more recent snapshots stuck in all around the inside of the frames—some of the snapshots
would be of Elias, he supposed, but it was too dark to see properly—
and the two stained lithographs of Genovefa, and the black left-alone
eyes of Elias's little son watching him over the edge of the hammock.

"You know why I am here," said Andreas at last. "I got the advance."
He waited a moment, but nothing was said. "Now I've got to get divers,"
he added.

Petros bent over the mackerel bones, picking about with his stained
fingers. His fingers were scarred from some sort of hard, dirty work, and
they were shiny with olive-oil where he had been dabbling in the platter
for scraps of fish. The women still made no movement.

"Vlikos wants the boat away before the Friday," Andreas went on
quietly, just as if his first statement had been answered. "I've got to
make up a crew list." Then, because he wanted to be honest with Petros,
so that he would know that he was not alone in being hurt, he said,
"They wouldn't have given me the advance at all except for that business
with the Thiakos boats."

At this Petros looked up, and nodded. He had a face more Turkish looking than Greek, with heavy brows and jet-black eyes that seemed to be set in a creamy, yellowish fluid, and a strong cruel jowly face that hadn't been shaved for a week. He had the sort of mouth that seemed to have suffered a lot and said little, and a thick moustache that curled arrogantly at the tips. When he looked up Andreas had expected him to say something, but he remained silent, so the captain glanced up and across to where Petros's wife crouched in the shadows. "It's work," he said.

Again the eyes met his without expression. She said nothing.

"There won't be another boat after me," said Captain Andreas. "It isn't good to sit around on this island, just waiting, all through summer. Better to get away. It's work," he said again. That was the truth. It killed men and it maimed them and it left scars inside them . . . but it was still work.

Petros was leaning across the platter, snapping the mackerel bones between his fingers, and his face was tightly twisted up, the way a face is twisted up when someone has you in a wrestling grip and your arm is hurting.

The captain, watching him, knew that Petros would have to say yes, but he knew also that he would have to sit there with the saucer of sweet syrup on his knees, just watching the eyes of the two women and waiting for the answer.

4

REPORT ON INSECTS

THE BUTCHER COSTAS had served his apprenticeship in the big market in Piræus (before marrying a Sileniot girl with a plain face but a good dowry), and although there was an easy-come, easy-go atmosphere about the *agorá* on Silenos he still liked to cling to the brisk, business-like methods of his earlier days. Thus on this morning, which was one of the three days of the week defined as "meat days," Costas had decked the outside of his shop with his special arrangement. It was not compulsory to buy meat on a "meat day," neither by convention nor religious observance, but since by not buying meat, which was more expensive than fish or vegetables or beans, a state of poverty might be betrayed, most of the townspeople were his customers—if only for offal or the cut-off scraps to go into a soup.

In consequence, Costas had all his pieces chopped and hung on the hooks outside the shop in a cleverly shaped abstract pattern of sides, half-sides, forequarters, hindquarters, brisket, hearts, kidneys, testicles, tails, heads, and so on. The pattern was mostly in the two colours of red meat and white fat, with a daring purplish-madder touch here and there where the inner organs were displayed. (Several naked electric bulbs placed strategically among the cuts would ensure that at dusk, when the town light supply was switched on, the effect would be even more striking.) Above the door, where there was a crude meadow scene executed in house paints, he had arranged the tripes like the loops and festoons of carnival decorations. The highlight of the day's display, however—since it was early spring and the lambs were small and supple—was a line made up of the carcasses of five very small lambs arranged on the chopping-block outside the shop like a row of puppets. With the hindquarters lopped off, the lambs sat up quite straight, like dolls, and a clever half-chop through at the back of each neck enabled Costas to manipulate the flayed and bloody little heads up and down, and even a little from side to side, in a most lifelike fashion.

He could thus create a strange burlesque of a marionette show with the slaughtered lambs dancing and singing to his own pantomime or to the rather hoarsely carolled choruses of popular *bouzouki* hits which he sang with more gusto than tune.

Sometimes, when a woman was passing, he would bob down and hide behind the chopping-block and suck out secret kissing noises from his pursed lips, or dance the lambs up and down with their heads nodding, or pitch his singing voice to a high quavering cadence, so that one could well believe that it was the little dead lambs which were singing and not Costas at all.

When he was not doing these tricks he was from time to time bellowing out the price of the meat—which was thirty-four drachmas the oka (the police set the price, and everyone knew it, anyway)—or stepping back into the *agorá* so that he might the more effectively admire his display of cuts. Whenever he did this he would spend a good deal of time going backward and forward to make slight improvements to the arrangement, or to tidy up the individual pieces by snipping off the untidily hanging fragments of fat or flesh or gristle, and again withdrawing across the *agorá* to stand in contemplation of his handiwork with his fists turned in against his hips, rather like a painter assessing his canvas.

Although Costas attempted to beguile and blandish every passer-by with his kissing and singing and shouting, he always seemed faintly crestfallen when somebody did buy one of his joints or cuts, because then the arrangement was out of balance and he was obliged to recreate the pattern again.

He was doing this—having just sold a small forequarter to the little servant girl of Stathis Vlikos the banker (a child of twelve who had been bought for a song from an impoverished and overlarge shepherd family who lived on the high slopes near the Black Vouna)—when David Meredith came to his shop and inquired for old Alecto, the goat woman.

"Why do you want Alecto?" Costas, being Greek, would see that the inquiry was made as complicated as possible.

"She has houses," said David. "Houses to rent."

"You have a house already," said the butcher, wiping his cleaver on his apron.

"My brother," David explained. "He wishes to rent a house."

"Your brother is here, on Silenos?"

"Yes."

"A house for the summer?"

"Well, for a month or two. Maybe for the summer also." Inside the door of the shop hung a calendar from the Genoa Home Laundry, with a picture in colour of the winter sports at Cortina d'Ampezzo. How would it have got to Costas's meat shop? David wondered idly.

"I'll tell you a good house," the butcher said helpfully. "Andreas's house. Andreas the sponge captain. He's sailing soon. He's signing crew now." On Silenos most things were known about just as soon as they happened. "He'll be down to Africa all the summer," said Costas. "That's a good house. His wife could do the laundry and keep the place clean."

"Maybe it will be too small. My brother will have friends with him also. A bigger house."

"Ah, *Kyrie* Tasséa," said Costas.

"Tasséa? Who is she?"

"In the street behind yours." The butcher smiled, an inward smile, as if he had a secret to conceal. "The pretty yellow-haired woman. Her husband is a tanker captain. He hasn't been home in four years now. That's a nice house," said Costas. "And your brother can get a bit of this from Tasséa." He made an unmistakably lewd gesture with his fingers. "She knows about it. She's good at it." He winked. "No husband in four years, eh? That's hard on a pretty woman like Tasséa. Maybe you've had a bit too, being so close to your house?" He grinned as he ran his thumb along the cleaver's edge.

"No, I've missed on that," said David with a smile, humouring him.

"It's available," said Costas. "Dionysios goes there every Thursday night. Sometimes Vlikos the banker goes too."

"Dionysios! He's nearly eighty!"

"Fffff!" Costas blew air from between his lips. "What difference. He's like a young bull, especially at night. You ought to try Tasséa," he suggested again.

"I've got my own wife," said David. "I'm satisfied."

Costas shrugged. "Soup, soup, soup all the time?" he said disparagingly. "You call on Tasséa some evening. She knows about it. She likes to do it."

"Yes. What about this house for my brother?"

"Better if you see old Alecto. She's got plenty of houses. Big, medium, small, falling down, standing up."

"Well, if you see her will you tell her I was asking," David said patiently. That was the way you had to do things on Silenos. Between points there was never a straight line. You could not even inquire about renting a house without touching on Captain Andreas again, or being reminded unpleasantly of Vlikos the banker, or crossing a thread with Dionysios the garbage man, or hearing about the yellow-haired wife of a tanker captain who had been left to her own devices for four years.

As he walked away Costas bobbed down behind the chopping-block to make the little dead lambs dance again.

Women left to their own devices. . . . Well, what was expected of a woman whose husband did not come home for four years at a time? And it could happen, of course, without there being a man away or a tanker sailing on the other side of the world. Women with their husbands at home could still feel lonely, neglected, left to their own devices. That was how Mark's marriage had smashed up, with Gwen left to stare at herself while he scrabbled for success. And in London even he and Kate had gone close enough to it. Not until afterwards—really not until they had come to Greece and had a chance to look at each other—had he realised how perilously close it had been. Nor how deeply he had wounded her. In a way, it was this that still lay between them, partly because, he supposed, it was always difficult to be forgiven, and partly because sometimes he could not help feeling that he too had been wounded in discovering that he had wounded her so much. But it was never any longer declared by either of them. There were not even oblique reproaches or criticisms—privately, perhaps, did she say things to herself about him?—and they were still very much in love with each other and their marriage was going on, and after all, with their responsibility to the children, these were the important things. Or so he told himself, with a twinge of uneasiness and even a subdued sense of resentment that the wound had still not healed, after all this time. Like the wound of Philoctetes. His wound had never healed and he too had been banished to an island, and then they had come looking for him, begging him to go back.

He tried deliberately to turn his thoughts away from the subject. He knew from experience that it led nowhere except into a kind of chain-reaction of disquietude, almost even of apprehension, and it never failed to have a very depressing effect on him. It didn't help his writing either, which was worse. Because that situation was bad enough already, now that he'd had to put his work aside so that he could listen to the pompous homilies of his brother or chase around the town trying to find a suitable house for him. With worse distractions still to come. And not even knowing that the damned book was any good, anyway. . . .

Perhaps the thing to do was to play distraction off against distraction, and send Mark and his friends off to live with the yellow-haired woman whose husband was away. A tempting thought. He smiled briefly at the intriguing picture of Mark in the house of *Kyrie* Tasséa . . . setting his brother in unavoidable rivalry with the garbage man, the local banker, and a sea captain who had left a cold bed for far too long! Surely this would be the direct way for Mark to find out how the island of Silenos lived . . . perhaps even to find out how he lived himself!

The house when he returned was empty. He assumed that Mark had taken Kate somewhere so that he could have the promised talk with her. It was still nearly two hours short of the time for the steamer's arrival, but Mark's baggage was heaped inside the door, ready to be taken across to the hotel. The baggage looked like Mark—solid, prosperous, unscarred by travel. On the kitchen table was a bunch of wild flowers which someone had evidently brought down from the mountains—iris and narcissus, wild hyacinth and crocus and spiky green things and small black-and-brown wild orchids that looked like cobras' heads. He put them in a jug with water, then went irresolutely upstairs to the high room he used as a study. The paper beside his typewriter had an uninviting appearance: the top sheet was dog-eared, slightly dusty, covered with scrawled notes. Reading them, they no longer seemed either coherent or sensible. Some of Jerry's coloured pencils were scattered across the desk, and in the typewriter was a sheet of paper headed *Report on Insects 29th June*. Another of the child's interminable withdrawals into his own strange and secret world. David smiled to himself as he read below the heading:

Had a jar with a PRAYING MANTIS and a FURRY INSECT. Added other insects at intervals. P.M. caught a PSALIDA and ate it. After, tried to climb the sides of the jar, but kept falling upside-down. Killed several small insects, but I noticed it would not touch the dead flies I had put in. Then nibbled its antennæ in a thoughtful way, and bit half off them. Then it started falling upside-down again. Several Psalidas tried (unsuccessfully) to get out of the jar. All the other insects involved in a free-for-all fight. Champions: ORTHOPTERA, Praying Mantis. DERMAPTERA, Earwig. COLE-

OPTERA, Furry Insect, Black Beetle (dead-heat). ARACHNIDÆ, Red Spider. MYRIAPODÆ, Millipede.

Perhaps, he reflected, he should get Jerry to write a report on the island of Silenos. Perhaps also, he reflected further, he should give a little more attention to the boy. He might even discover what a *Psalida* was.

He left the *Report on Insects* in the machine and, after another rueful glance at his own untidy papers, went downstairs and left the house and walked across the town to the street where Captain Andreas lived.

The door was opened by a small plain woman in a faded grey dress. She held in one hand a square of needlework and a needle with blue thread between the fingers of the other. She had sad, steady eyes set in a gravely sallow face. He knew that she was the captain's wife, although he could not remember ever having seen them in company at the port. In any case it was not normal in Silenos for wives to be seen with their husbands on the port—in all her married life, for instance, she would never have been to a tavern or a coffeehouse with her husband; and since the captain normally would be away at sea during the summer months she would have had no participation in the one connubial custom which island convention would permit them to share—the evening promenade along the *agorá* on summer evenings.

The captain, she informed David in a soft attentive voice, was working at his boat; nevertheless she motioned him to enter. He was taken to a small dark parlour which was immaculately clean and crowded with unlovely furniture precisely arranged. On a high chest were arranged numerous ornamental sponges mounted on sea rocks and decorated with shells and stringy loops of dried seaweed. On a varnished board behind the chest was a half-hull builder's model of the *Twelve Apostles*, which, according to the printed legend, had been built in Samos. There were many framed photographs on the walls, all retouched heavily, as if the humanity of the sitters had had to be painted out with great care. One was of Captain Andreas, much younger, wearing a beret and battledress and smiling beside the turret of an army tank.

David explained his mission: having seen the house and its furniture it had become no more than a formality, but he had to go on with the explanation. He was making inquiries in the town on the possibility of renting rooms for his brother and his brother's friends. The woman listened with a withdrawn patience while she prepared him a cup of camomile tea, then explained that there were only three spare rooms in

the house, that none of these was normally let to visitors, but that she
would discuss the matter with her husband when he returned from the
harbour.

As David took his leave the woman bent again over the square of embroidery with absorbed and careful eyes.

Women left to their own devices. . . . Thoughtfully he went down
through the bright sunlit lanes to the port.

Four landing-boats were already moving out to meet the steamer, slow-
rowing, with two men at oars in the bows. The two power launches were
waiting by the landing steps. They would leave last so they could pass
the pulling-boats near the breakwater. Once, from Silenos, the sponge-
boats had gone out, slow-rowing like these other boats, but with sixteen
men at the oars, rowing all the way to Africa and back. Harder times then,
before the internal combustion engine and the marine diesel . . . in those
days when a diver was paralysed by the sea pressures they would take him
ashore and bury him neck-deep in the African sands, and they would tell
him that the fierce Libyan sun working on the dry sand would cure
him. But they would leave him there and never go back. Harder times
then. It was odd how it stayed in his mind—sponge-diving, and Captain
Andreas, and the clean dull house with the quiet woman doing her
embroidery.

What would Mark and Mark's friend Janecek make of it all? . . . of
Costas the butcher with his dead lambs at their puppet play, and old
Dionysios rapping every Thursday night at the door for a pretty yellow-
haired woman whose husband carted gasoline in a tanker from Kuwait
to Rotterdam, and probably passed the beads of his *komlolloi* through
his fingers as he watched the girls in the *yoshiwara* at Yokohama, and the
anonymous wife of Captain Andreas sitting out her life in a clean and
respectable tomb where the passive forces of an unending loneliness
were to be distilled only through the alembic of shepherdesses and milk-
maids worked in cross-stitch on a square metre of cheap linen. . . .

The thought for some reason added greatly to his distaste for what was
ahead. He had no desire whatever to meet Feodor Janecek. Nor his party.
Mark already had sketched in, briefly and perhaps with a trace of reluctance—except in the case of Suvora (who, being a millionaire, would
have, in Mark's eye at least, a justifiable case for the benevolence of his
opinion)—the composition of what he called "the working party." In the
order of their importance, Suvora clearly came first, since he doubtless
was subsidising the working party's descent upon the island; then there

was somebody called Clem Kettering, whom Mark defined as "an interesting original," two figures almost devoid of outlines known as Brent and
Badger, and a woman dismissed rather coolly by Mark as "dear Clothilde."
The picture evoked sounded more ghastly than feasible. It seemed to have
no connection whatever with Silenos. It depressed him very much.

Poor Fegel, he saw, was already down waiting for the boat, sitting
disconsolately outside the Katraikis coffeehouse with Achille Mouliet.
Fegel was an inveterate boat-meeter. Despite a constancy of rebuffs he
had an unstaunched sense of expectation: always, with Fegel, there was
the hope of a cheque, of a good report on one of his verse-plays, of news
of a picture or a copper bangle sold, of a commission to translate something
from the Czech or the Hungarian, of an order for some specimen or
other of his pottery: if all else failed there would be a postcard from
somebody he had once known, or the latest copy of a literary review
with something in it that might interest him. Fegel was the paradox of the
born pessimist who insisted in believing that something was always likely
to turn up, a Rouault portrait of Mr. Micawber.

The young Frenchman sitting with Fegel struck the note of direct
antithesis; here was the enduring faun type, the ageless product of an
invincible narcissism, bathed in a golden sunlight which no shadow
could ever smirch. He had either reverted unseasonably to his costume of
a summer before, or he was intent on presenting himself *tout à fait* to the
newcomers. His feet were bare and his faded denim shirt unbuttoned to
the navel; the pair of shorts he wore were of the briefest cut consistent
with even a nominal evasion of nudity; the mid-morning sunlight gently
flecked the fine pollen-like down on his strong, handsome legs. The
golden earring glittered. The Roman cap of shining hair was crowned by
a battered old Florentine straw hat with a very narrow, ragged brim. A
small portable easel and canvas rested beside his chair.

David moved up under the awnings so that Fegel and Mouliet would
not see him. There was no sign of Kate or Mark. Alecto the goat woman
accosted him as he turned back along the quay in search of them.

*   *   *

They were, in fact, sitting not fifty yards away from him in the tavern
of the Two Brothers, where his wife was at this moment bringing to a
close her summary of a particular situation. "Listen to me, Mark," she was
saying, "whatever you think is best for him is beside the point, anyway.
He has to work this out for himself. And it's not easy for him. It's——"

"Nor for you," Mark put in warningly. He tamped the tobacco carefully into the bowl of his pipe. He struck a match. "This sort of life," he said, puffing.

"Oh, yes it is," she said emphatically. "It's much, much easier than it ever was in London. You don't know. I've no wish to change it."

"The children? Their future? Here, on a three-ha' penny Greek island, learning to be donkey-boys or fishermen? Come now, Kate, my dear, look at it straight! Are their chances for a proper, decent, organised future to be jeopardised just for some selfish, pigheaded whim of David's? It's not you, I know. You'd follow wherever he beckoned. But you have a loyalty to your children, Kate, as well as to him. Face up to it, girl, face up to it!"

"I've faced up to it," she said. "I faced up to it long ago." She carefully put down her wine-glass and studied across her clasped hands the dark, serious, bearded face of her brother-in-law. How different they were, how very different, these two brothers! And how impossible for her to serve as some point of communication midway between the two of them.

She tried to grapple with all the implications of what he had come to say—oh yes, it could be blundering, officious, tactless, all these things; yet in the troubled brown eyes that watched her across the cheap stained table there was genuine concern for all of them—but another reach of her mind observed him only in the unlikeliness of his setting, as a courier bringing auspicious news or dismal tidings from a foreign land might be looked at only for the difference of his complexion or the strangeness of his garb. On the wall behind him was the blackboard where the customers' tallies were chalked up in wobbly columns of strokes and crosses, the foreign-looking Greek characters painted on the *Timologion* board, the faded photographs of men with curly whiskers and stocking-caps and fustanellas, the flamboyant hero-lithographs of Canaris and Kolokotronis and the Boubalina. Seated beneath the blackboard was an old shepherd with splay-soled shoes, and a crook leaning against his chair. His eyes were contentedly closed. He sucked on a Turkish water-pipe, with the forefinger of his left hand stroking at his long white moustache in a rhythm pegged exactly to the bubbles rising and plopping in the ornamental bottle at his feet. A lean black dog, curled beneath the table, twitched in restless sleep.

"I can see your point, Mark," she said, "and we are grateful for your concern, but, after all, you can only personify one single attitude to the problem, can't you?"

"Surely the practical one though? Eh? I mean, it's pretty obvious he must be running dangerously close to the end of his capital. His book—this is another thing we have to face, Kate, don't we?—his book fell a good way short of being a real success . . . of being anything like a success."

"Well, at least he's still trying. I think the one he's working on now is really very good. And the reviews for the first were wonderful."

"Try spreading them on bread some time, my dear. Tell me the rate of exchange these days for kudos. You can't feed two young growing children on clippings from *The Times Literary Supplement* or *The Saturday Review*."

"You can't, I agree. Mark, I know what he's given up. I know the risk he's taking. But the children haven't suffered by it. And I haven't. And I think I've got a pretty good idea of what he's aiming at, what he's trying to prove to himself."

"You see his future then, here, on this island, quite clearly and optimistically?" She knew he had tried to keep the sarcasm out of his voice when he said, "You've lived with him eleven years, Kate. You must know him a good deal better than I do. Although I don't know . . . I was with Gwen six years and I knew a damned sight less about her at the end, when I had to kick her out, than I did when I married her."

"I don't see his future very clearly, no . . . nor mine," she said quietly. "But that's nothing to do with us being here, is it? Going back to his newspaper work, back to that other life, back to the city . . . that wouldn't make us more or less clairvoyant than we are, Mark. I don't know what's going to happen. Living with a man for eleven years doesn't give you that knowledge."

She knew that they were talking now about something infinitely more complex than either of them could ever understand. David, having asserted his right to a personal destiny, was no longer predictable. How could they, his brother and his wife, hope to understand him when he was grappling and groping to try and understand himself? He had been her husband for eleven years. She had lived with him and loved him and shared or endured all his changing forms of thought and belief and conviction. Yet now, more than ever, he was subject to a range of subtleties far beyond even her grasp. She knew his weaknesses and his strengths, the flaws of his character and the good hard ribs of it, his sensitivities and his obstinacies; she knew the dark side of him and the light. Yet with all this knowledge, nothing came out clearly. It was neither black nor white. It was neither the clear-cut divided circle of the Yang and the Yin,

nor the sort of computed exactitude of an insurance policy, where risk
and expectation were co-related factors. It was never a conclusive statement of purpose. He had left the herd, yes. Of his own choice, he had
turned his back on the brightly packaged securities which were the
slave-bait of insecure societies. He had become an individual in his own
right, answerable only to himself, yes. He had, a year or so before, liked
to point out to her how it was happening all over the world—the poking
up everywhere of what he called "these little nubs and knuckles of individualism" (was it, she had wondered at times, like a man seeking
safety in numbers?), and he would go on about the right of the solitary
seeker to reject those mass-patterns of society which, to his satisfaction
at least, had been proved invalid, banal, inhuman, stultifying, terrifying,
vicious, degrading, purposeless . . . there were a hundred words with
which he had defined its evils and its ill. Yet had he really escaped from it?
Or was his escape no more than a pretence, a weakness, a negation of
responsibility, and he was afraid to admit it and go back? How much, by
this time, had he become the victim of his own self-doubts? How far
was he committed? It was difficult to know. He had become lately much
removed from her, lost to his own perturbing self-examination.

Of herself, she could be more sure—much more sure. Yesterday, in
the kitchen, she had assured him that she had never been happier in her
life, and what she had said had not been merely an idle affectionate
cliché. But then it was easier for her—oh, so much easier than the nightmare years of London!

Her eyes drifted to the window, and outside against the sun and a
gull drifting and tilting on its wings swayed the pink and lemon mast of
an island schooner. London, the stark-black immensity of it . . . shep-
herding the wrapped-up children into the damp grey shroud of Kensington Gardens, watching their cold-pinched, disciplined little faces,
feeling the total dependence of their mittened hands in hers, sensing
the development of their patterned manners, hearing them cough at night,
seeing their slow inexorable moulding into the city shape. And seeing the
gradual—ah, but so quickly becoming less and less gradual—dissolution of
her husband in the hectic, tawdry violence of the daily struggle to meet
the issues, to stay ahead, to keep abreast, to survive. Survival. Conflict
and survival. And the cost of it? Gradually she had lost him, as the children earlier had lost him . . . gradually, then less and less gradually,
she had seen him as a figure growing dimmer and stranger, as tired eyes
meeting hers or evading them across a breakfast table which he never

saw; seen him as chemists' prescriptions, as benzedrine to stay awake and phenobarb to go to sleep; seen him as lies told in a thick voice on a telephone late at night, as car doors slammed by drunken friends, as tensions and stresses exploding in unreasoning angers or damp-squibbing into dreary silences, as bewildering terrors, as restless eyes staring from a cold bed at a darkened window; seen him also in the shape of herself, growing more shadowy, growing desperately lonely, growing colder, seated waiting on the edge of a bed—a woman left to her own devices, with nothing to devise . . . nothing to devise that was not in itself tawdry and temporary and worse than the alternative. To go back to this!

Oh no, for her the answer was an easy one. But was it easy for David? Did he really have the strength?—did he really have the ability, if it came to that?—to cut loose from the pattern of all his life? . . . this pattern which he was now trying so desperately to see. The first rejection had been easy, the cutting off, the slipping away . . . ah, so easy to turn your back on it and roll away on a great big gorgeous wave of audacity! But now it was harder. Now was the testing-time. The temper had gone off adventure, and he was no longer sure of himself. And this was the time that Mark had chosen to come.

She reached across the table and put her hand gently upon his. "Mark," she said, "I'm not even going to try to influence him. You're perfectly right. I'll go where he beckons. Always. It's easier for me, you see. But . . . don't make it more difficult than it has to be for him."

The schooner's masts swayed across the window. The gull had gone. A steamer's siren pierced the air, echoed from the surrounding cliffs, drifted away.

"Is that the ship?" said Mark.

She nodded.

"Ah!" He smiled. "Better get out there to meet my people, eh?"

The quay was already crowded. The first landing-boats were pulling away from the side of the steamer. She saw David along the *agorá* talking to a witch-like old woman in a black shawl and head-scarf, and she was about to go to him when Achille Mouliet intercepted her.

"Ah, it is you!" he cried, and after he had kissed her hand he held it a moment in his. "I 'ave been looking for you," he said. His voice was shy and warm. "This morning I visit your 'ouse, but you are not there. I leave some flowers which I pick myself on the 'ill above Fegel's 'ouse. I am so 'appy to see you."

"Kate, are you coming down with me to meet them?" said Mark impatiently. "Or shall I go on?" He had no intention of getting himself tangled up with this sort of accent!

"You go," she said. "I'll follow down with David." She turned again to Mouliet. How funny and odd he looked, she thought, with his earring and his funny straw hat and his childish shorts and the long V of a tawny nakedness showing between the faded blue denim—and yet how right for Silenos, where Mark, with his tweeds and crocheted tie and pointed beard, was so utterly wrong. "I'm so glad to see you again," she said. "My husband told me . . . we thought . . . well, here he comes now."

"Hallo," said David to Mouliet, with a lopsided smile. "You plan to chase that suntan early, I see. Kate, I think I've got a house for"—he paused with the smile turning wry—"for the man who did the sets for Vramantin . . . and party." He turned again to the young Frenchman. "Mouliet," he said, "who is Vramantin?"

"Vramantin?" Mouliet pursed his lips as if he had sucked on a lemon. "'E is of no importance," he said. "'E is very commercial. And 'e is a pederast." He moved a slow glance past Kate to her husband. "Vramantin 'e comes on this ship?" he asked.

"No. Well . . . God knows! Perhaps he does. I don't know. Our man is Feodor Janecek. Janecek, Suvora, Kettering, Brent, Badger, and dear Clothilde."

"Yes, Fegel tells me of this Janecek," Mouliet said morosely. "I think 'e also is commercial."

"Well, let's go down and find out," David suggested.

5

POSEIDON'S PLAYGROUND

THE ARRIVAL OF Feodor Janecek on the island of Silenos in archaic times would have called for some sign or omen for the natives: a tempest, the wild hurling of thunderbolts, a mysterious epidemic decimating the flocks, a trembling of sea and earth that might signify Poseidon's mood, an inexplicable jangling of the church bells, a fissure perhaps opening in the cliffs as if the entrance to Pluto's domain had been exposed.

Nothing of this sort happened. Janecek came in a crowded steamer, for the day was a Saturday and the tourist season was beginning, and two launches had already disgorged their straw-hatted, floral-shirted, blue-jeaned freight before the landing-boat that carried him made its own slow circling approach to the stone steps in front of the Katraikis coffee-house.

He stepped ashore, therefore, into a jostling crowd that was as chatter-ing, as vivid and ephemeral as parakeets darting in the sunlight, a mass so effervescent and confused that it was difficult to sift those who looked as if they might be intending to stay to write books or paint pictures from those who merely carried underwater masks and spear-fishing guns.

Silenos is no Juan Fernandez where Selkirk walked alone, nor even an incipient Capri. It has long since begun its walk towards sophistication, but has stumbled on the way. Its story roughly is this. It had been dis-covered, and abandoned, in the century of knickerbockers by a number of amateur archaeologists (drawn there by the presence of a ruined Temple of Artemis which Pausanias had mentioned) and by a select group of classically-educated Baedeker travellers who had revelled in its precipitous climbs and the magnificence of its views. Long after they had retired into the lay monasteries of South Kensington, rheumatoid arthritis, and the yellowing boards of old photographic albums, the island had been rediscovered by Impressionist and post-Impressionist artists, who for a time had flung futile pigments at its uncapturable essence: these in their turn had been followed by a group of intellectual camp-followers who had sought the lotus life at the minimum of cost and effort. They in their due time had moved back to the safer purlieus of Paris and Majorca, and now the island of Silenos—or, at any rate, a tiny section of it—has been abandoned to a very minor group of sincere, or professedly sincere cosmopolites who have turned their backs, for one reason or another, on the varying yet so-much-alike societies in which they were cradled. To these people, seasonally, are added the bright flocks of swift-skimming tourists who, in spring and summer, attracted by a tourist poster which describes Silenos as "Poseidon's Playground," briefly visit the island to take photographs, to swim and disport in the memorably clear and fantastically blue water which bathes the sheer-falling rocks of the island's outer shell, or to behave with a carefree immorality which the city conventions deny them.

It was within the very centre of a shoal of these gay creatures that Feodor Janecek arrived. It was not for some minutes, in fact, that his presence became evident to David Meredith.

And it was a presence. David knew instinctively and at once that this was Feodor Janecek: he had an insight also into how frequently the man would have been told of his startling resemblance to the Toulouse-Lautrec drawing of Oscar Wilde. The element of surprise was in the fact that the newcomer was not nearly as young as David had expected, for the man was clearly in his late thirties or early forties. Mark surely had described him as a "brilliant *young* man" . . . but then Mark himself was fifty, and that could explain it.

Janecek, as the crowd dispersed, stood beside a rising mound of baggage with the calm disdain of a landing conqueror—Mark's role could be seen now only as the advance agent, the keen-eyed scout: here was the real *conquistadore!*—and his composed gaze, riding above confusion, moved slowly over the rocky escarpment behind the coloured, crowded amphitheatre of subjugated Silenos. He stood rock-like and impassive, sublime in his stillness, impervious to chaos. He was a tall and excessively blond man with the teeth of a dentifrice advertisement and a cared-for complexion. He seemed to radiate a sort of contented fleshiness. His brow was smooth, his eye in contemplation of his surroundings as calm as a summer sea. His khaki shirt and khaki drill trousers, while testifying to pursuits less orthodox than the world of business and more earnest than the chase of pleasure, were neatly pressed and scrupulously clean. In his hand he carried only a very small flat tin box of German crayons labelled *Aquarell Staedtler.*

Contrasting with his majestic calm—indeed, giving it emphasis by the frantic tempo of his activity—the meagre figure of a lesser man, wearing a garishly-striped Mykonos shirt, fluttered around his feet like a humming-bird, a diminutive man with a young-old face adorned by a chestnut-coloured spade beard that jabbed dark wedges out of pigskin and rattan as he lunged and swooped amid the baggage. A gold Georgian monocle which swung from his neck by a thin black cord kept entangling with the blue overnight airline bag which dangled from his shoulder.

Mark, pressing forward to greet Janecek, said something in passing to the small furious figure, but whatever he said seemed to go unheard.

"Well, well, well, my dear Mark!" said Janecek warmly, extending a hand unmarked by travel grime or suntan. "I would scarcely have known you. You look ten years younger, my dear. And this is your brother and his wife? How do you do?" He had a voice that was charming and kindly and whimsical. "How enchanting it is here, Mrs. Meredith," he said. "How savagely enchanting!"

"You travel very light," said Mark, with an eye to the box of crayons.

Janecek's teeth gleamed. "I had thought to make some studies coming down on the steamer, but gave in to indolence instead. Actually it is I, I think, who have all the baggage. Clem travels only with his ikons, a box of caramels, and his Dramamine." His fine blue eyes rested for a moment with affectionate amusement on the spade-bearded young man at his feet, by this time red-faced and flustered as he struggled to protect a separate cairn of packages, folding easels, canvas in rolls, canvas on stretchers, and many bags of expensive and stylish leather.

"I'll go and help him," said David, also with a glance at the tin box of crayons.

"Oh, would you? That would be very kind of you, Mr. Meredith. He does get dreadfully upset and . . . and cranky when he has to look after the baggage. You will see him in a better light when this bedlam subsides." He smiled charmingly. "Come, Mark," he said. "Do please join us, Mrs. Meredith."

"Let me give you a hand with it," offered David, stooping, and the small figure arrested suddenly in its quicksilver activities, glared at him for a moment suspiciously. "I'm Mark's brother," David explained, offering his hand. "You're Kettering, aren't you?"

The man began to say something, then whipped around with a strange cry that began as a bleat, turned into a shrill wail at the sight of a crop-haired urchin scattering the cairn so laboriously established, faced into a sigh of resignation, then jetted again in a fountain of shrill instructions and expletives addressed to nobody in particular in French, German, Spanish and Italian—all delivered with spirited and remarkable fluency and a faint American accent.

David, knowing the rules, cuffed the boy away and retrieved the valises.

"Thanks," said Kettering. Flushed and panting, he stalked a vigilant circle around the re-established pile of baggage like a Roman centurion inspecting the last outpost facing the army of Vercingetorix, wiped his forehead with the sleeve of his gay shirt, and began pensively to caress his monocle. "Does your count of this stuff," he said, "come to twenty-three pieces?"

David made a slow circle, counting.

"Twenty-two, I'm afraid."

"That's fine," said Kettering. "Twenty-three with me. I always count myself as one. It makes the addition easier. If you don't count yourself in you never remember which one you've started with."

"You always take care of the baggage?"

"Always," said Kettering morosely. "And passports. And customs. And permits. Feodor deals with the human impedimenta. I am in charge solely of the inanimate responsibilities. Is there some place here," he said, his eyes roving, "where we might get a drink?"

"Why not? It's not so crowded inside. Half the island comes down for this, you see. It's the only event we have, the arrival of the steamer. It makes up for other things. There's no cinema, you see . . . no musical, no night clubs, no telephone even."

"Brother!" said Kettering, and followed him across to the coffeehouse. Janecek and Mark were in earnest conversation at a quayside table. Kate had detached herself from them, and was talking to Achille Mouliet in the shade of the café awning. Fegel had vanished, no doubt gone hopefully to wait for the clearing of the mail.

Kettering turned and tiredly blinked his pale, short-sighted eyes at the mound of baggage.

"Don't worry, the stuff will be all right," David assured him. "Let's go in."

When they were seated over their brandies at a marble-topped table, Kettering said, "You don't look much like your brother. What do you do?"

"I write."

"You do? Did Mark tell me that? You live here all the time?"

"Yes. Well, for the last three years."

"Brother!" Kettering said again. "Are we staying with you?"

"No."

Kettering nodded and stared down at his clasped hands. He wore scarab rings on three fingers. "Well," he said, "we won't be staying on Suvora's yacht either, that's for sure." He sighed. "Ah, well," he murmured, with what seemed to be an accustomed resignation.

A small boy wearing blue jeans and a grey turtleneck, narrow-hipped and tall for his ten years, pushed nimbly through the crowd around the doorway, came resolutely down between the tables, confronted Kettering squarely, and said, "Are you the millionaire?"

Kettering narrowed his eyes. "What's it to you if I am, Freckles?" he said in a low, threatening voice.

"Mummy said a millionaire was coming," said the boy firmly. "A friend of Uncle Mark's."

"This is my son, Jerry," David explained. "Jerry, this is Mr. Kettering."

"Hi, Jerry," said Kettering, then carefully lifted the golden monocle and favoured the child with a long, aloof contemplation. He saw straw hair and a honey-tan face, earnest grey eyes above dapples of tan freckles, a snub nose and a firm, well-modelled child's mouth.

"Why are you doing that?" asked Jerry interestedly.

"Just to see if maybe *you're* the millionaire. You're not, by golly! You've got a big darn in the left elbow of your sweater, there's a tear in the knee of your pants, one shoestring is undone, and you've got ink on your cheek. That's not millionaire stuff, not by my reading. No, Buster, you'll have to do better than that. You'll have to wait until tomorrow, too. To see a real one. That's when he's coming. He's coming in his yacht."

"Is that what you call an eyeglass?" said Jerry. "Do you always look at people through that?"

"Not always. Only when I'm intimidated. And it is not an eyeglass. It is what is called an affectation. Like this beard I wear. That is also called an affectation. When I'm intimidated if I don't have this"—he held the monocle between his fingers like an exhibit—"I stroke my beard. The effect is pretty much the same."

"But yours is a *very* handsome beard," Jerry said warmly. "It's much handsomer than Uncle Mark's. Yours is quite like the ones the ancient Greeks wore."

"You're smart, Jerry. You're smart. Once upon a time, thousands of years ago, the ancient Greeks made a sort of colony way up the other end of the Mediterranean, and——"

"I know. At Massalia."

"Was that it? Sure. Well, gradually these ancient Greeks moved up to the north and now you find their settlements all around a place called St.-Germain-des-Près, and the rue Bonaparte and places like that. They all wear beards like this. A fellow once told me that if you grabbed hold of all the beards in the St.-Germain-des-Près and laid 'em end to end they'd reach from Sodom to Gomorrah. Anyway, I'm the lucky one. I've got this eyeglass as well."

"But don't you think it's a very good beard, Dad?" appealed Jerry, slightly confused by now, but still admiring.

"I certainly do," said David with a smile. "A most impressive beard. Incidentally, why are you out from school so early?"

"Measles," said Jerry distantly. "In the second grade."

"My God! don't tell me kids have measles too . . . *here*, I mean!" said Kettering. "This earthly paradise . . . this other Eden."

"And mumps. And chicken-pox. It's just the same." David turned to his son. "Where is Simon?" he asked.

"Outside, with Mummy. I'm glad school got out early, because she's talking to a Frenchman with almost no clothes on, and *he* wears an earring!"

"Brother!" said Kettering, impressed. "Is this a big day for you! If only Suvora had come with us today." He paused. "Jerry," he said, "in my bag I've got a coonskin cap for you."

"For me!" The clear grey eyes widened into circles. An inky finger rubbed slowly at the inky smudge on the freckled cheek.

"Sure. And one of these make-it-yourself kits for your brother. It makes up into an interplanetary whizzbang of some sort or another, and I'm darned if I know why I should have brought *that* along here, but——"

"But . . . but how did you know about me . . . about me and Simon?" The small boy's eyes studied him with subdued, incredulous delight.

"Well, Mark told me his brother had a couple of kids, and . . . well, you know how it is with us ancient Greeks." For the first time Kettering smiled. His teeth were very small and white. The smile made him seem suddenly young and pleasant.

"Jerry, go and tell your mother we're in here," said David. "Perhaps she's looking for us." As the boy began to move away he said, "By the way, Jerry, what is a *Psalida?*"

"Earwig," the boy called back, and went out.

Thoughtfully, Kettering watched him go. His eyes were tired again as he lowered them to his clasped hands, where the three scarabs seemed to forage on his fingers.

"You're the lucky one," he said quietly.

"What?" David looked at him.

"It seems you're the lucky one," said Kettering. "Luckier than Mark, I mean."

"Oh, I don't know. I suppose so, yes."

"You only suppose so," said Kettering. "Brother!"

*　　　*　　　*

Within half an hour of the steamer's departure the waterfront at Silenos had resumed its appearance of normality. The parakeet flock had vanished without trace, absorbed into hotel rooms, public restaurants, narrow lanes, native lodgings, or the discreet isolation of remote and rocky coves.

Costas had gone back to the dance of his five dead little lambs, but the *entr'acte* provided by the arrival of the ship had sapped some of his enthusiasm, and his performance lacked its earlier liveliness. Moreover, old Alecto, whom he feared and respected because of his genuine belief that she possessed the evil eye, was tapping her stick up and down the *agorá* waiting for some decision about her house, and the constant passing and repassing of the crouched black figure made him uncomfortable. To David's explanation that there could be no decision at least before the evening she had turned a deaf ear. Outside the door of the tavern of the Two Brothers the big black mule, still harnessed between the shafts of the garbage cart, munched into a nosebag of chaff. Inside the tavern Dionysios drank resinated wine and grumbled about his wife to Tomás, a young man of the port who was rangy and cocky and given to indolence, although the best dancer of the *tsámikos* on the island. At a corner table by himself Captain Andreas waited for Dionysios to drink his wine and go, so that he could approach Tomás and see if he might be signed for the *Twelve Apostles.*

Mark Meredith had gone off to the hotel with Janecek, who had announced his wish to spend the afternoon in sleep after the rigours of the journey. Kettering had subsequently followed them, with the twenty-two pieces of baggage spectacularly lashed to three small donkeys. Achille Mouliet, whom Janecek had unaccountably missed, had made his indolent departure from the waterfront, his denim shirt discarded altogether. Kate had returned to the house to prepare lunch for the two children. Stathis Vlikos, lured from his office by the report that Suvora the millionaire had arrived, had returned disgruntled to his house, where he severely chided the little servant girl for buying the wrong cut of meat from the butcher. At a table in the sun outside the post office David sat with Conrad Fegel and a bottle of red wine.

The noontime had a drowsy summer-warmth, although the hard clear edges of spring still outlined the rock cliffs against the enamelled sky. There was a flittering, hesitant chirruping of early cicadas in the casuarina-tree like a tremulous beating of the air by invisible wings. The gulf sea was indigo with lacy streaks of white where the breeze struck between the islands, and three fishing boats with pink peaked sails slanted down from the reefs at Paralia.

The sun-warmth, the wine, and the lulling aspect of his surroundings must have dulled David's perceptions, for it was some little time before he realised the truth of the pain in Conrad Fegel's brilliant blue eyes.

"He was not, you might say, an easy man to meet," said David, in explanation. "He came ashore like . . . like royalty, or some visiting godling."

"I were not wishing to meet 'im," said Fegel harshly. "I wish only to see if 'e was the one. To make exact the impression I 'ave from the photographs in the magazines. So! 'E is the one, that is all. Oh yes, there is 'ere no mistake. When I see this I come away. I 'ave no wish to meet 'im." Fegel moistened his lips and scratched nervously into his mop of soft dun hair.

"Well, he's a Czech, like you. It would be rather interesting. You said you knew him."

"I am Czech, 'e is Czech—what difference is this?" said Fegel furiously. "Because you are Australian would you wish to shake the 'and of any murderer who 'appens to be also of this country?"

"Murderer?" David glanced at him. "Let's keep it within——"

"The same!" Fegel screwed up his nervous, sallow face into a grimace of disgust and anger. "The same, I say! What difference? You are not inform' on the story of this . . . this Janecek, my frien'. You are not inform'. I tell you the story of this Janecek, you will spit and go away."

"Really? You'd better tell it then." He filled Fegel's glass and waited.

The little man's head turned away quickly, and for a moment his eyes, catching the sun, looked as hard and as opaquely bright as turquoises. "You listen to me, David, I will tell you then," he said in a low taut voice. "I meet this Janecek first in a classification group near Jihlava after we are surround' by the Russians. It is to find out what work we are good to do, some to chop the wood, some to cart the water, some to attend the tanks and lorries, some to clean out the sewers, oh yes, some to do nothing and be the obstruct' so they are taken somewhere in the big lorries and we do not see these ones again. So! This Janecek 'e is young like me, and very pretty, and he looks then so delicate, and I am friends with 'im and I see 'e is very afraid, more afraid even than me. So I am taking care of 'im and I 'elp him with the questions and the way to make the act of doing things, so that 'e is not one to go away in the big lorries going east. And in a little time there is a Red Army captain who takes the fancy to Janecek, and I do not see 'im again in Jihlava."

He stopped and leaned across his clasped hands, cracked his knuckles nervously, nibbled for a moment at a hangnail on his thumb. "It is maybe six, seven months later when I meet 'im again. This time it is the big concentration camp outside Prague. It is called a . . . a redistribution centre, but it is the concentration camp just the same. It is a little better than Jihlava, because in Jihlava the war is closer and death is remember' better, but all the same it is not much. Ah no, it is not much! It is not very good there either. I think Janecek 'as fallen out with 'is Red Army captain, because 'e is there at first just like the rest of us, and 'e is only the number like everybody else, and sometimes 'e cleans sewers and scrubs the big ovens and digs ditches and shovels the stones from the bombed buildings. At first, yes—but then after a little while . . . no . . . oh no, he is transfer' to the office of the commandant, who is a big 'eavy brute from Georgia, and very cruel. Well, we are in the camp eleven months, and always it grows worse and worse. The punishment getting so severe, and still more severe. There is much flogging and bad confinement in the special cells, and there are some we do not see any more after they are taken to these cells and sometimes there is the firing squad to make the discipline in good 'ealth. At first we do not connect this with Janecek. Ah no, he is a Czech, like me. It is what you say, David—a Czech like me! We see 'e is in good favour with this commandant, but 'e is a 'ard worker, and very intelligent, and 'e is 'andsome, and"—he shrugged—"well, the war 'as been long, and the Russian officers 'ave the strict law against the . . . the fraternising. Ah, we 'ave seen much of this and we understand. Sometimes it is bitter to understand. Like Carel . . . 'e is my friend in the furnace-shop . . . and one day 'e talks of Janecek and says, 'Well, to 'ell with 'im,' and then 'e pushes 'is 'and into the chuck of the lathe so 'e loses three fingers and 'is thumb and this way 'e gets the long rest in the infirmary."

Fegel gnawed a thin sliver of nail from his thumb and stared at it a moment after he had taken it from the tip of his tongue, and then flicked. it away on to the sunlit cobbles where it glittered like a remote and tiny moon.

"It is in the spring," Fegel went on after an interval, staring across the harbour, "when we make the plan to fix the escape from the camp. It is not 'ard to make the short tunnel from the part near the kitchen grease-traps, beneath the wall and the wire. We 'ear the rumours that the French are across the frontier, near Gmund, which is a long way, but some of us know the country well, and we 'ear, too, that the Americans are coming to Pilsen. We 'ave no way of knowing it is true, it is false, but we think we will be better somewhere else. And nothing 'appens, David, because the escape plan it is inform' to the commandant, and thirty-six men and three women are put against the wall and shot, and two hundred and more others, they send them away in the big lorries going east. And the person who inform the commandant on this is Jane-cek. Feodor Janecek. 'E is a Czech like me, David. You are the one who says this!"

There was a long silence. "Go on," David said in a low voice. "Tell the rest of it."

"There is no rest of it," said Fegel tiredly. "I see this Janecek once more. It is at the camp outside Marseille. We are the displaced person, we 'ave no passport, no visa, but now we are names again instead of numbers . . . although, yes, we are numbers still as well as names, of course. We wait the permit and the ticket and the visa to take us away. Janecek is in the office staff. Very officious and of the big importance and walking around between the desks . . . 'e is in charge of interpreters and translation of documents, I think . . . anyway, 'e is very important. I 'ave to go to 'im because my documents are in Czech. 'E is very business-like and 'is temper is sharp. 'E says my name over and looks at me, looks

at me right in the eyes and up and down, but 'e does not remember me."
Fegel shook his head slowly and looked down at the ground.

"And you didn't make yourself known to him?" asked David quietly.

The little man glanced up quickly, his anxious little pointed face
twisted up, his blue button eyes gleaming.

"Oh, no, no, no! I say nothing. I do not make myself known to 'im."

"Why didn't you?"

"Because 'e is important, and 'is tongue is sharp, and I see 'ow 'e treats
some of the others who make the argument with 'im. If 'e knows who I
am 'e will not give me the permit and the ticket and the visa to go away.
So I say nothing. I just say thank you and walk away from this room.
I . . . I do not see 'im again until this morning."

"Well, you can meet him now. That sort of bastard shouldn't be
allowed——"

"I 'ave no wish to meet 'im."

"What do you mean? You'll still let him get away with it?"

"Now I see 'e is the same one . . . that is all." Fegel shrugged. "I 'ave
no wish to meet 'im."

"I'd bloody well want to meet him! I'd want——"

"But why, David—why? What is to be done, now, after all this time?
Fifteen years. . . . What can I do, David . . . to 'im? And 'e is important
still . . . of the more importance now. He——"

"Damn it, he can't have any effect on you now, Conrad! You're free!
Good God, man! you're not just a *number* any longer! You're an individual in your own right! You're free!"

Fegel raised his small neat hand with the dry clay embedded in the
nails and where the fingers joined. There was a far-away look in the pale,
gem-like eyes, and his thin lined mouth was twisted into a queer smile.
"David," he said softly, "'e is Feodor Janecek. And who am I? I am
Conrad Fegel. 'Ave you ever 'eard of this Conrad Fegel?" For all its
quietness the voice was impregnated with a brooding bitterness. "What
is the name of that sparrow there, 'opping in the gutter? . . . that gull
out there where 'e skims the boats? You see, David"—the low voice grew
thoughtful—"in a way 'e 'as justify what 'e did. 'E 'as been successful
. . . 'e 'as become the so important person. Yet after Marseille I suppose
we 'ad the same chance. And I 'ave failed. Nobody 'as ever 'eard of
Conrad Fegel. Ah yes, I make the pretend . . . I talk of this and
that. . . ." He shrugged. "We both get the escape, yes, but I do nothing
with it. Nothing!" He was silent for a moment, and then, "Also this,

David, there are the thousand and thousand files like mine . . . dusty files, tied around with the tapes. You think Conrad Fegel can undo the knots in one of them, eh? Bah! 'E cannot undo a knot, this Conrad Fegel . . . 'e bites 'is fingernails!" He stared down at the ground, searching with his eyes for the thin crescent of his thumbnail lying upon the grey cobbles.

*   *   *

It was mid-afternoon when David returned to the house. Kate was on the terrace in the sunshine, mending.

"You're late," she said, smiling. "Complications about the house?"

He shook his head.

"Shall I get you something to eat? I put yours aside in the icebox."

"Don't worry about it. I had wine and a bowl of *fasólia* with Fegel. I'm not hungry, really." He went across to the parapet and looked past the ruined windmills to the flanks of the Prophet's Peak. The sun, ruddy already and sliding down the blue sky, gave the higher flanks of the mountain a crystalline look, hard sharp edges of red and yellow and orange marking off the facets of the rock, embedded in a deep violet cement of shadow where the ravines and fissures came down. When he leaned forward across the parapet he could just make out the lava fields beyond, a thick, jet-black beading like a bold line drawn with India ink between the silver fuzz of the olives and the dark stand of distant pines. The Black Vouna, the local people called it, and shunned it when they could. It was a forbidding place, where nothing grew except asphodel and random clumps of wild thyme. It was strange to think that in the ancient days it had been a sanctuary for fugitives, because of the presence there of the temple of Artemis the Stranger.

"More patterns," he said to Kate, without turning. "Remember what I was talking about? Not me this time, though . . . it's Conrad." He turned to her, and said, almost musingly, "Everybody has these patterns, and some of them are strange. Bloody strange."

"Yes," she said. "I know."

"Fegel, you see, is all tangled up with this man Janecek . . . now, after all these years. Something slots together here, on a little speck of an island in the middle of the Ægean. Don't you find that strange?" He recounted the story he had heard from Fegel. She put the mending in her lap, and listened. The sunlight, slanting down across the mountains, gave a bright gleam to the high bone of her cheek and her loose tawny hair shone with coppery lights, so that on the side where the sun struck it had a metallic look, and on the other side, in shadow, where it fell in a long sweep to her shoulders, it had the bronze-brown look of a bird's breast. Even while he was talking he was conscious of the arresting quality of her beauty. He tried to think of what sort of bird it would be—some bird with that subdued burning glow inside it that would burst out in a ray of flame and light if it began to sing. Yet how long it had been since he had been able to make her sing . . . since they had been able to drown together in the wild flame and the light of it. How soft she looked! It was the same light lancing down from the deep-blue sky above the Prophet's Peak, yet it made her soft and warm and glowing, where on the rocks it struck off glassy glints of light that were sharper than teeth.

After he had finished what he had to tell her she was silent for a long interval, her grave, compassionate, sea-green eyes staring down across the cubed houses to the malachite shimmer of the harbour.

"Poor Conrad!" she murmured at last. "It just makes it all the harder for him, doesn't it?"

"Well, for us too, if it comes to that." David frowned. "After all, he's Mark's friend, his colleague. It's going to be a bit hard to take him, isn't it, knowing *that* story? Oh Christ! why don't people leave us alone?"

"Nobody is ever left alone, darling. Robinson Crusoe wasn't even allowed to be alone. It will work out."

"You know that the whole bunch of them are invited to Beth's tonight? She met Mark and told him to bring the others."

"Yes, I know. I was with him. I asked her if it mattered if Conrad and his friend came too. She said it was all right."

"Quite a soirée!" he said dryly.

"Oh, it'll be fun. We haven't met any people in ages." She smiled at him, then said, "Those two, the artist and his friend, are they queers?"

"What do you think?" He grinned. "I'm surprised you have to even ask. Dominance on the one hand and devotion on the other—what one might call a marriage of the old-fashioned sort. Now very chic, I understand, in those circles."

"Well, sometimes these days you can't *really* tell for certain . . . they just look and act that way. I think I like the little one, rather."

"Kettering? Yes. He thought to bring something for the kids. That jolted me, I must admit. Even poor old Mark didn't think of that."

"Mark only thinks of you, that's why. Mark's kind. He's good and he's kind and he's thoughtful—when he remembers. But he has too many other things on his mind. Mostly you."

"Yes, well . . ." David touched her hair as he went across to the door. "It's a pretty odd bunch, that's all I can say."

"But isn't it that people don't come to islands unless they're odd . . . a bit odd?" she said.

6

HIGH DUDGEON

THE HOUSE which the Sinclairs had bought twelve years before with part of Arthur's deferred retirement pay stood at the very ridge of the western heights, with a view that commanded all the amphitheatre of the town, the ox-yoke harbour of Silenos, and half the gulf beyond. It was a handsome house, finely built and square-set on substantial walls of hewn yellow stone blocks. The height of the walls and the colour of these blocks gave it the appearance of growing out of the very bedrock of the island. It had a broad and beautiful terrace which caught all the winter sunshine, but Arthur Sinclair, who had come to regard himself as a chronic invalid so that he should not have to go chasing up and down the precipitous steps of the town, used the terrace only during the month of August, which he considered as his annual holidays. Otherwise, he visited it only on four days of the year—on Greek Navy Day, on Trafalgar Day, on the anniversary of the Battle of Jutland, and on the eleventh of November, which he still solemnly commemorated as the Armistice Day of the First World War.

On these days he hoisted and broke out from the three flagpoles on the terrace the blue-and-white standard of Greece, the Union Jack, and the White Ensign, saluted each of them in turn, and allowed them to fly until sundown.

With a regrettable whimsicality, which must have been some legacy of his wardroom days, he had named the house *High Dudgeon,* and had taken the matter even further—no other house on Silenos had any name at all—by fashioning himself an entire wall by the front door where the name was boldly lettered in sea pebbles and shells embedded in cement. Beth Sinclair, many years earlier, had made some attempt to grow vines and creeping plants across it, but Arthur had cleverly countered this by training the cats to urinate in the pots, and all the plants had withered away.

Arthur was not in the living-room when the Meredith party arrived, but David could hear his quavering, high-toned, hesitant voice from a room beyond, and asked, "Who is in with him?"

"The admiral," said Beth Sinclair, and closed her eyes for a moment. "Admiral Mavro," she added, as if some additional information was necessary for Mark's benefit. "Or so they call him. He is retired also. He was famous," she said tiredly, "for an exploit in the war of 1912."

"He's wonderful!" said Kate, with enthusiasm. "I love him!"

"Even those one loves," said Beth, "can sometimes be tedious. Those two have been in there an hour already. They have been, as usual, discussing the Battle of Jutland."

"Beth's husband served at Jutland," David explained to Mark. "He was a midshipman."

"I have long since come to the conclusion that Arthur *was* Jutland," said Beth with a weary gesture. "Just listen to him now!"

The high thin voice drifted out to them: "Yes, yes, yes, my dear fellow, but the hypothetical question always remains. It is this, Mavro, it is this —what if *Warspite's* steering gear had *not* jammed? Supposing that when the line had made the——" The rest of the supposition was lost as Beth Sinclair moved across and firmly closed the door.

She turned to Mark and said, "At least, Mr. Meredith, this will give you the opportunity of meeting the foreign colony *en masse*. It would not do for you to see us only through your brother's rather prejudiced vision. Mr. Fegel will be here, with some French painter who is staying with him. Erica Barrington is coming. An interesting woman. No doubt you will meet my husband after Jutland is won or lost. Mavro, although ludicrous, can be rewarding. He is not, of course, foreign colony in the strict sense. He is, in fact, very Greek indeed . . . an impoverished Greek aristocrat. Greece, you will find, is full of impoverished aristocrats. They are always selling things—furniture, houses, jewellery, pictures. Mavro was forced to sell all the family portraits, except, of course, those of himself."

"David told me your husband was writing a book," said Mark politely.

"We indulge him in the conceit," she said without indulgence. "Arthur's last active appointment was aboard a light cruiser in the recent war which took some part in the battle of Cape Matapan, off the Peloponnese. Arthur has for ten years or so been writing what he calls a strategical survey of this operation. In other words, he is attempting to keep within a focus of reality a part of himself which has long since become totally unreal, even to him. The battle itself . . . well, nobody remembers it at all now. Still, we indulge him. It is preferable, I suppose, to the United Services Club—Ah! there is the bell," she said, pricking her ears. "Mrs. Barrington."

"How on earth did you manage to winkle her out?" David asked with a smile. "I haven't set eyes on her for weeks."

"Really? She has tea with me every Thursday."

David found himself watching the door with that subdued interest which the presence and sometimes the thought of Erica Barrington seemed to stir in him, although he knew her only slightly. Strictly speaking, she too, like Admiral Mavro, was not of the foreign colony, since she was Greek by birth and nationality. But she had been educated mostly abroad, and she had married an American, who had died some years before. The dead husband in some way intrigued him, for until he had heard of this he had harboured the vague notion that she might be Lesbian; indeed, even with her widowhood taken into account the feeling persisted. In any event she was a reticent woman and no subject for easy inquiry. She lived much to herself, working, it was said, on a history of Polycrátes the Tyrant of Samos. So the story went. She seldom spoke about herself, never about what she was doing.

She was at the door now, and he was immediately conscious—as he had been conscious before—of what a very striking woman she was. Although not particularly tall, her slenderness and the straightness of her carriage made one think at first that she was well above average height for a woman; an impression accentuated by the plainness, almost the severity, of the clothes she favoured. Tonight she was wearing a dark-brown linen dress with long sleeves and a plain curved neckline. The dress was beautifully cut and for all its simplicity looked expensive. From the top of the dress, rising from strong, well-modelled shoulders, a thin neck that seemed disproportionately long supported the head which formed the most striking feature of the woman. It was a head more of ancient Egypt than of modern Greece, and she must have realised this herself for her hair, black with blue lights in it like a raven's wing, was worn in a smooth straight bob, almost a pageboy cut, with a heavy

fall to a sharp edge at the back and a fringe cut dead-straight across her
forehead. Her complexion was dark, the brown-dark of rubbed wood. Her
eyes, beneath heavy, quizzically arched brows, were jet-black and large,
and again there was something in their long narrowing shape that reminded him of the ancient queens of Egypt. Her cheekbones were high,
planing the brown flesh sharply down to a chin that ever so slightly
protruded, her nose was long and thin above a mouth that was full,
richly moulded, and uncommunicative.

Standing beside him, Mark must have had similar thoughts, for he
touched David's arm and whispered, "My God! what a Cleopatra this
one would make!"

"Mark Meredith, David's brother," said Beth Sinclair briskly. "The
others you know. It's time Arthur made an appearance. I'll fetch him.
David, give Mrs. Barrington a drink."

"You've come out of your castle," David said. "We almost never see
you." She smiled slightly.

He went across to the sideboard to get the drink, as Mark, with all
the brashness of the newcomer, said, "David has told me about you, Mrs.
Barrington. What on earth do you do in that great house of yours, all by
yourself?"

David missed the answer, for at this moment the door swung open to
admit Admiral Mavro, Lieutenant-Commander Arthur Sinclair, and Beth.
The admiral looked dazed and foolish. Arthur Sinclair was chuckling into
a brown silk handkerchief. Beth was biting her lower lip. She made no
attempt to offer introductions, evidently feeling that her earlier comments
to Mark had covered the ground sufficiently.

The admiral was a very short and immensely stout man, with wide
shoulders, tiny feet in patent leather slippers, and a brown face that was
completely bald and circular. His eyes in the creased pouches of flesh
surrounding them were like little black stud-buttons pushed in as an
afterthought. Arthur Sinclair, as if the contrast was a deliberate act, was
ridiculously tall and thin, with a spiky tangle of sparse white hair above
a pale, mottled face that was excessively long and emaciated and seemed
to be covered all over with old duelling scars. He walked with a stoop
so pronounced that his arms always seemed to hang slack ahead of him,
as if he had borrowed them from someone else and was in the process of
returning them. With a series of hums-and-hahs, grunts, throat-clearings,
chuckles, and generally incomprehensible bonhomie, he moved among
his wife's guests. Admiral Mavro followed him dazedly until he reached

Kate, whom he grasped by the arm as a man who has swum a long time in perilous seas might grasp at a life-raft.

"Kate!" he said hoarsely. "You will get me an *ouzo*. A double *ouzo!*" He clung to her arm as she moved smilingly across to the sideboard. "If that man's strategy," he whispered fiercely, "is indicative of the training of the British Navy, then a very special providence must watch over its fortunes!"

"You mustn't take any notice of him, Admiral," she said soothingly. "He likes to tease you."

"By Christmas!" said Arthur, pushing between them with his head thrust forward and looking for all the world like an old and bedraggled wading-bird, "what's *this* I hear? Disloyalty, Kate? Disloyalty to the old red-white-and-blue! My godfather! I'll be beggared if I'd have believed it of you, Kate!"

Arthur was a master of uncommitted invective. It was always "my godfather!" instead of "my God!" He used words and phrases like "no flogging good!" "the fish," and "I'll be beggared." He firmly believed himself to be not only an outspoken man, but a bawdy one.

"You hold your tongue," said Kate, "and I'll get you an *ouzo* too." He looked cautiously over his shoulder to see whether Beth was looking, then nodded quickly and smiled at her. When he smiled the tip of his pink tongue came out from between his teeth, which were large and yellow and looked as if they would be soft to the touch. ("Arthur's teeth," Beth had once said, "look exactly like a very old silk tennis shirt.")

"How is your book coming?" Kate inquired.

"Revisions," said Arthur cheerfully. "Blessed revisions again!"

Admiral Mavro snorted and went away.

David stood irresolutely in the centre of the room. He would have liked to be with Erica Barrington, but she had already been cornered near the bookcase by Mark, who was talking very earnestly and stroking his beard with slow, approving fingers. Kate was obviously enjoying herself with Arthur. Admiral Mavro gave the impression of wanting to sulk it out by himself in the corner. Beth had retreated to the kitchen to organise the food. He went over to the sideboard and filled his glass with neat brandy. He had not heard the doorbell ring, and he was filling his glass again when he felt a hand tugging diffidently at his arm, and he looked down past a shock of dusty-coloured thistledown hair to the thin, sallow, worrying face of Conrad Fegel. His very bright blue eyes glittered like gem-stones.

"David!" he said urgently. He pronounced it Thaaavith, with a very long "a" and a last syllable like the bite of a buzz-saw. "This Janecek, 'e is coming 'ere tonight?"

"Yes, I think so," said David indifferently. "They're supposed to be coming up from the hotel a bit later. Why?"

"Then I will go away," said Fegel desperately. "I will not stay 'ere and 'ave to see 'im."

"Don't be so bloody silly! Have a drink." He looked across the room to where Achille Mouliet was bowing over Erica Barrington's hand and then Kate's. He looked brown, handsome, graceful, yet ever so slightly incongruous in a dark suit and white shirt, with a sprig of jasmine in his fingers and the little golden circle glittering at his ear. It was like him to have brought, uninvited, his own companion—a pretty little minx of a girl with tight black pants and ballet slippers and her black hair hanging in a horsetail and breasts that had the high arrogance of youth thrusting out her striped cotton shirt.

"Who's the girl with Mouliet?" David asked.

"Chloe," said Fegel dismally. "She is coming from Athens. A tourist, but she is as well the student at the polytechnic. She says this. I do not know. She comes 'ere on the same boat as Mouliet. It is all right, you think," he asked anxiously, "for 'im to bring this girl Chloe?"

"Oh, sure. Everything's all right in Silenos."

"I think," said Fegel, "I will go on the terrace for the air. I 'ave no wish to drink." He went away with a quick little nervous bow. David topped up his own drink and walked over to the corner group.

". . . the impossibility," Mark was saying, "of adjusting oneself to a totally alien way of looking at things."

"Your brother," Mrs. Barrington informed David, "is trying to find out why we live here. Perhaps you can tell him." Her voice was cool, controlled, rather deep in tone, without a trace of accent.

"I've tried." David smiled. "You might have more success."

"I've told him I live here because my house is here, my books are here, and because I have a very great desire to be left alone. It's all quite personal, you see, and rather selfish."

"Who was the little pixie you were talking to?" Mark asked.

"Conrad? He's a Czech. He makes ceramics, writes verse-plays, does translations, manufactures jewellery, paints in *gouache*, and reads all the little magazines. He's a total failure, and very, very poor. He's also a very nice bloke. He should make another case-history for your investigation on

'What We Are Doing It For.' " He was aware as he spoke of Erica Barrington's oblique dark eyes watching him interestedly. "It's time," he said, "I paid some attention to my own wife."

She smiled and said, "What do you think Mr. Fegel is doing it for?"

"I don't think," he said. "I know. He's trying to forget that once he was a number in a concentration camp, a cipher tattooed on a forearm, a filing-card in what was called a provisional settlement for displaced persons. He's doing it to be Conrad Fegel."

He was pleasantly aware of her eyes watching him as he walked across to his wife. "Hallo," he said, and nodded to Mouliet, and squeezed her arm, "how's young Kate?"

"I'm fine," she said happily. "Arthur and the admiral are feuding again. Erica looks gorgeous, doesn't she? It's going to be a nice party. It's fun being with people again."

"So long as Mark enjoys it. Is he?"

"What do you think? With Erica? He's having the time of his life. He's stroked his beard to about half the size it was." She laughed softly.

David left her with Mouliet and moved across to the girl called Chloe, who was standing by the door, rather self-consciously humming a calypso tune to herself. Her slippered feet moved absently to a *cha-cha-cha* rhythm. He made an attempt to engage her in conversation, but she had not much to offer in the way of response, and every now and then she would look across at Mouliet as if to reassure herself that he was still there—and safe. It was quite clear that she found the party stuffy and everyone dull except the young Frenchman: no doubt she had other ideas on how the evening could best be spent.

"*Epomoni,*" David said to her in Greek.

"What do you mean?" she asked listlessly.

"Patience," he said, with a dry smile. "That's all. Just that." He left her and walked across to the sideboard.

He could feel a sense of irritation stirring inside him: of irritation with himself mostly. In some queer way he felt isolated from conviviality. Almost the odd man out. Kate being vivacious with Mouliet. Mark sounding off to Erica Barrington. Arthur and Mavro, a truce declared, resuming their post-mortem on Jutland. Little sexy Chloe humming her *cha-cha-cha* tunes and waiting for the time to pass. He poured another brandy, filling his glass carefully to the brim, doing it perversely, aware of Kate's momentary glance at him across the Frenchman's shoulder, a look more of anxiety than of disapproval—but a look that had meaning, nevertheless, before her face was gone again behind the golden cap of the Frenchman's hair. It's fun being with people again, she had said. Each to his own taste, he reflected sourly. He had a childish pleasure in the fact that she had paused for a moment to be concerned for him. In the fact also that he was getting drunk . . . and that she knew it. He turned his attention to Mark. What was he talking about now? The bearded man with the reprieve in his pocket, stuffed into his jacket with the pipe and the pouch and the silver cleaning gadgets and the moral responsibilities. Come on, old man, you've got to go back to the *real* world, the world of boring platitudes and wasted time and languid slippers shuffling out a *cha-cha-cha* rhythm, away from this land of wops and goats and prickly-pear. He had a sudden wish to go up to Kate and tell her about it. "Come on, Kate," he would say, "we have moral responsibilities. So it's Land of Hope and Glory for us, my sweet." And she would say, "You go, darling. I'll stay on here with the children. We'll write to you every now and then." And perhaps she would say it with that soft, musical little laugh of hers, and for a moment press her cheek against his sleeve. Perhaps. How could you be sure? Uneasily, he resumed his examination of his brother. Wearing that beard, and with that intensity of expression, he decided, Mark should never talk to a woman a clear inch taller than himself. The thought amused him briefly. Coming in, Mark had wanted to make some notes on the appearance of the island. He had found its character very hard to define. Very elusive, he had said. What, David wondered, would he make of Erica Barrington?

He was aware without any particular interest that Janecek and Kettering had arrived, that Mark was doing the introductions, that Beth Sinclair had come back from the kitchen, and that the brandy was thicker than he had realised inside his head. Like Fegel, he felt the need for air. He had quite forgotten Fegel. He went stiffly to the French doors and out into the darkness of the terrace.

The little man was tucked away against the parapet in the farthest corner, the night wind stirring the mane of thin, dusty hair around his temples.

"This won't do, Conrad," David said sternly, and with a rather slurred, thick intonation to his voice that surprised him vaguely. "This won't do at all. Skulking. Come in and mingle. It's fun being with people."

"I think 'e 'as come," said Fegel fearfully. "I think I 'ear 'is voice in there."

"He has come," David agreed. "With fanfares of trumpets. Let's go in and tear him into strips."

"I am perfect' 'appy 'ere," Fegel said miserably. His sallow little face against the night seemed to have no features at all, only a smear made by fingers rubbing at something.

"Nonsense, man! What about your moral responsibilities?"

"I tell you I am very 'appy 'ere," Fegel insisted, very unhappily. "But I 'ave not the talent for . . . for parties."

"Then you must learn. It must be developed. Come here. Look at them." He took the reluctant little man by the arm and escorted him firmly to the door. "You are too shy, Conrad," he said chidingly. "Oh, I admit that contrived conviviality is something we should take in very small doses, but there are times when we have to hold our noses and swallow it down. It does us good, you know. That's what they say. It's the only time when we have licence to be insincere, banal, flirtatious, cruel, malicious, hypocritical, stupid, and boring all at the one time. So long as we present an appearance of being gay and bright we can get away with murder. With bloody murder, Conrad! The catharsis can be very good for the system. Fegel, can you do the *cha-cha-cha?*"

"No."

"Nor can I. We're behind the times. We're slipping back. We're waiving our moral responsibilities. We must go in there and learn."

"David, *please!* I 'ave not the desire to——"

"Shhh! Look at your friend M. Mouliet. Observe the intense, yet rather wistful lost-little-boy expression on that face, the glitter of that earring, the grace of that hand moving in emphasis, the charm of that posture. Witness the expression of enthralment on the face of my wife, and the anxiously subdued jealousy in the very lovely but rather bovine eyes of the young Chloe. Here, you would say, are all the elements of a romantic little sketch by, say, Colette. Yet Mouliet is undoubtedly being defamatory towards Bernard Buffet as a painter, and my wife is wondering whether Simon and Jerry will be bilious from having eaten all that ice-cream and chocolate cake which their Uncle Mark bought for them today. Now, see Commander Sinclair over there with our little admiral. You would say that Mavro is engrossed by this interminable anecdote, wouldn't you? Listen to him. Ah, they are off Jutland. I have heard this account before. It concerns an attack by Chinese pirate junks on H.M.S. *Cornflower* at Bias Bay in the expansive days of the Hong Kong station. It is almost utterly imaginative. But Mavro is not captivated by the tale:

he is merely stunned and bewildered. You see, Arthur *has* served in the
Far East and Mavro hasn't, and if Mavro attempts to question even a
point of detail Arthur will talk very sententiously about 'East of Suez' and
begin to quote Rudyard Kipling. Did you know that Mavro has grown to
dislike Kipling even more than he dislikes Byron? Now let us turn our
attention to the animated faces of Mrs. Barrington and my brother. Are
they engrossed in the intimate detail of some *affaire d'amour*? Or talking
about the best way of growing primulas in clayey soil? Especially, my
dear Fegel, take notice of my brother . . . the sagacity in those eyes, the
sense of profound wisdom in that hand stroking at the beard. The
weather, do you think? Or the best powder to take for stomach ulcers?"

"I think you are talking very——" Fegel began, but David checked him
with a gesture.

"This is your instruction, Conrad," he said. "You must pay attention.
Because we now must consider the others. Beth looks dreadfully bored.
Being the hostess, this is permissible—well, at her age it is, anyway. Janecek and Kettering also look bored. Janecek, I think, will be making a
deliberate point of it. With Kettering this is probably quite normal. He
has been to too many parties. The catharsis doesn't come any longer. He
is in a kind of state of permanent social constipation. We must be careful not to get like that, mustn't we?" He smiled down at the little man.
"Well, come on, now," he said. "Let's go in. I suggest we make our attack
on your compatriot. At the best he'll be vulnerable to our innocence. At
the worst we shall benefit by his experience."

"But I 'ave not the wish," Fegel mumbled desperately. "It is the best
for me——"

"Come along," said David, and took him firmly by the elbow.

Janecek was standing a little to one side of Beth Sinclair, waiting for
Kettering to bring a drink to him. He was making no effort to engage the
old woman in conversation, nor did she seem inclined to relax the
straight, stiff back which she was resolutely presenting to him and to
those others stationed behind the imaginary line she had drawn across
the living-room and which, as it were, confined within a boundary the
high-pitched, stammering cadences of her husband's tiresomeness. Moreover, she was not in the least interested in Feodor Janecek—whom she
had classified at a glance and instantly banished to that limbo of disinter-
est which she held in reserve for male homosexuals, Baptist missionaries,
Jesuit scholars, Indian hawkers, and all women social workers. Her interest was entirely in Kate Meredith and the young Frenchman, for she had

recollected that at Baden-Baden several decades before she had had occasion to form the opinion that no woman should ever trust a man who had eyes of that particular sea-green colour with yellowish centres—an opinion which later experience had given her no reason to revise.

"Mr. Janecek," said David cordially, "you have met, of course, your compatriot, Mr. Fegel."

"No, I have not," said Janecek, without cordiality.

"*Nazdar,*" said Fegel timidly.

"*Nazdar,*" said Janecek, and added condescendingly, "*Tak jak se nám dař̌i?*"

Fegel shrugged awkwardly, rubbed his hands together with a sound that was dry and nervous, and looked as if he wished to be very far away. Janecek, having distantly surveyed the thin legs, the baggy shorts, the rumpled seersucker jacket, the sad failure of a face, and the thatch of woebegone hair, had transferred his serene blue gaze to some far-away image visible only to himself. Fegel licked his lips and cast at David an imploring glance, like a dog on a leash pleading to be released.

"Janecek and Fegel were together in a concentration camp," said David quietly. "In Jihlava. Towards the end of the war."

In the sudden silence that fell between them other uninterrupted voices drifted on a muted level of independent interest: ". . . an Amoy junk, a jolly big fellow too," said Arthur's quavering voice, "coming up from Macao with all those blessed bandits hiding beneath a flogging great heap of gunny-sacks. . . ." And from the other direction, Achille Mouliet: "I am sad if you are not there to swim. Today I am there and there is also a girl from America and we 'ave a piece of chalk and we play this game they call tick-tack-toe on the rocks. It is a funny name, no? But I am sad it is not you who is there to play." His soft, gentle laugh drifted in the silence.

"Jihlava?" Janecek repeated the name slowly. "But I was never in Jihlava," he said in a tone of faint surprise.

"In Prague too," said David. "Outside Prague. At a camp for displaced persons."

"I think there is some confusion somewhere," said Janecek. "I was not in Prague at the end of the war, nor was I outside Prague, nor was I in a camp for displaced persons. Had you said Paris—yes."

"But I didn't say Paris, did I?" said David. "It was the camp where an attempt to escape was betrayed by somebody working in the commandant's office. Later, as I understand it, Fegel met you again at the redistribution centre near Marseille."

"Ah, but now I begin to understand." Janecek nodded and smiled and turned a quizzical gaze on Fegel's pale, stricken face. "So this is where we met, then? Yes, yes—but I do not remember. There were so many faces, so many people." He turned deliberately to include Beth Sinclair in the discussion. "I was stationed at this centre, yes," he said. "You see, Mrs. Sinclair, I was director of a panel of interpreters, and in charge of Czech, Rumanian, and Hungarian documentation. You may imagine what that entailed! Such a babble of tongues, such clamouring and pleading, such cajolement and bribery and intrigue. All seeking, of course, the ultimate haven, the El Dorado of the United States, all in conflict for the desired visa, all struggling in a beehive of consternation and hope and despair. Sad, yes—desperately sad. But how can one remember this face or that face, this name or that name?" Again he favoured Fegel with a glance that was faintly amused and faintly interested. "So that is where we met then?" he murmured with only the vaguest hint of patronage.

For a moment Fegel hesitated, with a wild, desperate glance towards David, then said, "We 'ad met before this," as if the words had been squeezed out of him by some uncontrollable force.

"Perhaps so," said Janecek equably. "I do not remember. As I have said, so many faces—so many desperate faces." He turned his back on Fegel and beckoned to Kettering. "Clem, dear," he called, "what is happening to my drink?"

*   *   *

"He's gone, has he?" said David morosely, and then, with impatience, "Yes, of course he'll have gone. He always runs away." He leaned over the parapet, twirling the glass in his fingers, staring down across the town. The houses seemed to give off a pale luminous mist from their white walls. Out to sea a deeper opacity blended imperceptibly with the metallic sheen of the gulf water. The island seemed adrift in a silvery veil of light.

"He went half an hour ago," said Erica Barrington. "I saw him saying good-bye to Mrs. Sinclair. I don't think he was running away. That Frenchman went with him. And the girl."

"He's still running away," said David stubbornly. "He never faces up to things."

"Is it necessary that he should?"

"Of course it is. Life isn't funny, but it has to be faced, doesn't it? Well, Fegel's life has been less funny than most, I suppose, but . . ." He broke off, and turned, and looked at her. "I like him, you see. But I get so damned impatient with him. He runs away from *everything*. He needs to be kicked into things. He doesn't ever seem to live in the world, not really—he just gropes around in it."

"But isn't that what we all do, more or less? In one way or another?"

"Do we? To the extent that *he* does?"

"Yes, but how can we put ourselves in his position? We still live more or less by the exercise of free will. We have the right to choose—or to have chosen. We can't know what it was to have been totally an outcast; we can't appreciate the absolute knowledge of *unwantedness*. To have been denied the very simplest right of choice. To have been nothing more than what you said to me a little while ago—a number tattooed on an arm, a filing-card in a dusty box; not a human being at all, just a displaced person."

"Displaced?" He gave her a long look. "We're all displaced. The whole world's displaced. Nobody belongs anywhere any more."

"Most of us still try, I think. It's important to try. I have the feeling that you try."

He was aware again of her oblique glance, of the quizzical interest in the jet-black eyes looking at him from beneath the blue-black fringe of hair.

"One isn't offered an alternative," he said.

"No. Not really." She smiled. "I came out here just to say good night. I must go now. I have a long climb, you know, to my house." She held out her hand to him, and surprised him by saying, "One evening will you come to my house for drinks? Just you."

"Thank you. I'd like to very much. I've been here three years, but I've never visited your house."

"My castle. That's what you called it earlier. It's not really as intimidating as people seem to think. Nor am I." Her thin brown hand with its long, transparently lacquered nails rested for a moment on his arm.

He was still on the darkened terrace, sipping at the last of his brandy, when Kate came out and joined him.

"We're the last," she said quietly. "They've all gone. What are you thinking about?"

"Unicorns," he said.

"Unicorns?"

"Well, it just happened to be unicorns. The quest for something fabulous. The unattainable quarry. Take no notice. I've been drinking too much brandy."

She came close to him and for a long time stared thoughtfully across the dark gulf. Then, "There's nothing there, you see, darling," she said softly. "There's only Silenos. There's nothing outside, just mist and shadows. Everything is here. Can you explain that to Mark? Everything you can touch and see, everything you want, is here. There's nothing outside."

He made no reply, but he put his hand on hers.

"David, supposing it works on him, too—on Mark. There is a sort of magic here, a strangeness. It works on everybody who comes. Sometimes I think it's like . . . like Prospero's island in *The Tempest* . . . it's not real at all, it's made up of magic and wishes and dreams. Unicorns, if you like."

"It's funny how you always think of being within," he said musingly. "Of being enclosed, secure. And I think of journeys. This movement through experience, whatever it is. Where we came from, where we're going, how we come to be in just this place at just this time." His mouth twisted slightly. "Philosophical reflections in the night hours. Signs of middle-age, I suppose. The male menopause? Something."

"No." Her fingers moved beneath his. "We all have journeys, darling. And at night it's always stranger, I think, because the night seems to stand there beside you, watching very quietly, and reaching all the way from the ground to the stars, and reaching right through you. So that you can't imagine a journey, *your* journey, as being just a movement from a point to a destination, wherever it might be, without its being a journey inside yourself as well. So we're really both trying to say the same thing, aren't we?"

"Are we?" He paused uncertainly. "I suppose we are. Yes, I suppose we are," he repeated the words thoughtfully. "I'm going to kiss you," he said.

He put his arms around her tightly, and he was surprised that her cheek was wet.

BOOK II

Suvora

THE MILLIONAIRE AND THE MAIDEN

Suvora—he had another name, but he was always called simply Suvora —was not a self-made millionaire except in the purely technical sense. He had inherited much wealth from his father, an Armenian, and he had, by clever investment and excellent advice, increased the six-figure fortune which his father had left to the seven-figure fortune which now, at the age of fifty, enabled him to live a life of busy indolence in a world of luxurious auxiliary schooners, the yacht harbour at Cannes, the Lido at Venice during the cultural or cinematographic *spettacolos*, the dress salons of Paris, various casinos, the islands of Greece, and the race tracks of Ascot and Longchamps.

The offices of his many companies, syndicates, subsidiaries and trusts were in Old Jewry and Lower Broadway, yet although he was a frequent visitor to both London and New York his calls at these business premises were infrequent and formal. The handling of his wealth had long since been delegated to a chosen army of talented lieutenants: what discussions were necessary between Suvora and his dedicated little bands could more comfortably be handled from his suites at Claridges or the Waldorf.

Suvora—unlike his father, who had begun his youth as an illiterate and had died with the reputation of being one of the world's finest translators of Persian poetry—had received an expensive education in a number of exclusive schools in England and Switzerland: this education had left him with no skill at translation and very little interest in poetry. He travelled on a British passport—since even millionaires must be registered as numbers in the transit from one territory to another (Suvora, not knowing the social and historical significance of this moment, had been born in the very year of the universal adoption of the passport)—but he was in every possible sense the most remarkable example of the true cosmopolitan.

He was an exceedingly handsome man by nature and he devoted a good deal of attention to maintaining this appearance. His strong, well-featured, masculine face was, for instance, always darkly suntanned, either by the natural actinic rays of the Mediterranean or the Bahamas or by recourse to an ultraviolet lamp. His teeth in this dark, good-looking face—all of them his own—were white and even, his smile was charming. He had a high sculptured brow and his black crisp hair was grizzled to perfection at his temples. His manners were impeccable. He was of average height with a strong, broad, vital body which he kept in a state of superb condition by massage, violent games of squash or volley-ball, by swimming and skin-diving and water-skiing—at all of these pursuits he possessed a competence that was seldom rivalled, even by much younger men—and by a studied attention to diet and to pleasures. He drank only moderately, smoked not at all, and attended to his sexual appetites (which, had he allowed them to run unchecked, would have been considerable, for he was by nature a full man) with a strict and systematic control which was almost, but not quite, like a monastic discipline. The strain of Oriental blood that ran in his veins supported his unwavering belief that coition as a regular exercise was medically essential: the strict discipline and cold showers of English prep. schools had taught him that it could also be the subject of a controlled routine, like anything else.

He had already had four wives—the score was even, since two had divorced him and he had divorced two—but now he was unattached, except for his much younger mistress Clothilde, whom he treated like an adored and spoilt daughter excepting on those occasions when his rigidly-enforced sexual programme permitted him to behave in an altogether different manner. Clothilde, naturally anxious as she was to assume the role of Suvora's fifth wife, would have preferred less of the father and more of the lover, but being twenty-eight she was wise enough to accept the curiously incestuous nature of their relationship with a commendable patience.

What she was perhaps not wise enough to know—but which her patron and paramour himself knew very well indeed—was that Suvora was beginning much to fear growing old, and he was becoming very tired of the intensifying tempo and the exhausting demands of the task of stay-

ing young. In other words, Suvora, at fifty, was for the first time trying
very hard to strike a balance-sheet with himself.

Beneath the after awning of his splendid staysail schooner *Farrago,*
cruising south towards the island of Silenos, he sat with a *Times* cross-
word puzzle on his lap, a gold mechanical pencil in his fingers, and his
thoughts moving around a dim strange figure remembered from his boy-
hood, the father whose name had been Silak who had ventured out from
a mud-walled village in Armenia with a roll of carpets on his back. For
a part of the new stocktaking of Suvora was a recently developed guilt at
having for so long been ashamed of the father who had made a fortune
as a carpet merchant.

Behind Suvora, on the soap-white, black-caulked teak deck of the
yacht, seated to port and to starboard in identical green cane chairs, and
equidistant from the pensive man with the folded newspaper in his lap,
were two silent, watchful, black-suited young men whose names, reading
from port to starboard, were Brent and Badger. Brent was American.
Badger was English. In a token sense they may be said to have represented
Lower Broadway on the port side and Old Jewry on the starboard; the
more accurate designation of their activities identified Brent as the millionaire's secretary, public relations man, answerer of telephones, and de-
cliner of invitations: Badger, being valet and therefore the man of the
bedchamber, was more intimately concerned with the personal life of
his master. He was therefore on the whole the more taciturn of the two,
although any contest in taciturnity between them would have been anybody's guess as to the outcome.

Clothilde was as far away as it was possible, on the sixty-eight-foot
overall length of the *Farrago,* to be from these three silent and thoughtful men. She was wearing a bra top which was little more than a swollen
ribbon and a pair of V's no more than a scrap of floral cloth. Her costume,
if such a word could be applied to so nominal a covering, did no more
than place in italics or enclose in quotation marks the long-legged, narrow-
waisted, full-bosomed, honey-coloured body of a born witch. With her
tanned and depilated legs spread wide she was stretched prone in the
very forefront of the schooner, her strong warm arms embracing for the
want of anything better the chromium-plated cap of the stem-post, her
topaz eyes bent upon the glittering ballet of countless whirling, leaping,
flinging, dancing beads of spray, sea-diamonds torn by the whitely shear-
ing cutwater of the yacht from the deep-blue, purple-woven iridescence
beneath. Her young mind, dazzled perhaps by the exuberant, splashing

play of water, flirted trance-like with her simple images—a glitter of diamonds on black velvet at Tiffany's, heads turning in admiration at Covent Garden, the fine profile and the speculative eyes of a young man called Louis-Paul whom she had met at dinner at *Tour d'Argent* on the quai de la Tournelle, and had not yet been able to quite forget.

"Brent," Suvora said suddenly, without looking behind him, "we shan't tolerate any nonsense this time with Janecek."

"No, sir," Brent agreed. No expression was added to his face, but his figure stiffened into a more rigidly attentive attitude. Badger aware that the matter concerned public relations, did not move a muscle.

"He is far too autocratic. I am getting very tired of his attitude."

"Yes, sir," Brent agreed.

"The night before last," said Suvora moodily, "his behaviour was indefensible. All right, a quarrel is a quarrel. We have had them before. This time, however, I'll be hanged if I am prepared to give in, to allow him to act as the arbiter of *my* tastes."

"No, sir," said Brent, then added for emphasis, "Certainly not."

"Brent—Badger, you listen to this too—he will want to stay aboard the boat, of course. I am not going to have him here, do you understand?"

"Yes, sir," said Brent and Badger in unison.

"I am sick and tired of his superiorities and his condescension. Besides, he rubs Clothilde the wrong way. He upsets her, makes her unhappy. Why should the child be unhappy just because of his presumptuous arrogance?"

"Oh, quite, sir—*quite!*" The matter having moved, more or less, into the bedchamber, the response this time came from Badger. The two young men, now equally rigid and attentive in their identical green cane chairs, had the appearance of bookends.

"I don't at all mind Meredith," said Suvora, less severely. "He's my sort of man. And, after all, it's *his* play, isn't it?"

"Yes, sir," Brent agreed. "Your capital, sir, but his play."

"I enjoy his plays very much. He has great talent. Well, it was he who insisted on Janecek. I didn't necessarily want Janecek. Burkin would have been as good."

"Better, sir," said Brent adventurously.

"Better, yes. You're absolutely right, Brent."

Brent smiled faintly and cast a sidelong glance at Badger, whose face, however, remained impassively set.

"My father," said Suvora firmly, "would never have put up with the sort of person Janecek is. He liked good, solid, trustworthy men around him. I don't trust this fellow Janecek. He pretends to have *my* interests at heart. Do you believe he has, Brent?"

"I am not in the position to say, sir," said Brent cautiously. In fact, he mistrusted Feodor Janecek very deeply, but he had some experience of the unpredictable nature of favouritism, and although, as Suvora had said, a quarrel is a quarrel, it need not necessarily be more than that—there had been tiffs before—and any committal of his opinion at this stage might well prove hazardous. "It is a hard question to answer," he said evasively.

"There are times," Suvora went on musingly, "when I wonder whether it is possible for a wealthy man to make friends with people, or whether he can only make contacts with them. There is a great difference, you know. It is very difficult for a rich man to be liked just for himself. That must be quite obvious, of course—and yet the more one thinks about it, the less obvious it seems." He sighed. "I am searching, you know, for a fallacy in myself. Perhaps if one finds the fallacy in Janecek one will find it in oneself. I don't know. I really don't know." His gold pencil doodled down the margin of *The Times*.

The philosophic tone of their master's voice as much as the fact that no direct question had been put told Brent and Badger that no answer was demanded. They remained silent.

"I think," said Suvora, "I shall put on my trunks and go up and get some sun with Clothilde."

"Yes, sir," said Badger, springing from his chair.

Up in the bow, with his strong brown body stretched beside the firm sun-warm flesh of Clothilde, Suvora had a violent momentary feeling of eagerness, which he quelled with admirable self-discipline. This little conquest of flesh and self left him intellectually more satisfied, although a deepening feeling of despondency and depression gradually possessed him as he gazed out across the tumbling blue towards where the faint, strange, double-pinnacled outline of Silenos stood upon a misty bar of sea-haze, creating that arresting illusion seen so often in the Ægean of an island riding in the air.

Suvora was no stranger to Silenos. He came often on his summer cruises, sometimes for an hour or two, sometimes even for a whole day, because he liked to show his yachting guests something a little different from Santorin and Mykonos and Delos and Hydra. He had a group of epithets which he reserved for the island. One was "odd," another was "quaint," a third was "uncharacteristic." He had even been heard to describe it as a "curiously sinister place," although upon what grounds was never made quite clear. In fact, although he had visited it often he knew nothing whatever about the island—he was far more familiar with the mooring basin at Cannes—but his feeling of a wistful sadness as he looked out towards its approaching outline could not possibly have been any premonitory knowledge that he was about to learn a very great deal.

He readjusted his position so that there was a strip of neutral, soap-white deck between Clothilde's flesh and his, closed his eyes, and resumed his interrupted reflections on Silak, the Armenian pedlar of carpets.

*   *   *

It was early afternoon, and even hotter than the day before, when the *Farrago* dropped her anchor in the harbour of Silenos; and David Meredith was at siesta. He was not awakened by the sound of the anchor cable, for the sleek oiled links and the patient windlass effectively muffled the usual sound of landfall. He was awakened by footsteps—quick footsteps on the cobbled lane growing louder, striking a tempo out of the warm, shuttered darkness, chipping sleep away in quick, rhythmic hammer-strokes. Was it his own familiarity with the stones, with each separate cobble, each step rising up, that made the footfalls part of himself rather than an intrusion from outside? The sharp rap of the doorknocker was the finality of reawakened consciousness. But outside the cicadas squeaked, a nervous agitation in the soft air that belonged not to him but to the coming of his visitor.

He rose naked, the sweat on his back cooling into a faintly prickly film across his skin, and pushed aside the shutter.

"Sleeping it off?" called Kettering, blinking up at him. Beside him was the ragged crop-pated boy who had guided him to the house; beyond, the town fell away towards the sea, a pale town without shadows, dreaming in light.

David shook his head. "Just a cat-nap. I was waking." He yawned.

"Suvora's yacht is coming in," said Kettering. "That's not what I wanted to talk to you about. It seems we have a problem."

"The door isn't locked. Push it open and come up."

He turned from the window and yawned again as he reached for his shirt. Other people's problems. The feeling of melancholy which always clung to him after siesta was heavier than usual . . . the sensation of still being entangled in sleep, yet also of being enveloped by other circumstances as insubstantial as the wrappings of sleep. He pulled on his trousers and fastened his belt and went barefooted into the other room.

"It's this house you got for us," said Kettering, coming directly to the point. "We looked at it. Feodor, I'm afraid, thinks it's too institutional. I'm quoting."

"Yes," said David guardedly.

"Another thing. There are also two rooms downstairs inhabited entirely by goats and sheep. And a crazy old hag who keeps cackling around the place all the time. I don't know whether all this is normal around these parts, but——"

"That's Alecto. She happens to own the house."

"And the livestock?"

"Yes, she owns them too."

Kettering grinned. "Too bad your brother isn't Tennessee Williams," he said. "He'd go for this sort of set-up. Mark doesn't care for it. Neither does Feodor."

"That's too bad. What about you?"

"Oh, it's fine! I'm all for local colour. And I adore goats. Heraldic, I always think."

"Yes." David thought of Alecto's goats going to the slaughterhouse, the burning yellow brilliance of their eyes.

"There are two other houses," Kettering said carefully, "which have caught Feodor's eye. That place we went last night."

"The Sinclairs'?" David laughed softly. "Are you out of your mind! The Sinclairs live there. They like living there."

"The other place," said Kettering imperturbably, "is owned by that old retired admiral we met at the party." He examined his monocle carefully. "We walked up this morning to have a look at it from the outside. Bougainvillæa over the gate. It's quite a house."

"It is, yes. It's been in the admiral's family for about three hundred years. The admiral was born in it. I don't think your Feodor will get that one either."

"Feodor has fallen in love with it. We hear that this admiral is very short of chips. *Very* short of chips." He stared hard at the three green scarabs on his fingers.

"He's a very poor man. You still won't get his house."

Kettering smiled. "Suvora will foot the bill," he said smoothly. "He has all the money in the world. And every man has his price. That's axiomatic. Oh!" he made an airy gesture, "the admiral could keep his own rooms. We wouldn't have to get in his hair. And we won't splash food on the walls or burn the furniture. We have our idiosyncrasies, but we express them internally, not externally. They wondered—Mark and Feodor—if you'd have a word with him."

For a long moment David studied him. "What would you think of offering Mavro?" he asked quietly.

"Brother, it's not *me*. I don't mind the goats. Well, Feodor put it this way—Suvora will foot the bill whatever it is, but there's no point in being madly extravagant just on account of that. On the other hand, the offer should be one which the old man must consider irresistible. You'd know about these things. As I say, every man has his price. You could work something out—enticing to the admiral, not too alarming to Suvora, pleasant for us."

"I'll talk to the admiral," David said, after a pause. "If that's what they want." The self-assurance, the cockiness, the incredible insolence of it! With what instinctive ease they assumed their superiority! Every man has his price, so all you have to do is snap your fingers, give the instruction, toss the money on the table! *Voilà!*

"That's fine," said Kettering. "Thanks. Mission accomplished. Feodor has kind of set his heart on it."

"Then we must try very hard not to disappoint him, mustn't we?" He made no attempt to conceal his sarcasm. The feeling of melancholy had changed to a much stronger sense of irritation and impatience. If they weren't satisfied, why didn't they go and find their own bloody houses? Just because he happened to be resident in Silenos didn't make him a kind of unofficial property agent, or some sort of lackey to be given his instructions through another lackey in a slightly more superior situation!

"You don't like him, do you?" Kettering blinked across at him, and began to rub self-consciously at his monocle.

"Janecek? Why? Is it compulsory?"

"I could tell last night. When you were talking to him. Or were you a bit high? I wasn't sure."

"I was a bit high. I still have a hangover. That makes me liverish. And I'm always at my worst after siesta. There you are, you have all the extenuating circumstances. And I still don't like him very much. Why should I?"

"Is that why you brought up this business about him and that little Czech friend of yours?"

"You know about that, do you?"

Kettering nodded.

"*All* about it? The whole story?"

"Sure. Well, I know enough about it." Kettering looked up at him and blinked short-sightedly. "It's a story you hear from time to time," he said. "Maybe it's true. I wouldn't know."

"Fegel isn't a liar. And it isn't the sort of thing you lie about."

"Maybe. Whether it's true or not isn't the point, though. The point is . . ."—he paused, and shrugged slightly—"was it worth while bringing it up? That's all I'm asking." Again he lowered his eyes to the monocle, and rubbed at it with his finger. "Did this fellow Fegel want you to bring it up with Feodor?" he asked in a quiet voice.

David hesitated. "As a matter of fact, he wanted me not to. What has that got to do with it?" His own hesitancy had the effect of increasing his anger. "Do you think a bastard like that should get away with it?" he said.

"He's not getting away with it," Kettering said tiredly. "He's already gotten away with it. A long time ago. Fifteen years ago. It's done. Finished with. Wrapped up in an old rag and stowed away. What's to be gained by dragging it out again?"

"Aren't you looking at this simply from the point of view of your loyalty to your . . . your friend?" He could not quite keep the edge of contempt out of the last word. "All right, he's your friend, not mine. Fegel's my friend, and my loyalty——"

"It's got nothing to do with loyalty. It's just a thing of dragging something out for ever and ever—dragging it out when it doesn't make sense any longer, one way or the other. Like some guy who killed a Jap on Guadalcanal in nineteen forty-two and is still talking about it when his son's grown up and gone to college and they're playing Jap musicals on Broadway and everyone's trying to be a first Dan at Judo or taking lessons on playing the samisen or brushing up their Zen. All I'm asking is, what good does it do?"

"You don't feel sorry for Fegel, for what happened?"

"*If* it happened," said Kettering carefully. "Maybe he's the sort of guy you'd feel sorry for, anyway. Just feel sorry for. He's a type. They exist all over. You might say he's the victim, the congenital victim. Did you know there's a school of criminologists who believe there's always a murderee as well as a murderer? A certain type that, in a way, just can't help getting themselves knocked off? Maybe. Who knows?" With an air of finality he put the monocle away inside his striped shirt and said, "I

hope I haven't messed up your afternoon too much. I'll tell them you'll
have a talk with the admiral. Thanks a lot."

*   *   *

Kate did not return to the house until the early evening, and when she
came back she was carrying a damp towel in a string-bag, and her hair
clung to her head in wet-dark strands, the colour of toffee.

"Where have you been?" he asked, surprised.

"Swimming," she said. "I went swimming with Achille and the children. It was wonderful. The water isn't a scrap cold. What about you?
Did you work?"

"Work!" He repeated the word sourly. "I didn't write, if that's what you
mean. I don't think I do that sort of work any more. I have a new job.
House-agent for the important people, general roustabout, errand boy.
The village Figaro, that's me. Janecek sends his little lackey to tell me
what to do. They're not satisfied with the house I got for them. Now
they want old Mavro's place." Behind the bitterness of his words lay the
arid hours of the wasted afternoon, the maddening frustration of staring
at a blank sheet of paper in an unresponsive typewriter, the leaden despondency of seeing all that he had written before as something contrived,
artificial, worthless, unpublishable . . . the dull ache that all through the
day had lain behind his eyes and the tormenting muddle of his thoughts.
And what a muddle they had been! He had stared at the blank white
sheet of paper in the machine until he had come to imagine that it returned his stare through an ever-changing pattern of other people's eyes
—the complacent eyes of his brother, the injured eyes of Fegel, the
quizzical, interested eyes of Erica Barrington, the tear-blurred eyes of his
wife, the blue disdainful gaze of Feodor Janecek, the pale unfocused
eyes of his slave Kettering blinking up at him above the golden geegaw
that he hung around his neck. Delightful distractions for a writer trying
to concentrate, trying to create! To create *what*? It was just as well, perhaps, that he had not known that Kate had gone to swim. In the state
of baffled anger and frustration which Kettering's visit had inspired the
contrast between her afternoon and his might have been just about the
last straw. To have imagined her body cool in the blue depths of the
sea and her hair fanning out around her as she floated, and to have heard
like a cry of mockery that special laughter that is the sea-music of summer . . . to have thought of her, while he glared and sweated, sprawled
sun-warm and salt-tingling on a grey rock, with a piece of chalk playing

—what was it he had overheard? . . . tick-tack-toe . . . noughts-and-crosses?—playing with Mouliet and the children. . . .

"Mavro would *never* let them have his house," she was saying. "What makes them think he would?"

"He might. He just might. He might, anyway, if *you* talked to him. Well, for God's sake, he needs the money, doesn't he? And they're flinging it around. They'll pay a thousand dollars for two months. I'm sure poor old Mavro can use a thousand dollars. Come to think of it, so could we!"

They would be aware of that, too, of course. To them, he would be very much the lesser of the two brothers Meredith—the unimportant one, the nonentity, the poor relation. And so, naturally, they would see him as somebody to be at their beck and call. They would expect to use him for their own convenience and comfort. Why not? The fact of its being to the detriment of his work would never even occur to them. What work? David Meredith's work? Gentle laughter—patronising, tolerant, amused. To them it was only their own work that had any importance: they would bracket him with people like Conrad Fegel. "*'E is Feodor Janecek. And who am I? I am Conrad Fegel. 'Ave you ever 'eard of this Conrad Fegel?*" The hopeless words of the dispirited little Czech came back to his mind with a new significance. To the newcomers the names of David Meredith and Conrad Fegel probably would be interchangeable.

"We saw the millionaire's yacht," said Kate. "And we met him. Mark was there. He seems rather nice, the millionaire. Everywhere he goes he's attended by two shadows—two strange, silent, very smooth young men with greenish complexions. They look like frozen peas. And there's a girl." Kate laughed softly. "She came ashore wearing a Hawaiian hula-skirt made of some sort of chrome-yellow plastic. The locals were very startled!" For a moment she was thoughtful. "It's funny, isn't it," she said, "to think that they'll all consider it's *we* who are the odd ones?"

How easily she had moved the conversation away from his problem —how deftly, how painlessly he had been manœuvred back to the distracting world of these self-important interlopers. The sleek yachts of millionaires. Plastic hula-skirts. Green-complexioned lackeys standing like attendant shadows. In all probability Kate adored it all, just as she had adored the party, welcoming distraction, fun, being with people—not seeing it at all as something destructive and humiliating. . . . He looked at her carefully, and—yes, there was no mistake about it!—there was a glow about her, like the radiation of some inner vivacity. With the flush of the sun on her skin and the long childish hang of her sea-damp hair she looked so much younger, like a being renewed.

He had a sudden violent desire to get away from it all, to find some touchstone of reality in the natural familiarities.

"Do you mind if I walk down to the Two Brothers for an hour or so?" he said. "I want to try to find Captain Andreas. I'll have to tell him that we won't be interested in that house of his."

SUNDAY NIGHT AT THE TWO BROTHERS

SUNDAY NIGHT on Silenos, as with most of the other islands of the archipelago, is traditionally the night set aside for carousal. On this night even Lieutenant Fotis, the police commandant, will take a glass or two of sweet red Lipsian wine, and there have been occasions when he has joined in the choruses of the songs and even danced a round or two. There is, on a Sunday night, a sense of divorcement from fixed rhythms. During the day the ikons have been kissed, the candles burnt in the churches. On the morrow the rigid pattern of labour must be resumed. The hours of the night that form the bridge between are for the men.

On Sunday nights the taverns where the wine is good, and where the music and the dancing are known to be enjoyable, are crowded as on no other night of the week. It is the time when music is loud, when guitars and *bouzouki* are taken from the nails on the wall where they hang amid the earthenware jars and water pitchers and galvanized iron bathtubs, when the *tsabuna* wails and the harp-like zither sings its song, when men warmed by wine will vie with one another in the intricate improvisations of the dance, when drunkenness is happiness, when song will run through the dark narrow lanes of the town like a river of joy.

Only on Sunday will Lieutenant Fotis relax his six-nights-a-week rule that tavern singing must stop sharp at eleven o'clock in the interests of sleeping residents: in the dusty folios in the dusty office of Theodoros Glyptis, the notary, no law is known to exist to specify the hour of a tavern's closing on a Sunday. At midnight—which normally is regarded as a very late hour on Silenos—lamps will be lit and candles stuck in bottles when the town's electric light supply is switched off. It is always better after that. In the jump of dim radiance and the flow of shadows the singing will always be richer, the music wilder, and the men of the quayside and the shepherds from the high *vouná* and the water-carriers from the Sweet Wells and the fishermen from Paralia will leap and spin in an abandoned revelry that is a good deal more pagan than they realise. Sunday on Silenos is always a good night and occasionally a memorable one.

David had forgotten that it was a Sunday when in the last of the dusk he came to the tavern of the Two Brothers.

It was not yet as crowded as it would become later in the night, but already there were only one or two tables in the big bare raftered room that were not occupied. Already four young men, linked hand to hand by their clean ironed Sunday handkerchiefs, were circling in the *tsámikos*, dancing it sedately with neat small steps and prim-pointed toes, dancing as daintily as girls, their faces absorbed in the leader's footwork, yet clearly holding in their energies for the wilder pacing to come.

At the end of the tavern, alongside a table stacked with glasses and shining copper beakers, seated directly beneath the thick, baulk-timbered shelf on which the five blue-painted wine barrels were racked, were the three musicians. There was a red-headed boy with a pinched face who cradled a *bouzouki* beribboned in blue and white and bellied like a melon, and with him were two gnarled old men with faces like dried apples. They were, although they looked like twins, the father and the grandfather of the boy with the *bouzouki*. The father's grey head was bent across the zither, the grandfather rested back in his chair and scraped shrill querulous stabbing chords from a battered violin. Above their heads Petros the drink waiter straddled a ladder as he filled the big blue enamelled jug with wine from the spigot.

The clientèle was mostly of Sileniots, although there were a few obvious holiday-makers from Athens with their women. The presence of the women established their alienness as definitely as the striped, tourist-weave shirts they all wore, for no local woman would ever be permitted to sit at night in the tavern of the Two Brothers.

At a withdrawn corner table beneath the barrel shelf another stranger was seated—a handsome, suntanned man of early middle-age. His clothes were good—what David always thought of as "yachting clothes"—and although he was seated alone there were two unopened bottles of Johnnie

Walker Black Label on the table. He sat with his chin resting on his cupped hands and he seemed totally absorbed in the dancing.

David waited until the circling dancers had finished their movement before he made towards an unoccupied table, but there was no chair and he was looking around for one when, to his surprise, he saw that the suntanned man was smiling across at him with an expression of recognition, and beckoning to him. He walked over to the corner table, and the man in the yachting clothes rose from his chair.

"You're Meredith, aren't you?" he said, offering his hand. "Mark's brother? My name is Suvora. I recognised you from your picture on the jacket of your book. Please join me," he said. "I am without company." He gestured to the vacant chair.

"I very much like to watch this island dancing," Suvora explained happily, as David sat down. "I find it very exciting. I had the pleasure, Mr. Meredith, of meeting your wife this afternoon. A most charming woman. And very beautiful."

David inclined his head.

"I have some Scotch here. You will join me?"

"Thank you." David shook his head. "Wine for me. Only wine."

"Ah, that is wiser, yes." Suvora glanced wistfully at the two unopened bottles. "I do not drink whisky myself," he explained. "Well, very seldom, anyway. I brought these from the yacht in case there is somebody who would like a drink. Do you come also to watch the dancing, Mr. Meredith?"

"Not really. Not tonight, that is. I like the dancing, yes. But there is a man I must talk to. I was hoping to find him here." He glanced around the tables, but there was no sign of Captain Andreas. The irony of the situation amused rather than irked him. He had come here for the express purpose of getting back to the simple truths of the island, of escaping from the disturbing elements of intrusion represented by Mark and his friends. And he had run smack into the symbolic focus of what it meant —this millionaire in his smart yachting clothes bearing his bottles of whisky like trade-goods for the natives! What would be his companion's reaction, he wondered dryly, if he were to say: "Alcoholic liquors not permitted as trade-goods. Glass beads, bolts of bright calico, yes; even Mother Hubbards if you like. But no grog for the natives. Makes them play up. Can't trust them, you know, when they get out of control!" Instead of saying it, he called Petros across to bring wine, and said, "You are expecting the others of your party?"

"Oh, no," said Suvora. "I am quite alone this evening. Your brother and Mr. Janecek have taken Clothilde to dinner at a restaurant. Clothilde —I think you have not met her, have you?—well, she has a passion for squid in sepia. It makes her teeth black, and her tongue. I do not like to see it. I pleaded an indisposition." He laughed softly. His face creased pleasantly with laughter, and his eyes seemed warm. "I think there are times," he said, "when it is very important to get away from women. Besides, I very much like to watch this dancing, but it seems to bore the others a good deal."

"Well, it's early yet," said David. "There isn't much life in it. When they get warmed up . . . later . . . a tip to the musicians, a half-kilo of wine here and there"—David smiled—"that's the quickest way to get them really dancing."

Suvora nodded. "Whisky?" He tilted his dark, good-looking head in inquiry. "They would like whisky?"

"Oh yes, they would like the whisky all right. But you keep it right here on the table. The wine is better, and very much cheaper. And they'll dance better. The whisky would spoil it."

"Yes, I see. My father—my father sold carpets in Armenia, Mr. Meredith—he had a saying, a village saying I suppose it was, that said, 'A pointed stick will plant seeds better than a silver fork.' There is usually a good deal of truth in these old adages." For a few moments he was thoughtful. "I like your brother's plays very much, Mr. Meredith," he said, changing the subject. "He has an excellent sense of the dramatic, a true talent for the theatre."

"I'm glad you think so. Mark's very clever."

"You also, I know. Mark lent me your book, and he has talked to me about you. I understand you will be returning to London with him."

David looked at him sharply. "That's not true," he said. "I have no plans to go back. I hope to go on living here."

"Ah, I have misunderstood the situation then."

David laughed softly. "You have been listening to Mark, that's all. He would like me to go back with him. He believes I'm wasting my time here."

"And are you?" The millionaire glanced at him quizzically. His eyes were a soft, dark-brown with a thin golden halo around the pupil; the blackness at the centre seemed to spread outward into rays. There were a few grey hairs curling out of the thick black brows.

"I don't know," said David. "It's too early to say."

"How long have you lived on Silenos?"

"Around three years."

"And still too early to say? Surely you should know by now? My conclusion therefore is that you are not. I am an authority, Mr. Meredith, on the subject of wasting time. It is a very, very difficult task to master. You must give your whole attention to it. It cannot be a hobby, a part-time pursuit: it's far too demanding for that."

David smiled, and was about to say something when he caught sight of the bulky figure of Captain Andreas at the doorway of the tavern, looking in. "Ah, there's my man now," he said, and began to rise, but as he did so the whole room stirred to a subtle difference in the atmosphere. He sat down again, and touched Suvora's arm. "Look," he said, "this man can dance. Watch him. This is Tomás. He's bone-lazy and he's a troublesome young bastard, but he knows how to dance. I should say he's the best on the island."

The *tsámikos* ended, the four men had put their handkerchiefs back in their pockets and sauntered across to offer their thanks to the three musicians. One of them had left a yellow ten-drachma bill hooked into the strings of the *bouzouki*. Now the banknote fluttered and flickered among the blue and white ribbons to the slow, jerky twangling of the strings, almost Oriental in rhythm and cadence, as Tomás advanced alone into the centre of the room, tweaking with nervous fingers at the knees of his threadbare blue fisherman's pants as he sought for the rhythm, the *levántikos* rhythm. Above the rolled neck of his frayed black jersey his thin arrogant face was tilted back. A lighted cigarette dangled between his compressed lips and his eyes were half-closed against the drift of smoke. For a long moment he stood in the centre of the room, as if he were looking at something high above and far away, and then his right hand moved up to finger the crotch of his trousers as he went down with bent knees, down and down very slowly until the palm of his left hand, extended outward, rested flat against the floor. For another even longer interval he remained immobile, almost in a position of obeisance, while the muted strings whispered a broken, staccato rhythm, his eyes tightly closed as if in prayer, his hand stretched out and pressing down as if he were feeling for the primal forces of the earth. And then with a strange grunting jet of a cry that spat the cigarette half-way across the room, he was a stiff figure bolt upright in the air, high above the floor, his thin body whirling into the spin, his hand upraised with his fingers clicking

. . . and all around the tables the other men were clapping out the rhythm with their hands.

For ten minutes he danced, poised in the air, turning and whirling, sinking to the ground, spinning and leaping, and in all of the dance and its infinite improvisations he never once trespassed on more than a square-metre of the floor.

When it was done he walked slowly back to his chair, his face expressionless, his back turned to the musicians. It was a man from another table who went across and slipped a ten-drachma note between the strings of the *bouzouki*. From the doorway of the tavern Captain Andreas watched.

"Good heavens! the man can dance!" cried Suvora excitedly. "I've never seen anything like it!"

"It's early yet," said David. "Wait until later." He pushed his chair back. "I must see Andreas now," he said. "Would you excuse me?"

"Please ask him to join us, if he would like to," said Suvora eagerly. "We have all this whisky."

"I'll ask him. He's not very sociable."

At the door he gave Captain Andreas the necessary information about the house, which was received with a polite inclination of the head, but without comment.

"I am sitting over there, with Mr. Suvora," David said. "Join us for a drink."

Again the sponge-boat captain inclined his head, and without a word followed David across the room. He did not look over to where Tomás was sitting, but Tomás's eyes above the rim of his wineglass followed the thick-set figure in the black peaked cap and the navy reefer jacket.

"Captain Andreas has a sponge-boat," David explained to Suvora. "He is getting his crew ready now to make the trip to Africa."

"How interesting," said Suvora. "The crafts of the sea are always fascinating. I am sure you have many adventures, Captain."

Again the response was a slight, polite inclination of the brown, weatherbeaten face, but although the gesture was the same there was depreciation in it this time rather than acquiescence. "It is work. Work is always work," he said.

"Please let me pour you a whisky, Captain," Suvora offered courteously.

Captain Andreas shook his head. "Wine, thank you," he said. "Excuse me. I will share a little of this wine with *Kyrios* Meredith."

Once more Suvora glanced sorrowfully at his two unwanted bottles. "You have been a long time in the sponge trade, Captain?" he asked.

"All my life," came the quiet answer. "First a boat-boy, then skin-diver, then a *skafendrós* . . . after that a captain . . . my own boat. I am fifty years," he said. "I began at twelve. Work it out. Thirty-eight years."

"Not all the time," said David. "I saw a photograph in your house. You in uniform beside a tank. The war."

"The war." The captain shrugged. There was no comment in his repetition of the words.

"So you are fifty." Suvora looked at him with deeper interest. "I too am fifty," he said, with almost a flourish in his intonation, as if something remarkable was to be found in the coincidence. Carefully he studied the dark strong face beneath the peaked cap, searching it for some evidence of a fundamental sameness or a fundamental difference. There was nothing in the face either to shock him or to reassure him. There were things in it, yes—a resolute hardness, a subdued dignity, a rock-like quality of endurance, but these were characteristics that had become subcutaneous, that were embedded in the hidden soul of the man, that were not related in any way to the self-searchings of Suvora.

There was a sudden wild screeching of chords, and a harsh scraping back of chairs as the *tsámikos* began again, but this time seven men were up, with Tomás leading them into the first prancing, experimental circle. The earlier *levántikos* had set the pace and given an electric quality to the atmosphere. The drift of tobacco smoke hung like a soft blue canopy beneath the shadowed parallels of the rafters, and at the far end of the room by the big tiled stove where the charcoal fire flung eddies of sparks into the dim-glowing, oil-smelling corner, Jumping Jack the epileptic, earning a platter of fish and a glass or two of wine by washing the dishes, wildly brandished a big black skillet in the air. All over the big room there was a muted, rhythmic rapping of fists and knuckles on the tables, and above the sound the taut breathing and the hoarse, grunting exhalations of the circling seven.

The music moved to a quicker tempo, jerkily, with sharp stabbing screeches from the violin; the pace of the circle, linked handkerchief to handkerchief, quickened, hesitated, swooped a tight dipping arc to pause again, swayed backward immobile, like a Greek chorus, as Tomás soared in a wild, whirling pirouette with his hand slapping at his heels. He came down from it, six feet down from his leap on to his bended knees, and kneeling there swayed forward slowly like a lingering death to strike his forehead on the boards and reach with his outflung palms for the secrets of the earth, and then, as if the hidden force itself had flung him off, he was high on his pointed toes, spinning the reverse, with every man in the circle gasping to follow him.

It was as memorable a *tsámikos* as any you would see on Silenos—or anywhere else, for that matter—and Tomás danced it with his lips compressed, as if he had no need to breathe, and his lean, flexible body changing at his will from the stiffness of a steel rod to the flowing subtlety of dry grasses in the wind.

When it was over, the six men who had tried to follow Tomás were staggering back to their tables, panting for breath, and the whole room was in an uproar, with fists and copper beakers beating on the tables, and the exuberance of the room's unanimous acclaim hammered at the ceiling. And Suvora the millionaire, as flushed as any of them, was standing on his chair waving a wineglass and shouting *"Bravo! Bravo!"* as loudly as the rest. David, caught by the enthusiasm, sat bolt upright in his chair. Captain Andreas did not move. His elbows were on the table, his shoulders bowed, his fingers linked so that his spread hands covered the top of his wineglass.

Tomás, staring around the applauding room with one hand casually arrogant on his hip, saw Suvora out of the insolence of his black eyes. Slowly, almost carelessly, he raised his own glass in response to the millionaire's salutation; and then, with the glass still in his hand, and all the cocksureness of the world in his walk, he sauntered across to the corner table.

"You were wonderful! Wonderful! Your dancing is really wonderful!" Suvora was breathless and repetitive, but his brown eyes were ashine with the genuineness of his admiration. "You must drink with me! You must have whisky!" His hands were shaking with excitement as he reached across and tore the tinfoil seal from one of the bottles.

David stared at the printed metal softly tearing away, at the brown, competent, cared-for fingers twisting at the screw-cap. Captain Andreas, motionless, his head still bent, looked down at his own hands clasped across the wineglass. His fingers moved slightly as he rubbed his knuckles, then were still. Tomás, unsmiling and disdainful, looked first at the whisky bottles on the table, then at Suvora, finally at his own wineglass. Casually he poured the wine out on the floor and offered the emptied glass to Suvora.

"Take it," said Suvora quickly. "Take it across to your friends. Take it all! Take the bottles! Both of them!" Nervously he thrust the two bottles across the table, and then he fumbled in his jacket pocket and drew out a pigskin wallet. "Here," he said. "You must have a present. I must give you a present for your dancing."

The banknote seemed to fall upon the table of its own volition. It lay there, midway between a dish of goat cheese and a spilt puddle of wine, a tan-coloured oblong, clean and starch-stiff from the Mint, a bill for a thousand drachmas. There was a long pause while it lay there, and David and Tomás looked down at it, and Suvora's eyes glanced across at them as if in search of something, and Captain Andreas stared down at his fingers linked across the wineglass.

Tomás nodded his thanks and bent over and picked up the money. He folded it with care and put it in his pocket, and then with the two bottles of whisky in his hand he turned away. He cleared his throat and spat on the floor as he left, and the white gobbet fell an inch or two to one side of the captain's seaboot.

Tomás held the two whisky bottles high above his head, like a man returning from the chase with trophies, as he walked back to his table.

A little later a group in the corner began drunkenly to sing the chorus of *Psarapoula*, and Captain Andreas, taking advantage of the din, left them. He went away quietly and politely, shaking hands, thanking them for the drinks, wishing them a pleasant evening. All the faces were turned to the singing group in the corner, and his departure was not noticed.

It was a few moments before Suvora spoke. "Your friend was not angry with me?" he asked quietly, almost with diffidence.

"I've no idea," David replied shortly. His fingers were cramped around his empty glass. He did not raise his eyes. He could still see on the stained table-top the spotless, tan-coloured banknote, the ornate decoration, the neat lettering, the fine engraving of the mosaic of Alexander the Great. He could see the blackened, stubby fingers of Captain Andreas clasped above the wineglass. He could smell the sweat and garlic smell of Tomás, standing there behind him.

"But I think *you* are," Suvora persisted softly, and with a trace of bewilderment. "I can sense your constraint, Mr. Meredith. What have I done that——"

"What the hell did you have to do that for?" David looked up at him sharply, his face flushed with anger. "What does *that* allow you to prove?"

"Mr. Meredith! I don't understand!" Suvora looked very startled. "I don't wish——"

"A thousand drachmas! Do you realise what a thousand drachmas *is?* That man probably wouldn't earn that much in two months . . . and then the whisky—that's damned near another month! God almighty! did you have to give him *that* much, just because you like his dancing!"

"I am sorry, Mr. Meredith," Suvora said with dignity. "If I have unwittingly upset some . . . some local shibboleth, I can only say I did it with the best intentions. The man is a superb dancer. In my view he deserved a reward."

"That much?" David repeated unforgivingly.

"I am in the habit, Mr. Meredith, of paying for my pleasures. The man pleased me beyond words. I wish him to be aware of my appreciation."

"Mr. Suvora, may I tell you something? Tomás is a very good dancer. I am not disputing this. But he is also a reasonably competent sponge-diver. He is also, basically, an opportunist . . . a harbour bum, a good-for-nothing. Most of the time his wife goes hungry and his kids starve because he likes to drink and to dance. That's one side of the picture. The other side is that our friend who was sitting with us, the captain, is a very good man. A good man who has been a little out of luck. Perhaps he can't dance very well. That's not important. What is important is that he's trying to recruit a crew for Africa. It isn't easy. All the worthwhile divers were signed on long ago. They've gone. He thought he would be able to get Tomás to go. You wouldn't rate Tomás as the best of them, but he happens to be about the best available. Well, do you think Tomás will go now?"

"I do not know, Mr. Meredith."

"He doesn't *have* to go now, does he?"

"Mr. Meredith, how do you know all this?"

"Because I've lived here a long time. And you can get to know everything that happens on this island if you take the trouble to listen. To look at people and to listen to what they say."

"All right, now may I put my case also?" said Suvora quietly.

"Oh, let's skip it!" David said with a quick, impatient gesture. "After all, you weren't to know, and——"

"I was not to know the details of this story, that is perfectly true," Suvora went on patiently. "But I have no intention of accepting an acquittal on the grounds of ignorance. I am sorry for any harm that may have been done unintentionally. At the same time, Mr. Meredith, I have the feeling that you consider my excessive tip to the man to have been a . . . well, yes, a vulgarity—a rich man's vulgarity."

"Look, I meant that——"

"When you are very rich, Mr. Meredith"—Suvora raised his hand— "vulgarities are expected of you. You have only the choice between being considered vulgar and being considered stingy. A poor choice, let us admit. On the other hand, you, I think, have elected to take sides on this matter. You have become partisan. You are biased, Mr. Meredith."

"Biased?"

"Of course. You are on the side of conventional reward for conventional labour. Let us examine the case. Now, you admit that this man Tomás is a sponge-diver of very average competence, perhaps hardly more than mediocre. You have to concede, though, that he is much, much more than merely a competent dancer. He is, in fact, an astonishingly gifted natural dancer. Yet you—even though you perhaps do not know these men very intimately—you consider that it is Tomás's duty to earn his thousand drachmas—what is a thousand drachmas? . . . thirty dollars or so—to earn this money by two months' work at a calling which is very arduous and so perilous that men are killed or maimed every season, even though at this work he is not notably proficient. As against this, you will not condone his earning of this thousand drachmas in one night by doing something for which he possesses an outstanding skill. Where is the logic of your argument, Mr. Meredith?"

"It isn't a question of logic. It's a matter of pride, of human——"

"Oh, come now! I think you are idealising, romanticising the situation too much. Another thing . . . touching perhaps on my vulgarity. I do assure you that I have on innumerable occasions spent far more than thirty dollars on a night's entertainment very inferior to what Tomás there has to offer."

"All right, yes. . . . I'm sorry for my outburst," David said. His apology was genuine. "I can see your point of view. It's . . . it's just that I hate to see the opportunist getting away with it."

"My dear Mr. Meredith," said Suvora with a soft laugh, "surely this is what the term implies? The opportunist, the true opportunist, always gets away with it. He fails only when he plans beyond the opportunity."

David looked at him a moment, then smiled. "We'll argue it out some other time," he suggested. "But right now, if you don't mind, I think I shall have to leave you. I'd like to try to find the captain. I imagine he'll be at one of the other taverns. I'd still like to . . . to sort of explain to him."

Suvora inclined his head. His face grew thoughtful as he watched the very tall thin figure moving towards the door, skirting the crowded tables, bending the brown head with the tousled spiky hair to pass beneath the lintel of the door.

Three separate groups of men were dancing now, but not very expertly, and the upper part of the pinched-faced boy's *bouzouki* was a yellow flurry of ten-drachma banknotes.

Suvora's brown, contemplative eyes moved from the three musicians and passed around the crowded tables, but he did not see Tomás nor any of the other men as isolated individuals but only as the confused, rowdy background to the sharply-defined, stooped figure of David Meredith plunging out into the night upon some indeterminate errand that was related in some way to integrity, or to mercy, or perhaps only to human pride.

The millionaire's fingers moved to the top pocket of his dark-blue yachting jacket, and from it he carefully withdrew a very small morocco-bound diary. He dabbed with his fingers to find a place on the table where the wine had not been spilt, and when he had found a dry space he put the diary down there to make his consultation.

Clothilde, his reference told him, strictly would not be available until the following night. However, he reflected, perhaps a certain latitude was permitted on Silenos: a point might be stretched. The thought gave him warmth and comfort as he returned the little diary to his pocket, and paid the account, and went across to the three musicians to leave a bill for ten drachmas in the strings of the *bouzouki*, and walked out of the tavern of the Two Brothers into the jasmine-scented night.

3

STREET SCENE

HALF-WAY ALONG the lane that led to the bright noisy door of the Two Brothers he heard the clock of the municipal offices strike ten, and the sound of the chimes brought him to an irresolute halt. He should have gone back home long since: if he stayed out any longer Kate would have her supper by herself and go to bed. To search for Captain Andreas through the taverns and the coffeehouses might take an hour or more—and supposing he did find him, what was he to say to him? What was there to explain to him? Nothing. Besides, he was getting very weary of being involved in other people's problems. Suvora was perfectly within his rights. He was entitled to spend his thirty dollars any way he liked. It was his money, his way of paying for enjoyment.

He walked on slowly, relieved that he had overcome his pique, and that he could see the subject rationally, both sides of it, without the need for intervention.

Did Vlikos the banker or Dionysios the garbage man pay the yellow-haired wife of the tanker captain for their enjoyment of her? There would be a variation in the rate, of course. There would have to be—if only to maintain the banker's standing. For a moment he flirted with the divert-ing thought of walking up to the street where the woman lived. If Thurs-day night was the night for the garbage man perhaps Sunday night was the banker's night. Logical enough. It was the night for enjoyment, and Vlikos was no man for singing or dancing or the tavern life. It would be amusing to catch him leaving the woman's house or to go there and rap on the door and involve him in some salacious Chaucerian situation. The Banker's Tale.

"Ah, *Kyrios* Vlikos," he might say. "I wished to see you a moment. Your sex life. It is below your reserve for credit. You must be careful. The dustman cometh. You asked me to keep you informed."

He had come almost to the quay when he saw Kettering, and it was the expression on the little man's face that kept him in the dark shadows, the overhanging balconies, watching. Kettering was alone and walking quickly along past the padlocked shops, his striped shirt flapping, his lips moving as if he were talking angrily to himself. His face was twisted miserably. He looked as if he had been weeping. He hurried the full length of the *agorá* before turning in at the door of the Katraikis coffeehouse with what, in a girl, would have been described as a petulant flounce.

David emerged from the shadows of the lane and walked slowly down the quay in the opposite direction, and it was at the junction of the mole near the vine-covered wall of the sailmaker's loft that he saw the explanation of Kettering's misery and agitation. Janecek and a young sailor in white drill were seated side by side on one of the heavy wooden chocks where the boats were slipped for repairs. They were caught together in a lattice of shadow cast by the surrounding masts. They were talking in low voices.

Other people had their problems too, David reflected, thinking of Kettering, as he turned around and walked back to the *agorá*. The two men on the wooden chock had not seen him.

Was it sympathy or sadism that led him towards the Katraikis coffeehouse? Perhaps something of each. Kettering was crouched at a table beneath the bright blue glare of the tube-lights, staring at a glass of brandy.

"Mind if I join you?" David asked, going to him. "I could do with a drink too."

"I was just going," said Kettering quickly. His fingers drummed nervously on the marble. "I was going along to the hotel."

"You haven't finished your drink yet." David took the chair opposite and clapped his hands for the waiter. "I wanted to see you, anyway. Mark asked my wife to see about some arrangement for your people to make a picnic up to the Prophet's Peak. She's fixed some mules for tomorrow, if that's all right."

"That'll be fine. Yes. I'll tell him." His voice was still agitated, artificial.

"You told him and Janecek I'd talk to the admiral?"

"Yes."

"Tomorrow I'll do that. *Tha thúme.*" He took the glass of brandy from the waiter's tray, and asked for two more.

"I don't care for another drink. I haven't touched this one yet."

David smiled. "I've been thinking over what you said this afternoon," he said. "You're right, you know. It isn't good to poke your fingers into other people's problems. Better for us to dismiss Fegel as a born no-hoper, and then we don't have to worry about things having a beginning, a middle, and an end. I have a bit of an obsession about continuity, you see, but I'm beginning to realise that continuities can get twisted up . . . snapped right off sometimes. Perhaps every now and then this is the way it *has* to happen, for the good of everyone concerned. Do you know the story of this island, about the old man and the basket?"

Kettering shook his head reluctantly. A moth pinged against the blue tube above his head, spun twice, and dropped to the table, a scrap of death that was dust-coloured and dry. Kettering stared at it a moment, then reached forward to flick it away.

"In the old days here, when life was pretty hard, they had this custom that when a man got so old and infirm that he'd become a burden on the community he had to be taken along the cliffs by his oldest son and bundled into a big basket and tossed into the sea to drown." David arranged the four brandy glasses in a straight line. "This went on for hundreds and hundreds of years," he said. "Then one day one old man got right up to the edge of the cliffs, and then said to his son, 'What are you doing? Are you mad? Are you going to throw away a perfectly good basket like that. Why, boy, the time will come when you'll need one just like this yourself, and then they'll have to get a new one! What a waste!' So the son took the old man and the basket back to the town, and they didn't observe the custom after that. It broke the continuity, you see."

"So what's that all about?" said Kettering uneasily.

"Continuity." David smiled. He was beginning to enjoy himself. He reached for the second glass of cognac. "Or the lack of it," he amended carefully, drank the brandy, and returned the empty glass to its place in the line. "Perhaps," he said, "we try to look for things that aren't there at all."

"You're a twisty sort of talker. You don't really expect me to follow you, do you? You've still got two more drinks there. I told you I don't care for any."

"Listen," said David patiently, "let's put it this way. The fact that

Fegel doesn't get his poetry published now needn't have any relationship at all to the fact that he got a dirty deal from your friend Janecek fifteen years ago. We agree on that, don't we? And you're absolutely right about it, Kettering. Even just to try to dovetail the two things together won't do either of them any good. It's something that happened a long time ago and then stopped happening. Like the old men and the baskets. Do you think that years after the custom had been dropped all the old chaps got together to complain, and said, 'Listen, whatever happened to that marvellous old custom we used to have with the boys and the baskets?' "

"I don't think anything," said Kettering evasively. "It's time I got along to the hotel. Feodor told me he'd——"

"Feodor's back there along the mole, with a sailor," David said. "I saw him before I came in here. We're not interested in Feodor." He waved his hand airily. "We're just interested in continuity." He felt drunk now, with the cognac on top of the wine—what Kettering would call "a bit high." "We're interested in continuity, aren't we?" he insisted. His hand moved towards the third glass in the row.

Kettering said nothing. He looked down for the dead moth, then remembered that he had flicked it away. On the table there was a faint powdering of greyish dust from the singed wings. He reached out and rubbed it into a smudge on the white marble.

"Or perhaps we *are* interested in Feodor," David said thoughtfully. "Yes. There is a man with continuity, at any rate. He's all of a piece —which is a bloody sight more than we are. We're all groping around in the dark, but he knows where he's going all the time. That's so, isn't it? He succeeds. He makes a special point of always succeeding." He took up the last full glass of brandy, and held it in his fingers for a long time, staring at it. "Kettering," he said at last, "why do you stay with Janecek?"

Kettering rubbed the last of the smudge away with his fingertip and looked up. For a moment his face with the square beard had the queer expression of an ancient mask, and then the expression was gone and it was just a tired young-old face that looked inward at itself and saw the skull beneath the flesh, the bones revealed, saw the ironies of existence clearly portrayed, and the indifference of the fates. "If you want to know," he said caustically, "I am the embodiment of the sick intellectual. Do you know what that means?"

"I'd like to hear your definition."

"It means I was born at the wrong time, in the wrong town, in the wrong country, with the wrong talents. I had the wrong parents, I went

to the wrong school and I mixed with the wrong company. I didn't even
turn out a genuine bum. So I took the alternative. I made the pilgrimage
to the proper shrines of decadence and spiritual negation, where I learnt
that while I was created equal it was easy to grow parasitical. So like
Little Tommy Tucker, I learnt to sing for my supper. I stay with Janecek
because it's not as painful as staying with myself. Shall I go on, or is that
all you wanted to know?"

David could only look at him, startled.

"Big fleas have little fleas upon their backs to bite 'em," Kettering
quoted, chanting the words mockingly, "and little fleas have lesser fleas,
and so *ad infinitum*. I'm the lesser flea, that's all. I guess it's a living."

"A good living?" David asked, without quite knowing why.

"Wonderful!" Kettering closed his eyes and threw back his head in a
mime of ecstasy. "Terrific!" he said. "I can't tell you! The places I've been!
The people I've met! The suppers I've eaten! Brother!"

He scraped his chair back suddenly, and hurried from the coffeehouse.
David was left with four empty cognac glasses standing in a row on the
table in front of him, and with a dry taste in his mouth, and with a vision
of a face contorted into the same expression of torment and misery that
had been there when he had seen it before, hurrying past the shadowed
lane, the padlocked shops, the unsuspected eyes watching him. . . .

It was well past midnight by the time he got home. The house was in
darkness, and Kate was asleep, with an open book turned down upon the
bedside table. Well, he thought with a queer little lurching stab of tenderness, here was another woman who had been left to her own devices.
As he lit the kerosene lamp his eyes caught the title of the book. *The
Brothers Karamazov* again. Kate's inordinate passion for very long books,
what he called her "tome complex." It was a passion she had developed
in London, when she had had a lot of time hanging on her hands. Understandable, in a way.

He had a sudden sense of the deepest solicitude and affection for the
sleeping woman, seeing her with a sharper clarity and a deeper sensitivity
than he had for a long time past. Her problems were as great as his—
greater perhaps . . . the children, the meals, charcoal stoves that put
smuts on the end of her nose, silly little infuriating paraffin stoves that
blew up in her face and burnt off her eyelashes . . . coping with all the
trivial checks and irritations that were the concomitants of the so-called
simple life—and God! how complicated the simple life could be! . . .
coping with him, if it came to that. Putting up with his moods, excusing

his obstinacies, forgiving him for those empty absences which had to be filled with Dostoevsky and Tolstoy, never questioning the rightness of his decisions. . . . Perhaps this was the clue to Kate's balance: her acceptance of all these things was so much more unquestioning than his: she seemed to have long since come to terms with her situation, whereas he, consciously or subconsciously, still questioned it, still grappled with it as if it were a beast to be subdued. The house and family undoubtedly gave to her that sense of permanence and security which to him was something dangling always just out of reach. Yet this, too, was understandable. It was so much easier for a woman. So much easier for her to see the purpose and the rightness of what she was doing. It was a little more difficult to find those reassuring symbols of permanence and security in a book written or yet to be written, in those terrifying moments of self-doubt when one saw with bitter clarity how far ability lagged behind ambition. Yet perhaps old Beth Sinclair had been right and Kate had already moved on beyond poste restante and learnt to belong. Was this the real difference between them? That she belonged? That he only wanted things to belong to him? Even those things that could belong to nobody—the future and fate and a sure shield against failure. . . .

The mood of tenderness had passed, and he felt himself afflicted by the deepest depression as he took the lamp and left her sleeping. Climbing the stairs to the study his shadow was thrown back into the room below, moved jerkily across the bed, covered her in darkness.

The divan in the study was hard and his stomach sour with the wine and the brandy, and for a long time he stared wide-eyed into the darkness afraid to close his eyes and embark on that nocturnal journey which would end in the grey light of another day. After a time he slept. His night was filled with fitful, half-recaptured dreams. He awakened nervous and liverish.

*   *   *

When Captain Andreas left the tavern of the Two Brothers he walked only to the next lane where there was a small wine-shop with three yellow tables set beneath a mulberry-tree. It was a place that never had music and where there was no provision for dancing, so that on a Sunday night few people went there. But Captain Andreas knew that Tomás would pass the shop on his way to his home on the hill, so he sat there beneath the tree with a beaker of wine and waited.

It was almost midnight before Tomás came, unsteady on his feet, uncertain of the shadows, clutching the two bottles of whisky which he had not shared with his friends.

"Tomás." The captain called to him in a quiet voice.

Tomás moved across to the wall and his head swayed stupidly as he peered into the shadows beneath the tree.

"You," he said. "What do you want?" His voice was thick with drink and insolence.

"I waited for you," said Andreas quietly. "I will have to give Vlikos the crew-list."

"You want me to write it out for you? To carry it down to him?"

"I want to know whether your name goes on it, that's all," said Andreas patiently. "You said you'd tell me tonight whether you'd come or not. I want to know, that's all."

He had never liked Tomás, and there had been seasons—those good seasons for Andreas which had been the green years for Tomás—when he would not even have considered approaching him, when Tomás could have come to him and been rejected out of hand. Yet Tomás, in a way, had always been there in the background, growing towards this moment in his destiny, a figure moving out of the assembly of the years and growing larger and coming towards him as the lurching figure had advanced along the lane towards the little wine-shop, to form out of the shapes of two men beneath a mulberry-tree another moment of expectancy. He remembered Tomás as a child on Silenos, growing up badly, growing from a ragged, bare-footed boy into a cocksure adolescent, cruel to the children, vicious with animals. Once, walking in the late afternoon along the breakwater, he had thought he might have been mistaken, because he had seen him sitting there all alone on the grey shingle by the slipways, and he had had a little mongrel terrier in his arms and he was caressing it and crooning to it, all by himself among the smooth pebbles. But then the dog had run off to chase a stick, and when Tomás called to it it didn't come back to him, so he had pelted it with rocks and the dog had fled yelping away behind the customhouse. A long time ago, before Tomás had become the big drinker and the big dancer—and now all these moments of long ago had run together and formed the shape of a man in the darkness imprinted against a starlit wall—a man with two bottles of whisky in his hands and a thousand drachmas in his pocket and no hunger in his belly and vindictiveness gathered into the pupils of his hard dark eyes. Captain Andreas waited.

"*Foniá!*" Tomás spat the word at him, dragging the last syllable out into a snarl of derision that sounded like 'fingernails tearing down his face. "*Foniá!*" He shouted the epithet this time like a howl of triumph, and then turned away and lurched into the shadow of the mulberry-tree, and out of it into the dim pallor of the starlit lane, and he went away along it, waving his bottles in the air and laughing as he went.

Captain Andreas shook two drachmas from his leather purse and put them carefully on the yellow table beside his wineglass. It was the first time in his life that he had ever been called a murderer, but there was nothing in the expression on his face to show what he was thinking.

When he was walking home he saw Vlikos the banker coming down from one of the lanes behind the church of the Virgin, but the street lights had been switched off and there was no need to make a greeting.

4

PROPHET'S PEAK

THE PICNIC to the Prophet's Peak had been Mark's idea. "We'll all go up there on mules," he had said, narrowing his eyes and tugging at his beard. "On mules! Marvellous!"

But as it turned out it was left entirely to David to organise the cavalcade and to act as its guide. Mark had been adamant that he should come. "Oh, skip your writing for one day, man. It'll do you good. You'll see it with a fresh eye." Kate had withdrawn at the last moment on the score that it was the day when the mainland market-boats called at Silenos, so it had been left to David alone to escort the grotesque column, left to him to meet the startled eyes and gaping mouths of the peasants, left to him to apologise for the roughness of the trail, the refractoriness of the mules, the hardness of the saddles, the lack of shade, the brackishness of the mountain water, the prickliness of the thistles, the differences from the Tuscan Hills, even for the absence of a tourist pavilion at the summit.

Now that they had come to the belfry terrace of the monastery of the Prophet Elijah, he had a feeling of distinct relief. Since the going-down-again obviously would be very much quicker than the coming-up had been, it was now only a matter of enduring the tedious passage of time until they should decide that they had had enough.

They were seated some distance away from him in the limited shade afforded by the gallery of five bronze bells, picking fastidiously at black olives, goat cheese, hard-boiled eggs and lukewarm sardines, and sipping with even less enthusiasm at tepid wine. Of them all, only Suvora seemed to be enjoying himself.

Of them all, in fact, David reflected, studying the group with a still-

lingering mixture of distaste and amazement, only Suvora looked normal
enough to be capable of enjoyment. There was something refreshingly
natural in his thick-soled brogues, the old grey flannels, the blue linen
shirt with the sleeves rolled up above his brown, sinewy forearms, the
wind and the sun in his greying hair. Next to him sat Clothilde, wearing
skin-tight blue jersey pants, high red boots, a tasselled cowboy shirt, and
a floppy Italian straw hat with a manufactured raggedness at the brim.
Kettering's garb was even more alarming, for he wore a lemon-yellow
baseball cap, a hunting shirt in green and purple checks, white moleskin
trousers, and Turkish sandals with turned-up toes. Mark was conventional enough in his dark-grey Daks, his white Aertex shirt, his Kangol
beret, and his sun-glasses, but his beard had lost its point with the jolting
of the mule and had become wispy and unimpressive, and when he took
off his glasses so that he could see the olives his eyes seemed rather
glazed. Mark, evidently, was feeling his fifty years and his lack of condition. Twice on the upward climb he had been heard to mutter, "Sedentary occupation, you see. Sedentary occupation." Janecek, dressed in very
pale-blue matching Dacron shirt and slacks and with his fine blue eyes
shaded by a white peaked golfing cap, had been generally silent and disdainful since they had set out. Clothilde looked sulky. Kettering seemed
very tense and tired, as if he had not slept well. There was an obvious
undercurrent of conflict within the party, but David was not interested
enough to try to determine the reason for it.

He turned his back on them and leaned across the terrace parapet. Below, in the unused courtyard of the monastery, old Aleksandros the
muleteer was refilling the nosebags of the animals. There, now, was a pair
of trousers for you! The old man was bent over so that every patch on
the seat of his pants was clearly and curvingly defined—patches in black,
in white, in blue, in brown, in checks, in spots, in stripes . . . right
across the broad buttocks and down each leg . . . squares, rectangles,
circles, ovals, bands, strips . . . an unintentional abstract purer than
Mondrian. Where now was the original material? Yet how Greek it was
—how different from the neat Dacron and moleskin and flannel and
gaberdine of the sophisticated world. On the pants of old Aleksandros
everything had merged and faded and gone into pebble colours, sea pebbles dried out and dappled in the hot sun . . . the way the colour-
washes on the houses faded into pale instinctive harmonies that took your
breath away. Accidents. The accidents of nature. The alchemy of sun
and light. Did it work that way with people also?

"Do they care for their animals well?"

The voice from behind him was tentative, interested. He turned to find Suvora standing beside him, looking down at the muleteer.

"They have to," said David. "It's their living. I was just admiring the old chap's trousers."

"Magnificent!" said Suvora respectfully. "And quite, quite outside my price-range," he added mischievously. "Did you find your captain friend last night?" He took an olive from his cupped hand and bit into it.

"Yes," David said, and immediately wondered why he had lied.

"I hope," said Suvora, "you were able to explain it all to him."

David nodded. "We talked," he said shortly. "We talked about things." Having already created the untruth, he had no wish to elaborate on it. Why had he lied? Probably some queer little spring of guilt that he had defected on his undertaking to find the captain and had tried to bait Kettering instead.

Suvora rolled the olive-pit in his fingers, studied it for a moment with great care, then flicked it over the wall. "I have enjoyed this morning enormously," he said, coming forward and leaning his arms on the parapet. "We must thank you for taking all this trouble with us. Sacrificing your time. Interrupting your own work."

"It's not all that important."

"Oh, one's work is always important, I think. Do you remember what the captain said to us last night? 'Work is always work,' he said. If we asked that mule man down there he'd probably give us much the same sort of answer."

"What are you two men talking about over there?" Clothilde called across to them. She rose slowly and came towards them, pouting her full pretty mouth.

"Only about work," Suvora said affectionately. "You wouldn't be interested." He put his brown arm around the girl's shoulder and kissed her lightly on the cheek.

"You pig!" she said indolently, and with a gesture as indolent as her words she put his arm away. For a moment her beautiful topaz eyes rested on David without a flicker of expression in them, and then she moved across to the parapet and leant beside him, her tall slender body tilted so that her face was turned to the sun, her long blue-sheathed legs stretched in front of her and spread wide. She had undone the two top buttons of her shirt, and through the opening of the cloth David could see the ripe firm swell of honey-coloured flesh, the paler yet more shadowy V between

her breasts like a bleached violet stain. A tendril of bronze hair lifted in
the soft breeze and fell across her temple.

"Oh, the sun! the sun!" she sighed. "I love the sun! I love the sun!"

"You complained about it coming up," Suvora reminded her.

"Sweet sun! Lover sun!" she breathed, ignoring him. "I'd like to take all
this off, every stitch of it," she said. Her fingers flicked at her shirt, so
that the opening of the cloth revealed still more of her bosom. "I'd like
to stretch out here and soak in it. Soak and soak and soak!"

"It might upset the monks," Suvora suggested dryly.

"There aren't any," said David. "The last of them left here years ago."

"Then it might upset us," Suvora amended. "Clothilde darling, your
buttons are undone."

Her shoulders moved in a faint shrug.

"Have you ever noticed, Mr. Meredith," said Suvora, "how utterly
naked these days a clothed woman can manage to look? If Clothilde
did, as she suggests, take all that off, every stitch of it, what would be
the gain? . . . except, perhaps, to the manufacturer of suntan oil?
Nudity has become such an unmysterious thing. They were so much
wiser a century ago, weren't they?" He rested his chin contentedly in his
cupped hands and stared out at the sunny view. "Hallo," he said, after a
few moments, "other tourists enjoying the day?" He pointed. "Down
there, do you see? Past the edge of all that lava, where there are two
white stump things sticking up. What are those white stumps, by the
way?"

"Columns," said David. "Ancient columns. Or what's left of them. It
was once a temple of Artemis."

"Ah? How interesting. The huntress. Clothilde should go down there
and make obeisance. Perhaps even a sacrifice. Kettering would be my
suggestion. Or Janecek?"

"This one was a very particular Artemis. Artemis the Stranger. The
precincts were a sanctuary for fugitives."

"Then we can not be sure *who* should go there to make obeisance,
can we?" He smiled to himself. "They are coming this way. Do you see
them? . . . just turning up past that sharp ridge."

"Yes," said David. "They aren't tourists. The one in front is a Greek
woman who has a house here. Erica Barrington. The other is the woman
who works for her."

"Barrington?" Suvora glanced at him. "Hardly a Greek name."

"She was married to an American. She's a widow."

"And a very attractive one," said Suvora, shading his eyes. "We have here an enchanting situation, Mr. Meredith. To be stationed here, on this wonderful eyrie in the bright sun, with the sea encircling us like a sapphire wall, and to find coming towards us across a fantastic field of lava a strange and lovely widow—coming, mark you, from a sacred temple of Artemis! Surely here, Mr. Meredith, is the stuff for your novels!"

Clothilde turned and stared down across the black slope of lava. Casually she fastened the two buttons at the top of her shirt, and then her hand went up and patted for a moment, tentatively, at her shining hair.

Mrs. Barrington had seen them. She waved and walked on and then was lost to sight behind the courtyard wall. It was several minutes before she appeared at the top of the steps below the gallery of bells. As she came across the terrace, Mark sprang to his feet, dusted the seat of his Daks, and hurriedly smoothed his beard. She was wearing a plain sleeveless dress of grey linen and thick-soled, single-thong sandals. She carried a leather writing-case. The woman who followed behind her, an elderly, withdrawn woman in a white head-shawl, with a face that was lined and leathery and patient, carried a soft basket of woven grass filled with wild flowers and upland herbs.

"You have a heavenly day for your picnic," she said, after she had greeted the others and been introduced to Suvora and to Clothilde.

"I should have sent you an invitation to join us," Mark said. "It never occurred to me. I didn't realise——"

"What does it matter?" said Suvora cheerfully. "She is here with us anyway. Do have some wine, Mrs. Barrington. It is a very strange wine, this Greek *retsina*, but interesting."

"It's really very good," said Mark loyally.

"It is, in fáct, quite beastly," said Janecek.

"Stick to the hard-boiled eggs," advised Kettering. "Take no notice of the black stain around the yolk. They go like that in the sun."

Clothilde, her face impassive, her golden eyes watchful, had nothing to say.

"What are you doing up here anyway?" David asked.

"I often come here . . . well, not here exactly, but over there by the temple. I like the atmosphere, the solitude. I do quite a lot of my writing up here . . . a lot of my thinking too. And Sevasti likes to come and pick flowers and hunt around for wild thyme and *fraskómolo*. You remember" —she addressed herself to Mark—"I told you about my selfishness, my wish to be left alone. Up here it's very possible."

"You have your own mule then?" said Mark, looking at the situation practically.

She smiled as she shook her head. "I walk up. It's much easier. My house is very high, you know. We have nothing behind us but the mountain, and this." She waved her hand at the landscape.

"Come and I'll get you a drink," said David, and he led her away deliberately. And with a certain sense of possessiveness, as if he were asserting a right that provided an intimacy between fellow-islanders that could not be extended to uninitiated newcomers. A sort of freemasonry of commitment, or involvement. He was childishly pleased when she said that she would not drink wine but would like a glass of cold water, because this meant that they would have to go to the very farthest point of the terrace, and draw the water from the old cool cistern which had a truncated marble cap carved with the peacocks of Byzantium. As he lowered the pail into the shaft and she stood beside him waiting he was conscious of the faint, cool smell of her presence—a smell that seemed to be compounded of the light and the air around her, and the spiky herbs in the old servant woman's basket, and the fine-woven dove-grey fabric of her dress, and the mysterious liquid darkness of the cistern below them, and the blue light caught in the jet-black fall of her hair. An astonishing woman, for the effect she created, this electrifying effect of drawing immediate attention upon her, was as faint and as cool and in its way as subtle as this intangible, evasive sense of her presence beside him. A magnetism born out of her very detachment, her stillness, her quietness. Yet how undeniable its effect! Mark jumping about like a puppet pulled by strings . . . Suvora polishing his suavity like a shoeblack brushing shoes . . . even Kettering forgetting for a moment whatever was tormenting him—all of them vying for her attention like children clamouring to give the right answer to the teacher's question. Not Janecek, of course. That would have been too much to expect! Nor Clothilde. Yet how instantly Clothilde, too, had seen herself in the presence of a real woman, how quickly the languor had vanished from her eyes and vigilance appeared. And how strange to think that once he had thought of Erica as Lesbian!

He filled the glass of water and handed it to her. She went to the parapet, and as she drank looked out across the field of petrified lava. "Up here," she said quietly, "is my part of Silenos. The lonely part. The strange part, I suppose. Do you like it?"

"Yes. I can see why you come here. It's more than just solitude, though, isn't it? You get more than that from it."

"Oh yes, I suppose one does. A kind of inspiration, a kind of magic . . . yes, and a kind of reassurance, in a way. An effect, at any rate. There is a beach down there," she said inconsequentially, pointing to the south, "that is covered with huge basalt rocks, and sometimes when there is a heavy gale great lumps of pumicestone are washed up there. Yet they say there hasn't been a real earthquake here for almost a thousand years. Only a little tremor every now and then to rock the houses with an old reminder. Only that and the shapes of the hills and this wasteland here. When you come to visit me"—and again the tone of her voice altered to shape the new tangent of her thoughts—"I must see if I can bring you up here at night. It is very strange . . . very wonderful. . . ."

"*When* I come to visit you," he said meaningly. "Your invitation was not definite. You didn't fix a date, remember."

"No. Well, Thursday, if you like."

He inclined his head in acceptance, and smiled at her. "You can tell me all about it then," he suggested, and for a brief interval he was silent, standing beside her, looking out across the Black Vouna. "Tell me," he said quietly, "do you think you could find a unicorn up here?"

"Unicorn?" The dark slanting eyes looked at him in surprise. "What do you mean?"

"Nothing . . . nothing, really. I'm old enough to be growing wistful . . . to want to catch a unicorn. Before it's too late. This looks to me as if it might be unicorn country." He grinned suddenly. "And that's something I'll have to explain to *you* some other time. I'm afraid Suvora is coming to rope us back into the official party."

"Mrs. Barrington," said Suvora, "would it be an imposition if I asked you to accompany me—well, to escort me, in fact—to that temple over there? If you are not too tired? It looks no more than a few hundred yards."

"I'd be delighted," she replied, and walked back with him to rejoin the rest of the party.

"The idea was," said David uncertainly, "for all of us to go there together and see the ruins."

"Well, why don't we do that?" said Mrs. Barrington.

"I had really hoped for a private showing," Suvora said, his brown eyes twinkling. "I wanted to make some rather personal inquiries about the rites of sanctuary."

"Are you a fugitive?" she asked.

"Oh yes, I'm sure I am. But I'm not at all sure that I know what I'm a fugitive from. Never mind. Let us all go together. I might trouble you, Mrs. Barrington, for a more personal consultation at some future date."

"I don't want to go," said Clothilde. "I'm tired. And I hate ruins. And I'd rather stay here in the sun."

"You should do that, Clothilde," Suvora said soothingly. "Strip it all off. Soak, soak, soak. Lover sun!"

A cryptic half-smile curved Clothilde's mouth as she again undid the two top buttons of her shirt. Her fingers were at the third as she turned away.

"I shall also asked to be excused," Janecek said rather distantly. "Like Clothilde, I detest ruins. They make me sick with melancholy. And they remind me of those dreadful Piranesi engravings in petit-bourgeois villas. I prefer my Greece without columns."

"I am sure Clothilde will be perfectly safe here with Mr. Janecek," Suvora said wickedly. "Shall we go then, Mrs. Barrington?"

For the first fifty yards across the solidified lava, petrified here into zigzag, glass-sharp ridges, the going was difficult, and David and Mrs. Barrington, being more at home on the terrain of Silenos—or this, at least, was the excuse David made to himself—went ahead together to show the others the easiest path.

"Your brother and I," Suvora was explaining to Mark, "were working out an entertaining plan to offer Kettering here as a sacrifice on behalf of Clothilde. . . ."

"Who is he?" Mrs. Barrington asked in a low voice.

"Suvora? He's a millionaire." David shrugged, as if the definition might explain everything.

"He is charming. I think I like him very much."

"Yes."

"He has a sense of humour, at least."

"Oh yes, as millionaires go, I suppose he's all right. I'm beginning to like him myself. On principle, of course, one doesn't *want* to like millionaires. It puts you into some sort of other category."

A slight smile touched her wood-brown, high-boned face and her eyes sought his for a moment as they had at the party. "Perhaps you search too earnestly for categories . . . categories for other people, even for yourself. Tell me more about the others. I scarcely spoke to any of them at the party, except your brother. I like him too."

"Mark?" He glanced at her in some surprise. "You don't find him pompous?"

"Oh, enormously!—but in such a nice way . . . such an honest way. I think he's sweet. I want to know about the others."

David glanced behind. They were well out of earshot, negotiating the glassy ridges with difficulty. "Clothilde explains herself, doesn't she? That only leaves Kettering and Janecek. They are more obvious in a way, but not so easy to explain. How would you define Janecek, for instance?"

For a moment she hesitated thoughtfully, then: "One is influenced, of course, by the story you told me about him. I suppose it's true. I think it is. The point is that one will always be inclined to read the story *into* him. I see him as a very clever man, egotistical, ruthless to a degree, the sort of person who won't allow anything or anybody to get in the way of his own success. He gives me the impression that he doesn't have any sort of soul at all."

"He cashed that in long ago, at that refugee camp near Prague."

"Perhaps. We can't really know about that, can we?"

"I think it's a fair assumption. I would say that if he sees any threat to his own interests he can be totally destructive. That's why I think he could be rather dangerous to poor little Fegel."

"What could he possibly do to Fegel?"

"What could he do that hasn't been done already, you mean," said David softly. He moved his shoulders in a slight shrug. "He could destroy him, I suppose. Basically, Fegel is destructible material. To Janecek he'd seem to be quite worthless, quite contemptible. Kettering thinks that Fegel is the born victim. Poor Kettering doesn't seem to realise that he is too."

"What do you mean by that?"

He paused for a moment to look back. Kettering was laboriously making his way on all-fours across a particularly difficult spur, with Suvora helping him. "He lives in this bitter servitude to Janecek," David said. "In a way it's a state of resented thralldom to this cleverer man, this smarter intellect, this exemplar of the talents he always craved for his own. But you see, the trouble is he loves him. I think he does, very genuinely. And that makes it more terrible than ever. Because it becomes a bitter love, hopeless, enthralled, tormented—all twisted up with resented persecutions, resented humiliations, resented jealousies of the little sailor boys that Janecek likes to play around with." He stopped. He could see Kettering's miserable face of the night before staring down at a dead moth lying on a marble table, the fingers nervously drumming, the eyes dull with pain. It was a face, he reflected, that had begun to grow very tired of itself . . . the face of a man nearly exhausted by the task of being him. Tired of chasing around after the right to participate in some brightly-lit world where the talents on display seemed more brilliant or more important than the ones he had had himself, or perhaps never had himself . . . tired of trying to escape when there was no place to escape to, tired of chasing himself away and then chasing himself back again. . . . In a way, the danger with Kettering was that he was still honest with himself . . . or was it that in this bright light of the island he had come to see himself more clearly?

"It's a funny thing, you know," he went on, "that Kate and I both like Kettering in some peculiar way, and he's very kind and sweet to our children, and yet—we've talked about it—we just don't want him to see too much of Jerry. That's unfair, I suppose"—he had an image of Jerry sitting up in his bed wearing the coonskin cap that Kettering had brought for him—"and yet one doesn't really want to see the child caught in that orbit. It's all one orbit, you see—Kettering's and Janecek's and the little sailor boys'. . . ." He made a long step across the last ridge and said, "There's a path from here on. Shall we let the others catch up?"

She nodded. Again he was conscious of the deep interest in her eyes. But she waited with him in silence.

Suvora came up to them at last and said admiringly, "Mrs. Barrington, you are as agile as the virgin huntress herself! And I thought I was in tip-top condition. That black stuff is very treacherous . . . slippery, like glass. Poor Kettering! With those ridiculous sandals of his!"

"Well!" gasped Kettering, stumbling up to them at last, and staring dismally towards the scattered ruins. "Closed for repairs! Is *that* all there is left?"

"Ionic," said Mark, narrowing his eyes and feeling for his beard. "The slenderness of those column drums . . . couldn't be anything else. Impressive, by Jove! Mighty impressive!"

"In fact, the temple was Doric," Mrs. Barrington corrected him gently. "Well, they believe it was," she added, to let him off tactfully, "although none of the capitals survive. Nor very much else, for that matter," she added ruefully. "You see, Silenos was settled originally by Dorian colonists; they came from Argos on the advice of an oracle. This, of course," she waved her hand towards three shattered columns and a litter of marble blocks and fragments tumbled among the weeds and thornbrush—"was much later than the original colonisation—around the early fifth century."

"B.C., of course," said Mark.

"B.C., of course," she repeated without a change of expression.

"Fascinating, by Jove!" said Mark enthusiastically. "What do you say, Suvora?"

"I will say nothing, my dear Mark, until you stop invoking the god by his Roman name! You are in Greece. You are standing within the sacred precincts of a pagan Greek temple. You have as your guide a very charming Greek lady who, for all we know, may be the very incarnation of Artemis's own high-priestess. And, by Zeus! you persist in tramping over all this like . . . like Cæsar himself!"

Erica Barrington burst into laughter—a laugh that was low and melodic and with a cadence in it that one felt to be memorable. Or so, at least, David Meredith thought as he turned to look at her. It was the first time, he realised, that he had ever heard her laugh outright. Beneath the straight fringe of thick, blue-black hair, her dark narrow face in laughter was startlingly lovely, with a flash of white teeth in the full red mouth, and the high cheekbones accentuated, and the strangely elongated eyes sparkling like polished jet.

"Well, let's put ourselves on safe ground," she suggested at last, "and leave the sacred precincts. That really is all there is to see. Of course, it isn't what is there or what isn't there. It's the atmosphere. But I think you can only feel it when you are quite alone." Pleasantly, without coquetry, she put her bare, deep-brown arm through Suvora's arm, an arm strong and black-haired and almost as brown as hers. "Come, Mr. Suvora," she said. "I shall escort you all the way back, as a reward for defending us against the Romans."

"Thank you." He bowed and smiled. "I warn you, however, that at the foot of the steps I must begin to sing very loudly. I have no voice at all, but I should give Clothilde the opportunity of stripping everything on again."

Together they went on ahead and David followed with Mark and Kettering.

"That," said Kettering, "is really quite a woman!"

"Quite a woman," Mark repeated reverently. "If I were Clothilde I think I should watch out."

"Watching out for other women comes to dear Clothilde like breathing," said Kettering. "Poor Suvora!"

5

KATE MEREDITH

AFTER HE HAD lit his cigarette he broke the match into three pieces which he assembled into a neat, tiny triangle on the kitchen table. The triangle formed the Greek *delta*: already with other fragments of match-sticks he had made *gamma* and *pi* and *lambda* and *sigma*. The letters made no sense, but the pattern of white wood against the almost black stain of the table and the geometric neatness of the letters gave him a sense of satisfaction.

When he had finished telling her of the outing to the Prophet's Peak —rather suprisingly, his account of the excursion came out favourably enough, after all—he looked across and said, "And what did you do with yourself?"

"Well, I marketed when the boats came in," Kate said. "The Soteri ketch brought loquats, the first we've had. Rather hard and tasteless, but the children, believe it or not, ate a whole kilo between them. After that . . . well, it was so warm and the sea looked so marvellous we decided to go swimming."

"Again?" He looked at her. "With Mouliet?"

"Not with him, exactly. I took the children. Yes, he was there. Well, there were lots of people there today. Crowds. It was almost like summer. One could swim every day now."

"You are swimming every day."

"Yes. It's something for Jerry and Simon to do. The school is to be closed for ten days, you know. It seems it's chicken-pox as well as measles.

They're loving it, of course. Simon would have stayed in for hours, even after all those green loquats."

David nodded, and rubbed his finger into the careful arrangement of broken matches, scattering them. "Will you come with me to see old Mavro?" he asked. "You have more influence with him than anybody else. He'll listen to you."

"Yes, of course," she said. "Or if you'd rather work, I can go over by myself and talk to him." Even as she made the suggestion she hoped he would not accept it: she had a sharp compelling need for his company. But he said, "Oh, would you mind? It would be a help."

"Of course I don't mind." She smiled the untruth away. "You've had a lot of interruptions. Too many. You should get back to your book."

"I know." He frowned as he scooped the fragments of broken matches into his cupped hand. "Yes, I know," he repeated. "Well," he looked up at her, "let's get the dishes done, and you can go across. You know what to say to him."

*   *   *

Alone in the dusk, walking across the town, her feeling of uncertainty, of being jolted out of accustomed rhythms, persisted. Deliberately she tried to analyse it. It was almost, she decided, a sense of something having been pruned off, a premonition of a new course that would have to be taken, or *might*—nothing yet so clear as "would"; oh no, not anything as decided as that, really . . . A subtle disturbance of continuities, rather, so slight as barely to be detected. And yet unsettling. A cat's paw of wind ruffling across deep waters before a squawl . . . the muttering of summer thunder . . . the fluttering instability of an earthquake tremor, containing within itself either no more than its own completion and totality or the alarming possibility of something violent and threatening yet to come. She was honest enough to sense, even directly to *know* (firmly she forced her introspection into implacable integrities) that the reason for her disturbed state of mind lay beyond her concern for David's own attitude of uncertainty, for the disruptive elements latent in the coming of Mark and the others. It was concerned also with Achille Mouliet.

The admission, finally expressed to herself in all its bluntness, startled her physically as well as mentally. She could imagine a quickening of her pulse, as if all the blood in her body had suddenly jetted to a swifter rhythm, as if a tiny dam of rectitude had been swept aside to free some wilder current. She could feel a tautening of her skin, a sharp sudden dryness in her throat. The sensation was not entirely unpleasant, yet it was unnerving and troubling, and she was tempted to push it aside, but again, resolutely, she forced herself to examine it.

That she found Mouliet attractive she no longer doubted, nor tried to doubt. The purely physical attraction of a man for a woman or a woman for a man was common enough. Yet this attraction was peculiar in its qualities: it was physical, yes, and yet not quite physical, as if there was something *of* the physical that lay beyond it. It was not something she had sought nor would necessarily want, if it came to an issue —on this particular point she was very definite—although even this was not altogether easy to express, because how could anything be fitted into a category of acceptance or rejection when it could not even be properly defined? The bodily beauty of the young Frenchman—sexual, if you cared to use the word—could be quite clearly seen for what it was, a source for admiration. At the rock pool where they swam, Mouliet's unabashed animality would have taken care of that; the eyes of men and women always followed almost every movement of that tawny graceful body, and if the expressions in the eyes of men and women were often very different, the eyes, nevertheless, were always upon him. And she could not be blind to his very particular attention towards her, his shy, sometimes almost childish flatteries, his own reciprocal and quite undisguised admiration for her. Yet nothing of this explained it. Nothing of this explained the other stirring forces that moved behind the obvious factors of attraction, the feelings of an unnerving restlessness, the faint flutterings of an undefined, indefinable fear, the fact that in the kitchen with David she had flirted with half-truth, moved along the edges of a lie.

And even this had its own peculiar quality of oddness, for while she did not question her own deep loyalty towards her husband, nor her love for him, nor even her reliance upon her own sense of simple honesty, yet she had not felt even the least trace of guilt about it until now. When she consciously set herself to examine it she *did* feel guilt, but at the time, when she should have, she could remember only a faint sense of exhilaration, a prickling of enjoyment, a sense of embarkation upon some new, thrilling, adventurous journey for which no course had been set.

It could, of course, be no more than that, she told herself—the thing that must happen every now and then, perhaps often, to any woman in her position: the subconscious rebellion against the long-sustained role

·of reliable respectability, the temptation to flirt, even to flirt safely, with an offered experience beyond the unchanging and frequently humdrum pattern which marriage imposed—that triple role, so satisfying at its best and so deadening at its worst, of wife and mother and companion. . . .

She brought her reflections to an abrupt termination for, to her sur-prise—and more than a little to her consternation—she found that uncon-sciously she had cut off from the transverse road leading to the steps and was walking along the narrower lane, the Lane of Roses, which twisted downhill towards the quay through quiet, high-walled houses. The lane, before it reached the waterfront, passed the Tavern Platinos, where she knew—for he had made a point of telling her—that Achille Mouliet liked to take his evening meal, sometimes in the company of Fegel, sometimes alone.

The knowledge of what she was doing brought her to a sudden halt, with her heart beating, and for an irresolute interval she waited in the dark scented shadows beneath a wistaria vine that cascaded heavy lilac clusters from a tall arched gateway. Above, in the thickness of the vine, a bird settled restlessly. She walked on more slowly. The tavern was quite empty. With a feeling of relief, stinging so sharply that it almost hurt, she retraced her steps and went uphill towards the house of Admiral Mavro.

*   *   *

"You see," she explained, "with all that money you could have the roof and terrace prepared for next winter, and the doors and windows fixed, and, oh, all sorts of little things attended to. You could save the house from damage, from ruin perhaps. And they won't affect you very much, Admiral Mavro. You can keep away from them; after all, the house is big enough. They'll have their own things to do. In any case, I should imagine they'll spend most of their time on that big yacht in the harbour."

The admiral moved himself gently back and forth in the big Thonet rocking-chair, his black, stud-button eyes fixed unblinkingly upon her. The rocker looked as if it had grown out of the swirling curves and tendrils of a vine from the hills around Vienna where it had been made a century before. There was a big hole in the woven rattan back behind his left shoulder, and from beneath his massive hindquarters frayed and broken tufts of cane protruded from the chair-bottom like inverted tus-socks of dried grass.

"You could even get that chair of yours repaired. If you don't, soon," she said with a smile, "you're going to fall right through it."

Admiral Mavro had kicked off his slippers, and he wriggled his toes in his cheap black cotton socks a good six inches above the uncarpeted stone floor (he gave the impression that had he not been so fat he would have tucked his feet up underneath him). His hands were folded across his splendidly spherical stomach. His bald, round face seemed to have sunk a little into his wide shoulders, where it appeared to balance like a brown leather ball waiting for somebody to kick it off. He looked exactly, she reflected, like one of those funny little Japanese toy dolls—David had once told her the name of them: was it *bi-jini?* . . . something like that—which had a round weighted bottom so that when you flicked them over they always popped upright again.

"Kate," he said at last, "I am not at all oblivious to the temptation. A thousand dollars, I agree, is a great deal of money. I could, as you have pointed out, have this chair repaired. I like this chair very much." His small fleshy hands patted the arms of the rocker affectionately. "It is my favourite chair. It was my mother's favourite chair. And my grandmother's. But that, my dear Kate, is not the point precisely." He coughed and fluttered his fingers. "We have never been in the habit of letting rooms, or taking in boarders." He coughed louder, and for the first time blinked his little pouched eyes. "Which is what it amounts to," he said gravely.

"But look at the house!" Kate protested. "The state of it! And, anyway, what have you been doing for years? Trying to live here on a naval pension. You've sold the furniture, most of it. You've sold the pictures, most of them. The jewellery, the porcelain, the cutlery, even the flowers and the bushes from the garden, some of them. Why? So that you can have the outside walls whitewashed, the steps cemented, the cistern repaired. There's no difference. This is the same."

"Not quite, Kate. I have never taken in boarders."

He looked at her carefully, as if to be sure she understood, then unclasped his hands so that he might lever himself into another position. The effort made him grunt and the rocker swayed wildly. When he had settled himself again he allowed his eyes to move slowly over the huge, high-ceilinged *sála* in which they were seated, he in the battered Thonet rocker, she on an old carved couch covered with very frayed, very tarnished, very faded Turkish brocade cushions. There was little other furniture in the enormous room—a circular brass-topped coffee table between them, against the far wall a much larger table littered with dusty books and periodicals, a monstrous Victorian hat-stand carved to simulate the antlers of reindeer, a Turkish water-pipe, two copper cuspidors long unpolished, and three cheap cane chairs that looked as if they might have been borrowed from a coffeehouse—which, indeed, they had been. On the walls, which were deeply streaked with the evidence of heavy winter rains and blotched even more darkly by mildew, were a number of framed photographs so old and faded as to be totally unidentifiable, a set of clearly unsaleable mezzotints of the Siege of Troy—all of the characters incongruously playing their roles in Swiss costume—and a very large framed painting of the Greek cruiser *Telemachus*. Only one of the warship's two masts and two of its three funnels were discernible through an inferno of gunsmoke and cannon-flashes, but above the martial holocaust the Greek flag was serenely and stiffly evident against a fortuitous cavern of clear sky that looked as if a whole broadside had cleared a passage for it, and the waves were painted in undiluted prussian-blue with a rigid, almost metallic devotion. (For a long nostalgic moment, Admiral Mavro allowed his thoughts wistfully to dwell upon an unforgettable few hours of nearly fifty years before when the six-inch turrets had filled up with shell-cases and the echo of the *Telemachus's* salvos had shaken the gulls off every cliff at Thásos.)

Yet the room itself, even now, even with the poverty of its tenancy and the frugality of its upkeep, was still magnificent. The gigantic ceiling, hand-carved by Spanish artisans and painted and gilded by Venetians, had miraculously survived the hazards of leaking roofs and crumbling masonry, and was still a museum-piece. The door- and window-mouldings—again the artistry of Venice—were superb in their chaste simplicity, and, apart from a cracked patch or two here and there, had survived the rigours of time. Against one wall there was built in a carved marble *lavabo* with a setting and canopy wrought in the form of the Byzantine peacocks amid arabesques of vine-leaves which would not have disgraced a palace. The great size of the room enhanced rather than disguised the delicacy of its proportions, probably because the far wall was broken by three arches supported by two slender stone columns with acanthus capitals. Since the house was not fitted for electricity and only a single kerosene lamp stood on the coffee table between Kate and the admiral, only the sweet outline of the arches was to be discerned; what lay beyond could not be seen.

"What do you advise, Kate?" the admiral asked at last.

She was silent.

"Come, Kate, tell me," he insisted. "Should I do this?"

For another moment she hesitated, then nodded. "Yes," she said quietly.

"Then I'll do it." He closed his eyes and nodded several times to himself, then, "And when they are gone, Kate," he said softly, "we shall have this chair repaired."

"The money will be useful," she said in a low voice.

"Very useful," he agreed. His voice as he spoke seemed sad and heavy, but in a moment he began to chuckle softly, and before long he was clasping and unclasping his hands and laughing immoderately.

"Why are you laughing?" she asked uncertainly.

It was a little time before he could control himself sufficiently to reply. "It . . . it may prove most amusing," he said at last. "With Alecto, I mean." He chuckled again and wiped his eyes with a not-very-clean handkerchief. "You did not know, I suppose," he went on in a steadier voice, "that Alecto is a cousin of mine?"

"A cousin? But——"

"Well, on Silenos virtually everybody is a cousin or a second cousin or a great-uncle or a nephew or a niece or something like that, and when they are not they are *kombáras*, godfather or godmother to somebody or other. Yes, yes, Kate, Alecto is a cousin of mine. A first cousin. There was a family difference many, many years ago, and so we have not spoken to each other for . . . well, let me think now—why, it must be thirty-five or forty years! So you see the possibilities?"

"No, not really. I mean——"

"Alecto will be angry, *very* angry, when she learns that they are coming not to her house, but to mine. She has always been an avaricious woman. She will be exceedingly disturbed to know that it is I who am getting the thousand dollars, and not she. She will believe, of course, that I have engineered this quite deliberately. So she will make trouble."

"What kind of trouble? What can she do?"

"Ah, on that point we must wait and see. Alecto, as I remember her, has a deep capacity for mischief. She is named, you know, after one of the Furies. An accident, no doubt, but the use of the name is far from common. She will think of something troublesome."

"Then I can't understand . . ." Kate shook her head in perplexity. "I mean, I don't understand what you can see in this that is funny. Surely it isn't a laughing matter if——"

"Kate!" He flicked his fat fingers at her. "My life has been distressingly dull for far too long. It is time I had some excitement. And to outwit Alecto we shall have to employ skilful strategy over the broad scope of the campaign and tricky tactics in the detail. It should be most amusing." He rubbed his hands together in anticipatory relish. "I can only hope," he went on thoughtfully, "that your friends will be able to cope with it."

*   *   *

When she left the house she was astonished to encounter Mark loitering against the moonlit wall at the bottom of the flight of stairs where the bougainvillæa hung in dark, drooping festoons. He seemed as startled as she at the unexpectedness of the meeting.

"For heaven's sake!" she said. "What are *you* doing here?"

He glanced at her awkwardly and felt for his pipe. "Oh, I was just taking a stroll around. Moonlight stroll. Contemplating. Felt like getting away from the others." He stopped and made a business of patting his pockets, looking for matches. "As a matter of fact, I walked up here to have another look at the house." He struck a match and bent his head and began to puff. "To tell you the truth, Kate," he said jerkily, between jets of blue, aromatic smoke, "I've quite fallen for this particular house." He looked up the flight of hewn stone steps leading to the panelled door, through the tunnel of the great earthquake-arches springing from the wall, black-shadowed in the moonlight, almost as massive as the buttresses of a cathedral. "If you want to know," he said, "I'm really the one behind us wanting it—more than Janecek."

"Are you? Well, I've just come from talking to the admiral about it. He's going to let you have it."

"He is! Marvellous, Kate, marvellous!" He looked as if he might throw his arms about her. "Well, my goodness, this *is* good news! I can't say——"

"You've never been inside, have you?" she asked cautiously.

"Inside? No."

"It might be disappointing," she warned. "It isn't——"

"It couldn't be! Kate, I know it couldn't be!" With the habitual narrowing of his eyes, he stared up the stairs again, but this time a glow of proud possession irradiated his expression. "Marvellous!" he murmured reverently. "Do you know, Kate," he went on in a confiding voice, "this is exactly the sort of house that appeals to me—something massive, enduring, beautiful . . . it's always been my dream." He paused, embarrassed. "And then . . . well, there is another aspect to it also, I suppose. I rather cottoned on to that fat old buccaneer Mavro the other night. He's a type, a character. I thought it . . . well, it might be a way of giving him a helping hand, you know, without his . . . well, you know what I mean. . . ." He coughed awkwardly. "Come on," he said abruptly. "I'll walk home with you."

For a moment she hesitated. Coming out again into the darkling silver of the night, she knew that the interlude in Mavro's house, the unexpected meeting with her brother-in-law, had changed nothing. "Mark," she said suddenly, "will you do something for me?"

"Of course."

"Take me down to the port, would you? Take me somewhere and buy me some wine."

"Why yes, with pleasure, if that's what you want. But shouldn't you——"

"I don't want to go home," she said. "Not yet. I want to go down to the port and drink some wine."

"What's this?" he said, glancing at her sharply, sensing the odd undertone of urgency in her request. "Something up?"

She shook her head, and shrugged slightly, and put her arm through his. "Come," she said.

"Well, at least it's downhill," Mark said lightly. "I must say that suits me perfectly. Kate, remind me never to ride a mule again! After our little jaunt today I don't think I could climb another step. I'm aching in every bone."

"Was it pleasant?"

"Instructive, let us say."

Arm in arm, no longer talking, they went down the flights of steps and through the empty lanes to the port, and Kate guided him to a small tavern next to a sailmaker's loft, overlooking the harbour. It was neither the Tavern Platinos nor the tavern of the Two Brothers, but a place where she and David often went together during the winter. Three fishermen sat at the corner table, dipping thick wedges of black bread into a communal bowl of fish soup. They and the unshaven, tired-eyed proprietor were the only occupants. As if to make a gesture to the newcomers, the proprietor began to wind the handle of an antiquated phonograph which had a long black trumpet-horn painted with a motif of cupids and chrysanthemums. On steel hooks above it hung cuts of liver and lights and a plucked chicken with its head wrapped up in blood-stained newspaper and a small side of lamb cut through lengthwise all the way from the head. A scarred cat sat on the floor beneath it, hoping something would drop. The proprietor selected a disc and put it on. A very thin, scratchy voice, which sounded tired and far away, began to sing *Sousouráda*.

They were drinking their second carafe of wine when Mark broached the matter with, "All right, Kate. What's bothering you? You've got something on your mind, haven't you?"

"Have I? Am I really as transparent as all that?" She smiled quickly, but her eyes remained serious. "At the picnic today, did you and David talk again?" she asked.

"About what in particular?"

"What you talked about before. His going back to London."

"Not a word." Mark shook his head. "Why?"

For a long time she looked down at her fingers, then in a low voice she said, "I'm not sure of this, not yet, but I think I might change my mind . . . I think I might want you to persuade him to go back."

"Yes?" he said guardedly, watching her.

It was some moments before she looked up at him. Her eyes were troubled and uncertain, but she seemed to have nothing more to say.

"I don't believe it comes into it; persuasion, I mean," Mark offered consideringly. "I've pretty much come round to your way of thinking. He'll make up his own mind. Best to let him decide for himself, without us interfering. Anyway, persuasion won't work with him. I doubt if it ever did." His shoulders moved in a slight shrug. He watched her eyes as he said, "Kate, what has brought about this change of face in you?"

"I . . . I haven't changed, not really." Her eyes dropped away from his. "I said I *might* want to, that's all."

"All right. That's a technicality. The point is why? There must be a reason."

Again she was silent for a long time. "Mark," she said eventually, "I can talk to you, can't I? Talk properly, I mean. As one might talk to a brother, not just a brother-in-law."

"I hope so, Kate," he said sincerely. "I hope so."

"Because I want to talk to you about David, and being married, and what it is—what it is *to me*, I mean."

"Go ahead." He leaned across and filled her wineglass.

She smiled her thanks and sipped at the wine and stared out at the dark harbour where the masts of the boats moved slow, soothing arcs against the ice-bright spatter of stars.

"You see, Mark," she began thoughtfully, "you think all this, living on Silenos, is escape for him . . . for us, I suppose . . . for me too. But it isn't. It isn't at all. Well, not for me, anyway. For me this is the direct opposite of that. For me, this is . . . well, *permanence* I suppose is the only word. It's stability, coherence, everything I've come to value—a sense of belonging, of family, of home, of children. Like that Chinese ideograph they use to write the word 'marriage' with half a dozen simple brush-strokes that show a man and a woman and a child beneath an overhanging roof. It's something like that—inked in very black, permanent, something you can't rub out. I . . . I never had this before, Mark. I never knew what it was until I married David: and then, even afterwards . . . well, I don't suppose it's ever really easy. You escape from the quicksands of adolescence and growing up and those early terrible freedoms, and then you have to walk for years and years along that narrow, imperilled beach of marriage and then you get to something like this which is important and . . . and secure"—her eyes moved lingeringly along the dark, quiet, light-studded quayside—"and then you discover how . . . how terribly *precarious* it all is."

"If you mean that the hardest job in the world to bring off successfully is marriage, I'm completely with you. Although you're not saying anything new. Mind you," he added wryly, "I wouldn't know. On matrimony, I never even got to the journeyman stage. But it's an entirely different matter, Kate, with you and David. Your marriage has been a happy one. Heavens, it frightens the wits out of old failures like me!"

"Happy?" She examined the word reflectively. "Yes, I suppose it's been happy. Some of it . . . quite a lot of it, really. And some of it has been miserable. And some of it has been dreary. I don't suppose it's been very different from most other marriages." She looked up at him. "But it has endured," she said quietly. "That is the important thing. It *has* endured."

"Obviously it has endured. So what's the trouble?"

"I'm frightened," she said simply.

He looked at her in surprise.

"If this doesn't make sense," she said with sudden vehemence, "then *nothing* makes sense! Nothing at all!"

"All right. Granted. But what are you frightened of? David isn't going to run off with some other woman. He's not going to leave you in the lurch. What is the matter, Kate?"

"But don't you see that some tiny little flick of this or that, something that you can't predict or expect, can change it altogether, smash it all to pieces?"

"And who's going to supply that tiny little flick? David? You?" He smiled at her and his hand moved to stroke his beard. "Kate, don't answer this if you don't want to," he said, "but the general relationship, you and David, it's all right, isn't it?"

She looked at him for a moment, then nodded. "Yes, it's all right," she said.

"You don't say that very convincingly."

"Well, yes, it is all right. Of course it's all right. But . . . but I don't expect you can go through eleven years of marriage without getting a few scars, a few bruises . . . on both sides, I mean. There are gaps left, little hollows, concealed wounds . . . I don't know quite how to put it. Gaps, I suppose is best. Certain little curtains of secrecy behind which we hide ourselves from each other. Maybe it's not secrecy . . . just confidence withheld, moments when——" She broke off. "Why am I boring you with all this?" she said.

"That's what we're trying to find out," said Mark patiently. "Go on."

"There are moments when we should talk to each other, and we don't . . . we skirt around it very carefully and come back to smile at each other, and the gap is left there behind us and we never have to look at it again. Lately it's been happening often. He's so preoccupied . . . worried, I think. He doesn't talk about it. We just move around the gaps. We're always very polite about it. We're so careful to consider each other's feelings that the feeling itself gets rubbed away to nothing."

"That could, of course, simply be something to do with this island," said Mark sagely. "You're too isolated, thrown too much into each other's company. It obviously must place a tremendous demand on your mutual resources—towards each other, I mean."

"Yes, that's true. That's very true," she said softly. "There's the light here, too. It's so clear, so terribly clear. You see people all the way through, as if they're transparent, almost. And you see yourself just the same way. It's a funny thing, isn't it, that everybody thinks we're escaping from something by living here, and really this is where you find that there isn't any escape at all, not from anything, not even from yourself." She sipped at her wine, and set down her glass and stared at the clear, pale liquid. "Least of all from yourself," she added in an undertone, as if it were her thoughts voicing a private reminder.

"But I wonder if we ever do—anywhere?"

"Perhaps not. I do think it's harder here, that's all. There's so much more time to consider things. And all the motions you go through, everything of contact and communication and experience . . . yes, and of self-examination too, seems to be stripped away by this light, stripped down to the bare bones. Like those sculptured friezes they used to carve around the ossuaries of medieval churches, with skulls and skeletons and everything of living stripped down to bones and two thighbones beating out on a drum the dance of death. . . . Well, no not that . . . not as chilling, not as macabre. . . ." She was silent for a moment. "But quite frightening at times, all the same," she said, and again hesitated, and then, "there's another thing too in that you don't have all the cushions around it here—around yourself, I mean, and trying to live with people. I'm beginning to think cushions might be better sometimes than always having the springs showing. They might be necessary. You see, Mark, even misery or uncertainty can be a cushion, or deceit . . . oh, I expect lots of things can provide the cushion. Then when you bump the bruises aren't so obvious, or anyway they don't seem to hurt so much." She looked at him and smiled thoughtfully. "Silly talk, isn't it? I haven't the least idea what I've been expecting you to say. Nothing, really, I suppose."

"Just as well perhaps. I'd hardly qualify as a Miss Lonelyhearts." He smiled and patted her hand. "Leave all that sort of stuff to Scott Fitzgerald, eh?"

Kate, a wider reader than he and a more retentive one, did not correct him. Scott Fitzgerald or Nathanael West, what did it matter? He had been patient, and sympathetic. She realised with a faint sense of surprise how quickly and how unexpectedly she had grown to like him.

"The question before the tribunal," he said cheerfully, "is that this darned jug of wine is empty again." His heartiness was deliberate. Strange talk for somebody so thoroughly down-to-earth and uncomplicated as Kate, yet he was sufficiently sensitive to her mood to know that she had no more to say to him, and he sensed that she had not said what she had really wanted to say. But he was glad that she had offered him a diplomatic and uncommitted withdrawal. There was something, he reflected, of very good value about Kate, something rare, something true and consistent and good. Now, if only poor Gwen had had a little more of the cut of Kate's jib. . . . "Shall we ask for another?" He lifted the carafe.

"No." She shook her head. "I think I want to go home now, Mark.

Thanks for listening." She pressed his hand affectionately. "You have been very sweet."

"Naturally. I'm trying to be. Kate, if you're looking for an eternal triangle, don't think I'm going to allow you to discount *me* as a third-party risk!"

She laughed and took his arm as they went out the door.

Going back through the darkness she was very conscious that she had skirted around a gap she had created herself, leaving the real issue behind them, unstated.

6

THE HOUSE OF ADMIRAL MAVRO

ON THE FOLLOWING DAY, when the occupation of the house of Admiral
Mavro began, David Meredith was himself concerned with certain as-
pects of the precariousness of living. He was as deeply perturbed as Kate
had been the night before, as uncertain of himself and where his destiny
was leading him as she had been. But the causes of his misgivings were
not the same, nor did he examine the core of his unrest with the same
degree of honesty as she had looked at hers. Perhaps there was a reason
for this. Kate, at least, had had Mark to talk to; David had only the
empty silence of his study, the dispiriting evidence of his unfinished work
scattered before him on the untidy desk, with a fine blown grit of almost
invisible dust covering the uppermost sheets of his typescript, as repel-
lent to his fingertips as a withered snake-skin, and a dead beetle upside
down on the cover of his note-book. A man will seldom make confession
when there are only his own ears to listen.

He did not, at this stage, even faintly suspect the danger that Achille
Mouliet added to the situation. True, he had observed, with not much
more than an idle wonder, his wife's enjoyment of the young Frenchman's
company. It had vaguely surprised him that she seemed to spend so much
time with him, but he had put this down to Kate's natural desire for
moments of distraction. There was always this stimulus and excitement
in the arrival of newcomers to the island after the aloneness and the
forced-togetherness of winter. New faces, parties, fun, being with people,
meeting the millionaire, going aboard his yacht, a girl in a plastic hula-
skirt . . . he had even remarked to himself on the reawakened vivacity

of his wife since Mark and the others had come to Silenos. Something
different from being left along with *The Brothers Karamazov*. Any
woman after a time would have to become bored with *The Brothers
Karamazov!* It never occurred to him to imagine Achille Mouliet as an
alternative distraction.

His picture of the Frenchman, indeed, was to some degree an imagined Mouliet, conjured out of memories of the summer before, of in-
ferences he had drawn from his behaviour, of the girl Odette hung with
dogs' jawbones sharing his golden masculinity with a swarm of other
girls who all looked exactly like the Chloe whom the Frenchman had
brought to Beth's party—breasty girls with horsetail hair-dos and willing
legs sheathed in tight black pants waiting their turn at the semenal well-
spring. In this picture he had of Achille Mouliet the presence of his own
wife was unimaginable. When he thought of Mouliet at all, in fact, he
thought of him in relation to poor little Fegel. The self-invited guest.
The cuckoo in the nest. And poor Fegel having to cough discreetly every
time he entered his own door! It was so sadly in character for the little
Czech to have even his own house usurped by someone more confident
than himself. . . .

His uneasiness—and this time he allowed the chain-reaction to develop
into that familiar but feared feeling of apprehension without really trying to check it—therefore had no direct reference either to Kate or to
Mouliet.

It began the moment he seated himself in front of his typewriter, and
it was, at first, concerned only with his work. The dusty feel of the paper,
the dead beetle, the dog-eared pages discarded, the uncompromising
blankness of the now-yellowing sheet curling up from the roller of his
Remington, all seemed symbols of the fact of failure . . . dumb witnesses
to a lost confidence. Unhopefully, but with a sort of obstinate desperation, he tried to allay his misgivings by going back to that first section of
his novel which, written so many months before, might easily surprise
him, he thought, by its unremembered freshness. He had not read two
pages before he closed the folder and put it away. For a long time he
stared at the blank white wall above his desk. He knew that today he
would write nothing. There would be nothing more to add, nothing to
say. Quite suddenly he felt the task to be beyond him. He had a feeling
of being adrift, without any sense of direction, without belief in himself.

It was a feeling so absolute that it first shocked him and then frightened
him. The possibility of failure had always been there, of course, lingering

in the back of his mind. How precarious is freedom! But he had always
seen that. The risk was the price you paid for the right to strike out in
a new direction, in your own direction. But the feeling before had always
been under control. Only now was the actual *fact* of failure there in front
of him, right under his eyes, as visible and as tangible as the fact of death
represented by the dry, black, brittle, stiff-legged beetle up-ended on the
cover of his note-book! He had a swift strange image of the beetle swollen
to the size of a man, the dead, bent legs rigid in mid-air, the black
carapace emptying itself to nothing, and Mark and Janecek and Kettering standing around in a silent group looking down at it . . . Mark's eyes
narrowed in the scrutiny of success, Janecek's unpitying survey, Kettering's eye grotesquely enlarged and blinking within the square golden
frame of his monocle, and the three green scarab beetles on his fingers
holding the glass—the beetles of death—staring unseeingly at the dead
black beetle of failure. . . .

Well, it was their fault, he told himself resentfully. It was by *their*
coming that he had been interrupted, thrown off his balance. They had
distracted him, fractured the continuity, destroyed his concentration with
their piddling problems, their endless demands, their taken-for-granted
assumptions of superiority! If they had left him alone. . . . *If!* There were
no ifs. If there were no picnics, no parties, if there were no talks with
Mark, if there were no inquiries to be made about houses, if there were
no millionaires throwing largess to the natives—would all these ifs add
up to there being no dead beetle on the cover of his note-book? How
could one be sure about that? The dead beetle was a *fact* of death, not
an *if* of death. . . .

And the cold uncivil smile on the lips of Vlikos the banker—that had
been there even before Mark or any of them had come. A fact of in-
civility, not an if. Perhaps bankers were able to smell failure from far
off . . . did bankers become bankers because of this special prescience of
lost causes and bad risks? Logical enough. There were old fishermen still
living in Silenos who were said to have the power of smelling the approach of death, and the people of Karpathos and Kassos—the peasants,
anyway—could smell an earthquake coming. Much, oh much more important for a banker to be able to smell failure in the wind! And certainly Vlikos had been able to catch a whiff of it in Andreas the sponge-
boat captain. So why not in David Meredith? He wondered what failure
would smell like to a banker. Faint and sweet, like melons rotting in
the harbour water. . . .

Perhaps Lieutenant Fotis would be able to smell it too when he went to him at the police station to renew the residence permits. In less than a month it would have to be done. Aggravating. A nuisance. But this was the way you had to kotow for time to live, for slices of your own life. Stamps, rubber impressions in indelible ink, three passport-size photographs, the Christian name of your father, your mother . . . religion, date of birth, occupation . . . the dry voice of bureaucracy that was the deafening sound of the spinning twentieth-century globe . . . the force that kept people pressed inside their cardboard fences, docketed away, filed where they belonged. And then the questions! The interminable, dreary, unsympathetic interrogation of officialdom. And Lieutenant Fotis looking down at his blotter and tapping with his cheap little ballpoint pen, with that sweet, faint whiff of failure in his nostrils . . . Fotis in the ascendancy, tapping with his pen, as if the life of David Meredith was a little round peg to be tapped back into the little round hole where it belonged. . . .

"What is the purpose, *Kyrios* Meredith, of your wishing to remain an additional year in Greece?"

"It will take me an additional year, Commandant, to complete the next sentence of a book I am writing."

"This is a book dealing with Greece?"

"No. This is a book dealing with beetles. Dead beetles, to be explicit."

"This book could be written in Athens, of course?"

"Of course. The reference sources would be better."

"Then why is your application for continued residence on an island like Silenos?"

"My wife and family are here. My brother is here. Freedom is here. Freedom of course is everywhere. One reads about it all the time. It is fashionable now to find freedom of a special sort on distant islands. Freedom to fail even. Quietly. Without fuss. Just roll over on your note-book and poke your legs in the air."

"Why do you not wish to fail in London, or in your own country, *Kyrios* Meredith?"

"There would be too many people watching. Here there are only three or four."

"You would be more free in your own country. You would belong with the people. You would not have to fill in forms as an alien. Your situation would not be so precarious. There, people would understand your

habits and your customs. What is the purpose, *Kyrios* Meredith, of your
wishing to remain an additional year in this country?"

"I have no alternative, Commandant. Mr. Vlikos, the banker, will explain that our account will not stand the fare out—not for all of us. And
I must finish my book."

"This is a book dealing with Greece?"

"This is a book about my grandmother's cough. She was very old, and
blind, and bedridden. Some years before she had fallen off a tram at the
corner of Glenhuntly Road and Kooyong Road, right in front of the
sweet shop. We lived in a very small house called *Avalon*. My bed was
in a small, wired-in sleep-out where my mother also kept ferns. It was
dark and I was always rather frightened, especially by cocks crowing. I
would put my head under the blankets and keep it there until my grandmother began to cough. Her bedroom was next to the sleep-out, with
only a thin door between. She always began to cough just before dawn,
and the cough would stay with her until eleven o'clock, when she would
send me up to the corner sweet shop for a bottle of lemonade. 'It cuts the
phlegm,' she used to say. 'It cuts the phlegm.' When she began to cough
I could take my head from beneath the blankets, because I knew daylight
was coming and the cocks would stop crowing. Then I would hear the
alarm clock in mother's bedroom. It would ring just for a moment or two
and cut off, and I'd sense—yes, sense rather than see—that somewhere a
light had been switched on. Time for my father to get up and go off to
the tram sheds. And then I'd turn over on my side and go to sleep. My
mother's name was Minnie, but you have that down, haven't you? I still
remember my grandmother's cough. It was dry and faint and scratchy,
exactly like the sound a beetle makes."

"Earlier you told me your book was concerned with *dead* beetles. A
dead beetle cannot make a sound like your grandmother's cough. It cannot make any sound. There is a penalty, *Kyrios* Meredith, for making
deliberately misleading statements or giving false information."

"There is a penalty, Commandant, for almost every bloody thing under
the sun."

*   *   *

In the meantime, occupation of Mavro's house had begun quietly
enough with the arrival of Mark, Kettering, a mule-load of baggage, and
Kate Meredith as attendant interpreter and escort.

The admiral welcomed them courteously with a brief, somewhat

stilted, and very formal speech in Greek, winked slyly at Kate, delivered
to Mark a medieval-looking front door key, ten inches long and weighing
a good two pounds, and tactfully withdrew himself to the Sinclair house,
where for the remainder of the morning he played cribbage with Arthur
while Beth prepared for him a light luncheon of artichokes and cole-
slaw.

If Mark was startled by the internal appearance of the house—which
in the revealing light of day he might well have been—he betrayed it neither by his expression nor his attitude. (Perhaps, Kate reflected, watching
him as he hurried from room to room, exploring, exclaiming, pointing out ceilings, fireplaces, mouldings, niches; discovering, all by himself it seemed, the huge arched stove in the kitchen; apostrophising the
splendour of the view from the terrace, he did so genuinely love the old
house that he was blind to all its defects, as a true adorer may be blind
to all the blemishes and shortcomings of his mistress. Within twenty
minutes he had taken proud spiritual possession of the property.)

Kettering was obviously apprehensive of what Janecek would think of
it all when he consented to make his appearance—"I will come in the
afternoon," he had said. "I would like the place thoroughly aired first"
—but he tried to force his wit to overcome his misgivings. "I take it,
Kate," he said, after Mavro had withdrawn, "that this is the House of
Usher *after* the fall?"

"The weather is warmer now," Kate said blandly. "You will do most
of your living outdoors."

"Brother!" said Kettering. Again he surveyed the *sála* through his
monocle. "You will excuse us," he said dully, "if we skip the entertaining while we're here. There aren't any chairs to sit on."

"Cocktails," Kate suggested cheerfully. "Everybody stands at cocktail
parties. You can clear off that big table and put the savouries and bottles
over there."

"Yes." He rubbed his fingers over the monocle, stared at it a moment,
then said, "Well, shall we get the worst of it over now and go look at
the toilets?" At the door he paused and looked back into the room, his
wan, shortsighted eyes blinking at the patina of rain-stains and mildew
on the far wall. "Jackson Pollock," he said absently, "would have been
crazy about that wall."

At eleven o'clock a discreet but firm rapping at the front door disclosed
the presence of the man Brent from Suvora's yacht. He was dressed incongruously in a dark-grey houndstooth suit with a double-breasted waist-

coat, a white shirt and black silk tie, and, as a concession to the climate, an off-white Panama hat. In his hand was a thick sheaf of envelopes.

"Ah, Mrs. Meredith," he said gratefully, "this will save me a journey. I have one of these for you and your husband. And for Mr. Mark Meredith and for Mr. Kettering." He bent his head and fingered carefully through the envelopes.

"My goodness," said Kate, watching him, "you have quite a batch there to deliver."

"Mr. Suvora," Brent explained, "is giving a small party tomorrow aboard his yacht. He wishes to invite all the foreign residents."

"How nice," said Kate, taking the three envelopes. "I see you have one there for Mr. Mouliet, and for Mr. Fegel. Their house is quite a long way round the cliff. I'll be seeing them after lunch. I can take them for you, if you like."

"That would be very kind of you, Mrs. Meredith," he said, with obvious relief, and rummaged through the stack for two more envelopes.

Inside, handing their messages to Mark and Kettering, she said, "We're all invited to a party."

Her message, written in Suvora's neat, small hand, read: "My dear Mr. and Mrs. Meredith. Do come for cocktails aboard my boat, the *Farrago,* at about five-thirty tomorrow, Wednesday. Bring your children. There will be something teetotal for them and they can climb the rigging. X. J. Suvora."

"There you are!" She turned to Kettering. "Cocktails, you see! It's the chic thing to do."

"What on earth," said Mark wonderingly, "could 'X' stand for?"

"The spot where the body was found, usually," said Kettering.

"A name, I mean. Suvora's name. Xenophon, I suppose. Or Xavier."

"What's wrong with Xerxes?" asked Kettering.

"Xanthippus," Kate offered, and Mark grinned at her and said, "You're cheating." "I'm not," she retorted. "He was an Athenian general. He succeeded Themistocles." Kettering said, "We bow to classical scholarship." Suddenly they were all laughing together.

She felt astonishingly gay, exhilarated. How much she liked being with these two nice men! The invitation had filled her with a quick, childish pleasure: the specific inclusion of the two children—how thoughtful of the man!—somehow made it that much more exciting. A party on a millionaire's yacht! Jerry would be beside himself. And Simon . . . she could imagine the child's wide grey eyes trying to take it all in. And then there was the problem—heavens! how long since she had had to face it? —of what to wear.

It was not until she was walking back to get lunch for David and the children that she found herself looking down at the other two envelopes in her hand . . . M. Achille Mouliet, M. Conrad Fegel. . . . Only then did it occur to her to consider the possible complications that might arise out of Suvora's invitation.

* * *

She sensed David's mood soon after she returned home, but left him to his thoughts while she washed the children and prepared the meal. At luncheon he was morose, withdrawn from all of them except in momentary spurts of crossness; with Jerry for slouching at the table, with Simon for slopping his glass of milk, even with her for unspecified offences, never made vocal but harboured in his eyes. She saw with a sharp stab of concern for him that he had already been drinking—not wine, but brandy . . . he seldom really began to drink before the evening.

She sent the children off to play and took their coffee into the garden, beneath the plum-tree, and said, "We're invited to a party tomorrow, aboard Suvora's yacht. All of us."

"Marvellous, marvellous!" he said, mimicking his brother. "Party after party! The social whirl! Any day now we'll see our pictures in the *Tatler!*"

"The children are asked. It'll be heaven for them."

"Bliss," he agreed sarcastically. "I suppose we'll have to take our turn, and throw something lavish. A masquerade perhaps. What do you think?"

"We organised the picnic for them."

"*I* organised the picnic for them," he corrected her carefully, and bent over to stir his coffee.

She had a sense of deep sadness, desolate sadness, of an aimless movement through lonely, empty places, as she looked at him. How drab and grey and dispiriting it had all suddenly become, how different from that jet of rapture in the admiral's house when she and Mark and Kettering had laughed together, holding their invitations in their hands.

"I want to walk over to Conrad's house this afternoon," she said. "I have this invitation to give him. And there's something rather special I want to talk to him about." She waited. He was staring down at his coffee cup over his clasped hands, and he seemed to be paying no attention. "Mark told me that Suvora is very interested in ceramics," she explained. "I thought I'd show him some of Conrad's things. You never know. It might be a way of helping. I feel so desperately sorry for him now that this . . . this other business has come up to worry him."

"I organised that too," he said, without looking up. "Or is that what you're getting at? Still, it's a nice idea. More largess for the natives. I was thinking about that this morning. The *fact* of the largess, not the *if*. Make him buy Fegel's pots. No ifs about it. *Make him!* Suck the juice out of him while we've got him here. Remember what Kettering said to me. Suvora will foot the bill, whatever it is. Every man has his price . . . that's axiomatic. You might even see if you can get a cut off the joint for me!"

"You're in a funny mood, darling, aren't you?" she said gently. "Did you work this morning?"

"Of course I worked," he said shortly. It was her routine question every day now, he reflected irritably. Work, work, work! Like some bloody left-wing slogan battering at his brain. *Were you able to work, darling? . . . Did you work this morning?* A phonograph needle caught in the groove, squeaking out its idiocies. *You must get back to your work, David.* You have a wife and two children who depend on you. . . . Work, boys, work and be contented. . . . Press on, deserving poor. . . . "I don't plan to do any more," he said deliberately. "Not this afternoon, anyway. I'll go across and see how Mark's making out."

"Do you really want to?" she said quickly, sensing the aggressiveness of his mood. "They're managing all right, you know. They were fine when I left them."

"I'll go over, anyway," he said obstinately. At least it was a way of escaping from the dead black beetle upstairs. Was this the beginning of it? he wondered . . . the first step in running away from it, in giving up? . . . to find in anything that was offered an excuse for withdrawal? "I might as well make it easy for them," he said sourly. "I can be there on the spot with my little note-book to jot down their complaints."

"Darling," she said softly and compassionately, and there was pain and tenderness in her eyes.

"What?"

"Darling, don't let them rattle you," she said.

*   *   *

With an expressionless face, Janecek examined the *sála*, then walked slowly through the arches to the next room, glanced through the opened doors at the terrace, returned languidly to the *sála,* and made a beckoning finger at Kettering.

"If you have not already done so," he said, "I suggest you pack our baggage again."

"Pack what baggage?" said Kettering. "Where are we supposed to be going? We're here."

Janecek smiled faintly. "Of course we are here. But you are not suggesting, surely, that we are *staying* here?"

"Oh, yes we are," said Mark firmly.

"Clothilde," said Suvora admiringly, "just look at that exquisite ceiling."

"Mark, are you out of your mind?" Janecek asked gently. "Darling, we cannot possibly live in a place like this. Not possibly. None of us can work. We shall——"

"Well, whether we can or we can't, that's what we're going to do," said Mark determinedly. "I signed the lease with the admiral before we came up here. And I paid him in advance five hundred dollars of the amount we agreed on."

"Then you *are* out of your mind, Mark. You mean to say you had not even *looked* at the place before you signed this lease?"

"We all looked at it. Didn't we? You, too. You were as enthusiastic as I was."

"We examined the house from the outside," Janecek said patiently. "We had no idea of—" he paused and spread his hands expressively—"of *this!*" He turned. "Clothilde," he appealed, "could you live in a place like this?"

Clothilde shuddered.

"Suvora?" Janecek said with a smile.

"Oh yes, I could live here for quite a long time. I would very much like to own it." He returned Janecek's smile, and took Clothilde aside to show her the *lavabo.*

"Coming to points of detail," said Janecek, "we are, after all, here to work. There is no *place* to work. No place at all. Unless one were here to draw Charles Addams cartoons, or to illustrate Poe."

"Work on the terrace," said Mark. "That's where I plan to work."

"That will be pleasant for all of us, darling. Let us try to be very civil to each other when we jog elbows."

"Have you *looked* at that terrace!" said Mark angrily. "We could play tennis on it, and still leave room enough for you to paint da Vinci's 'Last Supper'!" He took a deep breath and tugged his beard. "What are you suggesting? That we start all over again looking for another house? Damn it all, man, my brother has gone to all sorts of trouble for us already! Do we toss this one back now and say, 'Oh no, I'm afraid this one won't do either. Please find me another!'" He took another breath. "He's not a house agent, you know."

"That's true, he's not," David said from the doorway, smiling in at them. "You left the front door open," he explained. "I came in on my cue, didn't I? What's the trouble now?"

"Clem dear," said Janecek, "what is the position about the baggage?"

"Yours," said Kettering, "is there in the hall, where I put it. Mine is all unpacked, in the room I've chosen."

"Then do hurry and get it all together again. The smell here is very unpleasant. Mildew. Rats. Bad drainage."

"Have you looked at it all?" David asked mildly. "Surely there must be an attractive corner somewhere for you. The place, after all, is very large."

"So was the Cloaca Maxima."

"Well, you'd possibly know more about that," said David, joining battle. "If this place doesn't please you, I suppose there's nothing to stop you going back to the hotel."

"Only the fact that I regard the hotel as almost equally offensive."

"Oh, for God's sake, stop this bloody humbug!" Mark said in sudden anger. "If we go on like——"

"May I suggest," put in Suvora in a tone of moderation, "that the decision is really up to Mark. It is his play, after all. I am merely an interested investor. You, Mr. Janecek, have accepted a commission to provide the essential décor for the production. Mark should be the one to say where he thinks the work can be most harmoniously carried out."

"We are staying here," said Mark flatly.

Janecek made a little *moue* of resignation. "With your permission, Suvora," he said, "I shall move my effects aboard your yacht."

"You may move them wherever you please," Suvora replied smoothly. "There is ample storage space in the forward 'tween-deck, behind the chain locker. Unfortunately, I cannot accommodate you personally. We do not have the room."

No more than a flick of curiosity in Janecek's fine blue eyes betrayed his recognition of the fact that battle had been joined on a second front. David came into the room and walked across to the chair beneath the painting of the *Telemachus*. Kettering rubbed nervously at his knuckles.

Mark cleared his throat. Suvora smiled from one to the other of them and said, "I have decided to invite Admiral Mavro and his friend Commander Sinclair to spend a few days with me aboard my boat. They are both old seafaring men. I think they'll enjoy a little spell of shipboard life again, feeling their sea-legs and so forth."

"That's a wonderful idea," said David, with a quick glance of admiration in the direction of the millionaire. "They'll be tickled pink. However, that doesn't solve Mr. Janecek's problem, does it?"

"I appreciate your concern for me," said Janecek pleasantly. "The best plan, I imagine, is for me to rent myself another house. We may all be happier, I think, if we are apart from each other. When something arises which calls for general discussion, Mark can always call us together."

Mark frowned. Kettering rubbed his knuckles harder.

David said, "Islands can be pretty disruptive places, particularly with creative people. Your idea might be the practical one. You can't expect to discover an ivory tower to rent, but maybe if you look around you can find some sort of little *pied-à-terre*. After all, you'll have Kettering to run up and down with messages and so on."

Kettering looked uncomfortable.

Suvora said, "In that case, I'm afraid Mr. Janecek will have to be responsible for his own personal property negotiations. My basic investment allocation for essential accommodation I have already entrusted to Mark."

"I've got a nice room here," Kettering said suddenly. "I'm happy with it. I'm staying on."

Janecek looked at him gravely, and then his face softened into the expression of amused tolerance which an over-fond parent might display towards a spoilt and mutinous child.

"Bravo, Kettering!" said David. "Good for you!"

Kettering planted his feet firmly on the uncarpeted stone floor, took a firm hold of his monocle, and blinked defiantly.

Janecek shrugged, and turned his glance slowly around the room, his fine eyes pausing in turn on the Swiss mezzotints of the Siege of Troy, the anonymous photographs, the antlered hat-stand, the embattled splendour of the cruiser *Telemachus* in its peeling gilt frame, the shabby coffee-house chairs. The last time, he recalled, that he had stayed in a place as large as this had been at Venice, in the *palazzo* of Ricci and the countess. There had been liveried servants in powdered wigs, and lanterns dancing their reflections in the canal, and the gallery with its

Carpaccios and the Bellini and the Giorgione. Vramantin had been there to talk of his plans for *Semiramis* . . . the people from the Biennale . . . Isidore with the score of his new opera. . . . Kettering had been there too. Had he forgotten? He had so loved it all, too! Had his sensibilities been so affected by this savage, crude island, by the uncouth aggressiveness of these two bourgeois brothers Meredith, that he could actually choose to live in this . . . this Castle of Otranto? To express his happiness with it? Or was it only a jealous petulance because of the young sailor Vassilis whom they had met under the pines? He turned and examined the small, bearded, awkwardly rebellious figure with a studied concern.

"My dear Clem," he said gently, "I shall stay where you want to stay. We are committed to this thing together. We'll try to make the best of it. You have my sympathy, you know that, but I was trying to——"

"Oh, I don't want your sympathy!" cried Kettering wildly. "To hell with your sympathy! To hell with your sympathy, I say! Or anybody else's!" He sounded almost hysterical. "If I want sympathy, brother," he said in a lower voice, "I can find it where I've always found it—in the dictionary, between 'sin' and 'syphilis'!"

Shaken by his outburst, he gulped as if all the words might be swallowed away, blinked uncertainly, and hurried from the room.

"Well!" said David.

"All right," said Mark. "What *all that's* about I don't know. As far as you're concerned"—he looked at Janecek sternly—"the question is quite simple. Do you wish to pick a room for yourself?"

"I'd adore to see Clem's quarters," said Janecek, quite unruffled. "And if today is the day for viewing the dungeons, darling, I must say I'd rather like that."

"By my count," said Mark unequivocally, "there are sixteen to choose from. Take your choice. Except for Clem's," he went on mercilessly, "none of them has a bed in it. We can organise you a camp stretcher. And no doubt Suvora will let us borrow one or two Li-los from the yacht."

"I should be more than delighted," the millionaire said, as Janecek, without a glance to right or left, went through the arches in search of Kettering.

"Mark," said David admiringly, "I never knew you had it in you!"

"I'm beginning to grow very bloody tired," said Mark, "of all this

bunkum!" He looked uncomfortable for a moment, then turned away
from them, fingering his beard.

Soon after, Suvora left. He was in the highest of spirits as he went
down to the port with Clothilde on his arm.

David, too, went back to his house with a rare feeling of exultation—
exulting less in the defeat of Feodor Janecek than in this sudden rise of
unexpected forces of non-conformity. How good to see old Mark digging
his heels in! How suavely Suvora had played his role! How astonishing
to see little Kettering making his own private stand for independence!
Pathetic too, in a way, like a tearful child stamping its foot in anger.
Yet it was his little surge of rebellion that had taken the real courage.
Mark and Suvora, after all, held all the cards in their hands. Kettering
had had nothing except some glimpse of the flickering spirit of freedom
. . . perhaps a desperate wish to escape from this love-thrall that bound
him to the icy personality of his master. Well, the three of them together
had effectively taken intention out of his own hands, for he had been
willing and eager to join issue with Janecek on any number of points:
yet their having done so did give a special pungency to the situation.
There were weaknesses also, it seemed, in the formula-patterns of success; cracks in the façade of superiority. And in some way their little
outbursts of rebellion gave validity to his own rejection of the conventional.

He was in good spirits when he reached his home and called to Kate
so that she might share his better nature. He had called her name three
times before he remembered that she had gone to Fegel's house. He went
upstairs to the study and flicked the dead beetle from his note-book and
put a sheet of clean paper in his Remington.

By this time the occupation of Mavro's house had been almost completed. The word "almost" is used advisedly, for it was at the first faint
darkening of twilight that old Alecto forced her entry into the lower
floor of the huge, crumbling mansion. Her approach was made through
a gap in the western wall opening on to a neglected garden where she
had long been in the habit of illegally pasturing her animals. From this
it was a simple matter for her to effect entry into the lower levels of the
house through the broken French doors that hung askew on their hinges.
By seven o'clock she had established her grim and vengeful tenancy of
the lower floors with a herd of nine goats, a flock of eleven thin sheep,
and one black sow.

From the high terrace of the Sinclair house, Admiral Mavro followed with intense interest this extraordinary operation with the big pair of old naval binoculars which Arthur had treasured since Jutland.

He, too, was in excellent spirits as he went in from the terrace to make his report to his old colleague.

BOOK III

Fegel

THE HOUSE ON THE CLIFFS

CONRAD FEGEL's little house stood at the very edge of the sea cliffs about a mile to the westward of the town and quite a distance beyond the last hilly sprawl of the Silenos cottages. It was a small whitewashed building crouched into a high ledge of rock about thirty feet above the sea, so that from a distance it looked like a strange deposit of guano.

On a ridge above it were two stony cylinders, old ruined windmills that looked for all the world like the crumbling watchtowers of some medieval fortress, and the rocky escarpment behind had the look of a high castle wall, and so added to the illusion.

The house itself, below this forbidding tellurian backdrop, was invaded on three sides by all the desolate manifestations of the island's wildness beyond the hammered pathways of the town. Old rock slides filled eroded gullies that dropped down from the ruined mills and at one side a bank of shale cast a flinty glitter from the sun; everywhere, to the very walls that sheltered the house and its parched and limited little garden, was the dry encroachment of asphodel and thistle and spiky thornbrush and sage and acid-coloured plants with milk-oozing leaves and vines that crept out of crevices in the rocks and tangled, thirsty growths that had a wet and glossy look yet rubbed into dry dust at the touch of a finger. The earth itself was hard-baked and spread with flints and dry snail-shells, and there were lizards flicking on the rocks and big pale butterflies spasmodically fluttering above the brittle vegetation. In it all there was a queer, frightening sort of beauty, but it would not be easy to accept unless one were to cast a glance every now and then to the eastward, for comfort or reassurance, to the random scatter of the outlying houses of Silenos, drifting over the last hill like laggards of an army in retreat. To the westward the empty landscape would give little comfort —nothing but steep cliffs and brassy mountains, broken by a snout of lava-black rock falling like a chute into the sea, a smear of distant pines, a sharp-fanged spur of the stony uplands that seemed to stand on edge against the sky—nothing arable or fertile or populous, an emptiness filled with the scratch and scurry of insects, the slither and flick of snake and lizard; land of the burrowing hedgehog and plated tortoise, of the stiff-pinioned eagle high above and the gull winging in from the sea.

The house, given both grandeur and insignificance by its setting, looked northward across the gulf and the scattered islands, so much a part of the sea that the whitewash on the northern wall had flaked under the crust of driven salt. The house would shudder and shake and groan in every storm, and the leap of blue and white or the flung silver of the spray was as much a part of every window frame as the cracked timber that formed it.

It was a small, unpretentious house that had once been the cottage of a poor fisherman. On the lower floor were a tiny kitchen primitively equipped, a small bedroom, and the larger room where nets and tackle and bait and fish-boxes had once been stored and where Fegel now had his clay-bins and potter's wheel. This room was dark and cool and damp and smelt of wet earth, the smell of the soil after rain, quite different from the sea smells of tannin and marline and iodine which once had permeated its smoky, wattled beams and rafters. On the floor above were two other rooms, pleasant rooms with windows open to the sea and the air. In one there was a goatskin rug spread on the floor where Achille Mouliet slept, and nothing else in it except his few clothes hanging on nails, and his pencils and brushes and colours on an upturned box near his portfolio and papers, and abstract sketches in jewel-like colours pinned up around the whitewashed walls. The other room was Fegel's own, and one end of it was stacked almost to the ceiling with battered books and dusty periodicals, while the other end of it was piled high with finished pottery, old canvases, tied-up manuscripts and unidentifiable bundles of paper, so that only a little space was left in the centre of the room for Fegel's camp-stretcher and blankets and two rickety cane-bottomed chairs and a sort of makeshift easel contrived out of old packing-cases. This was the extent of the house itself with the exception of a built-on privy that was really only a hole in the ground with two cement foot-shapes for positioning, and a small terrace which served as a catchment for rain-water, delivering it through a complicated series of pipes and channels to the underground cistern.

The kiln was outside in one corner of the scraggy garden, and beside it a great heap of two tons of mountain brushwood, to make the fires with, and next to this a heap almost as large of fragmented pieces of glazed and unglazed clay which had broken in the firing, for the kiln was a very primitive one and it was always impossible to maintain the temperatures exactly or even constantly with the flary, resinated brush-wood from the mountains. Fegel obstinately fired a kiln about once every month, but his percentage of loss was never less than one-third, and often was more than half when the wind changed while the ceramics were baking.

When Kate reached the house Fegel was in his room writing by the open window, but he took her down to the tiny kitchen to make her coffee while she explained to him the object of her visit.

"It's a good opportunity," she said, "because you can have a talk with him tomorrow at the party."

"I 'ave not the intent to make the presence at this party," he said firmly. "I 'ave no wish for it. I do not 'ave the enjoyment of the other party."

"But, Conrad, you *must!*" she protested. "It's important to you."

"'E can come 'ere, and I will show 'im what there is. It is the same. Except we do not 'ave all these other people."

She protested again, but he remained inflexible, so finally she said, "Then what you've got to do is pick me out two or three nice pieces, and I'll take them and show them to him. If he's interested, I can bring him here."

"Come," he said. "We will make the good selection."

Going up the stairs she said casually, "Where is Achille?"

"Oh, 'e 'as gone along the rocks . . . he swims with this girl." Fegel shrugged.

"Which girl?" She had a queer, quick little prick of jealousy.

"This one 'e brings to the party. It is 'er last day 'ere. In the morning she 'as to go 'ome to Athens."

This time a definite sense of relief. First jealousy, then relief. But how ridiculous! The situation was absurd, almost schoolgirlish. As if she cared, or even had the right to care, about who he swam with! "Has she been—" she paused, then went on—"been staying here with you?"

"Staying?" He looked at her. "Oh, no, but we 'ave not the room. No, no, no. She comes. She goes. Not staying exactly." He moved some magazines aside and said, "'Ere is one which 'e should see, Kate. I try 'ere for the Persian glaze, the blue with the green like the . . . the music of the sea. I 'ave the good impression of this piece. It is not bad, eh?"

"It's beautiful," she said. "Put that one aside. That's one we'll show him." She looked out through the open window at the quiet blue rhythm of the gulf: the bowl he had showed her seemed a part of it, solidified, and yet with movement within its stillness. "Conrad," she said, "supposing he does like your work, and supposing he pays you quite a lot of money, what will you do?"

"Do? I buy more clay, of course. Better clay. In Ægina the clay is better . . . 'ere it 'as too much of the silicate."

"I don't mean just enough money to buy clay, or chemicals, or things. I mean quite a lot of money. Enough, say, to take you back to Paris, or to Milan."

"Then what 'appens to my work 'ere . . . to my 'ouse?" He looked up at her in surprise.

"But you haven't really been successful here, Conrad. You've been lonely, miserable. And you're too far away from everything. You need contacts with people and with things, with critics, editors, exhibitions, books. It might be a lot better for your work to be back there. Where——" She stopped suddenly. "Where you belong," were the words she was about to add. The words Mark had used to David . . . words, in any case, that had no application whatever to Conrad Fegel, who belonged nowhere.

He noticed her hesitancy and perhaps sensed the thoughts behind it, for he said quietly, "You 'ave this same thing to say to David, eh?" He looked at her intently, cradling in his thin arms a tall yellow jar glazed with a black design of brush strokes that looked like rushes standing.

"No. It isn't the same with us."

"Why is it not?"

"It's harder for you, being alone . . . being just one person."

"Ah, Kate, we are all the just one person most of the time. Eh? Is it not this way?"

"You don't understand what I mean, Conrad. We're a family, a unit . . . we're organised . . . we have each other. It isn't so hard for us."

"Oh, I understan' very well. But even when we are with the unit, when we are the organised we 'urry to each other because we 'ave the crazy fear we are alone, just one person. Eh? In Paris, in Milano, do I grow into two persons, three, four? I am not less alone, am I? No, no, no. I only 'urry more. I am begin' to learn this 'ere on Silenos, Kate. If I 'ave the better clay from Ægina, maybe I learn it better."

He went across the room to find some old newspapers which would serve to wrap his offerings in, and Kate crossed to the window and looked along the cliff rocks. Far away she thought she saw a figure moving, too minute to be identified, scrambling around the black snout of lava that fell like a chute into the sea.

"You will wait 'ere for Achille?" he asked, rather anxiously.

"Oh, well . . . I don't know. Will he . . ." She broke off and shook her head quickly, moved by a sharp little flurry of panic. She had no desire at all to wait for him, nor any reason for it. And she had no wish to see him coming back to the cottage with that girl. "No, of course I don't want to wait for him," she said firmly, and her heart quietened.

"Sometimes 'e is back early, sometimes 'e is not," said Fegel disinterestedly. "It is of no importance to you to wait for 'im. I can 'and to 'im 'is letter to make 'is presence at the party. Of course 'e will go. 'Is friend she will 'ave gone 'ome to Athens, and 'e will 'ave nothing to do except sit 'ere with me. Ask 'im to talk to this man Suvora. Mouliet 'e knows very well my ceramics."

"Yes, I'll ask him," she said.

"Kate?" His sallow face was worried as he handed her the wrapped-up yellow jar. "You be careful of this Mouliet, eh?"

"Careful?"

"Careful." He nodded. " 'E 'as the liking for you too much."

*   *   *

Returning to the *Farrago* along the western mole of the harbour, Suvora saw that a small faded caïque, painted pink and lemon-yellow and with a blue strake at the waterline, was warping into a berth directly alongside the big white schooner. It was not until he had climbed his own gloss-varnished gangplank with its stainless-steel stanchions and pipe-clayed, turksheaded hand-rope, that he realised that one of the two men working on the deck of the caïque was the sponge-boat captain he had met with David Meredith in the tavern of the Two Brothers. The man working with him was shabbily-dressed and middle-aged. He had a strong, swarthy, unshaven face that looked more Turkish than Greek. The two men were warping in by hand, straining at the thick manila rope, letting the slack drop heavily to the cambered deck behind them.

Brent and Badger were attentive busts, heads and shoulders, perfectly immobile in the shadow of the midships and after companionways, waiting for his orders. Clothilde had already taken up her magazine and moved herself to an Arabian Nights arrangment of Li-los and pillows on the deck behind the foremast. Suvora waved his hand and the disembodied faces of Brent and Badger dissolved into the shadows, rather like the Cheshire Cat vanishing in *Alice in Wonderland* except that neither of them left a grin behind to disappear last of all. Suvora went to the *Farrago's* starboard rail and leaned upon it and looked across the narrow strip of water to the shabby *Twelve Apostles*.

The two men had made the warps fast to the thick wooden bitts in the bows and were now putting over the side the old automobile tires they used as fenders.

"Good afternoon, Captain Andreas," Suvora called across, and the thick-set man looked up quickly, his big blunt hands gripped along the edge of the weather-cloth. "When you're finished there," said Suvora, "come aboard and have some coffee with me. Or a drink."

For a long moment the Greek looked across at him, and then he inclined his head in acquiescence, and said something to the other man and together they went across to the starboard side of the caïque to put the other fenders over.

Suvora, watching the two blue-jerseyed backs—working backs these, backs that had suffered the knout of circumstance—bent over the patched canvas of the weather-cloth, seeing the play of hard sinews on the thick brown forearms, was touched again by the feeling that he had had lately very often when he thought of his father Silak tramping to the muddy villages with his roll of carpets on his back. A feeling not of guilt that he had tried so long not to remember his father, but a regret, a kind of regret, a strange regret, that he had not somewhere participated. Perhaps Silak, even at fifty and wealthy then, would have had a back like these two men and arms still corded by old labours, a back configured and marked for ever by the burdens he had borne, not physical burdens only, but those other more brutalising burdens of ignominy and failure and fear and the greyness of rain-spattered roads that twisted through a dismal landscape towards unfriendly villages. Of his father he had little visual memory, scarcely more than the lamplit shape of an old man confused with an image of glass cases and rare books, a figure of quietness that never chided nor made demands, yet never, either, established any communication. He had been a child, at Harrow, when the telegram had

come to speak of his death, and they had let him go away from the school
for five days. Of that strange, rather frightening interlude nothing was left
but the memory of a sense of surprise at the extent of the crowds outside
the Russian Orthodox Church in the Buckingham Palace Road and a
more singular astonishment that around the altar there were arum lilies
and not rolls of carpets. Now memory could re-assess the scene, and paint
it as it would, so that around his father's bier, in place of the trumpet
blooms, were stacked the folded rugs and carpets in the wild Armenian
weaves, smouldering their fiery yellows and scarlets through the drab
greyness of a London day.

Suvora the millionaire, staring across a gap of garbage-covered water
at a shabby pink caïque, felt a desperate need to know this Captain
Andreas, to understand him, to hear his story.

It was twenty minutes before the sponge-boat captain came aboard
the *Farrago*. He had washed his face and hands with a bucket of harbour
water drawn from over the side, and the hair above his temples was still
wet and spiky.

Boarding the schooner, his thick fingers moved exploratively along the
spotless hand-ropes, touched the stanchions; his eyes roving everywhere,
deeply curious but not in the least envious, made a sailor's estimation of
the caulking of the deck, the sunken binnacle in its gimbals, the tubular-
steel masts, the angled wheel, the open charthouse with its lettered
cubicles and the formica-covered chart table, the prone figure of Clothilde
among the heaped gaiety of the cushions, the three deck-hands up forward, talking together, with the white symbols, FARRAGO—R.I.Y.C., printed
across their neat blue jerseys.

"Well," said Suvora, welcoming him, "what will it be? Coffee or
drinks?"

Captain Andreas inclined his head. "What you are taking," he said.

Suvora went to the corner of the charthouse and pressed a bell, and
Brent appeared as if he had been released by a hidden spring.

"Ask Giuseppe to make coffee. Turkish coffee," he said. "And bring a
tray of drinks." He turned back to the captain. "It's pleasanter up here
on deck," he said. "Down below it is very cramped. You have to pay for
this sleek, sharp look. Your boat, now, is workmanlike. It's got beam and
bilge. How many do you accommodate, going down to Africa?"

"Sixteen," said the captain. "Eighteen. It depends."

"There you are now! My boat is more than twice as long as yours, and
if I have fourteen aboard we're tripping over each other." He smiled and

motioned the captain to a deck-chair. "Our friend Mr. Meredith told me
a little about you," he said. "He told me you were looking for men. You
have filled your crew?"

"I still need five."

"But you will get them, of course."

Captain Andreas lifted his heavy shoulders in a shrug. He stared up
along the soaring elliptical metal mast to where the yacht club burgee
rippled against a deep blue sky. "God will decide," he said. He made the
statement as a thing of fact, without any flavour of piety.

Brent came with an elaborate display of drinks on a silver tray, set
out bowls of *pretzels* and crackers and caviare on the cover of the sky-
light, and withdrew unobtrusively.

Captain Andreas glanced at the drinks and the food and said, "You
have never tasted *galétes?*"

"*Galétes?*"

"It is the bread of the sponge-boats, the bread we take to Africa. I
have aboard . . . I can call to Petros to bring some if you would like to
try."

"Well, yes," said Suvora eagerly. "If you can spare. . . ."

"Petros!" the captain bellowed, without moving from his chair. "Bring
galétes."

The man with the Turkish face came aboard a few minutes later with
six of the hard, brown, round biscuits.

"But isn't this what they used to call hardtack?" Suvora asked, examining one carefully.

"Perhaps. They are hard enough. They ask strong teeth." He spoke
without humour. "They are good," he said, "with beer."

"Brent!" Suvora yelled, in a voice as loud as that which the captain
had used. "We have no beer! Bring beer!"

"They are not very good," added the captain, "after you have been
eating them for six or seven months." He picked up one of the biscuits
and bit into the hard, crunchy arc. "These are fresh ones," he said, as
Brent appeared with the beer in tall, frost-dewed glasses.

Ten minutes later, when Suvora had succeeded in nibbling his way
through a whole *galéte*, he said, "I heard from our friend Meredith that
you had a difficult cruise last year."

The captain shrugged. "We had a cruise," he said.

"You must tell me the story some time."

Perhaps Captain Andreas would have told his story then, if Kate

Meredith had not at this moment appeared on the mole at the foot of the gangplank with her burden of three misshapen packages wrapped around with old newspapers. A story, after all, to Captain Andreas was only a story. He would tell it not as a thing of vainglory or entertainment nor as a plea for understanding, but simply as a thing that had happened. He would tell it, because he was an unimaginative man, as somebody might describe to a stranger a town or village he had passed through; and, indeed, all experience to Captain Andreas was simply part of a single journey. He was not indifferent to the varying shapes and textures of each separate part, nor unaffected by their unpredictable reactions to the course of the journey as a whole, but it was the journey to him that counted and not the towns and villages that were touched at on the way.

But since he was a shy man in the company of women, and even more taciturn when they were not women of his own world, Kate's arrival prompted him to excuse himself. "It is time I went back," he said, rising from his deck-chair. "Petros is waiting. He'll want to go home now. His wife has made *fasólia.*"

Suvora, concealing his disappointment, walked with him to the head of the gangplank, where Andreas paused for a moment with his thick, brown hand on the pipe-clayed rope. "It is a fine boat you have," he said, looking back along the schooner's deck. "Clean. Beautiful. It is fast, too, I suppose?"

"Yes, it's pretty fast."

"But it is not a working boat. You could not work on it."

"No, it is not a working boat," Suvora admitted. He said good-bye, and went slowly back along the deck to where Kate was sitting. His face was very thoughtful.

"Mrs. Meredith," he said, "why does that man intrigue me so much? Why does he fascinate me?"

"Which man? The captain?"

"Yes."

"He fascinates my husband too." Kate smiled. "He always has fascinated him."

"Really? Do you have any idea why?"

She hesitated, then shook her head slowly. "You'd really have to ask David," she said. "I could guess, but I couldn't be sure. I think . . . well, I have the feeling that to David he sort of symbolises some particular aspect of individualism . . . he's the raw, natural thread in the pattern . . . almost a sort of mark that you can check yourself against." She stopped and frowned. "I don't know that this explains it at all. It's very difficult to explain, you see, because it's something one senses rather than knows."

"They are good friends, are they, your husband and this man?"

"No—not really. David used to spend quite a bit of time with him, drinking together and talking. But not recently. Not now. I don't know why."

"All three of us were together two nights ago. In one of the taverns. Your husband introduced us. Unfortunately"—a rueful smile touched his mouth—"I am afraid I offended him."

"Offended who? The captain?"

"I don't know whether he was offended also, but your husband was. Anyway, they both left."

"My husband is very nervous at the moment," she said, quick to defend him. "He is trying to finish a book and he has a lot of things on his mind. He tends to take offence easily, but you mustn't pay any attention to it. He's really the nicest person."

"Yes, of course. And I'm not blaming him at all, Mrs. Meredith. He was perfectly justified." He looked at her carefully. "Supposing," he said, "we try again? Supposing we drink some wine together in a tavern this evening? Just the three of us. Just to talk."

"I think that would be marvellous," she said.

"Good. You arrange it with him then. And now—tell me all about your friend Fegel."

*   *   *

It was a quiet night in the tavern of the Two Brothers. Only half a dozen tables were occupied. The three musicians were absent. A guitar and a *bouzouki* hung neglected from their pegs between an empty bird-cage and a copper frying-pan. There was no dancing. A light breeze coming in from the sea made the Olympic Airways calendar swing backwards and forwards on its nail.

From the table by the window where they were seated they could look out across the dark harbour towards the mole, where the green beacon flicked on and off and the two slender masts of the *Farrago* and the stumpier mast of the *Twelve Apostles* seemed to be separate parts of a single ship. Far across the gulf a string of lights marked the slow passage of a flotilla of boats flare-trawling out from the mainland.

"Mr. Suvora has become very intrigued with your friend Captain

Andreas," Kate said to David. "He was aboard the yacht this afternoon, teaching him to eat *galétes*."

"I hope your teeth survived." David smiled at the millionaire.

"Perfectly. I took it very carefully." Suvora's smile gave flashing testimony to the statement. "But your wife is quite right. The man does intrigue me. Perhaps it's the fact that we are exactly of an age and have lived such totally different lives. I feel very humble when I am with him, and yet I don't quite know why. I'd very much like to know his story."

"He told you his story the other night, when we were here. You heard him. Boat-boy, skin-diver, *skafendrós*, *colazáris*, captain, owning his own boat. . . ."

"Not that, particularly. That's rather like playing tinker, tailor, soldier, sailor, isn't it?" For a moment he stared down at the table, and moved his wineglass like a chess-piece across a crack in the wood. "I should very much like to know the story, for instance, of that last cruise of his," he said quietly.

"That's a long story," said David. "And complicated. And you couldn't get him to tell it—not all of it. You would have to piece it together. From other men, from here and there . . . bits and pieces. Even then you could never piece it together just the way it happened. The main fact of it is that Andreas had to go down with a knife and cut the air-hose of one of his divers, and leave him there to drown in the mud, thirty fathoms down."

"Good heavens! But why?" Suvora looked up at him sharply.

"Ask that man over there in the corner—the swarthy one, drinking by himself."

"But . . . but surely that's the chap who brought the *galétes* aboard!" Suvora exclaimed. "He was working on the boat this afternoon with the captain."

"That's right. He's poor. He has to eat. The rest of that game is rich man, poor man, beggar man, thief." He sipped at his wine and said, "He was there. Earlier, on the same cruise, his brother was drowned, when a coupling broke on the air-pump. It was an unlucky cruise all round. Andreas had to go down and cut the air-hose of the other diver. He had got himself trapped in the mud beneath an old wreck. Andreas went down through the mud to try to work him free but he couldn't do it so there was nothing else to do but cut through the air-line and leave him there. By that time they had been twenty-six weeks at sea. You have to imagine that. Sixteen men cooped up all together in a boat not ten metres long for twenty-six weeks in the summer heat along the North African coast. That's quite a test of human relationships! And it just wasn't Andreas's lucky season."

"I see. So this is why the bank penalised him by withholding his advance money?"

"The bank penalised him for not bringing back enough sponges. It's the people who penalise him for the other thing. He tried to save a man's life, you see. But he failed. He had to kill him instead." He stared down at his glass, and he could imagine Andreas, naked, dragging himself down along the air-hose, hand over hand into that terrifying thick blackness, feeling beneath his palms the air pumping through the hose like a soft heartbeat . . . his icy fingers groping and fumbling down along the hose, trying to feel for the lock-nut on the other man's helmet . . . the mud thickening over him like jelly. Black jelly. And that terrible moment of knowing that he could go down no farther—the pain spreading to his chest, little pricks of pain at first like pins-and-needles, as if the casing of his lungs had turned into raw wool, but then growing into a deeper, duller pain like bone being hurt—and the mud flowing thickly over his body like black jelly, and the knowledge that he would have to take the knife and use it, that he would have to kill a man in such a darkness, with everything turned to pain and black jelly. . . . The knife would have gone into the hose as if the rubber was bread or a soft sausage, and Andreas would have twisted his wrist to make the slicing cut, and the air from the hose would have exploded the jelly and the blackness over him as if the sea had burst apart, and he would have gone back up into the light to face the eyes of the other men. . . .

"Why does he have to be penalised if he tried to save another man's life?" Kate asked, and David looked up with a start.

"Why? He tried to do something and it didn't come off. You see, it becomes part of a pattern of failure . . . of bad luck, if you like. They have penalties for either. He drowned two members of his crew. He didn't bring back too many sponges. He'd had bad results the season before, too, and bankers have a knack of smelling a bad risk."

"And the people?" Suvora asked quietly. "Your theory is that the bank penalises for commercial failure, but the people penalise for some other thing. What other thing?"

"*Pou ton matiásane,* is the way they put it. They think he's afflicted by the evil eye. Nobody wants to sail with him. They're afraid of the contagion."

"Then what will he do?" Kate asked anxiously. "He's a good man. He's strong and brave and——"

"What's that got to do with it?" said David quickly. "Failure is failure. It's almost something you can smell. Well, that's Captain Andreas's problem. It's something he's got to work out for himself, I suppose. We can only look at it as an interesting exercise in cause and effect. Sixteen men all cooped up together in that boat out there for months at a time—and then one of them left alone to his own fate, and his own thoughts. This old problem of blame and punishment. The ancient Greeks wrote whole cycles of plays about it. Cause and effect. The journey there and the journey back. *Pou ton matiásane,* if you want to be superstitious. Crime and punishment, if you read Dostoevsky. Kate does," he said to Suvora. "All the time. So let's bang for some more wine and drink to Dostoevsky!"

*   *   *

The change of plans affecting Suvora's party was conveyed by notes to those who had been invited, carried again by the man Brent in his houndstooth suit and Panama hat. The party would be for dinner and it would be held in a restaurant ashore; the *Farrago* in the meantime would make an overnight cruise around the gulf islands under the command of the yacht's captain, and with Brent and Badger on hand to look after the four special guests—Admiral Mavro, Commander Sinclair, Jerry and Simon. A postscript added to the note sent to Kate Meredith said, "I would be grateful if you could take me along to Fegel's house tomorrow morning. I am very interested."

The dinner party was quiet, pleasant enough, and whatever forces for disharmony existed among the guests, they were subdued by the benevolence and hospitality of Suvora as host. An independent observer would have been left with the impression that here was a group of people brought together within a very normal frame of relationships, talking compatibly, happy in each other's company. There were jokes, laughter, compliments, intelligent observations, with decorum and conviviality preserved with the formality of a balletic rhythm. "A very civilised dinner," Mark said later. "Society's protective camouflage," David offered. He had sat between old Beth Sinclair and Kettering, with Clothilde opposite him, yawning at the company. Erica Barrington had sat at the far end of the table, next to Suvora: Kate, deputising as hostess, had taken the opposite end of the table, next to Mouliet and Janecek. David had had little to offer, either to the gaiety or to the bonhomie of the company.

Going home with Kate he said, "No crises. Rather remarkable when you consider the undercurrents that must have been there. I suppose the mask is the symbol of what Mark calls being civilised."

"Or perhaps you over-estimate the undercurrents," said Kate, taking his arm.

"I usually do. Then I never get taken by surprise." He grinned. "I wonder what made Suvora change his plans. Wonderful for the kids, of course—and the old boys. I can imagine them all out there in the gulf playing pirates! But what made him do it?"

"I know why he did it. He told me before we sat down. It's part of what you told him last night, in the tavern. He just didn't want that sort of thing going on, what he called 'a show of splendid vulgarities,' with that sponge-boat lying right alongside and the men working on it."

"You're making this up," he said, glancing at her.

"I'm not making it up at all, darling. That's what he told me."

"My God! A sensitive millionaire! He's beginning to learn, isn't he?"

2

LE VIEUX MOULIN

CONRAD FEGEL was out of bed as early as if it had been a firing-day, although the kiln was cold. Achille Mouliet had come up from the kitchen to watch him sorting through his ceramics, and he stood now by the window clad only in a very brief bikini, spooning raw egg from a cracked cup and munching on a crust of bread. When he and Fegel were together in the house they ate mostly raw eggs and fruit and black bread, but they drank a lot of coffee, and every second day they had fresh sheep's milk delivered by a peasant who came down from the mountains with the milk in two tin cans slung over the back of a donkey. Except for the coffee they never cooked anything but would usually eat a proper meal in the evening in one of the taverns, with wine to wash it down.

"Show it all to 'im," Mouliet advised, scraping at the bottom of the cup, then licking both sides of the spoon. "You do not know what 'e will prefer. Let 'im see it all. You pick out just what *you* like it is never the same."

"But if 'e buys 'e must see the best," said Fegel anxiously, and flicked his finger at the rim of a shallow dish with a glaze like a peacock feather. "Oh yes, 'e must see only the best."

Mouliet shrugged. "'Ow is 'e to know? A rich man's taste, what is that?" His mouth pulled in a grimace of contempt.

"Oh yes, 'e 'as the taste," said Fegel angrily. "So would 'e like my work if 'e 'ad not?"

"Pouf!" Mouliet repeated the grimace. "*Tant pis.* Show it all." He tossed the spoon to the window ledge. "You know that Katherine she is bringing 'im to the 'ouse?" he said casually, and when Fegel nodded rather sulkily he smiled to himself and said, "You will stay 'ere with the rich man and show 'im everything and make 'im pay the big price, and I will walk with Katherine and we will pick the flowers and I show 'er the old mill. There is a song, *'Le Vieux Moulin,'* a love song. I will sing it to 'er." He began to hum the tune softly.

Fegel peered up at him worriedly across the rim of a shell-glazed platter. "You will play no tricks, eh?" he said warningly. "No tricks, Achille. No more making the trouble like last year."

Mouliet smiled his slow, remote smile, and slowly shook his head. "Now I make for us the coffee," he said. "The coffee I make. The trouble I do not make. After this, I arrange the paintings on my wall—not all, a little selection. Like you, the best. When you 'ave finished with this Suvora you show 'im my pictures, and sell them to 'im for 'is collection. I pay you the commission for what you sell." He laughed as he went downstairs to the kitchen.

By ten o'clock, when Kate came with Suvora walking slowly along the rough cliff path, Fegel had rather pathetically arranged his "selections" in an orderly display against the stacks of old books and magazines. His face was drawn and white and he felt very sick, partly because of nervous excitement and partly because of his anger that Mouliet, despite his protests, had refused to add any other clothing to the scant loincloth he was wearing. "But why?" the Frenchman had protested with a spread of hands. "It is what I am wearing when I swim, when fifty people, a 'undred, are looking. What difference 'ere? . . .'ere, when we are friends. Besides, it will give the *rehaussement* to the setting; they will not notice the condition of our bedding, those bundles of the dirty books, the stink from that yard."

So that it was a tawny, near-naked Achille Mouliet who met them at the door with all the studied charm and grace of a *boulevardier* and ushered them up the stairs that creaked and gave out little sighing puffs of dust at every footfall and into the cluttered room with the sea behind where Conrad Fegel waited in an agony of despair and hope. Suvora caught sight of the vivid ceramics stacked against the battered books, and he sucked his breath in with genuine pleasure, but his frown was a pretence when he said to Fegel, "I see we're to be in for some bargaining. I warn you I'm almost a Levantine."

Now, coming around the path from the town, Suvora had talked with Kate. "There is a matter of pride in this," he said, "and a matter of another man's pride. I am beginning to see that individual pride is a question of very great importance. I have to be more careful than most people. It is easier for me to give offence to another man's pride than it is with most other people."

"Like David, the other night?"

"Yes. Or the reason why I changed the venue for the party. You see, Kate—I do prefer calling you Kate, by the way—I have the feeling that this man Fegel has one or two skins fewer than the rest of us. He can be hurt very easily. He can read into our visit the bitterness of charity, the rich man slumming, if we give him any cause for offence. I do wish to help him, yes. But that's beside the point. I admire what I have seen of his work. I want to see more of it. I shall then form my own judgments and make my own assessments. So there is one favour I should like to ask of you. When we are there, should the opportunity arise, leave us together, will you? Just the two of us, to discuss and compare and haggle about prices and so forth. I think I shall buy his ceramics, anyway. But I would like also to sell him back a remnant of his pride."

That was why when Mouliet suggested brewing up some more coffee it was Kate who shook her head and said, "No, I'm going out to sit on the rocks and look at the sea, and leave these two to their business."

And Fegel looked from her to Mouliet with a flash of alarm, and said, "Oh, no, no! Kate will be most 'elpful in——"

Suvora cut him short with a quick gesture. "Let them go," he said, with a dismissive wave of his hand. "We are going to get down now to brass tacks. So—supposing we consider the large, plain platters first."

*　　　　*　　　　*

A slow, easy swell lifted long dark grooves out of the blue and moved them tirelessly across the gulf. On the rocks below the house the edge of the sea breathed and creamed over weedy platforms, and folded under with a soft hissing almost at the base of the cliff, and slid away again to mark the rim of each ledge with a curve of purple glass. And the sea would suck down at the sharp rocks, and then breathe up and cream again and move the emerald weed in slow green fans across the rocks.

"I should have brought my bathing suit," said Kate wistfully. "I could have swum while we're waiting."

"Ah, the rocks 'ere are not good for the swimming." Mouliet shook his head. "The goémon is very thick and it is 'ard to get out because everywhere there are the little spikes, the sea-urchin." He squatted beside her,

sunk upon his haunches, settled down on to the flat of his bare feet with
his arms loosely hanging, a still, passive figure sitting the way a savage
sits. "Down there not too far"—his green eyes turned to the western
emptiness—"there is a little bay where there is the sand. You can swim
there if you wish. The bathing costume—pouf! Who is to see?"

"Oh no, it doesn't matter." She spoke a shade too quickly, too aware of
the almost naked body beside her. "It was just a thought," she said. "I
can swim later, when we go back."

"Now I swim in the night," he said quietly. "Ten o'clock, eleven, midnight . . . when I feel it. I swim by the cave. Now there is little moon.
It is very, very dark, and the . . . the *phosphorescence?* . . . you call it
that?"

"Yes, the same word. We pronounce it differently."

"The *phosphorescence* it is very beautiful. With me it 'as the magic,
the peculiar magic." He smiled gently and glanced at her. "For *me*
it 'as the magic," he repeated. "For you I do not know. Come!" He rose
suddenly in an effortless, weightless movement, and stood looking down
at her, a golden figure sculptured against the sky. "Since you are not to
make the swimming I take you up there to see the mill. '*Le Vieux
Moulin.*' I sing you the song. You know it? In Cherbourg when I am a
little boy we 'ave it in the school." Softly he began to sing the lilting,
childish words.

"But shouldn't we stay nearby?" she said. "They may want—"

"Bah! They will 'ave an 'our with Conrad's things, and then there is
the pictures by me to be shown. Come. We will go. The view from the
mill it is *enchantement.* Come."

He offered his hand to help her rise, and although her body offered
no resistance the physical contact of his fingers conducted to her a sharp
stab of panic—this arm and hand reaching down to her from this seem-
ingly naked figure planted golden and godlike against the dazzling
morning sky, these brown and gentle fingers that touched her and made
a shell of her body, a shell that was empty and yet burning, that trembled
and yet was quiescent and unresisting. A stinging pain possessed her as
she rose towards him.

But as they began to walk away from the house, moving diagonally
across a thistled spur that lay between the bank of shale and a rock-choked
watercourse, she repossessed herself, and her feeling as she followed him
was almost a sense of anger with him that in that fleeting moment he had
dispossessed her of her will, that he should want to do it like this, throw-

ing his nakedness at her, flaunting it in the sun. She wanted to smile at her own foolishness . . . better still, to laugh at him, to laugh at him for the clumsiness of his approach, for the utter *naïveté* of this blatant, animal sexuality of his method. Did he think he was luring some teen-age virgin to her first seduction? The word, framed in her thoughts, startled her, and the spurt of derisive anger faded. She felt strangely unsure of herself as she followed him.

He was leading her now down a narrow gully. The house was no longer visible. The sea had vanished. They might have been in the heart of some strange arid continent, a land compacted out of all that was bizarre and fantastic, where there were only the two of them in a glittering, flinty landscape of rocks in the strangest shapes and tangled growths that were like the plant-forms of a dream. And before them was only the great slanting ramp of red earth and stone crowned by two squat ruins against the sky. Ahead of her, moving upward now, the brown, naked feet scuffed the dust in tiny golden puffs and crunched against the hard sliding gleam of the flints and heedlessly pressed the thistles into the baked earth and crushed the brittle snail-shells into powder, and above the feet the golden body moved, and the buttocks moved with it in an onward driving rhythm, two moon-segments of faintly paler flesh revealed and vanishing, revealed and vanishing on either side of a ridiculous scrap of Paisley-patterned cloth. Brown and orange and grey. Printed cotton in the Paisley pattern. How ridiculous, she told herself, the Paisley pattern! She wanted to laugh aloud at the absurdity of it, to make him see how ridiculous he was clad like that, clambering out of the burning gully as if they were at a *plage* on the Riviera, and those sickles of pale, firm flesh coming and going, coming and going. . . . Yet she could not laugh at all because her mouth was dry and her eyes were stinging with the glare of light that compressed her and her heart hammered hollowly in the emptying chamber of her body. She felt dazed, sunsick, helplessly drawn on behind him without will or reason. Was he still singing that stupid, childish song? Or was it no more than the lingering memory of the touch of his hand drawing her up to him? If he would go over a ridge and even for a moment drop out of her sight it would be all right. She would be able to look at the thing reasonably, calmly, without this heart-hammering, flesh-tightening, dizzying enchantment that had so inexplicably seized her. Enchantment . . . *enchantement* . . . yes, the same word—we pronounce it differently . . . *the view from the mill it is enchantement . . . come.* . . . He was still climbing upward, ahead

of her, making for the nearer of the two ruined mills. You are Kate
Meredith, she told herself. You are Kate Meredith and you are the wife
of David Meredith the writer and you have two children of school age
and you are acting like a fool. . . .

Deliberately she kept her eyes upon his feet moving in the golden
drift of dust, but even this was of no avail to her because she instantly
began to imagine that the feet were cloven, and she had the absurd
feeling that if she dared to raise her eyes again to the moving buttocks
she would see there a cropped tail in the place of the Paisley rag and the
hairy animal hams of the satyr. The ridiculousness of the image jolted
her sense of reason, so that she was able to raise her eyes, and at this
moment he stopped and turned and smiled back at her encouragingly.
It was that same smile again, faint, remote, scarcely curving his lips . . .
no more than the memory of a smile that had derived its amusement from
something that had happened long ago in time. He had almost reached
the crest of the ridge so that from her lower viewpoint his body again
was thrown against the sky, a complete form that was tawny-brown and
capped by gold, silhouetted godlike against the empty shining hugeness of
the sky, and smiling that haunting, far-away smile at her, and calling to
her, "Come. We are almost there. Come. You are so slow."

He looked exactly like the bronze image of the god Dionysos she had
seen once in the Louvre, the god young and naked and beautiful . . . he
needed in his hand the wand of fennel, the mystic emblem of the *thyrsos*,
and the fillet around the gleaming cap of his hair, and his bare feet laced
in hunting-boots. Memory was evoked with a piercing clarity; she recalled that the little bronze statuette had been incomplete; one arm had
gone and the right foot had been broken off; yet in her mind's eye she
saw it as a totality of beauty—a body of exquisite harmony yet of a man
who, like this man calling down to her, probably would not have been
particularly tall. But there was no double image in what she saw: the
real and the remembered had become fused into one form—flesh and
bronze alike in this identical godlike shape of the proud, youthful set
of the chest and shoulders, the swing of the arm, the thick strong thighs,
the hard curve of the naked belly dimpled at the navel and tapering to
the triangular mat of the uncovered loins, and the head that was tilted
forward slightly as if to summon somebody up to him, and the face that
was this face, this very face, swelling in her vision, growing closer, emptying her of sanity. The downy curl of hair on his chest and belly had a
soft sheen, like rubbed silk dusted with gold. Was this how the ancient

women had felt, following him upwards and upwards into the lonely mountains, these women in *ecstásis*, the mad women, the Mænads, the Thyiads, lost to all but the sense of an orgiastic licence, of frenzy and abandon and the naturalness of physical love? . . . *There's a brute madness in that fennel wand—reverence it well.* . . . The lines of Euripides, read so many times, heard in the theatre once when she had gone to Epidaurus with David, spun in her brain. *Dionysos will not compel women to control their lusts.* . . . *In the rites a chaste-minded woman will come to no harm.* . . . Kate Meredith, stop being a fool. . . .

"I go on a'ead of you," he said, "because it is easier to climb this way. But you follow so slow," he chided her gently. "And you are flushed and sweating and yet pale also. It is too much for you, the climbing?"

"The sun," she said faintly. "The sun, I think. Down there in that gully, it beats at you. It's . . . it's like an oven."

"Ah, no matter, we are there already. Come. This is the path. You see?" He shrugged. "So we are there," he said, and gestured towards the crumbling ruin of the mill.

The thick circular wall was a conglomeration of cut stone, cemented rubble, and old clay bricks set in dried mud; the truncated cylinder rose to a height of about thirty feet, where the roofless wall ended in irregular gaps choked with dandelion and thistle and the trailing greenery of wild caper. At the base there was a square wooden door set within a frame that was cracked and bleached bone-white, like driftwood. The door itself had weathered to a grey, stone-like texture, and the little flecks of old paint still embedded in grooves and cracks gave the worn surface the look of one of those archaic statues where the polychrome is still here and there faintly to be seen.

"And 'ere is the view," said Mouliet softly and with reverence. "*C'est magnifique, c'est formidable*, no?"

"Yes, it's very beautiful," she said, without enthusiasm, her voice still choking a little, as she turned to the panorama which he was presenting with a wave of his hand. The sea seemed to surge up at her, engulfing her in a blue mist that was like a burden of all encompassable space, too vast to be comprehended, too impossible to be borne. "I think . . . this sun. . . ." she began in a low voice that faltered away. "It's . . . it's too much," she said. "Do you mind? . . . I'm sorry, but . . . but do you think we could find some shade somewhere?" Below, in the walled tangle of Fegel's garden there were strips of shadow, and at one side a thick bar of cool darkness where the russet-tiled roof ended.

"Ah, but of course," said Mouliet quickly. "We 'ave much shade 'ere. It is very cool." He pushed at the ancient door and it opened with a rasp of the broken latch against the stone and a sharp little squeal of hinges. A sliver of decayed wood dropped from the broken lintel, and Mouliet kicked it off the threshold with his bare foot. A small yellow lizard flicked down across the stones and vanished among the weeds. Through the square doorway Kate looked into a deep, dark cavern of coolness.

"I come 'ere very often to sleep," said Mouliet. "Often at night, sometimes when the day is very 'ot. It is my *lit de plume*, my feather-bed. *Voilà!*" he said, and laughed softly.

The floor of the mill was deeply spread with hay. Obviously the hay had been there for many years, for it was of the palest colour, like old paper, and in some parts it had been crushed almost into a powder. It gave off a faint, indefinable odour, trapped sunlight and salt and grass and flowers and the lingering ammonia-tang of a barnyard, a smell that was very pleasant and in an odd way exciting. At one side, very high on the towering arc of stonework, there was an elongated ellipse of sunlight which exposed weeded crannies and the webs of spiders, but elsewhere was only a well of shadow that was deep and cool and fragrant.

Timorously yet thankfully she passed through the doorway. Her body was suddenly weak and boneless. Without attempting to resist she sank down to the soft cushion of the hay. Mouliet followed her inside, and pulled the door to behind him.

"Why do you close the door?" she said quickly, but weakly. "There will be a breeze, and——"

"There is no breeze," he said. "Also I wish you to smell. With the door closed you can smell it." He raised his hands and sniffed, and smiled down at her. "It is very beautiful this smell. Around the *midi*," he explained, "two hours maybe at the noon, the sun is right above, and all of this is filled up with the sun. It is very 'ot 'ere inside and 'ard to breathe even, then the sun passes over and it is cool again. But the smell of the sun stays 'ere on the straw, on my *lit de plume*. It never goes away. It is always 'ere, even at night, late, the smell of the sun. Like a great bottle that never becomes empty . . . always full, right to the top. This is a good vintage, eh? this sun that stays with you when it is cool and sweet and dark and soft." She heard his soft, inward-sounding laugh as he stepped across her limp body. He moved some little distance away and stretched himself out on the hay, his hands linked behind his neck, his dark-gold body relaxed, his eyes squinting up at the stone-rimmed circle of the sky. "Ah yes, the rare vintage," he said musingly. *"Mis en bouteilles au château,* but the *château* is of the gods, eh?"

The coolness, the softness of the scented couch, the gentle reflectiveness of his voice, the distance that physically separated his body from hers were all blissfully soothing things—had she expected when he had closed the door that he would leap upon her like a lusting satyr?—and her own voice was softly lulling, dreamily remote, as she said: "It's funny you should talk about the gods. Coming up here, walking behind you, I was thinking of Dionysos leading the Bacchæ into the mountains. Strange thoughts. And then I realised that you looked exactly like a little statue of Dionysos I saw once in Paris."

"Ah, then I am glad," he said, and smiled as if the observation had given him secret pleasure. "If I 'ad a god to believe in it would be 'im, I think." He glanced across at her. The filtered light reflected from the carpet of hay gave a curious flowing colour to his eyes so that they seemed alive with mysterious green movement, like tidal rock pools. His lips were parted slightly and between his small white teeth was clenched a thin, pale straw. "But I am not a good Dionysos, I think. You come very slow be'ind. You are not in the frenzy to 'urry, like the women of Bacchus in the time long ago."

"It was much too hot to hurry," she said practically. If he knew the truth! If he even guessed at the madness of her thoughts as she had followed him up and up across the flinty rises! And, feeling the same strange stirrings rising again within her, she quickly moved the conversation to a different plane. "You say *if* you had a god," she said. "You do not believe in a god then?"

"No, no, I believe in life, in existence, that is all," he said calmly. "In being what I am. It is enough. I 'ave no god."

"If you did, it *would* be pagan, I think. I've thought that, ever since I met you."

"Perhaps," he said thoughtfully. "I think they were better, these pagans. They were not concerned, as we are concerned, with sin. Only with mistakes, with errors. It is better that way. It can be understood. It is so stupid to call it sin when it is only a little mistake of the judgment, a slip, an error." Again his soft laugh drifted across to her. "You must not listen to me," he said. "I do not 'ave the much respect for this. For anything."

"Except life . . . existence?"

He spat out the straw and made a little grimace. "Oh no, not that even.

I 'ave not the respect for it. I enjoy it when I can, but I do not 'ave to respect it. It is what I say—I 'ave not the respect for anything."

"It's very necessary to respect some things," said Kate firmly. "To believe in them. Otherwise, if you didn't respect these things you wouldn't have them, and then everything would be in such a hopeless, hideous mess."

"Tell me these things," he said sleepily. "Tell me what they are." He put another straw in his mouth and closed his eyes.

"Lots of things. Morality. Family. Law. Building. Things like that."

"Of course," he agreed. "For some people these things are good. For me, no. What does it matter? I 'ave no family. I suppose I 'ave no morality . . . well, it is what Fegel believes; it is what 'e says to me. I do not make the offence to the law. It does not bother me." His shrug caused the straw to crackle softly. He opened his eyes and looked at her. "You are cold now?" he said. "You shiver a little, I think."

"No, I'm not cold," she said quickly. "I'm cool now, but not cold. Not a scrap. But we should be going back, shouldn't we?" She knew as she spoke that her voice was too jerky, too nervous. If she could stop her hands from trembling. If she tried to push them deep into the loose hay he would know what she was doing and he would make some comment. She turned her head a little away from him. She must not look at him. That was the important thing. She must not look at him at all. She could · hear the sound of the straw crackling more loudly with some movement of his body.

"What you wish," he said agreeably. "It is pleasant 'ere. We can stay a little longer, if you are not cold."

She did not reply, but neither did she make any attempt to move. Her body was tense and stiff, her nerves tautened to a pitch of expectancy, waiting. For what? Again the straw rustled, and she could imagine the brown-gold body, this body that was virtually naked, moving in the pale, soft hay. Moving towards her? Rising up, so that they could go away together, out of this place, back to the conventional safety of Fegel's little house on the cliff? Which? She dared not look. Her head was still turned away: in front of her she saw with the exaggerated microscopic vision of eyes too closely focused bleached tubes of straw that looked like peeled logs, as if the world of Lilliput had been thrown suddenly on some Brobdingnagian screen. A ruddy-bellied ant struggled across the logs with a crumb of something; nearby a bizarre insect with filigree wings and legs of twisted wire balanced itself teeteringly for a moment, fell, and flew off with a stinging buzz of wings. A brown and cream butterfly fluttered down from the ellipse of sunlight and perched at the edge of a stone, rhythmically opening and closing its wings like . . . like—how grotesque the images of her mind!—like chopsticks picking at Chinese food.

"Katherine." He called her name with the same unemphasised intonation. From the sound of his voice he seemed no closer than he had been. "Do you wish me to make love to you?" he said quietly.

She closed her eyes against the straw logs and the labouring ant and the sensual beating of the butterfly's wings, and a red mist whirled behind her eyelids as she thrust her hands deep into the loose hay, clenching them until the fingernails bit into her palms.

"We can do it 'ere," he went on in the same soft, uninflected voice. "No one is to see, no one is to know. And it is very pleasant 'ere. But I do not want to do it, you see, unless you wish." The straw rustled.

"What are you talking about?" The words came in a low, choked voice, hardly audible even to herself. Her head was stiffly turned away, her cheek stinging, the muscles of her throat hot with a dry, desperate pain.

"I am for a long time very much wishing to kiss you, perhaps to make love with you, but then I know that if I kiss you I 'ave not the strength then to wait for you to decide whether you wish or you do not wish. And I do not like to 'ave it this way. *You* must wish it to 'appen. You must ask for it to 'appen. I 'ave the respect for you, you see. For you, yes, I 'ave the respect."

She lay silent and rigid, her eyes closed tightly, her head averted, willing her nerves to subdue the inward trembling which, should it come to the surface, would expose her as utterly, as shamelessly as if she were to rip the clothing from her body and throw her nakedness unresistingly at his. How unfair, how cruel for him to do it like this! The walk from the sea, the sun on his body, the sun trapped here within this cool and fragrant column of stone, the silence, the softness, the withdrawn, ineffable gentleness of his voice. God! what *chance* had he given her! What chance for the respect he talked about! For respect or dignity or responsibility or common sense! For anything save surrender, for the abandoned frenzy she had imagined coming up with him, for the shame, the sweet shame, of compliance. . . .

"Katherine, you 'ave nothing to say. You do not look at me. You say nothing. Your 'ead is turned always away. Katherine, you must turn and look at me." His voice was still low, but it moved now to an undertone of urgency.

Why should I, she thought numbly. What need? What need to turn and look? Through the red, racing film behind her closed eyelids she could see it all, the naked body sprawled on the soft cushion of the hay, this union of gleaming bronze and golden flesh, of god and mortal, of the real and the remembered . . . all of it, to the least pore, the last gleaming tendril of hair spread like a fine silken mat from belly to chest— her nails dug pain deeper into her hands—the circlet of gold below the golden cap of hair, the fluid mystery of the sea-green eyes, and that secret, haunting smile that seemed to dwell upon the pleasures of a long-lost time . . . that long-ago time when there was no sin, only errors, slips, mistakes. . . .

Her fingers loosened limply and a shudder like a spasm of shock seized her body as she opened her eyes and, all control spent, turned her face towards him.

They had no words to say as they faced each other, and then she saw him slowly rising up from the pale straw that rustled and crackled and fell like dust from his skin. He was erect now and coming towards her. A small, noiseless slide of powdered hay, dislodged by his movement, drifted down and partly covered the cast-off rag of Paisley. She heard as if from across some immeasurable distance his murmured words, "Ah, Katherine, *ma mie*, you 'ave told me. You 'ave said nothing but you 'ave told me!".

He was standing above her, his skin gleaming where it was not dusted by the dry powder of the chaff, a figure framed within a stone circle against a disc of stainless sky, and then he was bending over her, pressing her down, down, down into the soft, yielding, sun-smelling bed of hay.

On the ledge of stone the butterfly lingered, opening and closing its wings, fanning in and out, a brown and cream brilliance purposeless upon the wall, a senseless fragment of colour and rhythm that seemed to flood her with a wild, delirious intoxication as she closed her eyes.

3

SILENOS BY SUNLIGHT

RETURNING TO THE PORT with Suvora, walking slowly around the cliffs
through the thickening clusters of the houses, she found herself still
wondering about that quick glance he had cast at her—had it been quizzical? questioning? amused?—when they had come down from the mill
to the house on the cliffs. She had then the curious feeling, an almost
adolescent welling up of sudden and uncontrollable guilt, that what had
happened must certainly *show,* and show in some absurdly mundane way
—the tell-tale rumpling of her dress (which, in fact, she knew to be perfectly in order), or a chip of hay caught in her hair (which she had had
Achille check before they left the mill), or a smear of lipstick (which she
never used). But then perhaps her very expression had betrayed her.

Still, Suvora, after that first suspected glance of examination, had been
no different from his normal self. He had insisted that she should take
lunch with him aboard the *Farrago*—how pleased and how relieved she
had been to accept the invitation and thus to build a bridge of something
different between what had irrevocably happened and what was un-
predictably to come—and had sent Brent off to fetch David and the children. So that there was also this interlude of waiting in which to recover
that self-possession which was still inwardly in chaos as a result of this
experience which had been so strange and yet so natural.

Suvora had gone ashore to arrange for a donkey-man to bring back his
ceramics and so she was left on the midships deck with Clothilde, where
she was able largely to recover her composure by going through a stack
of French magazines, *Elle* and *Match* and *Réalités* and the rest, and

engaging with the other woman in that formally desultory conversation
which, among women, seems to germinate spontaneously from any pile
of French magazines—a kind of soporific intermittent commentary on
the colour pages, the fashions, the food recipes, the cosmetics, the articles
on movie stars, and those lukewarm scandals involving royalty and titled
people which have become the obsessive mania of Parisian editors. It was
a conversation which was not demanding even when it jetted into sudden
artificial spontaneities. It was, in a very definite way, the perfect con-
valescence from that Bacchic madness which had possessed her less than
two hours before on the burning slopes above Fegel's house on the
cliffs. Clothilde, who made little attempt to dissemble her boredom,
was never very much inclined to put herself out conversationally when
the company was only feminine (indeed, her vocal virtuosity was at any
time limited, since even in the company of men it was her firm belief
that actions spoke louder than words), and Kate, for all her outward
composure, was still profoundly shaken by feelings which she was unable
to sort out, one from the other.

Guilt and shame were there, yes, but so was a lingering feeling of that
earlier *ecstásis*, and a sense of something recaptured that was eternally
young and still held captive, flutteringly, impermanently, like a wild bird
imprisoned within the hands which sooner or later must be released: but
these were subordinate undertones to those more chilling feelings of apprehension of what was yet to come, of issues as yet unspecified which
would have to be faced, of doubts as to how deeply she had in fact committed herself, of conflicts within her own being which had already been
declared but the outcome of which were hopelessly beyond the range of
even her darkest premonition.

Yet when at last she saw her husband coming, her heart leapt at once
with a spontaneous kick of relief and joy—not with doubt at all, nor with
apprehension. He was coming around the curve of the quay, a very tall,
very thin figure in a white shirt and khaki shorts that made his lean brown
legs seem grotesquely long, and his shoulders were stooped a little and
his head bent to the two children who walked beside him, holding his
hands. Suvora was with them, stepping briskly, his solid, broad-shouldered
figure contrasted to David's gangling thinness.

"Here comes my husband now," she said quickly. "There are the children with him, and Mr. Suvora." It was necessary to say something aloud;
the triteness of the remark was of no importance.

Clothilde adjusted her sun-glasses languidly, stared without interest across the harbour, nodded vaguely, and took another sugar-powdered cube of Turkish Delight from the box beside the Li-lo.

"How was it at Fegel's?" David asked Kate when he came aboard.

"Very pleasant," she said. "We had a nice morning. You heard what happened?"

David grinned. "Conrad made a killing, it seems. Good luck to him. It's time he had a break."

"What a bargainer that little chap is, eh?" Suvora winked slyly at Kate. "Eleven hundred dollars this little excursion cost me. And perhaps Clothilde won't like these things any better than the last lot. What about you, my sweet?" He smiled down at the sprawled figure of his mistress. "If you sun-bake much more you are going to look exactly like a Negress."

"I'm that colour all over," she said. "Everywhere."

"Fascinating!" observed Suvora happily. "Where are our friends, the admiral and the commander?"

"Badger took them in the launch," said Clothilde tiredly. "They've all gone fishing. Thank God!"

"God bless them, yes, but why 'Thank God'?"

"You had a pleasant morning spending money," said Clothilde acidly but also with a certain basic honesty, since her connotation of pleasure invariably involved the spending of money. "I had that old fat man for a solid hour drawing me diagrams of the different rigs of sailing-ships. And then that old thin one for the best part of another hour giggling at me and telling dirty stories about Shanghai and Yokohama."

"But how instructive!" Suvora exclaimed, his mouth twitching. "And how fortunate that the lectures were not concurrent. Imagine trying to digest barquentines *and* brothels all together! Well now"—he rubbed his hands together briskly—"let us see about some drinks."

David took the deck-chair beside Kate, arranged his brown, bony knees, and said, "Suvora tells me you were a jolly good salesman for Conrad. That was nice."

"But . . . but I didn't have anything to do with it." She looked at him in surprise. "They did it between them."

"Well, that's what he says. It was nice, anyway. I'm glad for little Fegel. It could make all the difference."

She nodded, and for an interval was silent. It would seem then that there *had* been significance in Suvora's studied glance when she had come back from the mill. Or did it mean this, or anything at all? It could mean no more than her having in the first place talked to him about

Fegel's work and shown him some examples . . . or the element of complicity in their talk together on the way to the house . . . or even no more than his way of sharing his philanthropy among them. Yet the doubt persisted.

"What about your morning," she asked. "How did it go? Your work, I mean. Were you able to?"

"Struck a blow," he said. "As a matter of fact, yes, I had a good morning, a very good morning. The kids went swimming. The house was quiet. Nobody called."

She nodded and smiled at him with a sudden warmth. They were across the bridge. The safe, banal usages of marriage had carried them across. That agony of waiting for him to come, of having to confront him again in a normal way after what had happened, after *that* had happened —in one moment of insane panic she had half expected that her guilt would have been as evident on her person as if the scarlet letter of her shame had been branded upon her brow!—had vanished in the accustomed commonplaces of their association. Did you sleep well? What sort of morning did you have? Were you able to work? Did you take a look at the children? How banal the questions, mannered exchanges as commonplace as shopping lists, yet how infinitely precious, how infinitely reassuring!

Her eyes were wet as she looked along the deck to where Jerry and Simon were manning the wheel, staring upward with wide wondering eyes as they sailed their imaginary seas. She blinked quickly and lowered her eyes, and saw the worn sandals on her husband's feet. Brown, bony feet, with tiny coronets of hair on the knuckles: on the right foot he had cut a little V in the nail of the big toe because of his ingrowing toenail. She had never loved him or the children so deeply, never loved them with so much feeling or understanding, as at this moment.

"It took me quite a while to get used to the quietness of the house without you there puttering around below," he said. He was crouched over his clasped hands, looking down at the deck, so that he did not see her eyes. "And then no visitors! Can you imagine that? Do you realise this is the first time for days when nothing's happened, when we haven't had some bloody crisis or other, somebody's mess to be sorted out? Ah, peace, it's wonderful!" he said, and looked up and grinned at her.

*   *   *

The same sun that cast its high-noon shadows in diminished pools and strips of blue-black ink on the scrubbed white glare of the *Farrago's* deck was screened from the banking office of Stathis Vlikos by the grilled window and the drape of the vine outside. It invaded the stuffy interior room only through a gap where two tiles were missing from the roof, and since the aperture occurred directly above a flaw in the ceiling a slender pencil of sunlight was directed almost vertically through the dinginess to the surface of the big oak desk, where it formed a pool of light almost exactly the shape and size and colour of an old gold guinea.

Captain Andreas, waiting for the banker to return from the barber shop, had been watching this coin-like disc of sunlight for quite some time—long enough, at any rate, for it to have travelled a good few inches, all the way from the edge of the blotter almost to the base of the black plastic inkstand. Captain Andreas had no watch, and the pendulum clock in the broken glass case on the end wall, next to the Keranis calendar with the old views, had been fixed at five minutes to six ever since he could remember it. He knew that he had come, as instructed, at a quarter-past eleven, and had sat there in the stiff chair beside the desk, where the banker's girl had put him, long enough for the little gold circle of the sun to travel all that distance from the edge of the blotter.

By the time Vlikos came, bustling into the room with the frown of a man bearing the brunt of the world's affairs, the sun-disc had begun to tip up along the edge of the inkstand, so that it did not look like a coin any more and was beginning to take the shape of the mouthpiece of a Turkish smoking-pipe, a gilded mouthpiece like the one on the pipe in the Katraikis coffeehouse.

"Ah, Andreas, I wanted to see you, didn't I?" the banker said, drawing his big chair up behind the desk and immediately taking up his usual position with his right elbow on the table and his hand up over his bald head with the fingers spread, and his eyes turned to the window through which a green light filtered between the vine leaves. "I have had a busy morning," he said sombrely. "There is to be a meeting of the town council. There is a move for the dismissal of Dionysios. A strong move. He is a drinking crony of yours, is he not?" He took his hand down from his head and shot a quick glance at the captain, not yet a censorious glance but one with the possibility of censure in it. The stain of pink fingermarks was left on his head, making a curiously chromatic criss-cross network with the few sparse strands of thin black hair which the barber had rubbed with brilliantine and combed across the sallow scalp in very much the pattern of the lattice grille which divided the banker's office from the ante-room.

"He is a friend of mine," Andreas admitted simply. "We have a drink together sometimes."

"His drinking is a disgrace to the town. A scandal!" Vlikos stared angrily at the window. "He will be removed. Oh, yes, he'll go, don't make any mistake. That fool Phrontis, the mayor, tries to protect him simply because he has his vote. We shall see about that!"

"This isn't what you wanted to see *me* about, is it?" Andreas asked patiently. "You told me to come at quarter-past eleven. I've been waiting."

"I want your crew-list. And the victualling accounts."

"You had the victualling accounts yesterday. As far as we've ordered. There isn't any crew-list yet."

"What's this!" Vlikos dropped his hand from his head, drummed on the desk with his pudgy fingers. "My telegram must go to Athens this afternoon." He stared at the window with a set face.

"There isn't a crew-list," Andreas repeated with undiminished patience, his dark eyes staring at the sun-shape on the inkstand, which had not turned out at all like the gilt mouthpiece of the pipe. "Not yet," he added. "You sent me to Phrontis. You said he'd find men for me."

"Did I? Well, didn't he find them? He needs votes."

"Maybe." Andreas shrugged. "I still need men. He didn't find any. That's why there's no crew-list. Your girl went through the victualling accounts yesterday. She said they were all right."

"All right! What the devil do you mean, *all right!*" The banker turned in a sudden explosion of anger, and brought his two fat fists thudding down on the desk, so that the inkstand jumped a little, and the sun-shape jumped with it, and then was quite still on the black pedestal and exactly the shape of the gilt mouthpiece on the pipe in the Katraikis coffeehouse. "You've spent *our* money on victualling without even having a crew. And you think that is all right!" Vlikos glared at him from his little pouchy hazel eyes, but he must have been discomfited by the dark, even, deep-set gaze that met his, for he clapped his hand across his scalp and turned his head and glowered at the window.

"I told you I didn't think it would be easy to get men," said Andreas calmly. "I warned you of that. I've got eight who've signed. Even that's better than I thought it might be. I need four more. We'd still be short-handed, but we could make the cruise, I suppose."

"You suppose! If you don't make this cruise, my friend, you'll never make another!"

"That's right." Andreas nodded, and a slight smile touched the corner of his mouth and vanished. "Two bad cruises, then left behind altogether for a season, that would rub out the years before, all right. That would be a good *kaput* for me. So?" He shrugged. He was by nature a laconic man, and at this moment, unlike the man who sat across the desk from him, he was without anger; yet there was some deep sense of inequality of the values that had been presented to him which made him wish to express himself with an almost formal clarity. At the back of his mind he knew well enough that even if he did fill his crew-list and make his cruise it provided no guarantee that he would make another cruise next year. Indeed, the way things were, it might even be a guarantee that he *would not,* since the rest of the fleet would have a clear month's start on him, and he would have to voyage with a short-handed crew and a team of second-rate and third-rate divers, and therefore could hardly expect to have anything but a lean season—the third lean season in a row. And it was not probable that the Thiakos brothers would again lose two boats off Crete next year. . . . All this he saw, but this was not the particular thing that was in his mind and which he wanted to express. It was something to do with Dionysios the garbage man, and with Phrontis the mayor, who was looking for votes, and it was something to do with the power that was gripped in the fat, pink hands of this man who sat across the desk from him.

The fat, pink hands were at this moment taking the Ronson lighter from its little purple velvet slip-case. As no cigarette was offered to Captain Andreas he was not given the opportunity of refusing it.

"*Kyrios* Stathis," said Captain Andreas, careful to be respectful because of what he had to say, "you must tell me where I am to get these four men. You must try to help me, *Kyrios* Stathis, because if I have spent some of the bank's advance on victualling and then have to stay in port all summer, you will have to make the big explanation. Maybe they will not be angry with me at all, but only with you."

"What sort of talk is this?" Vlikos said sharply, setting his jaw more firmly, but keeping his face averted because he knew how strong and stern it looked in profile.

"People make trouble for other people," Andreas quietly went on to explain, "sometimes for their own reasons, for selfish reasons. Like Dionysios. He works hard. He's a good hard worker. I've seen him working away before the sun comes up, and right through the day up to nearly dusk. Twelve, fourteen hours a day he works and he's nearing eighty. Who's to blame him if he drinks an oka of *retsina* at night? You can't say he doesn't work for his wine. And he's always there in the morning to do his job, isn't he? Nearly eighty, and up and down those lanes, climbing those steps with his donkeys . . . who's to clear the garbage away if he doesn't do it?"

"We are not discussing his donkeys or his drunkenness. We are discussing your crew-list."

"I'm coming back to that," said Andreas patiently. "Besides, it's the same thing in a way. Your group on the town council wants to sack old Dionysios not because he doesn't do his work all right, and not because he drinks too much wine once in a while, but only because it's one little way of showing that you don't want Phrontis to be mayor again. In a way, that's why you sent me to Phrontis too. You'd have guessed he couldn't find any men for me, so then you'd be able to say he wasn't a man with much influence around the port."

"You should be in politics, Captain Andreas," the banker said with cold sarcasm, and his hand came down to tap with nervous anger on the desk-top.

"I like to be at sea. The sea and politics don't mix. What I was going to say was that sometimes these things aren't what they seem. You can kick Dionysios out of his job, and that'll make things very hard for him, but the victim you want, the real victim, is Phrontis. Maybe if the bank gets angry it will work like that with you, too—with you and me. Maybe up in Athens there's a sort of group of the town council in the bank too, and they don't think about how hard you work for them, they only think that you spend too much time talking politics in the corner barber shop or in the coffeehouses playing *tric-trac*. Then when they hear about me spending the victualling money and not making a cruise, it'll go hard with me, yes, but you'll be the real one to suffer."

"Enough!" said Vlikos curtly. "I've given you a hearing. You're wasting my time and yours. The affairs of my bank are not for you to discuss, however idiotically you talk. I want your completed crew-list by six o'clock this evening. You will sail on Friday. As instructed."

Captain Andreas shook his head slowly. "It won't be Friday," he said. "I'll sail just as soon as I can, if I can get the men. I'll keep trying, even if you can't help me. I won't promise anything, though. You've seen that big yacht out there in the harbour, the one the millionaire owns. And all those tourists coming. And the weather's hot now, like summer already. I think most of the men who are still around would like to stay on now. They can run little boats for the tourists. They can make good money. Easy work, too. They can have a nice summer."

"Well, run *your* damned boat for the tourists, too!" said the banker angrily. "And get out and find those men and stop wasting my time!"

"Maybe that's what I'll have to do, if I don't find them." Captain Andreas rose, squat and thick-set from the hard cane chair and put on his black peaked cap. "Or maybe you can hurry this business up with old Dionysios and Phrontis. Kick them out of their jobs quickly, then maybe I can sign them for the *Twelve Apostles*."

*   *   *

Nothing very much could happen on Silenos without it being fairly generally known in quite a short time and so it was not surprising that by the time exact noon was marked on the ancient Venetian sundial in the courtyard of the monastery of the Virgin, old Dionysios the garbage man was immovably established at a corner table in the Tavern Platinos, and he was roaring drunk.

The Tavern Platinos was the place he liked best to drink, but during the middle of the day he usually took no more than a glass of *ouzo* in passing. His more copious drinking, when he would take only wine, was a thing for the night hours, a kind of protracted warding-off of something which ultimately he knew to be inescapable—return to the shrewish old woman who waited for him in his little cottage up the steps. In this there were all the elements of a vicious circle. Had he just once returned home early and sober it is quite possible that out of sheer astonishment she would not have been shrewish at all; this thought had once or twice passed through his mind, but it was a thought he dared not entertain for very long, for there was the danger that she would still be shrewish and he would be sober—a situation which he found impossible to imagine. So that by drinking to postpone the shrewishness which he detested he made absolutely certain of its continuance.

Nevertheless, it was seldom before that he had ever been as drunk as this at midday. The reason, of course, was that he had heard of the plot being hatched by the political enemies of Phrontis the mayor and, knowing his local politics and his people, he had no doubt whatever that if he had been chosen as the scapegoat, then the scapegoat he would be,

and there was nothing at all that he could do about it, except get himself
as drunk as a lord.

By noon, Dionysios had passed through two successive stages of his
sad carousal. He had been angry and inflammatory at first, but since
this had raised no obvious support for his case he had moved into a brief
phase of fist-waving truculence. This too having failed to impress, he had
by noon lapsed into a pitiable state of maudlin tearfulness. And since it
is very difficult for a drunken man in this condition to give of his best
without an audience he had invited Costas the butcher to his table. It
being a meatless day on the *agorá,* Costas, out of boredom and the need
to be entertained, for there were no beasts to be slaughtered nor little
lambs to be danced, had joined him willingly enough. Indeed, Costas,
who had a good generous heart, was the one who was paying for the
wine. He did this really out of good fellowship and for the amusement
he derived from Dionysios's tears, since he was of the faction opposed
to Phrontis and therefore not too sympathetic to the garbage man's
grievances.

By the time Captain Andreas was leaving the office of Stathis Vlikos,
and Kate and David Meredith were sitting down to lobster and cold
chicken aboard the *Farrago,* and Conrad Fegel was rather dazedly re-
sponding to the toasts to his good fortune offered by Achille Mouliet in
a fishermen's tavern on the outskirts of the town, and Admiral Mavro and
Arthur Sinclair were returning in the launch with Badger and seven or
eight kilos of good fish and enough camaraderie left between them for
them to be singing *Blow The Man Down* in chorus, and Beth Sinclair
was enjoying a blissful solitude in her own garden, in a deck-chair, with
no luncheon to prepare, and a box of caramels on her lap and an old
copy of *The Queen* to go through—while all these things were independently happening, Dionysios, through tears and hiccups, was giving
a detailed account to Costas of the precise motives which had impelled
him, forty-two years before, to stab his first wife to death with a bone-
handled fish knife nine inches long.

He had lived then on the island of Andros, which at that time, with
the war coming to an end and the blockade opening, was a big time for
foreign-going ships. Andros was then—and to some degree still is—a busy
port for freighters, and there were big wine taverns in the port which
were frequented by seamen who knew not only most of the ports and
islands of Greece but were familiar also with distant places like Genoa
and Rotterdam and Tampico and Kobe and Cardiff. Conduct therefore

in the taverns was inclined to be on a level rather more worldly than in
most Ægean seaports, and at this time you could even see local women
at times drinking in the taverns with the sailors. (Even to this day you do
not see this custom observed on Silenos, although foreigners with their
own women may do so without the least offence.)

Dionysios was employed at this time, with a string of five mules, in
bringing charcoal down from the kilns in the mountains. When a kiln had
burnt slowly or had not dried out from its wetting, Dionysios sometimes
would be delayed overnight on the *vounó*. His wife was pretty. She was
twelve years his junior. She had come from a family of mountain shepherds, and in comparison the port of Andros was to her a place of constant
glitter and enticement. So that it was natural enough that on lonely
nights she had taken to visiting the waterfront taverns where she might
expect to find an hour or two of bright company with some lonesome
sailor passing through.

It happened one night when the moon was full and so bright that the
mountain trails were almost as clearly defined as in daylight that
Dionysios, although delayed on the uplands, decided to make his journey back to the port that evening rather than to wait for sunrise. The
clear brilliance of the moon had made him feel very restless, and he had
developed a strong craving for a shared bed and the marital pleasures to
which, having worked a long day, he was certainly entitled. Unfortunately for him, the moon was no less bright on the waterfront of Andros
than on the pine-smelling *vounó*, and it worked a very similar magic
upon the glands of a certain French-born Greek from Marseille who at
this time was bos'n aboard the tramp steamer *Ekatontakis Drakoulis*,
which had come to Andros with a cargo of asphalt from Trinidad. The
pretty wife of Dionysios the muleteer, susceptible as only a shepherd's
daughter could be to the light of the moon on the sea, was also very much
taken by this Marseille bos'n, who was a curly-haired, well-set-up young
fellow who knew sophisticated ways, carried small bottles of exotic scents
in his pockets to use as gifts for women and, as a result of his Gallic birth
and upbringing, had come to look on the practice of cuckoldry not so
much as an adventurous pleasure as a firm duty.

"Yes, yes," said Costas the butcher with some impatience. In magazines
which he bought Costas spent much time examining the pictures of
film-stars, but he never read the text of the articles about them. "So what
happened?" He reached across and shook Dionysios by the shoulder.

"They were in a tavern by the customhouse," the garbage man said thickly. "They did not see me. They sat very close together, closer than we are sitting." His bloodshot eyes grew wet again.

"Holding hands?" said Costas, who was interested in details, but not in scale details. "Rubbing their legs together? That's what they do when they're working up to it."

"Embracing," said Dionysios darkly. "Kissing." A slow tear filled the crevice beside his nostril. "Then he paid the bill and took her away, back to our house."

"You did nothing? You just watched?" Costas studied him in some bewilderment. Dionysios nodded dismally. "Why?" asked Costas.

"I wanted to see what would happen."

"You could have guessed. I would have guessed. When they're going on like that you always know what it leads up to. Well, go on—what next?"

"He took her inside and climbed into bed with her."

"Ah, what did I tell you?" said Costas triumphantly. "Isn't that what I said? It's inevitable. One thing leads to another. So then?"

"So then I waited, and——"

"You what?" Costas stared at him in blank astonishment.

"I waited," Dionysios insisted hoarsely. "Not long. Just a minute or two. I thought Nomiki would scream and throw him out."

"But she didn't scream?"

Dionysios shook his head numbly.

"You heard nothing?"

"Oh, I heard things. Oh, yes, I heard things! That's when I went in. I thought it had gone far enough. The fish knife was lying there on the kitchen bench. I picked it up. She was there in bed with him, and she didn't have any clothes on and—"

"You waited too long, I think," Costas said with a disapproving frown. "That always takes time. It must have been longer than a minute or two."

"I don't know how long it was," said Dionysios miserably, and again the tears welled. "I thought she would scream," he explained again. "But she didn't scream at all, not even when I stabbed the knife into her. She was naked. She didn't make a sound . . . not a sound . . . not even a little sound. I . . . I stabbed her thirteen times, and she didn't make a sound." He was shaken by a spasm of sobs and hiccups. Costas nodded over his clasped hands and waited. It occurred to him to offer the comment that it would be difficult to make much noise when one had been stabbed so many times, but instead he said, "Come now. You must not upset yourself. It was a long time ago. And she deserved it, going on like that with that man from Marseille. What happened to him?"

Dionysios choked back a sob and said, "He jumped through the window."

"And escaped?"

Dionysios nodded.

"That was a mistake." Costas pursed his mouth in censure. "You mean nothing happened to him?"

"He tried to get away by climbing over the wall of the cottage next door, but he lost his foothold and he fell head-first into their toilet-hole."

"Ah, well, that was something, wasn't it?" The butcher nodded his gratification. "That would teach him his lesson, anyway. He would not want to try that sort of funny business with your wife a second time, eh?"

"She was dead," said Dionysios heavily. "Thirteen thrusts I gave her with that knife. Thirteen thrusts!"

"You must not dwell on that part of it. What does it matter whether it was one or thirteen? Or did the magistrate make a point of that?"

Dionysios shook his head morosely.

"Well, he acquitted you, anyway, so what *does* it matter? Now, don't start crying all over the place again! You did what any honourable man would have done. That's why they acquitted you, isn't it?"

From Dionysios there was no reply. His head was buried in his arms in a puddle of slopped wine. His shoulders shook, but more slowly now, for grief and misery were exhausting him, and his brain was too fuddled for him to work out what it was exactly that he wanted to explain to his companion.

What it was, in fact, was no more than this: that in the state of maudlin misery to which he had been reduced by the wine and by his foreboding of what was in store for him, he had come to see all the darkness of his fate pegged to the single fact of his having come to Silenos in the first place. It is true that he had not come of his own free will, for the magistrate of Andros in acquitting him had also ruled that Dionysios should remove himself to some other island, to forestall the possibility of a feud developing with the shepherd brothers of the murdered woman. His steamer fare to Silenos was paid from the municipal treasury.

Thus Dionysios saw his present abjection, the plight in which he found himself, the poverty which he could see as inevitable, the ugly scold of a wife whom he dared not face, the long hours he worked, the injustice of his fate—he suddenly saw all these things as the fruits, the bitter fruits, of that affair in Andros forty-two years before.

"Oh, Mother of God!" he sobbed suddenly, "why did I do it? What a fool I was!"

Costas, who had been watching him without much interest, since the spice had gone from the tale, reached over and shook him firmly by the shoulder. "Sit up!" he said sharply. "Be a man! Stop blubbering! Look at the state of your shirt! And don't go on making these idiotic remarks. Of course you had to do it!"

"I wish I hadn't." Dionysios wiped his eyes with the back of his hand and sniffed. "I'd be on Andros now. Respected. Prosperous. With a good, pleasant woman to cook for me and warm my bed. Fine, strong sons too. They'd work for me. They'd buy my wine."

"That's all you think of. The woman deserved it. She wasn't warming *your* bed."

"It wasn't her fault. She was weak, that's all. She was pretty, too. And . . . and it was that man . . . he made her do it. It was only a mistake she made. It wasn't a crime."

"Not everybody would agree with you about that. And anyway it's too late to worry about it now."

"Yes, it's too late," Dionysios agreed dismally. How long the time, and through what devious channels of torment, it took a man to realise that a comely, warm-blooded woman with a weakness to be fickle is at least preferable to an ugly, cold-blooded shrew with the virtue of being chaste. So the garbage man of Silenos lamented to himself in his drunken anguish, seeing through all his tears and terrors and befuddlement a fact which wiser men than he have seen—that vice and virtue are but the two faces of a single coin which can be spun this way or that with the flick of a finger. "Yes, it's too late now," he moaned, and put his head down again on the wine-slopped table.

By two o'clock the garbage man had entered the fourth stage of his melancholic debauch, for his weeping had ceased and he had fallen into so deep a stupor that all of Costas's efforts to awaken him were of no avail.

With the assistance of two passing labourers, the butcher and the proprietor of the Tavern Platinos carried the sodden, wretched figure behind the rack of painted wine barrels and stretched him out of sight on the floor to sleep it off.

*   *   *

At almost precisely this hour of two o'clock the storm broke in the house of Admiral Mavro, on the hill.

It broke in an atmosphere which had been singularly peaceful. Kettering and Mark had been sharing the sunshine on the broad terrace which so splendidly overlooked the town. Mark, with tobacco-pouch, a spare tin of Three Nuns, all his cleaning instruments, and three pipes set out on a small table beside his chair, had for some time been meditating over three sentences which he had written down in a careful hand on the first page of a large, loose-leaf writing block. Kettering, in an attempt to transform his sallow, grey-pink skin into something roughly resembling a healthy complexion, lay spread-eagled along the parapet, wearing only his monocle and white jockey briefs. His head was tilted back, his eyes closed, and his chestnut beard appeared to jab at the sky like a burnished bronze javelin-point.

"How does this sound to you?" Mark said thoughtfully, and cleared his throat and began to read: "'SCENE: The rattan-screened veranda of a somewhat weatherworn bungalow at the edge of a tea plantation near the village of Chabua, in Northern Assam. It gives the immediate impression of a careless disorder, a kind of masculine slovenliness betrayed by the scattering of prosaic, tropical-style furniture—cane lounging-chairs, a frayed rocker, low wicker tables upon which glasses, bottles and siphons are haphazardly arranged, and to one side (upstage left) a bamboo whatnot crammed with magazines and old newspapers. It is between seven and eight in the evening and through an open swing-door (down-stage right) the thick straight trunks of two lofty dahl-trees are seen standing above the stunted tea cultivation, dramatically side-lit against a threatening monsoon sky.'" He nodded to himself, selected the long-stemmed meerschaum from among his pipes, put it to his mouth, waited a moment, then said, "Well?"

Kettering grunted.

"Well, what do you say?" said Mark with a touch of impatience. "How does it sound to you?"

Kettering grunted.

"Like Somerset Maugham. Or *White Cargo*. I thought you were going on. I was trying to guess which would be the one to come in out of that threatening monsoon sky—Sadie Thompson in those bulgy white boots or Tondelayo with her sarong slipping off."

"Clem, be serious, please! What do you really think?"

"I don't think anything. I never read stage directions, anyway. So how would I know? All I know—if this is of any interest—is that Janecek will have a fit. His sets are always cubes, cylindrical forms, abstract pastiche in light and colour to symbolise the hidden meaning of the play, and perhaps a soupçon of *collage*. It's just possible he might meet you half-way and arrange them in slovenly disorder, but he just wouldn't be seen dead with a bamboo whatnot!"

"This is to give him the *sense* of what's to be conveyed," Mark explained carefully. "Once that is absorbed he can treat it in as avant-garde a manner as he pleases." He paused rather doubtfully, failing to visualise the two lofty dahl-trees treated in cubes or cylindrical forms; failing, in fact, to visualise dahl-trees at all, since he had never visited Upper Assam and therefore had never seen one. "What was wrong with the sets for Vramantin?" he asked, choosing a defensive tangent.

Kettering gestured weakly with one hand. "Totally different thing," he said. "Symbolic satire on Lesbianism, freely based on *Lysistrata*. Perfect for cubes and cylindrical forms. Did I ever tell you," he said reflectively, "of my first meeting with Vramantin? In Venice. He set himself out quite instantly to dislike me. He adored Feodor, of course, and it was quite obvious he wanted to come between us. So when we were introduced his immediate gambit to me was, 'Oh, my dear, but your beard reminds me so much of my old grandmother!'" Kettering fluttered his hands in mimicry. "Crude, I thought."

"You didn't let him get away with it, I hope."

"My dear! Are you crazy? I tipped off all the English newspaper men— it was at the time of the Biennale—that Vramantin's play was to be done in London at the Stoll under the English title of *The Rod in Pickle*. Vramantin and I had no further intercourse." Kettering smiled in pleasant reminiscence.

"Is he as big a bastard as people say?"

"Big is too loose a word. He's vast."

"You know," said Mark musingly, "that's not really at all a bad title for a play. *Rod in Pickle*. Not bad at all." He stroked his beard carefully.

"Mark, you must do *some* of this yourself, mustn't you?" Kettering protested mildly. "You can't steal your brother's story, and my title as well."

Mark laughed and took up his pen again. Kettering cautiously turned himself over on the parapet to do the other side. A placid silence fell between them. Mark scratched out part of the last sentence and substituted "Dramatically side-lit against a sky in which monsoon clouds are piled in the weird forms of a cubistic nightmare." On the page opposite he began to doodle piles of monsoon clouds in the shapes of geometric solids and advancing cylinders, and he had almost developed the sketch to a satisfying nightmarish point when Janecek came. He stood in the doorway of the terrace, his sketch-block and box of crayons in his hand, his face a little pale but carefully composed.

"To whom am I indebted," he said quietly, "for the very amusing little practical joke? I have just come up from the port. I have just been to my room. Terribly amusing. Was it you, Clem?"

"What practical joke?" Kettering asked sleepily.

Janecek did not reply, but he continued to look across at Kettering with a faint smile at his mouth. After a few moments Kettering turned over with a grunt and sat up, his short legs dangling from the parapet.

"What are you talking about?" he said. "What joke?"

"Oh, come, Clem," said Janecek tolerantly, "you really must try to control this childlike flair you have for carrying diversion to a point where it becomes a bore. I know you enjoy being funny at the expense of others, Clem, but the good clown should always know when to terminate the slapstick and take up the other mask. A joke protracted is simply too tedious. So come, my little Grock. I wish to make some sketch notes this afternoon. So if you would go down immediately and get those things out of my room and clean up all the mess. *All—the—mess!*" he repeated, spacing the words for emphasis.

Kettering blinked at him wearily, then drew his legs up and linked his hands behind his neck, and lowered his head gently to the parapet. "I'm enervated by the sun," he said. "I'm just not in the mood for guessing-games. You work it out."

"What *is* this all about?" Mark asked with a placatory curiosity. "I assure you we haven't the faintest idea of what you're talking about. If you'll only *tell us.*"

Janecek shrugged. "I'm sure it will not come as a revelation to our little jester here"—Kettering was again favoured by the faint blue smile—"but there are three animals tethered in my bedroom. A goat." He compressed his lips, but his eyes still smiled. "A sheep." Again he compressed his lips. "And a pig. The filth," he added in a voice of gentle reproof, "is quite indescribable."

Kettering sat up this time with such a start that the monocle swung wildly about his neck.

"I would suggest," said Janecek imperturbably, "that you take lots of water, and a large pail."

"There you are!" Kettering stared at Mark in wild triumph. "Didn't I say? I *told* you I heard animals! You said I was crazy! You said I had to keep in out of the sun! You said I had a hangover from all that vodka!"

"You see, he *did* know," said Janecek blandly. "He kept mentioning it because he would not wish his jest to go unnoticed."

"Oh, shut up!" said Kettering. "I told Mark I heard these god-damned things below us, and——"

"If you ask me, you're all crazy!" Mark said distinctly. "Clem, for God's sake go down and see what all the fuss is about."

"You will need a large pail, remember," said Janecek. "As for me, I'm going down to the boat while you are cleaning up. I shall have a word or two with this man Mavro. And Suvora will let us have some disin-fectant, I expect."

He left as calmly and as disdainfully as he had come. It was ten minutes before Kettering returned to the terrace. His face was rosily flushed, his eyes startled. "Brother!" he gasped weakly, and paused for breath. "He's right!" he said. "He's dead right! The god-damned place is overrun! The whole house stinks like a manger! Goats and sheep every-where! A big bastard of a ram with great curly horns and the nastiest yellow eyes, and in Feodor's room"—he broke off to take an even deeper breath—"there's an enormous black flitch of a pig the size of a hippopota-mus who looks like the union boss of all the Gadarene swine you've ever imagined!"

"A flitch," said Mark dazedly, "is only half a pig." It was all he could think of to say.

*   *   *

At five o'clock in the afternoon, when the long triangle of shadow cast by the Prophet's Peak had pushed its apex all the way to the lower slopes of the High Lady, and the lava fields of the Black Vouna gleamed like obsidian in the western light, David and Kate, having returned from the yacht and sent the children on an errand to the port, were having tea by themselves in their garden. They sat beneath the plum-tree. In the cool, high shadows the bees still droned busily, as tirelessly foraging among the leaves and flowers as they had at the zenith of the day.

"Lemon?" said Kate.

"Thanks." David took the cup from her and put it down on the bench beside the watering-can and lit a cigarette. "By the way, I forgot to men-tion this," he said, "but can you amuse yourself for a while this evening? I promised to go up to Mrs. Barrington's."

"Tonight?" She looked up at him quickly. She could feel her throat tightening, and a queer coldness prickling at her fingertips.

"Yes. She suggested tonight."

"She meant just you? Not us?"

"No, she made a point of it being just me. I suppose it's something to do with her writing . . . something she wants to talk about."

"Yes, I see . . . well, if you've made the arrangement I suppose you'll have to go," said Kate doubtfully.

"You sound as if you'd rather I didn't." He glanced at her curiously.

"Of course not. It's just that in a way I'm rather sorry it's tonight, that's all. I . . . I wanted . . ." She did not complete the sentence.

"What?" He waited. "What were you going to say?"

"Nothing." She shook her head quickly. "Is it for supper?"

"I'm not sure. She didn't actually say. Drinks, she said—that's all. Oh, I expect there'll be something to eat. If one has to climb all those steps to her eyrie there should be some scrap of sustenance at the end of it." He smiled. "I must say I'm quite looking forward to it. I do like her. And we never have seen inside that mysterious house of hers. I'm sorry we're not both going."

"It doesn't matter," Kate said. "It doesn't matter in the least." But she knew that it did matter. It mattered terribly. Not tonight. Some other night. Let him go some other night. Almost she found herself forming it into a little childish prayer: "Please God, let him go some other night . . . make him understand that tonight he has to be here, *to be here with me!* Please God, don't let him leave me tonight . . . don't let him leave me alone tonight!" But the prayer remained inside her, and she summoned a quick smile in which the tremor was scarcely detectable, and said, "You're very privileged, darling. You're the first she's asked to her house."

"Nonsense. Beth's been there, I'm sure."

"I don't mean Beth. Beth's been everywhere. One doesn't count her, really. What I mean is you're the first who is . . . well, who is sort of . . ."

"Eligible?" There was amusement in his grey, deep-set eyes. "Is that the word you are seeking, Mrs. Meredith? Bedworthy?"

She pulled a face.

"Am I eligible, Kate?" The lopsided smile creased his face as he studied her affectionately.

"No!" she said, accepting the superficial safeties. "And don't you get

the idea into your head that you are! Nor bedworthy, either! But you
are very nice. So you see that you behave yourself."

He burst into laughter. His long, lean, sunburnt face was very attractive when he laughed. "Not eligible," he said. "Not bedworthy. But nice.
There are some men, you know, who would regard that as defamatory.
Still, I am, as you say, the privileged one—the first. He was the first
who ever burst into that sunless she!" he parodied, then said, "I'm sorry.
It's a dreadful pun. It sounds like something Mark would say. Or Kettering." He snapped his fingers and said, "By Jove, that's an idea. Why
don't I call round on Mark and ask him to drop by and take you down
to the port? He's the wealthy member of the family now. He can buy
you lobster."

"No." She shook her head determinedly. "If you like, I can wait for
you."

"I shouldn't. I'm pretty sure I'll eat up there. She'd hardly expect someone to slog up a thousand steps in the dark just for a glass of *ouzo.*"

"Then I'll have supper with the children. And there are any number
of things I can find to do later."

"Well, eat with them, yes, but why couldn't Mark take you for a drink
later, after you've put them down?"

"But I don't *feel* like Mark, darling," she said with a touch of impatience. "Really I don't. Not tonight. Why all this fuss about me, anyway?"
She looked at him quickly, then dropped her eyes. "I shall be perfectly
happy, darling. I've been left alone before."

"Yes, but I just hate to think of you sitting here by yourself while I
am being richly entertained by the enigmatic Erica." He grinned at her,
then looked around as the gate squeaked. Jerry and Simon sidled in, the
legs of their blue jeans splashed by water, carrying between them a
string-bag in which was enmeshed a quarter-block of ice. "Ah, the ice-
men cometh," he said, and went down the garden to relieve them of
their burden. "I'll put this in the ice-box," he called up to her, "and then
I'd better go up and shave and change. Will you take over the kids?"

Gratefully, she said to herself. Oh, so gratefully! Here, at least, were
her other securities—the children, the house, the garden, the damp
trousers that had to be changed, the shirt to be mended, the button to
be sewn on, the supper to be prepared. "Simon! Jerry!" she called. "Come
and have some tea with me in the garden. And then we'll make supper
and have it out here too, with the lamps."

Jerry came through the garden, scuffing the fallen leaves, and went to the bench and took the disc of lemon from his father's tea-cup and popped it into his mouth. Simon said, "Mummy, there was a block of ice at the *pagopoleion* with a fish inside it. A whole fish. A big one. A cod, Jerry said."

"I didn't say it was a cod," said Jerry. "I said it was *like* a cod. It's quite different for a thing to *be* a thing or only to be *like* a thing. I'm always explaining that to Simon, but he just doesn't listen. He'll never be a scientist, you know, and that's what he wants to be. Do you think we could have egg-toast for supper?"

"Darling, you can have anything you like for supper," Kate said happily. Her childish little prayer had been answered after all. It was a different answer but it served the same purpose. Nothing had crumbled away after all: the walls of her security were safe around her . . . just as safe as ever they had been.

"Come on," she said, reaching for their hands. "Let's go in and get started. And you can take it in turns to use the egg-beater."

4

SILENOS BY STARLIGHT

THE ISLANDS of the Ægean, scattered in luminous air within their running seas, are specially vulnerable to the nocturnal witchery of the stars. Here sleeping towns float above their dusky terraces, and the sea slides silver in the starlight, and pale, silky mountains seem to hang like an arras against the sky. The violence of these Grecian nights is only in the incandescence of the stars so prodigally scattered against the emptiness of space, where Venus blazes like a warning brand above a hill where a single fig-tree stands, and the Pleiades are gathered at their conference like seven old women gossiping by a summer door, and Orion in one bound vaults the steely strip of sea between two islands, and Betelgeuse throws his blue beam from the silver pollen of the Milky Way. . . .

It is the stars that are real and we that are ethereal, Kate Meredith reflected, staring up from the terrace of her house into the glittering, explosive brilliance of the night. Below her and around her silence filled the secret labyrinth of the lanes and the streets. The women had gone from the well; the murmuring of their voices from the porches was no more than a shadow of sound: the insects forced a more determined loudness. Or the bats, flicking down from the high dark cliffs behind, printing the black angles of their flight in a hallucinating pattern of squeaks and shapes.

In the distance, across a gulf of darkness and airy space where no shape declared itself, a dog howled and a donkey harshly spent its paroxysm and the sheep bells jangled and the little owl, the little owl of Pallas Athena, dropped globes of liquid music to make one think the stars were falling into the shrouded valley and chinking as they fell.

A cockerel in the house next door flapped its wings and crowed. The sound was too loud, too raucous for the night, and it startled her, and when birds near at hand and far away took up the strident challenge, she found herself suddenly uneasy and out of harmony with the night. "Cocks crowing when they shouldn't." That was what David had said. Well, that was the way the cocks *did* crow on Silenos. Did self-respecting roosters anywhere else in the world begin their crowing almost before dusk had ended? She struck a match to light a cigarette, then held it to her wrist to see the time. Still only eight-thirty! She had thought it later. The children had been asleep for only half an hour, and already she was restless, nervous, unable to settle to anything. From the house below her there was no sound, from the night around her only the irritating, unnerving cries of these ridiculous birds. She could understand now how they had come to have such a fearful significance in David's childhood, even to see how through all his life, right through to his present maturity, all his inner restlessnesses, all his perplexities and fears, were imprinted with the mysterious savagery which he associated with this strange, private symbol of the night. Poor David!

She stared curiously at the lighted end of her cigarette. Why poor David? Why had she thought that? Slowly she shook her head, then flung the cigarette over the parapet and walked to the far corner of the terrace. She knew as she looked up the tilted tiers of the town in darkness that Erica Barrington's house could not be seen, but as she leaned out across the parapet she almost expected that the heavy domed bulk of the Church of Saint John the Theologian unaccountably would have moved some distance to one side along the spur of the hill to reveal, higher still, the big square house of stone with its lighted windows. Or would they be, like her, on the terrace, under the stars, looking down over the quiet nocturne of the town? As she moved back across her own terrace she found herself taking another cigarette.

Strange. She had just thrown one away. She had not wanted another. Queer to detect a part of one's mind acting independently of the conscious processes of thought, moving out of harmony, even mutinously, as if there were secret compulsions which moved to private rhythms, unsuspected until they had become acts. Nervousness? Nervous reaction? Reaction to what? To the night, perhaps, and to her own solitude. Did David think like this during his own secret, baffled communions with the darkness? Had she become affected by that same unexpressed, uneasy self-searching which lately in him had worried her so much? In the last half-hour, since Simon and Jerry had gone to sleep, she too had been prowling alone through the dark and silent house. What was the difference between them? Cups of coffee drunk in solitude in the empty kitchen. A cigarette lit and tossed away after two puffs. Another one taken from the packet. A book picked up and set aside. A door opened stealthily to peep in and make sure that the children are all right. A plan to make more coffee considered solemnly and nervously rejected. And then, inevitably, the terrace—to stare dumbly at the chinking brilliance of the stars, to hear the flung challenges of the cockerels, to lean over the parapet and sink unresistingly into this darkly-charmed and strangely terrifying starlit world of bats and owls and bells from far away and the forlorn distances of an infinite loneliness that sank away into those empty recesses which lay beyond the light—to wonder about journeys . . . where we came from, why we are here, where we are going. . . .

She struck another match to look at her watch. Twenty minutes to nine. Only ten minutes! A slow journey this one, she told herself wryly, wherever she was going! She would take a walk then. The children were safely in bed and sleeping soundly. In a way she was sorry now that she had not accepted David's suggestion to have Mark call for her. It would be pleasant with him now, strolling down to the port, sharing a bottle of wine with him in a tavern on the waterfront with nothing to do but look out upon the dreamy dance of the caïques at their moorings. With nothing to think about, with everything put aside, lulled away, subdued. Well, she would go for a walk, anyway. It was still early. David would not even have begun to eat yet, so there was no point in even expecting his return before midnight.

At first, walking slowly down the shadowed lane that led past the well, she had no goal in mind, no more than a vague thought that she would climb to the hill by the cemetery where the cypresses grew. The port did not lure her particularly. The garish lights in the windows of the shops, the bright open doors of taverns, the festoons of naked electric bulbs along the quay, would all be inimical to the charmed, dark magic of the night, to this queerly disturbing continuity of aloneness which she had come now to cling to as something very private and very precious.

Yet her footsteps, aimless footsteps scarcely connected to her thoughts, took her through the narrow, white-walled alleys to the Lane of Roses, and she followed it, slowly walking, as it twisted down towards the harbour, past the wistaria and the vine-hung gates and the quiet secrecy of tall, enclosed houses, down to the doorway of the Tavern Platinos.

He was seated alone at a table in the centre of the room, beneath a lamp-bulb shaded by a spill of paper, and he was the only occupant of the place. Fegel was not with him. He was leaning forward with his tawny-brown arms elbowed on the table, one hand dipping a crust of bread into the bowl of thick bean soup, the other holding the pages of a paper-backed novel open to the light.

For a long moment she stood in the darkness outside the doorway, her heart hammering, her fingers tightly clenched on the handkerchief which she had wrapped around the little bundle of hair-pins she had taken from her dressing-table. Only now did she realise *why* she had brought them. To pin up her hair. To pin up her hair if she should go swimming, so that it would not get wet! A handful of hair-pins to pin up her hair, clenched so tightly in her hand that the little points of steel seemed to be drilling little agonising holes through her palm. The pain flowed like a burning stream through all her body as she went in through the door.

He looked up from his book and saw her and smiled. His smile made it seem as if he had been expecting her to come.

Stretched on the floor by the wine-stained wall, hidden from both of them by the long rack of barrels, Dionysios stared up at the tarred beams of the ceiling, blindly fighting the pain that seemed to cleave his skull in two, blindly groping for some shred of comprehension and meaning, blindly struggling to find a pattern of reality in the flickering confusion of the images that swelled and vanished in his poor sick brain.

*   *   *

It was obvious from the laden table so carefully prepared in the stone-arched dining-room which looked like a nuns' refectory that Erica Barrington's invitation, even if unstated, had included dinner.

It was obvious also, David reflected with satisfaction, that his hostess and Sevasti, her woman, had gone to some pains about it. This gave him an added pleasure because it was evident from the dishes and the napery, the six slim candles set at either end of the table in two three-branched candelabra carved from jadeite, and the meticulous arrangement of glasses and bottles of wines and liqueurs on the sideboard, that this would be a meal over which one would be expected to dwell lingeringly: the sort of meal which, had one thought of it, one might have expected to

share with Erica Barrington. Selfishly, he was glad now that Kate had
not come with him: what was now, in a sense, an adventure would then
have been no more than a visit.

Earlier, on the terrace, with Sevasti bringing ice and offering platters
with such unobtrusive silence that she might have been a shade hired
for the evening from some Elysian underworld, he had without even an
inward objection allowed himself to sink luxuriously into the unaccus-
tomed pleasure of being totally civilised. Far from being only the "glass
of *ouzo*" which he had prophesied to Kate, the *apéritifs* on the terrace
would not have disgraced the bar at Maxim's. For the pure novelty of it
he had lingered long over his choice, finally settling for a dry martini
which, somewhat to his surprise, Sevasti prepared with a professional
skill. It gave him an even sharper sting of pleasure when Mrs. Barrington, as if to give the final varied touch to this totally un-Sileniot
sophistication, asked for Byrrh.

She was wearing the plain clothes that he had come to expect of her
—a black dress of such simplicity that he knew when he was asked by
Kate (as, of course, he would be) he would have no way of describing
it—and no decoration save a single small yellow rosebud upon her bosom.

Unexpected also had been the fact that there had been no "showing"
of the house. In Silenos people were almost expected to "show" their
houses, and since so much mystery attached to this particular house he
had come to it with the definite feeling that a detailed viewing would
be inevitable. Yet, until he was taken to the dining-room, he had seen
only the entrance hall—high ceilinged, massively stoned, and grandly
proportioned, with arched niches in which, in the brief survey he was
granted while he passed through, he was able to identify an exquisite
little Cycladic figure of a seated woman in cream marble and a slightly
larger bronze of a serenely standing woman (a Demeter, he had thought
—which surely must have been stolen from some museum) and the broad,
dark terrace which seemed to be suspended closer to the stars than to the
spread-out town of Silenos below.

The view, he realised, was worth the thousand steps one had to climb
to reach it, for this was the topmost of all the houses of Silenos, with
nóthing above it but the rocky slopes and terraced plots and a ruined
windmill. It was a breath-taking panorama that was spread out below,
yet as he looked down upon it he had a sudden juvenile stab of pique
that the cut-out black shape of the Church of Saint John the Theologian
on the ridge below completely obscured the view of his own house, so

that he was not able to see a light burning in a window there to signify the familiar presence of his wife.

They had sat together on the darkened terrace for more than an hour, talking of this and that, and sometimes falling silent and enjoying the shared loveliness of the scattered stars above and the dreaming town below. And inevitably, after one such silence, they had begun to talk about the stars, and he had come to realise again what a truly remarkable woman she was. He had never met a woman before who could look up into the heavens and know Rigel from Aldebaran, and point out Procyon and Betelgeuse, and talk of Orion standing guard at the edge of Eridanus, the river of stars, and discuss the Roman addition of the Scales to the symbols of the Zodiac, seeing an almost mystical significance in the fact of its being the only inanimate object among the twelve signs.

Interesting talk, curiously detached in a way—there had been the thought in his mind at one point that she had been talking *to* the stars rather than to him—and with her extraordinary range of knowledge ("extraordinary for a woman," he had almost found himself adding!) never forced, as if her erudition was something to be set on display for his admiration; and yet with it all she somehow conveyed a sense of warm and peaceful intimacy of communication. There had been several times during that hour when he had caught himself glancing across at her with a quickened interest, sensing in some particular cadence of the soft, deep, mellow voice a hint of another thing, another meaning. Yet all his glances had been abortive. There was nothing to discern save a dark shape that gave only token substance to the voice, for with her black hair and black dress and the darkness of her complexion she was physically no more than another half-detected shape in the sombre pattern of the night.

It had been after nine when Sevasti had come to her like a silent shadow and whispered something, and she had said, "Perhaps we should go in. Sevasti is ready."

Only now, in the soft glow of the six slender candles capped by their six dancing droplets of light each the colour of the rose at her breast, could he search again for this quality in her that he found so elusive.

"I'm intrigued," he said, "to know why you asked me here tonight."

She said simply, "I thought I should like to know you better."

"My guess was wrong then," he said. "I had it all worked out that you would want to discuss something about your writing."

"No." Since she added nothing to the blunt negative he assumed that there was to be no further elaboration of the subject of her writing.

Strange. Most people, given the lead, would have wanted to make some comment.

"That was why," David said, aware that he might be pushing it perhaps too far, "I thought you had confined your invitation to me. I couldn't see another reason."

"Your wife? I like your wife very much," she said, and smiled at him. Sevasti brought fish soup, the steam fragrant with egg and lemon.

"I would have thought," he said, "that the way to know a man, to really see him in his true colours, is to see him in the company of his wife."

She laughed. "Only at the times when it *isn't* possible to see him. When he is *just* with his wife. Not with an audience. Or a private observer."

"I'll take your word for it," David said, and laughed too. "It's possible, of course, that one can't really know anybody except through a truly intimate association. Actual involvement with a person. Not mere observation. By observation you can know all there is to know about the behaviour of a single-celled amoeba. I doubt if you can do it with a man."

"Or a woman?"

"Woman is implicit in the word man," he said, and thought that Kate would have understood that without having to question. But then Kate knew his talk patterns so well. As he knew hers. They could complete each other's sentences probably. "Woman, of course," he said. "Certainly. By observation what can I possibly know about you? I can see you are an unusual person. I can see that you are beautiful. I can see that you have intelligence, taste, background. I can assume that you are wealthy." The focus of his eyes changed as he looked past her dark, attentive face to the cloister-like stone arches which marked the end of the room, where fragments of marble and bronze, the black curlicues of wrought iron, the honey-sheen of old wood gave subdued excitement to the texture of the stone. "On observation alone," he said, "I have no further reference. Incidentally, this is my favourite soup."

"Would you like more?"

"Please," he said, and helped himself from the old Spode tureen. The ladle was Georgian. It was all very civilised. Over his soup he studied her carefully, sensing that their companionship had moved subtly to a different plane. He enjoyed the sophistication of the setting, the "civilisedness" of their being together: how sharply in the last hour or so he had been reminded of that afternoon in the garden on the day of Mark's arrival when suddenly he had seen again the world of good living, of Bond Street shops, of sophistication and the exhilaration of success. Yet the woman herself was still remote from him. Between them was warmth, pleasure, an instinctive easiness of communication, a mutuality of interest, even something that *seemed* like intimacy. Yet the evening somehow remained a visit. It was not yet an adventure. And he was still not altogether sure how far he could go with her.

"When I first met you," he said deliberately, "I thought you were Lesbian."

Amusement glinted in her long eyes. Her mouth twitched. "I see. And you are thinking of a 'truly intimate association' as a sexual intimacy."

"Well, not entirely, of course. Other things too. But that has to be included, I think."

"I am not a Lesbian," she said, still amused.

"I said I thought that when I first met you. I didn't say I thought it now."

"It doesn't necessarily follow that because a woman turns away from men she must become a Lesbian. There are other substitutions one can make."

"I agree. Of course. For a time, anyway." He was still aware of the glint of laughter in her eyes. "You have what I would give my right arm for. This house—this retreat away from the pressures of the world. Spiritual and material independence. You have total privacy in surroundings that are completely lovely. You can do the work you want to do on your own terms. Perhaps you—" a faint smile twisted his mouth—"are the Blessed Damozel."

" 'And the stars in her hair were seven,' " she quoted. Sevasti removed the soup tureen and brought a casserole of meat and vegetables in an earthenware pot. It smelled delicious. "I'm sorry it is not more exciting," she said. "The meat is so tough that one daren't take risks with it. But then you know that as well as I do."

"It's wonderful," he said, tasting. It was. For a second he felt aggrieved that Kate never made casseroles for him. But then Kate did not have an oven. They could not afford an oven yet.

"The Blessed Damozel looked out from her golden bar of heaven and longed for her lover on earth, remember," she went on. "Heavens aren't enough sometimes. Nor ivory castles." The smile lingered at her warm full mouth. "But you were aware of that, weren't you? That was why you said the substitutions were satisfactory *for a time*."

"Are you longing for your lover on earth?" he asked, meeting her change of mood with a strange feeling of exultation rising in him.

"Just for earth," she said, surprising him. "I'm longing for earth. That's all. I've come to think that it is foolish to be an islander, and then to want to build another island within the island, and another within that, like a Chinese puzzle-box."

"Sometimes we have to do that, wherever we are. Protection."

"Yes. But not all the time. Not as a permanent way of life. For six years, when I was married, I had to do it. Even then, not all the time. There were intervals."

"Who was your husband?"

"He was an archæologist. You might have known of him. Brandon Barrington. He did some important work. He was wealthy also. And a collector. Many of his things are here in this house. They are archaic things, far too old for them necessarily to harbour any associations with him."

"Why did you say that?" It was his turn for curiosity.

"Our marriage—what you would call our deeper intimacy of association—was not particularly happy. That was one of the things one thought one was able to escape or evade by turning one's back on it." There was a queer, detached quality in her voice, the same quality of remote association that she had had when talking about the stars. He had the uncomfortable feeling that she was reviewing what had happened less as a woman than as a historian—that as far as personal emotion was concerned she could have been discussing her book on Polycrates. It was vaguely disconcerting to realise that both her dead husband and Polycrates had fallen into the same slot—they were men who had lived once and whose stories were ended; the difference was only in detail and a span of time.

"How long ago did your husband die?" he asked.

"Almost four years."

"That's a long time for grief or——"

"Grief?" She seemed to examine the word. "But I am not sorry that he is dead," she said calmly. "I have no grief for him. But sometimes—sometimes I wonder which of us defected on the other, and to what degree. In an intimacy of association"—she seemed to underline the words—"one often neglects to look for one's own defections. One is so certain of the flaws of the other. One doesn't realise until later . . . perhaps too late . . ." Her dark shoulders moved in an almost imperceptible shrug

over the scoop of her black dress. "I suppose the hardest thing of all is
to recognise ourselves," she said. "Wouldn't you say that? We live most
of our lives in the skin of a stranger. And never realise it."

She moved her eyes and Sevasti came to take the casserole away.

*   *   *

It was in a rather dazed fashion that Conrad Fegel had begun drinking in the tavern with Achille Mouliet. He had then had no intention
of getting drunk. He was aware that in his pocket-book were five one-
hundred-dollar bills and a cheque on the Chase Manhattan Bank made
out for six hundred dollars and signed by X. J. Suvora. The full import
of these facts had not altogether penetrated his bewildered brain, although he did see, with Mouliet, that there was a basically valid cause
for celebration. The Frenchman was, in fact, genuinely pleased for Fegel,
so much so that it was he who had insisted on the dollar bills being kept
intact—"you must go back to Paris, and you will 'ave another start there"
—and the wine in the tavern had been paid for out of his own scanty
funds. This gesture, in turn, had touched Fegel very much, so that for
fear of giving offence to his friend he had gone on drinking beyond what
he knew to be his capacity. Like most men of apparent moderation
Conrad Fegel was always highly susceptible and even vulnerable to
emotional extremes.

To this point, therefore, it had been a perfectly normal example of
conviviality with a reason: a libation, as it were, poured in thanks for a
stroke of good fortune received by a man who in his lifetime had known
little enough of it. It was afterwards, in the middle of the afternoon,
when Mouliet went back to the house to finish a small *gouache* he was
working on, that the strange thing happened. For Conrad Fegel, the
timid and moderate man, for whom even the middle way had always
been a treacherous razor's edge between abysses and quicksands, had become utterly obsessed by a single aim. He wanted to go on drinking!
More, he *did* go on drinking! And the more he drank the less effect it
seemed to have upon him—or so he thought as he made his progress from
tavern to tavern along the inland road towards the centre of Silenos,
although this is an opinion which may well have been disputed by those
villagers who saw him pass.

The fact remains that by nightfall, when he lurched from the tavern
of the Two Brothers, he was still upright. And he was possessed by an
immense anger. It was an anger of Euripidean proportions, for it in-

volved man, God, fate, injustice, persecution, martyrdom, sacrifice, and
murderous impulses. And it was an anger directed towards and totally
concentrated upon the person of Feodor Janecek.

As he made his way slowly and laboriously up the steps towards the
house of Admiral Mavro—and painfully, too, for often he stumbled on
the rough steps and at other times it was only by rasping his shoulders
along the white walls on either hand that he could remain upright—he
had no doubt whatever that his new-found courage would not flag in
the face of what he had to do. But he cursed the weariness of his thin
legs and his frail body, and he cursed the darkness of this night without
a moon, with only the chilly light of far-away stars to light him on his
way to this moment of retribution which he saw like some golden mirage
that lured him on.

*   *   *

No ripple stirred the silk-dark surface of the sea, so that all the stars
were mirrored in it, but mistily. Like eyes seen through tears, thought
Kate. For all its stillness the sea breathed slowly, with a slow, soft sucking at the rocks below her bare feet and every now and then, at intervals that had no expectancy or rhythm, there would be a muted, running lap of water against the reef that hooked out from the entrance
to the cave. He was in there somewhere, swimming in the darkness, but
she could neither see him nor hear him because she knew that he would
still be swimming in that same slow soundless way.

When he had gone in he had lowered his naked body very slowly and
very carefully from the overhanging ledge of rock, inch by inch, as if
it would be a sacrilege to mark a ripple upon the silken surface, or to
draw the least sound that might make an overtone to the liquid sucking
at the rocks. And he had swum away with a very slow breast-stroke that
did not break the skin of the water save where his head emerged, silver-
sheening in the starlight. Yet all the sea around had been alive with his
movement—the jump and dance of the stars reflected flicking, vanishing,
reappearing, like living things, one moment brilliant as in the heavens
above them, then misted again like tears, darting from place to place in
the blackness like freed spirits; and in those strangely opaque, strangely
transparent depths below the skin of silk, where depth or shallowness
were only abstraction of a substance that was of another world beyond
understanding, a trailing, curling wake of fire moved sinuously behind
him. So sparkling was this phosphorescence, so coldly fiery, that one

expected it to hiss its incandescence as it spread, and yet it glittered and vanished without sound, and behind him as he swam farther and farther away the fiery comet's tail pursued him, as shimmering and as intangible as galactic dust.

And then he had swum past the reef and into the black cavern of the cave. At the moment when he passed beneath the overhanging lip of stone the phosphorescence burst like an exploding star, and then the blackness swallowed him.

It was not until then that her fingers reached for the zipper of her dress. Dreamily and without haste she took her clothes off, folded them carefully, set them neatly upon a flat shelf of rock. In what she was doing she had no sense of immodesty. Indeed, from the moment when they had left the tavern together and had tacitly set out for the sea-cave around the cliffs, it had seemed as if they had been drawn inexorably towards some impending adventure of the spirit that had nothing to do with physical intimacy, that had no connection at all with what had happened that morning at the ruined mill above Fegel's house. And Mouliet, when they had come to the rocks above the cave, had gone a long distance away from her to a fissure in the rocks to take off his clothes, and then, without a glance towards her, or even a word to encourage her to follow, he had gone into the water and slowly swum away.

She rose naked and walked slowly to the edge of the rocks and for a long time she stood there in the cool, dark air, her lips parted and her teeth clenched on three of the little metal hair-pins. And slowly, almost reluctantly, her hands moved to her head as she began to pin her hair up. It would not do to go home with wet hair. She could enter the water as he had entered it, lowering herself inch by inch, carefully, so that her head would not go under. And she would swim as he had swum, with only her body immersed in the cold fire and the wet tangle of the stars in the black water. It never occurred to her that she could still withdraw, that she could walk away and put her clothes on, and go back home.

She had a slight sensation of surprise as the water opened silently beneath her feet and allowed her legs to sink down. There had been a half-expectation that one would need to press down forcibly to break this smooth, thick, shining skin that lay across the sea. Below her, even with the slightest movement of her feet, the sea boiled with a sparkling churn of incandescence, and specks of cold fire clung to her skin or danced away across the blackness, to flick on and off erratically, like distant lights.

The sea seemed warmer than the air above, and as she swam slowly towards the cave, creating her own churning aura of mysterious sea-light,
it caressed her body like the softest hands, oiled hands, stroking her.
There could be no sensual experience more tenderly perfect than this,
she realised, no intimacy that could transcend the quiet rapture of this
mystical and total intimacy with the night and the sea and this strange
glittering effulgence that bathed her body in the stars.

Inside the huge black arch of the cave the phosphorescence glittered
even more brilliantly. The interior of the sea-cavern was bigger than a
church, yet she could see Achille swimming on the far side of it, swimming very slowly and silently, his presence manifested only by the pale
wraith-light enfolded about him and trailing behind him which myste-
riously the passage of his body fashioned from the presence of these
millions of minute living organisms which possessed the secret of the
sea's nocturnal radiance.

Towards the back of the cave the sea grew shallow and here it was
not totally dark, for high above the roof of rock was punctured by a
great, jagged hole which seemed unnaturally light with the brightness
of the starlit sky, and as she swam, looking down, she could see the
coralled, leaf-like, sponge-like, convoluted forms of the sea-bed, and although this strange other world was a shimmering thing of black and
silver pricked here and there with the blue and yellow lights of the
plankton flicking, it seemed to Kate that she could see the colour beneath the chiaroscuro—the pale lavenders and pinks and lilacs and blues
and soft greys which were its true palette.

After a time she turned on her back and floated, her pale naked body
stretched still upon the dark, quiet water, her arms and legs spread wide,
her eyes and thoughts upon the night sky revealed above through the
jagged aperture of stone.

Mouliet made no attempt to swim near to her, nor was there any
speech between them: he, too, seemed to be involved in his own quite
private communion with a mystery which was not to be shared, with his
own secret Eleusis of the sea-night, with the "peculiar magic" which he
had mentioned to her that morning.

She swam out of the cave before him, and when she climbed out of
the water on to the rocks there was an instant when her whole body was
bathed in a cascade of blue-green fire, and then the phosphorescence
ran down her legs in a sparkle of tiny gems, and only a single gleam of

light, cold and glittering as a diamond, clung to her knee for a long time and then vanished.

He followed her from the water a few minutes later, drawing himself out in another flood of light on to the rocks a little distance away from her, and then he clambered to a ledge and sat there with his arms gripped about his knees staring out across the shrouded gulf.

"We 'ave not brought the towel," he called to her. "We will sit and the air will dry us. It is warm air, and soft. Better than a towel."

And so they sat apart in their nakedness for a long time, looking down upon the dark sea, and after a time Kate found that she had taken the little hair-pins from her hair, and it fell loose and dry about her face.

5

SEQUELS TO STARLIGHT I

DURING THE whole course of the night Conrad Fegel remained perfectly conscious of everything that happened.

As he sat on the hard wooden bench in the stone cell of the Silenos jail, staring up at the cold light of day filtering through the narrow, iron-barred window, he saw all the chain of horrible events with an anguished clarity. No merciful amnesia had obliterated these events. The physical pain that racked his head and body had not, as he had prayed it might, formed into one great burning blade that would cut through him and end instantly and for ever the terrible realisation of his shame, his guilt, his foolishness, his humiliation. Desperately he wished that Fotis, the police commandant, would come and get it over with, and then he could go away and find his own remedies to the situation. . . .

At the time he had reached the house of the admiral, Feodor Janecek had been alone there, seated stiffly in the *sála*, with the doors closed against the animals of Alecto. Mark and Kettering had left an hour before to try to find David Meredith or his wife so that they might suggest some solution to the problem. Therefore Janecek, in privacy, had no reason to dissemble the depth of his disgust nor the coldness of his anger. Indeed, as he sat in the wan light cast by a single kerosene lamp in the sordid vulgarity of this room he hated, Feodor Janecek was a man possessed by thoughts almost as venomous as it is possible to imagine.

These icy broodings he had begun to concentrate mostly upon the absent person of Kettering—this little graceless parasite to whom for so many years he had given protection, sustenance, affection, even some caricature of position, and who had now turned upon him, betrayed him, tricked him. *You must kiss the hand you cannot bite* . . . the Chinese proverb moved bitterly through his mind: but when the opportunity to bite was presented it must be a deep bite and a savage one. He could see now the whole sly pattern of Kettering's treachery—his fawning upon this third-rate playwright from the Colonies, his cunning undermining of Suvora's interest, his deliberate disloyalty on the question of this frightful house, his whisperings and deceits. More, he could see the reason for them. Jealousy. Plain, downright jealousy! Had anything but cheap, petty jealousy been the reason for his hatred of Vramantin? His nasty little innuendoes about Isidore? His absurd hysterics about a common sailor . . . Jealousy! Jealousy of all abilities, all talents, all sensibilities that were in any way greater than the meagre, atrophied shreds of intellectual values that lingered in his sick little brain: it had reached the point now where he could find compatibility of spirit only with a person like this man Meredith, a descendant of transported felons, a third-rate, plagiarising pedlar of banality, of the safe commercial cliché, of the tawdry trash that in England and America—thank heaven! not yet in Paris nor in Berlin!—had barred the door of Theatre against real art. Kettering quite obviously was seeking a new master—successful enough to allow him to preen in the warm glow of reflected glory, prosperous enough to support him in the effete sloth which had become his way of life, and without any demands whatever upon his intellectual values. *In the kingdom of the blind the one-eyed man is king!* This second proverb, reflected upon this time with contempt rather than with bitterness, was in his mind when he was startled by an erratic rapping of the knocker and a soft thud as of something solid falling against the front door.

Assuming the sound to signify the return of Meredith and Kettering, he went to the door unhurriedly, allowing his anger and contempt to settle into a hard, cold core of enmity which gave no reflection to the composed image of his face. But when he drew the bolt and opened the door he was momentarily disconcerted to find at the top of the flight of stone stairs a frail, wildly dishevelled figure that swayed in the darkness and stank revoltingly of cheap wine, a figure that muttered something incomprehensible, lurched to one side, then seemed suddenly to swoop at him with a demented tossing of horrible, dusty-looking hair, a mad contortion of the sallow face, an insane rolling of pale, glittering eyes. The unpleasant little compatriot he had met at the English party!

With profound repugnance Janecek extended his arm to thrust him off, but the small fragile body seemed to roll off his hand without any sense of weight at all, staggered to one side, and fell in a heap upon the broken tiles of the hallway.

"What do *you* want?" Janecek said coldly, staring down at the wretched, crumpled figure on the floor. From it came a sound divided between a sob and a whimper. Janecek prodded at the wine-reeking figure fastidiously with the toe of his shoe. "Get up!" he said. "Get out of here!"

Fegel shook his head and lifted himself with an effort to his hands and knees.

"Kettering is not in," Janecek said distantly. He had no doubt whatever that Kettering's malicious, twisted mind was behind this visitation also. Obviously this explained his prolonged absence on an errand that should have taken him no more than five or ten minutes. Another aspect of his childish little war of nerves. "Will you please get up and go!" he said sharply.

"I did not come to see Kettering," Fegel mumbled thickly. With his hand against the wall for support he pulled himself erect. His head swayed slowly from side to side, and his breath came in heavy gasps. "I 'ave come 'ere to speak with you," he said at last.

"How kind of you!" Janecek smiled frostily. "I am not at home," he said distinctly. "I am not at home to drunkards."

Fegel blinked and gulped and wiped his hand heavily across his eyes. "You . . . you will be at 'ome to me," he said huskily. "We will 'ave the talk about Jihlava . . . we 'ave many things to talk about." He paused to catch his breath, and again he rubbed at his eyes as if to rid them of some monstrous image. "We will talk of you and of me," he said in a hoarse monotone, "and we will talk of the camp outside Prague and of Karel Foltyn and of the commandant Alskionov . . . you will be at 'ome to talk of these things, no?"

For a long interval Janecek looked down at him, his blue eyes without expression other than a detached surveillance of an object which can be recognised yet is of another species, the examination a research scientist might give to a familiar disease bacillus seen through the lens of his microscope. Finally he said, "You had better come into this room. If you are capable of walking, that is." His face was thoughtful as he returned to the *sála*. He made no attempt to give any assistance to the reeling figure which, with an effort, loosened itself from the peeling wall and stumbled after him.

"Sit there," he said curtly, pointing to one of the two cane chairs. He did not even look at the woebegone figure swaying in the doorway as he seated himself in the frayed Thonet rocking-chair. He waited deliberately, his eyes lowered to his folded hands, until Fegel had lurched across to the shabby chair and had slumped into it, his arms and head loosely hanging. "I have no intention of wasting my time on a drunken man's delusions," Janecek then said evenly. "I seem to remember that we have already discussed the matter. What I *am* interested in is why you persist in trying to annoy me in this childish way. Kettering has put you up to it, hasn't he? Am I right?" His heavy, well-kept face lifted slowly, his blue, cold eyes contemptuously studied the wretched little man across the room.

"Kettering?" Fegel mumbled the name thickly. He had the sensation that his brain was clouding with nauseous vapours, sour and sick-smelling. He could feel the nerves of his stomach hard-knotted and pressing sharp pains into his diaphragm, and a thick, bitter taste of bile was rising into his throat. His head lolled forward until it was almost on his knees.

"Kettering?" He repeated the name stupidly, as if it were some magic catchword that might clear his head and bring back to him that burning flame of audacity which had swept him here through the night-cloaked town. Why did this man have to ask questions? He had not come here to answer questions . . . that would make it all go back to the distribution camp outside Marseilles. Questions, questions, questions! What is your name? Place of birth? Full name of father? Were you of a partisan group? What is your name? Your name? Your name was not Kettering, no, not Kettering. But it was not for this man to ask the questions, like in Marseilles. It was for him, for *him*, Conrad Fegel, to ask the questions . . . the questions about things that went back further . . . earlier than Marseilles. . . . The fumes thickened around his thoughts, and his head lolled forward even more.

"But then perhaps you have really come here for charity," Janecek said dispassionately, carefully watching the slumped small figure on the cane chair. "Have you come to rap your little begging-bowl on our door also?" He waited, but the only response from Fegel was a loose shaking of the head, not so much a gesture of negation as an attempt to shake a vision from before his eyes. A slight smile touched Janecek's strong, well-modelled mouth. "I visited Mr. Suvora's boat this afternoon," he went on, his voice even and pleasant. "Clothilde told me of your singular good fortune. I am afraid she was rather angry that you had been able to trick him so easily, but I must say I was amused. You were clever, Mr. Fegel, to be able to extract so much money from him for such a trumpery little heap of scraps. Still, he is rich. He can afford to give alms to the needy."

Fegel lifted his head laboriously. His face was grey-white and filmed by sweat. The whites of his eyes were bloodshot and watery, the bright blue centres glazed over and without focus. He tried to say something, but the sound that came from his throat was a hoarse, incomprehensible croak. His hands, thrust down now on either side of the chair-seat, were trembling uncontrollably.

"Ah, yes, clever of you, Mr. Fegel!" said Janecek admiringly. "Not so much in getting your begging-bowl filled—Suvora has a good heart and he likes to scatter his largess among the beggars—but in getting it filled so copiously! A thousand dollars, was it not? Would you believe that he paid only that amount for the last painting of mine he bought for his London collection? And you were able to squeeze the same out of him for your funny little pieces of art school craftwork!" Janecek laughed softly, then shrugged tolerantly. "Bah!" he said good-naturedly. "Why worry? He can afford it. They like to play God, these rich men. They enjoy their little games with the lepers of society, with the lost, the needy, the under-privileged, with the sad people."

Fegel had risen now and taken a staggering step forward, but this was obviously the extent of the effort of which he was capable, for he stood there swaying from side to side while his shaking hand fumbled in the pocket of his jacket. His eyes were tightly closed and his mouth worked as if he were saying something, although no sound came from his lips. Like a blind man he fumbled with the battered pocket-book in his hand, like a blind man he felt for the thin bundle of banknotes and the long, narrow oblong of grey-green paper signed with the name of X. J. Suvora, like a blind man he crumpled them all together in his trembling fingers.

"Good heavens, man, what are you doing!" Janecek cried in alarm. "Don't be absurd, Mr. Fegel!"

But already the banknotes and the cheque, crushed together into a hard little greenish wad of paper, had struck the floor and rolled away across the cracked stone flags.

"Ah, but why should you be so foolish?" Janecek said with gentle reasonableness. "Come now, pick it up. It is *your* prize. You have worked for it, haven't you? Why should you be the one to worry about absurd little trivialities like principle or pride? My dear, it is your——"

Fegel lurched to one side, retched once, and vomited, and then his knees buckled and he vomited again as he fell headlong into the mess of fluid and gobbets spread across the floor.

"Why, you . . . you filthy, disgusting swine!" Janecek, white with anger and revulsion, leaped to his feet and stepped back. "You foul, dirty, loathsome little creature! Get out of this house! Get up this minute and get out of this house!"

Fegel, sprawled face downwards in the sour and nauseous pool, retched again and began to sob. His right arm was flung forward beyond the splashed vomit, and the fingers clenched and unclenched on the cold stones as if he was trying to drag himself away. But all his strength had gone, all his will borne away in this dizzy whirlwind of mist that filled his brain.

Janecek, his face contorted into a mask of loathing and disgust, stooped over him with his legs braced wide apart and seized him by the shoulder and lugged him shuddering to his feet, and then, holding the filthy, fearful, trembling figure at arm's length he propelled him out of the room and through the hall and the front door, and roughly down the arched flight of stairs to the gate where the bougainvillæa hung. And from there he flung the frail, stinking bundle violently into the darkness.

Fegel rolled down the last three steps into the narrow lane. There, spread-eagled in a pile of mule-droppings and still weeping softly, he was found five minutes later by the two patrolling police corporals of the night watch.

*   *   *

When Mark and Kettering returned to the house three-quarters of an hour later, it was to find Janecek seated rigidly on a cane-bottomed chair in the desolate hall, his fingertips together and his face set.

"What are you supposed to be doing?" Kettering asked in surprise. "Playing charades?"

"I am waiting for you," said Janecek calmly.

"Well, here I am. I'm sorry we've been so long. We've been looking all over for Kate and David. They aren't at home. We searched around the taverns and the restaurants. They aren't there. God knows where they are." He blinked short-sightedly and rubbed tiredly at his eyes. "We called around on the boat too. Nobody there, either. Except dear, dear

Clothilde. And, brother, is *she* bitchy!" He grinned evilly. "It seems she is suffering from chronic neglect. All that gorgeous, meaty, all-over-crispy-brown body going to waste. Brother!" He yawned. "Well, do we go inside, or is this where we hold this year's convention?"

"You may go inside," said Janecek agreeably. "I shall remain here."

"You aren't going to be very comfortable," said Mark, frowning. "I imagine you've got quite a time to wait. There's not much we can do about those infernal bloody animals until daybreak. Damn David!" he said, with a petulant tug at his beard. "He's never around when he's wanted!"

"Well, you can please yourselves," said Kettering wearily, "but for me it's bed, bed, bed! I grew up on a farm in Illinois. We never had goats that I recall, but we kept a hog or two, and sheep, and cows, and a big run of white Orpingtons. I'm a product, you might say, of the mid-West midden culture. That's why I get on so well with anyone who's even half-way to being a horse's ass. Well, 'the lesser Sunne at this time to the Goat is runne to fetch new lust, and give it you, enjoy your summer all.' John Donne, if you want the quote reference. Sleep tight."

"In that room," said Janecek quietly, "there is another filthy mess for you to clean up. It was left by a friend of yours. He paid a visit to me while you were away. But why do you look surprised, my dear little Clem? He is your little scapegoat, is he not? Your little jumping Pinocchio who dances to your clever twitchings of the string? All you have to do is to prime him with your sly tales, so that he will come here and aggravate me . . . isn't that the scheme? He was very effective tonight. Yes, very effective. He did aggravate me. His nuisance value was profound. As you will see when you go in there, the filthy little wretch was sick all over the room! I am afraid you will need water, and another large pail, Clem."

*   *   *

Kate Meredith lay wakeful in her bed in the house by the well watching the pallid light of another day marking window-frames and latches and the tracery of the vines and the spindly furniture of the room and the bowls and jars upon her dressing-table—watching these things and yet not seeing them as she waited for her husband to come home.

Dionysios the garbage man sat despondently in the gutter of the Lane of Roses, sick at heart and confused, but wakeful also; and he was waiting for the Tavern Platinos to open its doors. He knew that already it had passed the hour when he should have harnessed up his big black mule and roped the double baskets to his donkeys . . . passed the hour even when he might have expected his sweet coffee and his little glass of cognac at the Katraikis coffeehouse. The thought of the cognac brought hot, stinging tears to his eyes. But how could he go there now? . . . without his mule and his donkeys and the battered cart and the baskets for the garbage? How could he explain to Nicholas the all-night waiter or to Constantinos at the bakehouse? What questions would they ask him? And how could he find the answers when he could not even see the answers himself?

It was all too confused, that was the trouble—too confused altogether. For some of the things he had seen seemed not to be real at all but only memories of things that had happened a long time ago . . . In Andros, such a long time ago . . . and then even the real things—things he *knew* to be real—were somehow all tangled together with things that had long since stopped being real. Even when he had watched them from behind the barrels, even afterwards, when he had followed them along the road to the cave by the sea, it had not really seemed as if anything was actually *happening* but only as if it was still part of the story he was trying to explain to Costas the butcher. That was the trouble, that everything was tangled together, and so you couldn't make any sense out of it no matter how hard you tried.

Dionysios put his throbbing head down upon his gnarled old hands and waited for Mitso to come and open the door of the Tavern Platinos. And Mitso would give him wine because he was a man of good heart and sympathy and understood confusion.

6

SEQUELS TO STARLIGHT II

"You CAN almost imagine it," said David, "as the background to one of those old steel-engravings. Doré's, I think. Perhaps Dante. Or Genesis. No—the Book of Revelation, that's it. In this landscape you can smell the Apocalypse . . . you can see the Four Horsemen riding out of it. Don't you think so?"

He looked out across the shadowy waste of the Black Vouna. It was true that in the calm, dim, eerie emptiness of their surroundings one could imagine that spectral shapes were moving; that at any moment the dark-gleaming sky above might split in portent and shine with fantastical, blinding doomsday images; that the solidified writhings of spewed-out basalt spread before them might suddenly begin to seethe and melt all these halted, petrified current-courses into crawling live tongues of fiery lava.

"Yes, perhaps," Erica Barrington agreed musingly. "A steel-engraving, yes, I agree with that. It's the blackness of the basalt, and that soft thin pallor of the limestone peaks across there—so much paler than white, really—and the black sky above it again."

"And you in a black dress," he said softly, "and the starlight on your face, and above that again the blackness of your hair. You see, you're a steel-engraving, too," he added with a smile.

Her laughter was almost inaudible as she turned her head away.

"And up there," he went on, "you even have the meteorites scratching lines across the picture, as if the engraving-tool slips every now and then." He stared up into the night sky, and as he watched a pinhead of light appeared out of nowhere, scored a flat-curving line of light down through the stars, burst in a momentary flash of incandescence and snuffed out above the pallid pinnacle of the Prophet's Peak. Never before had he seen such a display of meteorites, showers of meteorites, sudden scatterings of meteorites, as if some cosmic enemy had got among them and sent them fleeing, solitary suicidal plungings that burned down out of the heavens to die in the darkness above the silent girdle of the hills.

If it were not for the meteorites, he reflected, one might have thought that even the night was poised around them in an expectant stillness, as if it too was watchful and waiting for some revelation of fiery, mystic wonders . . . waiting, perhaps, not merely for the revelation but for the actual cracking roar of doom's finality. Such a strange, arrested stillness, as if the globe had ceased to spin and had faltered on its orbit and all the stars were rushing down to drown their brilliance in this jet-black lake where the guts of the earth were frozen into the weird shapes and the spasmic patterns of that long-ago moment of parturition.

"What time is it?" he asked suddenly.

"I've no idea," she said. "Late, I think."

How late? he wondered. He had no idea, either. It must have been only a little before midnight when she had suggested that they leave the house and climb the mountain behind to the old temple of Artemis. And then they had walked along the edge of the Black Vouna, and he could not even guess at how much time had passed since then. Certainly it would be nearer to daybreak than to midnight: there was in the stillness and the texture of the night this odd feeling of termination, of something running to a preordained conclusion. Even without the crowing of the cocks, for a silence deeper than death hung above the lava fields, it was a feeling that he found familiar enough. Time, and the texture of darkness—the things he had tried to explain to Kate. Yet what was this thing of time? . . . this plastic substance that stretched, compressed, expanded, contracted, advanced, receded, that moved past with callous remoteness, that sprang upon you like a ravening beast? What logic framed its form? Why, already it seemed years since he had tried to convey to Kate these fumbling attempts to understand, to see if by talking with her he might succeed in shaping the conclusions he had failed to reach: and yet it had been no more than a few days ago, a week at the most. Or had it been years, really? Had it been years that he had been trying, and he had made it articulate only when he felt himself to be within reach of comprehension?

"Are you worried about getting back?" she said. "Do you want to go now?"

"No." He stared up into the sky. "No," he said again. He knew that if he talked to this woman seated beside him she would understand. For so many hours now he had wanted to talk to her. "No," he said a third time, "I don't want to go back." For a while he was silent, then he said musingly, "What are other people doing, do you think, right at this moment? Down there, I mean . . . oh, and everywhere. Sleeping mostly, I expect. Although some will be drunk and some will be sick and some will be staring at dark windows waiting to die, some copulating, some thieving, some shivering their way thankfully out of nightmares, some desperately struggling to return to dreams. Policemen examining door locks. Fishermen rowing slowly. Burglars prowling. All sorts of people doing all sorts of things." He had a vaguely resented picture of Kate asleep, her hair spread across the pillow.

"And you?" she put the question softly. "What are you doing?"

"Dreaming too, I suppose. It won't be until later that I'll want to try to struggle back to it. Heavy ponderings, really—not dreams. Time. The cosmos. Meteorites. Apocalyptic visions. And you, of course. Very much you, as a matter of fact."

"How do I fit into your cosmic ponderings?" she said, a slight smile playing at her mouth, her long black eyes studying him curiously.

"I want to know about you—about you, the woman, I mean. It's perfectly fair, you know. You did it to me." He sat up and looked at her. "I don't want just to admire you," he said seriously. "I don't want to do nothing more than respect you because you know where to find Aldebaran in the sky or because you can tell me the difference between clinker lava and tube lava or explain to me that this . . . this wasteland here came out of the earth at a temperature of seventeen hundred degrees Fahrenheit, or that——"

"Stop it, please!" she protested, laughing. "You make me sound like a quiz-kid!"

"That isn't what I'm saying. I *want* to listen to you. And I want to talk to you. But also"—he paused—"I want to know you."

Her face was turned a little away from him, so that he could see, against the pale limestone ridges in the distance, the sharp upward slant of the cheekbone, the casque-like fringe of hair that capped her high, arching brow, the hair falling to her brown bare shoulders in a smooth straight sweep of jet that still shone with the blue, dim radiance of the stars. Her loveliness, he realised, was something profound and special, and in an almost mystical way it was related to the strangeness of this night, to the prescient qualities of this watchful hour, to the bizarre desolation of their surroundings, to the lost, obscure mysteries of this ancient and forgotten temple whose few white bones still stood upon the dark spur beyond, to the dance of celestial light above them—even to the very improbability of their being in this place together, suspended high above the sleeping world. His lips felt dry, his throat tightened as he said, "I would have to be your lover to know you. To really know you." He moistened his lips. "Erica," he said, "you know what I'm saying, don't you? You know what I'm asking?"

"Yes," she said. He thought her face was sad as she turned to him.

For a long time she looked at him. Her head was lowered a little and the dim light of the stars did not fall upon her dark-complexioned face, so that he could detect nothing of her expression, but in her silence, and immobility he seemed to feel the sense of her sadness persisting.

"What good would it do?" she said. It was in her voice too. "To you? Or to me?" Again he was conscious of her remoteness: her questions, concerned though they were with the ultimate intimacy of their being together, might have been addressed to the stars above them.

"What do you mean?" he asked, his voice as low as hers, but with a harsher timbre. "That isn't a question you ask, is it?"

"It's one you have to ask. Yes, it is, David—I know it is." Her cool thin brown hand touched his gently and rested there a moment and was then withdrawn. "I think I would like you to be my lover," she went on thoughtfully, and paused for a moment and said, "If it was only that. But it isn't only that, is it? You have to ask what good would it do. It couldn't be any answer to your problem . . . or to mine."

"What are our problems?"

"Shall I tell you?" Her deep soft voice moved like a caress in the darkness, filling him with pain. "I think we have lost the way, David," she said gently. "I think that's the real problem."

"What do you mean, we've lost the way?"

"Just that. We sit here. We talk about it. *Talk!* We look at love as if it's something we see from a distance, not as something that bursts inside us. It isn't a natural act any longer. It isn't a thing *happening*, whether we wish it to happen or not. You do see what I mean, don't you?"

"I'm not sure that I do. One doesn't expect to retain an eternal exuberance about it, if that's what you're suggesting. It can't always be coy shepherdesses surprised, or wide eyes and wet lips, or those first swift palpitations of rapture. There's an intellectual quality to love, too. You grow to realise that." He felt thwarted and angry, but he kept his voice under control.

"Perhaps you do. Perhaps there is. But why try to substitute a formula for a mystery? You can't define love by a calculus. And even if you could the essential mystery would still remain, for someone. David, listen to me. Tonight we have been together, just the two of us, for . . . for how long? . . . for hours and hours. We have dined, we have drunk wine, we have talked, we have laughed together, we have come into the solitude, we have wished on shooting stars, we have considered the universe above and the petty world below, and now we are ready to talk of love . . . to talk of it as an intellectual overture to the actual, or at any rate possible process of copulation. . . . Having played our intellectual roles we are ready to be physical. Do you see what I mean? We are not immersed in it at all. We are not involved even. We are standing away, looking at it, as if we were watching meteors skidding down the sky, or examining the flaws in a limestone outcrop, or seeing in this lake of lava here the solid evidence of some geological statement we've never been quite sure about. What good can we expect to get out of that? What good will it do us?"

"It's really *you* who are taking this thing to the nth degree intellectually," he said. "I simply said I wanted to make love to you. Perfectly simple. It didn't involve the calculus, I assure you, nor geology, nor astronomy, nor any other damn thing!"

"David, don't be angry, please." Her voice was very gentle and soothing, with a tiny uncontrollable throb of laughter in it. "If you want to, I'll let you make love to me. I would enjoy it, I think . . . it's been a long time. . . . But I wonder is it worth it to you? For the pain it will cost you. For what you will fail to get out of it."

"Surely that's the risk *I* take?"

"It's the risk we both take. Because if there is pain it hurts the both of us, you see. And I wouldn't be your coy shepherdess, David, and there wouldn't be those wide eyes and wet lips you spoke about, or those rapturous palpitations. And afterwards we would go back down the mountain together and we would talk about the stars and the rocks and the trees, and we would hear the clocks chiming and the church bells ringing for another day that wouldn't be the same as any day would be ever again. So . . . do you want to be my lover, David?"

"I want a cigarette," he said gruffly, and sat up very stiffly and began to pat at his pockets. "Will you smoke?" he said.

"Thank you." As he struck the match and held it out, the loveliness of her face in the warm flickering radiance hit him like a physical blow, and he knew from the expression in her oblique black eyes that her thanks were for more than the cigarette.

For a minute or two they smoked in silence, lost in their own thoughts, their eyes brooding over the quiet, death-still plain. Although there was no perceptible lightening of the sky, the brilliance of the stars had faded, and thin ribbons of mist were forming around the base of the Prophet's Peak.

"David," she broke the silence at last in a voice so low that it seemed no more than a reverie, "it is true, you know, that we have lost our way. We have to find it again. We have to find our way."

"To where?"

"To where we're going."

"And where is that?"

He was aware even in the darkness of that quick, sidelong, quizzical look of hers: her soft laugh wavered for a moment on the threshold of sound. "On our journeys," she said. "Yours and mine. They aren't the same journeys."

"They have the same destination," he said. "We all die. We all die alone."

"We all travel alone, too. Except for little intervals. Sometimes we meet somebody, have a partner in the deck-games, share a cabin, sit together at the bar. Little intervals that are shared. Not many . . . and even then . . ." Her voice faded. He waited for her to go on. Not until she had finished her cigarette and rubbed it slowly into ash on the rocks beside her did she speak. "I think ours are different journeys, David," she said. "You are outward-bound. You are still sailing in search of something that lies over the sea-rim, beyond the curve. I went there, too, but I didn't know what I was looking for, or perhaps I did, but I didn't find it anyway. And now I want to sail back. Perhaps you *will* find what you are seeking, and recognise it when you do find it, but I think you'll still want to sail back, too. We aren't just blind plungings like those meteorites up there: we have a sort of purpose that we have to try to fulfil. You made me see that, you know." She glanced at him quickly. "You and one other person. But you were the first. That night at Beth's party, when you were talking about Mr. Fegel."

"And the other person?" he asked curiously.

"Your friend Suvora," she said.

"Suvora?" He looked at her in surprise.

She nodded. "When we were all up here together. Walking back from the temple. I went on ahead with him, do you remember? I had asked him the usual platitude—how he was liking Greece or enjoying the island, or something like that—and his reply was very strange. He said, 'Oh, it's too early to say yet. I'm journeying in search of a fallacy, you see, and I'm not sure yet that I've found it.'"

"What did he mean by that?"

"That's exactly what I asked him. He said, 'Well, it seems to me that everyone has to call a halt at least once in his life, so that he can take a good look at himself and see where the weakness lies.' He didn't enlarge on that, because then he began to talk about his father, who apparently used to peddle rugs and carpets round the Balkans."

David nodded, and after a pause said, "What was it I said about Fegel that made you . . ."—he paused, his mouth twisting in a wry smile—"that made you see the light?"

"I don't even remember what you said exactly. But you made me realise that even this funny little man—so sweet, really, and yet so pathetic and weak and . . . oh, and hopeless, in a way—that even he was fighting his battle, trying to make his journey succeed. He wasn't turning his back on it. He wasn't running away and hiding from it."

"Like you?"

"Yes, like me," she said quietly. "Do you remember on Beth's terrace? You said to me, 'Life isn't funny, but it has to be faced.'"

He remembered Beth's terrace. He remembered how drunk he had been, how he had tried to stop Fegel from turning his back on it, from running away and hiding. He remembered Kate, and the tears on her face as he had kissed her. He had talked then, too . . . talked of unicorns, and of journeys. And Kate had said the real journeys were inside yourself. The thought of Kate filled him with a strange uneasiness—not guilt, but a sense of the night's waste, of sterile words withdrawing into an emptiness, of an adventure that had never occurred drifting back into nothing.

"Look," she said. "It's getting light. In half an hour it will be daybreak."

He looked up with a start and stared around. He could make out the colour of her lips, the startling yellow of the rosebud pinned to her breast, the rich, wood-dark sheen of her flesh.

And beyond her the sage-green streaks and mustard-coloured puffs of the harsh mountain vegetation that marked the black edge of lava. In the clear, greying air above, an eagle glinted bronze as it turned on a slow, questing circle to the stiff canting of its wings, but a deeper obscurity still shrouded the surface of the earth in what was still no more than a promise of light. It imparted to the Black Vouna an atmosphere different again from that of the retreating night: above the frozen convulsions of the plain a light, airy mist seemed to have solidified, while the lava field itself appeared to be flowing down towards them with a light wind making weird rippling patterns in the stone. The solidified cinder-cones, which in daylight so resembled ant-hills, looked like sinister, black-cloaked figures huddled together, sharing secrets.

"Would you like to walk up to the Prophet's Peak?" she suggested. "To see the sun come up out of the sea? We would have time to get up there, I think, if we go now. And up there the sun will strike *us* first. We can be the first people on Silenos to touch this particular day. Shall we go there?"

"Yes," he said. A slight shiver seemed to pass through his body, less the dawn chill than a physical reaction to her words, an almost atavistic hunger for reassurance that the sun *would* rise out of the sea and he would feel its warmth upon his face.

As they went along the spur past the temple of Artemis he could see the pearly sea-mist already forming on the gulf, and the port far below them in the rocky bowl of the valley. It was a town still sleeping in its quiet, dim shadows, a place insubstantial and colourless and as filled with mystery as if it had been fashioned from the stuff and texture of a dream. Anxiously, guiltily now, he thought about Kate . . . about his wife, waiting for him, wondering. . . .

He heard very, very faintly from the distant depths below the repeated triple-tone ringing of the church bells in the town and the crowing of the cocks.

7

SEQUELS TO STARLIGHT III

"HALLO THERE!" he called at the gate. "Anybody up yet?" He was conscious of the forced heartiness of his cry, and of the falsity of the question. It was past eight o'clock: of course they would be up! He went into the courtyard, uneasy that there had been no response to his greeting.

Inside he found the kitchen empty and the breakfast dishes not yet cleared away. The square-cased clock on the wall was silent, the hands stopped at twenty minutes past three. He had not been there to wind it and Kate had not remembered. Still, it was a thing he had always done; why should *she* have thought of it? He took the clock key from the shelf above the water-jar and went over and opened the glass case, but he had only turned the key twice when Jerry came in from the garden.

"Hallo, where's your mother?" he said.

The child looked up at him for a moment with great interest in his eyes. "You didn't come home all night," he said, obviously deeply impressed. "You didn't sleep in your bed at all."

"That's right," said David. "I asked you where your mother was."

"I think she went to look for you," said Jerry. "I suppose she did. Well, she told Sim and me to play in the garden until she came back. Were you," he asked respectfully, "out *all* night long?"

"Yes," said David shortly. "All—night—long," he said, spacing the words sarcastically. "I went walking."

Jerry nodded. "Yes, that's what Mummy said. But I said to her that that was a jolly funny time to walk, when you can't see anything, and there are bats and things everywhere. And Simon said he thought you were dead. I'm glad *that* wasn't true. He got scolded for saying that. Not a very bad scold, though." He rubbed a grubby finger against his freckled nose. "If you've walked all night you must be jolly tired."

"I am pretty tired, yes. And hungry, too. You run out now and play with Simon and I'll get myself some breakfast."

"We had ours ages ago. Last night we had egg-toast."

There was still some cold toast on the plate, and David made a pot of coffee and fried an egg, and after he had eaten he cleared the dishes away. He had smoked the last of his cigarettes coming down the mountain, and he grew more irritable as he searched vainly through the house to find a spare packet. After a time he went into the garden and called, "Jerry, I'm going down to buy cigarettes. You wait here and don't get into mischief. If your mother comes you tell her where I've gone." The garbage cans, he saw with distaste, had not been emptied.

On his way down to the port his irritation increased. The sense of anti-climax, which had begun with not finding Kate at home, had grown stronger. He felt disturbed, depressed, empty. The dry scratchiness of his throat, the tiredness of his eyes, the heaviness of his limbs, the sensation of fuzziness in his head, all contributed to a feeling of futility and anger, but without resolving itself into any particular target towards which the anger could be directed. Against himself, probably, he thought moodily. Out of practice for these all-night sittings! At thirty-nine one lacked the old resilience for that sort of thing . . . and all that climbing and clambering, and the food and drinks, and too many cigarettes, and those hours of verbal fencing . . . For what? he wondered sourly. Wiser to have stayed home with Kate and read a good book and gone to bed early. Oh, much, much wiser! Looking back on it now, with all the conscious physical discomfort of not having slept at all, he could find little consolation in the experience. He saw it now only as a series of disturbing memories to consider—he flushed inside himself, with shame as much as with anger—of gauche questions asked and inane responses offered, of his ridiculous attempt to involve himself with the woman in a sort of hit-and-run seduction—and, my God! how neatly she had put him in his place for that!—and of his pretty lamentable failure to really find out any more about the enigmatic Erica than he had known before! Hardly the night of triumph for young Lochinvar!

And there still had to be explanations! Kate, naturally enough, would want to know. He had felt the evening before that she had been a little resentful of the private nature of the invitation, so that her curiosity understandably would be intensified since he had stayed out all night. He could hardly plead now that the intimacy of the evening had been purely on a professional writer-to-writer basis! Oh, God! how impossible the situation had become! How fantastically different a thing looked in daylight from what it seemed in the secrecy of darkness! What the devil *could* he say to Kate? We just went walking on the mountains . . . we were discussing astronomy . . . we were interested in the lava formations . . . we wanted to have a look at the old temple. On a dark night, without a moon? We were talking, that's all—just talking . . . All night? About what? The hell of it was that *these were the facts,* the ludicrous truth of the explanation! *There wasn't even anything to hide!* Unless he told the whole truth, which just made it more absurd than ever! Oh, yes, I tried to make a pass at her, but she wouldn't play. So you kept trying for the rest of the night, did you? No, no, we just sat and talked. . . .

Kate, he felt, would be difficult. Already her attitude was a little to be deplored. Why was she chasing around looking for him, as if he were an errant child? And why talk to the children about it? Why should she want to make a *thing* of it, before he'd even had a chance to talk to her? Dashing out of the house as if there'd been some terrible crisis, with the bloody place left like the *Marie Celeste*—dishes unwashed, food left about for the flies, the clock run down, all the cigarettes taken, garbage cans not emptied. . . .

His mood was sombre as he strode down the narrow lane towards the sea, his step firmer now that he was beginning to assemble the target for his anger.

After he had bought his cigarettes he walked aimlessly along the water-front as far as the post office, then back to the Katraikis coffeehouse, without any sign or report of his wife's whereabouts. He ordered a double brandy, to see if it might steady the jangle of his nerves. It served only to thicken the fuzzy feeling in his head. He was about to quit the table and return to the house when Fotis the police commandant came up to him, swinging his *komboloi* of little yellow beads, smiling his quick little diffident, nervous smile. David returned his greeting rather churlishly. He was not in the mood for Fotis or bureaucratic officialdom.

Nevertheless, there was nothing to be done about it; the police lieutenant had made his apologies and drawn up a chair. There had been, it seemed, an unfortunate incident during the night, and since *Kyrios* Meredith was a good friend of this other foreign gentleman, *Kyrios*

Fegel, permission would please be granted for a brief personal discussion on this matter.

It took Lieutenant Fotis quite a long time to explain—and David, with his heavy head and his involved personal thoughts, a long time to understand—the full import of the problem. It amounted to this. Fegel had been picked up during the night on a public thoroughfare in an extremely distressing condition of intoxication—a spectacle, in fact, which could not but set a very bad example to the town and provoke fear and disgust among respectable women who must use these thoroughfares on their way to and from the port. All this the police commandant had explained to *Kyrios* Fegel himself in a most serious reprimand before permitting his release from the jail and allowing him to return to his home. The police commandant, being himself a travelled man, completely understood that different customs were observed in different lands by different people. It was even understood that the custom of the *xénos*, the foreigner, living on Silenos might be different from that of the local resident—but, even so, there could be only one law applying to them both when excesses of conduct came into the public domain. Since *Kyrios* Meredith, among all the foreigners, was respected as a temperate and good family man, he, the police commandant, would be most obliged if this matter could be taken up with his friend, *Kyrios* Fegel, to ensure that there was no future repetition of such shameful and unfortunate conduct. In the event of a second similar offence, drastic measures—perhaps the revocation of *Kyrios* Fegel's residence permit—would have to be taken.

David promised that he would talk to Fegel about it, but Lieutenant Fotis, having completed his official business, had moved on to some nostalgic reminiscences of war-time cabarets in Alexandria. It was over an hour before he took his leave and went briskly back along the waterfront, twirling his yellow beads.

As a result of the encounter David was in an even worse mood when he returned to the house to find that Kate had still not returned. He found two aspirin tablets on the kitchen shelf, swallowed them with a glass of water, went into the garden, smoked another cigarette, moved the garbage cans into the shed, toyed with the idea of getting the bellows out and giving the vines a dusting with powdered sulphur, decided it would take too long, then stared up towards the plum-tree. Jerry and Simon, obviously aware of his mood without understanding the reason for it, were playing there in a way which, for them, was unusually subdued.

"Come on!" he called to them suddenly. "Let's all go for a walk. It's our turn now. We'll go out and look for *her*."

But there was still no sign of Kate anywhere along the quay. It was not until after he had bought ice-creams for the children that it occurred to him that in all probability she would have gone to see Mark. The realisation came to him with the rather sour thought that if she had the smell of scandal in her nostrils she would at least be tactful enough to want to keep it in the family, so to speak.

"Let's try up at the admiral's house," he suggested, and together they turned off the waterfront into the Lane of Roses. They had walked some little distance past the door of the Tavern Platinos when he was aware of the scampering shuffle of footsteps behind, and he was already turning when he heard his name breathlessly called in a hoarse, thick voice. He saw Dionysios the garbage man lurching towards him, waving his arms wildly about. The old man was very agitated and very drunk, and a coarse white stubble covered his face, and veins like dyed threads stood out on his nose and forehead, and the black centres of his eyes seemed to swim in a filmy redness, like new coals added to a glowing fire.

David frowned as the reeling apparition staggered up to him, gasping his name. Jerry and Simon moved a little to one side and waited, their eyes alight with an intense appreciation of the spectacle.

"What is it, Dionysios?" David said, vaguely sympathetic to the man's condition, yet not quite able to keep the coldness from his voice. "Come on, we're in a hurry." The police commandant had tried his patience enough; he was in no frame of mind to put up with one of the garbage man's drunken supplications. "Come on, what is it?" he said curtly.

Dionysios lurched wildly, pulled himself together with an effort, took a deep, quavering breath, wet his brown-coated lips with an unnaturally bright pink tongue, and twisted his face into an idiotic leer.

"She's in there," he said at last in a slurred, thick voice. "She's in there with him, the *Gállos* . . . that's where she is! With *him!*" He hiccuped and tried to wink, then lifted a wavering finger to make a circle at his ear in mocking simulation of Mouliet's little golden earring. "I've been watching them," he whispered hoarsely. Again he hiccuped, and blinked, and laboriously worked his mouth around to pull a solemn face. "Embracing," he said hollowly. "Kissing. Rubbing their legs together under the table. You know what that leads up to. You've seen——"

"Jerry! Simon!" David called to them sharply, suddenly remembering that their Greek was as good as his, or better. "Go away, both of you! Go on! Run off somewhere. This is nothing to do with you."

The two boys hesitated, and then moved off with reluctance. They went towards the port, but they walked slowly, and they kept looking back over their shoulders with solemn, resentful eyes, and they stopped again and turned when Dionysios began to perform a crazy, stiff-jointed mime of lovers embracing and kissing, his eyes closed, his wrinkled sun-blackened face turned up grotesquely. "Don't stand there gaping! Go away, I said!" David yelled to the children, then turned and took the old man by the shoulder and began to shake him. "Now, what the devil are you talking about?" he demanded fiercely. Dionysios whimpered like an animal and began to sob.

"Stop snivelling and tell me," said David furiously.

"They . . . they're all the same, these *Gállos* people," the old man whined. "All the same." He squirmed as he tried to free himself from the strong brown hand that clutched him so painfully. "They are!" he wailed. "They see a good man married to a good woman and they have to spoil it all. They . . . they can't leave a pretty woman alone, that's why. They——"

"You're drunk! You——"

"Drunk, yes. Drunk, that's right." He whimpered again, like an animal in a trap, rocking his head from side to side. His eyes were swimming, his mouth fell open to reveal horribly the rose-pink tongue beteween the toothless, blackened gums. "Last night I followed them," he whined, and sniffed, and said, "I wasn't drunk last night when I followed them. Oh, no. They went down to the sea there, by the cave, and he . . . he made her take her clothes off. All her clothes. She stood there. I saw her all right. You couldn't make a mistake. All her clothes . . . just the way this other *Gállos* did with my Nomiki. That's——" He groaned as David pushed him around and flung him against the wall. A powdery shower of flaked whitewash fell over his hair and shoulders as he slid to the ground and lay huddled and sobbing in the gutter.

"Daddy! Daddy! She *is* here! We've found Mummy! She's in here!" The high-pitched, childish, excited voice seemed to come to him from very far away, through a blinding tunnel of white light. Slowly, almost reluctantly, he turned and saw the two small figures standing at the door of the Tavern Platinos, and Jerry's thin brown arm waving and beckoning . . . slowly, almost reluctantly, he turned his back on the shuddering, sobbing figure in the gutter and walked down to the tavern.

After the glare of the whitewashed lane, the interior of the cool, low-beamed little tavern seemed as dark as a cave, and it was a moment or two before he could make out the two figures seated at a table in the far corner of the room. Kate and Mouliet, seated very closely together, side by side, their arms touching, and on the square green table in front of them two glasses and a copper wine-beaker and a pile of papers.

"Darling!" Her voice, soft and affectionate with a welcoming surprise, came to him through the cool wine-smelling shadows as he took the children by their hands and led them away.

*   *   *

He had to wait in the kitchen for more than fifteen minutes before she returned, and in that time the terrible circle of his thoughts had completed itself. He was able now to add a lot of things together: the way she had always seemed to seek out the Frenchman's company, on the waterfront, at Suvora's party, anywhere at all where he happened to be . . . and even when he was absent—he remembered the day Mouliet had arrived, and the party that night at Beth's place—she had to ask for him, to see that he was invited too. . . . Oh, yes, the little intrigue was very plain to see now! Mouliet's strange familiarity about her, the flowers left at the house, the secret little swimming assignations, his smarmy way of bowing over her hand, his endless bloody compliments! And her withdrawal from the picnic party to the Prophet's Peak on the excuse that she had had to do the marketing, when all the time it had been a device to enable her to go swimming with him again. A pretty piece of hypocrisy, that! And the other cunning little ruse to interest Suvora in Fegel's pots so that she could go out there to the house and see him. . . .

He looked up quickly, and placed his hands carefully on the table among the white chips of matches he had broken and scattered on the dark wood. She was standing in the doorway, holding a bundle of torn envelopes in her hand. Under the fall of soft, coppery hair her face seemed pale, but her expression was grave and composed and her eyes seemed to search for him with a tender solicitude.

"Well?" he said quietly.

"Why did you come back?" she asked wonderingly. "Why didn't you come in and have a drink with us?"

"You don't seem to have been in any hurry to find out why," he said coldly. "I've been waiting half an hour for *you* to come back."

"Not half an hour," she said quietly. "Not as long as that."

"Long enough. Long enough for me to work a few things out. Long enough for you to get pawed around a bit more by your little Nature Boy before you felt it was time to come home and give a bit of attention to your husband and your children and your house. The place was like a pigsty," he said viciously. "I cleaned it up as best I could."

"Thank you," she said, and came into the room and walked past him and went to the stove. She struck a match and lit the fire and put some water on and without turning said, "Are we going to discuss this like intelligent people or——"

"Of course," he said tensely. "But surely we *are* intelligent people. Aren't we?"

She turned slowly and looked at him. Her face was paler still, her eyes troubled by a deep compassion.

"David," she said, "I went out because I was worried about you. I went to look for you. I met Achille on the quay and we——"

"By arrangement, no doubt," he said sarcastically.

"Do you want to hear what I have to say first?" she asked quietly. "There has been some trouble about Conrad. They kept him in the jail all night, and——"

"I know about Fegel," he said impatiently. "That isn't what we're discussing."

"Yes, it is. They let him go quite early this morning, but he hadn't come home, and Achille was worried about him, and——"

"Yes, you both looked terribly worried, I must say, sitting in that tavern guzzling wine at half-past ten in the morning! And you practically sitting in his bloody lap!"

"We were sitting there waiting for one of the fishermen to come back. Achille had sent him. And while we were waiting he was sorting through some old letters for foreign stamps he'd promised to Jerry. French stamps. Algerian. Spanish." Her hand moved in a slight gesture towards the tattered bundle of envelopes on the table. "That's all. I was looking at the stamps and I didn't see you go past with the children, or I would have called you."

"And last night, on the rocks, down by the cave?" he said cruelly. "Was that another meeting of the local philatelic group?"

He saw the shadow of a deep sadness pass across her face, and the flush that came after to deepen the colour of her cheeks.

"Well?" he insisted. "You don't have anything to say? You were with him, weren't you? Naked! A pleasant little intimate nude bathing party on the rocks at night! Doesn't some explanation come pat about that? Don't you have another packet of foreign stamps to produce?"

"David!" She whispered his name, and the pain deepened in her eyes as she stood quite motionless beside the stove, and she looked across at him with her lips compressed as if she were trying to stop them from trembling. Stirred by some vagrant current in the air, the bunch of bay-leaves dangling from the roof-beams began to twirl slowly behind her tall, slender figure; the same fugitive breath of air lifted a coppery tendril of the hair that fell loose and shining about her face.

"David, I love you," she said in a low, flat voice. "I love you more than anything in the world . . . more than I can say. That's all I *can* say."

"What do you mean, that's all you can say?" he said angrily. He scraped the chair back and rose, and he could feel inside himself that same pain that was in her face tightening around him, cramping him, sapping his strength, as if all his organs were turning into liquid, dissolving into a racing, burning tide of tears that could not be shed. "What sort of bloody explanation is that?" he said.

"It wasn't supposed to be an explanation," she replied quietly. "It was just something I wanted to say, that's all. Something important." She turned away. "I'm making myself some coffee," she said. "Shall I pour a cup for you?"

"I don't want coffee. I want to know what you were up to last night with this bloody Frenchman! I want you to stop this damned stalling and give me an explanation!" He turned with a furious gesture and swept the litter of broken match-sticks to the floor, then went across and took her by the shoulders and twisted her round to face him. Her arms were pressed rigidly to her sides, her fists so tightly clenched that the knuckles made white ridges on the sunburnt skin. "All right, Kate," he said softly, "let's hear all about it."

"Let me go, David. Please let me go." He released her unwillingly. She stood her ground, facing him, so close that he could see his own image reflected in the dark, green, even pools of her eyes. "I did go to the cave with him last night, yes," she said quietly. "We swam there. We weren't even together really . . . but that isn't important . . . we could have been, I suppose . . ."

"Nude?"

She nodded. "Yes; if you want to use that word. It's a horrible word . . . but, yes . . . we swam like that. I don't think that mattered, really. That's all. Nothing else happened."

"What do you mean, nothing else happened! God almighty, woman! You go around frolicking in the nude with this——"

"Stop using that word," she said tightly. "Please!"

"Naked, if it suits you better," he said tartly. "It means the same thing. There aren't any clothes hanging on either word, are there? You know this man's reputation just as well as I do—so you go and make a public exhibition of——"

"It was not a public exhibition," she protested, and her voice shook a little with her effort to retain control.

"Oh, wasn't it? It was quite private then? With the town garbage man watching it all . . . seeing him taking your clothes off!"

"He did——" she began, but he cut her short with a gesture, and raised his own voice louder:

"So you think it's pleasant for me to have the bloody rubbish collector going around playing town-crier to your cheap, sordid little cavortings? Whether it was a public exhibition or not, my dear, you can be damned sure it'll be all over Silenos before the day is out!"

"Shall we try to keep our voices down?" she suggested. "The children are out there in the garden, and——"

"Isn't it a little late to worry about that? Do you think *they* don't know? They've had splendid entertainment! They've *heard* all about it! They've listened to Dionysios. They've watched him making his imbecile pantomimes in the street of your cheap little love affair! They've seen you in a public tavern, crawling all over your pretty little Casanova. Rubbing yourself against him like a randy school girl. Do you think——"

There was no expression in her pale, set face as she raised her hand and struck him a stinging blow across the cheek; no expression as she pushed past him and went to the chair and folded her arms across the table and put her head down. He turned to look at her, his shaking fingers rubbing at his cheek, a red mist whirling and burning behind his eyes.

"All right," she said, her voice thick and muffled by her arms. "What do you want me to say? What do you want me to tell you? Go on, ask the questions."

"You're in love with him, aren't you?"

"Is that what you want me to say? I'll say it if you want me to. It wouldn't be true, but I'll say it if that's what you want." She did not raise her head. Her voice was low and toneless, as if she had no interest at all in what he might ask her, nor what she might reply. "I love you," she said dully. "I don't know why I do, but I do. Only you. Only you and the children . . . *us*, really." The pronoun was the only word of emphasis in all that she had said. And it seemed to take a special significance as she said it, for she lifted her head from her folded arms and stared at the wall and repeated it softly, *"Us,"* she said.

"So you have to have an affair with . . . with a bloody over-sexed little creep like Mouliet!"

"I haven't had an affair with him. I'm not having an affair with him. I like him, yes," she said musingly. "I like him very much, if you want to know. He's not a . . . creep at all. And I like him, but——"

"All right," he cut in bitterly. "I'm perfectly aware of your peculiar affection for the little bastard, but——"

". . . but I'm not at all in love with him," she went on in the same flat monotone as if he had not spoken at all. "I love you, David. I can't be in love with somebody else when I love you. Can't you understand that? Last night we swam together. That's all. Nothing else happened, David. Nothing at all."

"There hasn't been only *just* last night, has there?" he asked savagely. "He's been sniffing around you for days . . . ever since he came here!"

She lifted her head very slowly and turned to face him. Her hair had fallen across her brow, and he saw that her fingers were trembling as she brushed the loose strands back out of her eyes. He had never seen her face so drawn and pale, and her head came up wearily, as if an almost insupportable burden of trouble and suffering had to be lifted by the movement. He had thought she had been weeping with her head buried in her arms, but her eyes were dry and intensely brilliant, and they seemed to harbour a queer expression of pity, of infinite pity. Pity for whom? he wondered . . . for herself? . . . for him? How could he know?

"Darling, what do you expect me to say?" she asked in a low, tired voice. "If I tell you I am innocent you won't believe me . . . because you don't *want* to believe me. If I tell you that he has been my lover it means that this, all this, *us* . . . all of it is destroyed, smashed to smithereens. All the years together, trying to make it work . . . all rubbed out as if they haven't meant anything at all . . . as if they haven't even occurred. You, and being in love, and the children, and this home we've tried to put together . . . all these years of *trying*. David, what do you want me to tell you?"

"The truth," he said stubbornly. "That's all. It's quite simple. I want you to tell me the truth."

She looked up at him for a moment, her mouth trembling, her eyes at last misting with tears. "All right," she said evenly. "I'll tell you. I'll tell you first that I love you, though . . . only you . . . and then——"

"*Pardon*, please," said a voice from the doorway. "I 'ave to make the interruption."

David swung round and stiffened with anger at the sight of Achille Mouliet standing in the doorway in his tight blue jeans and unbuttoned shirt, and with the battered straw hat on his head, and the little golden circle glittering at his ear. His tawny-dark face was set and heavy, and he looked directly at David, without even a glance at Kate's ashen face and tear-filled eyes.

David made a move forward, his fists clenched. "What the hell are you doing here?" he said in a low, strained voice. "What the devil do *you* want?"

"I 'ave come to get you," said Mouliet quietly. "I 'ave been sent . . . it is not my wish. They 'ave insisted to send me for you. They 'ave found Fegel, you see. They say you will 'ave to come."

*   *   *

He was sprawled where he had fallen, tilted downwards towards the sea on a sloping shelf of rock, his arms and legs flung out at odd angles and in a loose way, so that they looked more like the freely-jointed limbs of a puppet than of a human being. Indeed, from the rim of the high cliff above he looked so small and rag-like that he could have been a shabby doll tossed away by some spoilt child, and the shock of dun-coloured hair that capped the curiously twisted head and stirred softly in the wind looked as if it might have been teased out of old rope. It was only the right hand that imparted any semblance of a living reality to the discarded little figure, for it hung over the lip of the rock, and it could not yet have stiffened, because at each surging rush of the sea sucking at the rocks, it would move in a weak, dismissive gesture, as if Fegel was still trying to get rid of something that was tormenting him.

On the cliff path above, with Lieutenant Fotis and the fishermen, waiting for Mouliet and the others to come back with the rope and the tackle, David watched the rhythmic movement of the hand and wondered whether the sea by this time would have washed it clean of the dye-stains and the dried clay embedded around the fingernails.

8

THE DIALOGUES

IT WAS GETTING on towards evening by the time Kate climbed the last
of the steps and reached the high arched door with a knocker in the
shape of a woman's hand holding an apple. She hesitated for a time, then
rapped on it, and while she was waiting for her summons to be answered
she ran her fingers curiously over the pebbles and sea-shells embedded in
cement to form the name *High Dudgeon*. Labours of love, she reflected
wonderingly, were often extremely puzzling.

The door opened with a soft creaking of old hinges, to reveal Beth
Sinclair standing in the dark hall shadows as rigid and as arresting as an
exclamation-mark, and almost as thin.

"Hallo, Kate," she said gravely. "I thought you might come."

They said nothing to each other as they walked along the quiet, cool
hall which on either side was flanked by ferns in tubs and a jungle of
climbing begonia. When they went into the drawing-room Beth said,
"Shall I make you some tea? I have taken Arthur his barley-water, so he is
out of the way for the moment." She went across to pat the cushions and
tidy the stack of old *Scottish Fields* on the table. "He came home absolutely drunk at midday, reeking of rum, and mumbled something about
drinking damnation to the Furies. He is in a disgusting condition. And
he has the temerity to complain about his spondilitis! I am giving him
compresses. *Very hot* compresses." For a moment she stared down at the
pile of magazines. "Would you rather wait here?" she said, "or would you
come into the kitchen with me?"

"I'll come with you," said Kate listlessly. "You know about everything,
of course?" she added in a low voice.

"Yes. A dreadful business about that poor man Fegel." She compressed her withered mouth. "Suvora called on me this afternoon," she said.

"Suvora? But what——"

"He has some tormenting feeling of guilt." She led the way into the clean, big, old-fashioned kitchen. "He feels in some way responsible. He was trying to ask me what *causes* things to happen. He said he wanted to talk to me about it because he felt me to be a wise woman who would no longer be moved by the wilder passions, by those impulses which in younger people, according to him, are never quite under control." The slightest smile touched her lips, and then the pink roughened skin at her throat worked a little, as if she had swallowed the smile away like an acid-drop.

"What did he mean by that?" Kate asked.

"I don't think *he* knew. I gathered that he assumed that the intrusion on Silenos of himself and his party had caused things to happen which otherwise might not have happened. That they had, as it were, flawed the mirror . . . dropped a stone into the calm of the backwater. He seemed to want to take the blame largely upon himself. I told him it was a stupid and thoroughly conceited attitude to take. I asked him did he wish to usurp the prerogative of the gods."

She had poured her tea and taken it across to the high-backed kitchen chair, where she now sat very stiffly, holding her cup and saucer at a precise horizontal with one hand and her teaspoon in an exact vertical of reproof with the other. The combination of the chair, her thin angular limbs, the line of the saucer, the upright of the spoon, and her sharply ridged features, made Kate think of the diagrams in school text-books illustrating the Euclidean theorems. She half expected to see little numerals at Beth's armpit and the crook of her elbow saying 90°; almost found herself waiting for her to round off her statement with the unequivocal words, *Quod erat demonstrandum!*

"Beth, I know it's awful about poor Conrad," she said suddenly, bringing the words out quickly because her throat was dry and her eyes were burning, and she knew that if she did not talk she would have to cry. "I know it's . . . it's terrible and ghastly, but . . ." She stopped and moistened her lips. "But it's not . . . this isn't what I came to talk to you about."

"I know," said the old woman quietly.

"You *know!* About——"

"About David and you and the French lover. Of course, I know. I am

neither blind nor deaf, my dear. I saw it coming, and I have now heard
a number of varying accounts of the·manner of its coming. Tidings of
this sort, Kate, travel very rapidly in a place like Silenos. This is another
thing which afflicts Suvora with his sense of guilt."

"But why Suvora? He——"

"The flawing of the mirror, as I said before. I told him he was talking
a lot of arrant nonsense. People, I said, were affected on this island in
exactly the same way as they are affected anywhere else. Possibly here
you see it rather more clearly, and you certainly find out much more
quickly. So much the better. Get it over and done with. I told him that
you were three grown-up people, and that what had happened is entirely
your business—not his, or ours. In any case, I said, the thing had been
perfectly predictable for days, and now that it had come to a head you
would all have to work it out for yourselves." She sniffed. "I told him,"
she added dryly, "that the situation was not at all unusual."

"Yes." Kate nodded slowly, her head bowed over her teacup. "What
did he say?"

"Say? Nothing, of course. What could he say? Oh, yes, he went on with
his but-but-but this and but-but-but that, so I cut him very short. I told
him the affair would do both you and David the world of good. I said it
might make you look at each other for a change, instead of looking around
each other. I also said it might teach you both that it is very foolish to take
either oneself or other people for granted. How is your tea, dear? I find
the second cup has always drawn better." She came gauntly across to
take Kate's cup and turned stiffly and went over to the kettle.

"Beth, did you say all this to him, or are you only saying it to me?"
Kate asked in a low voice.

"I said it to him—and I am saying it to you," she said without turning
her back. "Not in the form of advice," she added quickly. "I never give
advice."

"Would you give me advice if I asked you?"

The old woman turned and stared at her. "No," she said, after a pause,
and the rough pink wattles at her throat worked.

"Not even if I told you that I desperately needed it?" said Kate softly.
"It's why I came, Beth. You know it is."

"My dear Kate, I have a Sibylline capacity for sitting and watching,
but unlike the Sibyls I am not prophetic, I offer no oracles, and I give no
advice. On the other hand, I have no objection to making an observation
or two." She returned to her chair and seated herself stiffly. "You will go

off, I think, with the Frenchman," she said. "That's all right. It's probably precisely what you need. An experience of that sort might do you a world of good. And David too, in the long run." She sniffed. "Rectitude as a constant diet can sometimes be as tiresome as an uninterrupted appetite for depravity. What in my younger days used to be called 'a fling' is sometimes a very beneficial thing all round."

"But. . . but what if I don't want to go off with the Frenchman?" How safe the anonymity of the term—*the Frenchman* . . . as if he were a character in a play, a puppet figure.

"That is your problem, Kate, not mine. My observations are concerned only with the more practical elements of the issue. The Frenchman is young. He has not yet graduated in the more Machiavellian practices of his sex. When you have a body like his you do not necessarily need the other more intellectual subterfuges. For a time at least I am sure you would find him a refreshing change from . . . well, from all sorts of things." She shrugged impatiently.

"David?"

"Naturally, David. *Primarily*, David, if it comes to that."

"But supposing I love him?"

"Listen to me, Kate," she said carefully. "I have no doubt whatever that your husband is at this very moment puffing himself out with moral indignation and self-righteousness. You must always remember, Kate, that puritanism was not the invention of a woman. Nor was the chastity belt. If David is left alone, and if he is given time, and if he is sufficiently frightened, it is quite possible that he will come to see that he has merely been displaying the usual stupid masculine attributes of selfishness, intolerance, self-assertion, the total inability to see another person's point of view, and, I very much suspect, that propensity for guilt-transference which men have developed into such a highly-refined skill."

"It isn't the answer to it, Beth," said Kate unhappily. She shook her head slowly. "It isn't, you know." God! how difficult it was to explain. And how tired she felt—how desperately tired! Not just a tiredness of *now*, but a tiredness that stretched right back through the years . . . the tiredness of a burden supported too long—this strange, shapeless, meaningful, heart-rending, terrible burden of home and family and purpose; this beloved burden, believed in utterly. Yet for how long was she expected to be its foundation and its prop? How long? how many years, lives, moments? Moments—yes. For a moment she had put it down, for a little breath of time she had relaxed, for a magical instant she had been young again and carefree and lost to an unburdened love . . . and it was over and done with and she would take up the burden again. If David would allow her. *If!* But had he never been involved in a magical moment? There had been Sara in London, other women, occasional women. Had they been moments of magic for him or only interludes of escape from tension and fear? Had *he* never sought the enigmatic, the unattainable, the mysterious? Was it all earth to him? Had he never tried to pluck a star? Sorrowfully she looked across the room to the old angular woman seated stiffly in her chair. "You see, Beth," she said, "you don't know David. You don't know his obstinacy. You don't know the burden *he* has to carry, the problems he has to wrestle with, the responsibilities . . . without *this* being added to it. The load might be too heavy for him now. When you are unsure——"

"I know David very well," she said quietly. "And I know you." For an interval she paused, and her face worked slightly as if she were trying to stop a smile from rising to her mouth and eyes. "Kate," she said, "has David ever talked to you about his unicorns?"

"Unicorns?" She shook her head uncertainly. "Why, yes, once he did," she murmured. "Out there on the terrace. The night of your party. The others had gone. I asked him what he was thinking about, and he said unicorns. Something fabulous, he said. Something unattainable." She looked questioningly at the old woman.

The smile touched Beth's face and vanished. "He talked to me two nights ago. At Suvora's dinner party. We were sitting together. He was looking along to the end of the table, where Erica and Suvora were sitting. And he talked to me about unicorns—the delirious, heady excitement of such a chase, with *such* a quarry. So I said to him, 'But what on earth would one *do* with a unicorn if one did catch it?' Do you know what he said? 'As if that matters,' he said. 'As if that matters.'"

"I . . . I don't understand what you mean by this."

"I mean that I think he has his private images, too—visions, dreams, things he can't share. People must have. Give him time, and he'll see that. He's not a fool, Kate. And he does love you. Do you want me to give you advice now, my dear?"

"Yes, please."

"Go to the Frenchman," she said. "Go to him. And wait."

After she had seen her to the door, Beth Sinclair waited on the porch, watching the slender, solitary figure slowly descending the steps. A faint smile hovered around her withered lips. She felt that she had done what she could. The problem now was committed to the men. The smile remained at her mouth, and her old, wise, raddled face looked almost happy as she went inside to prepare the hot compresses for Arthur.

* * *

Both brothers were pale and their eyes wary as they went together into the lamplit living-room. Mark, his tubby bulldog pipe clamped grimly between his teeth, could not help being reminded of two offended adversaries walking on to a duelling field. He strode firmly across the room to take his stand beneath the old map of Tartary, his arms folded, his legs well apart, his beard thrust out, his pipe drawing, and his eyes filled with determination.

The elder brother stance, David reflected sourly, as he went heavily across to the old leather arm-chair and seated himself tiredly. He was not finding it easy to contain either his anger or his impatience. It seemed years now since he had slept or rested—the night without sleep, the shadowy vision of the Black Vouna under the stars seemed as remote as Suzy Chinnery's lemon biscuits, or riding into Rokewood Junction behind the four sweating bays, with Rudge Midgeley cracking his long whip from the box of the coach . . . as far away as this, and as meaningless. There had been too much since then—this ghastly business with Kate, the horror of Fegel's death, the hours with the party on the cliffs, with the police, with Suvora, with almost everybody under the bloody sun! If only they didn't feel they had to *interfere!* If only they would leave him alone for half an hour, even for ten minutes, so that he could try to work things out for himself . . . try to hack his own way out of this stifling, clogging jungle of thought . . . try to banish the always-recurring sequence of horrible images that jerked behind his brain, one after the other, like mechanically operated slides—the frozen emptiness of Kate's face as she had struck him across the cheek; her mouth quivering as she had looked up at him from her folded arms; Fegel's hand moving to the stir of the sea in that sad, limp gesture of rejection; Dionysios prancing his lewd and drunken jig against a stark white wall; the soft golden tendrils of hair damply gleaming against the half-exposed body of Mouliet standing in the doorway. . . .

"I insist on making it perfectly clear that she did not come to me," Mark said gruffly, examining the bowl of his pipe with great attention as he resumed the discussion. "If you don't choose to believe me, ask her for yourself. Where is she, anyway? She should be in on this."

"How should I know where she is?" David said without interest. "There was some suggestion that she was packing her bags. Or perhaps she's still running around, tattling the bloody story all over the town."

"Or perhaps she has gone to *him*," Mark suggested darkly. "Has that thought occurred to you?" When there was no reply, he took a deep, controlled breath and said testily, "You really are the most pig-headed man, David! You won't even listen! I tell you she said nothing to anybody except old Mrs. Sinclair. She is *not* tattling the story all over the town. You do her a very great injustice by suggesting that she is. I have already explained to you that she never sought me out. I made it my business to go looking for her after Suvora told me what was happening. It was Suvora who suggested that I should. Do you know where I found her?"

"I don't know and I don't care."

"I found her quite alone on the cliffs, almost exactly at the spot where poor little Fegel tossed himself over. Suvora had said——"

"It's nothing to do with Suvora, and it's nothing to do with you!" David cut in angrily. "Why don't you all mind your own bloody business? This is a personal problem that concerns my wife and myself, and I bloody well resent it becoming a matter of common gossip all over the town!"

"Do you? But why should you? You've reminded me often enough that you can't do anything here without everybody knowing about it in ten minutes' time. Do you expect some special dispensation for your own affairs and the policy of the goldfish bowl for everybody else's?"

"I expect to be left alone to work it out for myself, that's all."

"To make a confounded great ass of yourself, you mean! God almighty, David! haven't we had enough trouble today over that poor bastard Fegel without having to get ourselves involved in *all this* as well?"

"Nobody asked you to involve yourself in *all this* as well," David retorted caustically.

Mark snorted, and began to search through his pockets for his pipe-cleaners. "You're very mistaken," he said, "if you think I'm going to allow you to mess up your whole life over one little difficulty. After all, I'm your brother. What do you expect me to do? Sit back and enjoy the fun? Remind you of the time you offered me some hindsighted advice on the way I should have treated Gwen? Stand to one side while you deliberately throw your own wife—a wife like Kate!—into the arms of a detestable, decadent little Frog who wears a bangle in his ear? You don't seem to realise that she made it pretty clear to Beth Sinclair that you'd left her with no alternative but to scoot off with him. *With him!*"

"That's for her to say, isn't it? If that's what she wants——"

"What damned chance have you given her to decide what *she* wants?" Mark tugged at his beard angrily. "You tell her you're going to sell all this up"—he jabbed his pipe irritably around the room—"go back to London, take a job, smash into fragments everything you've worked so hard to put together. Everything she believes in. Never mind about you. Everything *she* believes in. Listen, I've talked to her about this, David," he said earnestly. "I know what it means to her. And, by God! *you* know what it means to her too! So you try to frighten the wits out of her, you try to break her heart by pretending that you propose to rub the whole thing out and start all over again!"

"I'm not pretending. I *am* going back to London."

"You're out of your mind!"

"But I thought you wanted me to go back to London. I thought that was the idea. We talked about it in this very room only a little time ago, didn't we, Mark? You were so insistent, so persuasive. Now, when I agree with you, you say I'm out of my mind."

"So you are. Listen to me. You don't go back to London, or anywhere else, on those terms. You don't go back, you don't go forward, you don't go anywhere. And another thing, while we're on it—the one who will suffer most will be you. Not Kate. *You.* And shall I tell you why? Because she's got deeper dignities than you have. Her values are better. She's got more to fall back on. In the long run she has a sounder capacity for survival than you have. She actually believes in certain things that you only believe you're supposed to believe in. She's got more honesty than you have. And she's got a lot more guts." He broke off, breathing heavily, and knocked the cold pipe ash into his cupped hand as if he were hammering at a nail.

"Exactly what do you mean by all that?" David asked in a tight, low voice.

"I mean just what I say." Mark lifted his head high and looked sternly down at his brother across the spiky point of his beard. "Kate isn't a coward. And you are."

"Am I?" David straightened his long figure carefully. The smile at his mouth was twisted and without amusement. "In what way?" he asked quietly. He rose without haste and walked across to the sideboard and took down a glass and the brandy bottle. "I'm waiting for you to explain, Mark," he said patiently.

"Then put that damned drink down!" said Mark irritably. "You've had enough to drink already. You don't need any more for the moment!" David looked across at him curiously, then made an almost imperceptible gesture of obedience, and with a faint, mocking smile at his mouth returned to the leather arm-chair. The glass of brandy remained on the sideboard. "Go ahead," he said calmly.

"Certainly I'll go ahead," said Mark firmly. "Since you have brought up that earlier discussion we had in this room, you may also recall that the question of cowardice was discussed. It was the one point upon which you conceded that you had doubts. Do you still have your doubts?"

"I'm waiting for you to put *your* case."

"Unless I'm very much mistaken, you won't like it. However," he coughed and narrowed his eyes, "it shouldn't take long."

"Don't worry, I'll give you a hearing."

"I'll state it very simply. You're scared of yourself, David. Of an incompleteness in yourself, really . . . of not having *quite* come off, if you want to put it another way. You're scared of failure, too, but that's part of it, of course. And you're scared, most of all, I think, of having to admit your own weaknesses and shortcomings. What I am trying to say is that basically you're very unsure of yourself and this has made you frightened. So you want to scuttle back to cover. You want to get back in where it's warm, out of the wind and the rain. You're afraid of the dark, and you want to pull the blankets up over your face. There really isn't anything in this to be ashamed of, but you can't look at it honestly, and make an open admission of it. You aren't prepared to confess to an element of failure—although for Christ's sake! what is there to be ashamed of in having *tried* and failed?—and you aren't prepared to accept the compensation of other standards which you think are below those which you've come to believe in—or to *think* you believe in—as your own little banners of integrity. In other words, you cannot *on your own terms* scuttle back to those nice safe little prisons of security which society fits out with all modern conveniences for the not-quite people, like you and me. Are you with me to this point?" he asked, filling his pipe.

"I'm listening," said David curtly.

"Good. Because I'm coming to the real point now." He struck a match and lit his pipe, puffing the blue spirals of smoke unhurriedly from his pursed lips, holding the match above the squat thick bowl until the yellow triangle of the flame sank back into the bent blackness of the dead stick. "You see, David," he said quietly, "your real weakness is that you have to always look for causes and reasons that are outside yourself. You have to twist things around to try and find explanations that will stand as proxy for your own uncertainties. Some may be valid enough, I suppose—I'm no Freudian expert—but I'm pretty sure some are not. Nobody can be the judge of that except you. What I *do* know is that you have this obsession about patterns of things . . . as if you can pin life to a board like a set of dead butterflies. Kate told me about this business with the bloody roosters, and how you're always trying to find an excuse for *now* in something or other that happened when you were a kid way back there in Elsternwick. As I say, I'm no Freud and I'm no Jung, and I don't even pretend to be half-way to becoming a quack psychologist, but——"

"You're making a fairly brave attempt," said David dryly, and put his head back against the soft leather and closed his eyes wearily.

Mark stared at him for a moment in silence. "All right," he said evenly. "I'll cut the jargon. My advice to you then, David, is quite simple. Stop trying to find scapegoats for your own weaknesses. Stop trying to shove your little guilts off on other people, on other factors. Take the damned things on your *own* shoulders. They should be strong enough. Go back to London if that's what you want. But don't make Kate the excuse for it. Don't delude yourself, or think you can delude anybody else, by blaming it all on her . . . by crawling in under the blankets and saying that *she's* the cause of it . . . by suggesting that one trivial moment of weakness on her part has ruined your life, destroyed your hopes, forced you to go running back to the bloody herd!" His voice now was very low and quivering with real anger. "Why, you bastard, David, *you're* filled to the gills with weaknesses! Kate's the real strength in this set-up—*not you!* She's worth a hundred of you. She's——"

"That's enough!" said David tensely, and pushed himself up from the chair, his face drawn and pale with strain and anger. "You've had your little say. Now——"

"No, by God, I haven't!" Mark stormed, jabbing the air with his pipe as if he was bayoneting an army. "You sit down and listen to what I have to say! You try and think what *she's* put up with on this island. Oh, I've learned a lot about islands in these last few days. Kate's right. You see things very clearly in this light. You see yourself. You see other people. Well, you try and look at yourself, too—but take a proper look this time.

Don't try and squint around the other side of the glass. Try to understand what she's had to go through while she's been waiting for you to get to grips with yourself, while you've been looking around her to see if you can find your own shadow. And try and think what she had to put up with in London while *you* were cavorting around the town and she was stuck at home with the two kids. It's she who's made the damned thing last—not you! Don't you realise that? And don't you sit there like . . . like some complacent Grand Panjandrum telling me that my marriage went sour because I didn't take the trouble to get to know my own wife!" He took a long, deep breath, glared furiously at his brother's startled face, marched across the room, took the glass of brandy from the sideboard, and drank it down in one gulp.

"Pour one for me too," said David quietly.

"Pour one for yourself!" Mark snapped.

David made no move to rise. He was sunk deeply into the chair, his hands motionless on his thighs, his head tilted back exhaustedly against the leather, his eyes closed. In the sudden silence Mark had the sensation that everything of life had been siphoned out of the dim, lamplit room, but then he could hear the drift of little sounds from the town outside, the slow ticking of the clock in the kitchen, the scratching of a twig against the window-pane, his own heavy breathing, the thudding of his heart. From the slumped figure in the leather chair there was no sound at all. Resentfully he took another glass down from the rack and tilted the brandy bottle.

"What do you think I should do, Mark?" His brother's voice, low and toneless, drifted across to him. He turned. There was still no movement from the lean, thin-legged figure sprawling in the chair. The eyes remained closed.

"I suggest you show a bit of guts, for a change," said Mark. "Some real guts. Go out and find her. Go out there in the dark and look for her." He picked up the glass of brandy and walked heavily across to the chair. "Here's your drink!" he said crossly.

*   *   *

"But why did he do it?" said Kate again, in a voice so low that it was almost less than a whisper. "It doesn't really answer anything, does it?" She stared down beyond the rim of the stony cliff path, seeing the sea and the rocks below in two degrees of darkness, and between them the sheen of a slow-curling serpentine wraith that hissed and sucked around the ledges where the waves folded into slow foam and dipped away.

Far away across the black gulf two red beams flickered where they were burning charcoal in the mountains, and the fire ran towards them across the water in scribbly reflections.

"Oh, yes, it is an answer," said Mouliet quietly. "For some people it is an answer. Sometimes. For Fegel, I think, yes, it was an answer."

"When I came here first I had the funny feeling for a moment that it would be the answer for me, too," said Kate thoughtfully. "But then straight away I knew it wasn't . . . it couldn't be."

"No, no—for you, no. Conrad was different, and 'is case was different. Sometimes it was very painful for 'im to live. For you it is important to live . . . ah, yes, there are the people who belong to life and the people who belong to death. I, too, am of the people who 'ave to live whether it is a pleasant thing to do or a sad thing to do. And you." He was silent for a time, squatting beside her among the flints and the thistles, looking down into darkness. "No, Katherine," he said at length, "we will sit 'ere together for a little time longer, and we will talk, and then you will go back. You will 'ave to go back, Katherine. You will 'ave to go back to 'im. And I . . ." He broke off with a tiny shrug that seemed less a gesture of renunciation than of acceptance of a role already cast for him.

"Yes," she prompted softly. "And you?"

"I will go back also. I will go back to 'is 'ouse and I will tidy up for 'im very well, and put 'is things away. And then . . . well, I 'ave my own things to pack up also."

For a long time she was silent. "Do you know what I've been thinking?" she asked at last in a low pensive voice. "I've been thinking how sad poor Conrad's death was—sad in a special way, I mean. It happened, and then there was something else that got in the way of it. Us and David, I mean. There's been no time to think properly about it, really . . . well, not in the way it should have been thought about. It's suddenly subordinate to something else. It doesn't even seem dramatic any longer, because of all these other things happening. The others won't be talking about poor Conrad at all; they'll be talking about us. That's very sad, I think . . . yet, in a way, I suppose, it's like Conrad was himself, when he was alive."

"It is what I say to you. When you 'ave the problem of life you do not 'ave the time for the dead thing. It is past, finished. It is no longer the thing to take into account. Why should it be? What claim does it 'ave?"

"Just now you said the only thing that anybody has said that makes it all seem real and terrible—when you said you'd go back and tidy up his house and put his things away." For a time she was quiet, then, "You will go away?" she asked. "You *must?*"

"Of course. What else? It is 'is 'ouse, not mine. I 'ave no 'ouse anywhere. So?" Again the little shrug.

"And you wouldn't want to . . . to look around for some other place?"

"Oh, no, not now. And already I am making the arrangement to go away from 'ere. Tomorrow I think I will know about the arrangement, and then I will go."

"You don't want me to come with you, do you?" She spoke as if she was anxious to know for certain.

"But yes, of course. I *want*. But it would not do. I explain to you this, Katherine. I want, yes. But what do I give you that takes the place of all this other? I 'ave no 'ouse. No place anywhere at all. I am *le rôdeur*, the wanderer . . . it is what I choose. And what do I give you for all those years you 'ave 'ad? Eh? For the children? Me, I do not 'ave the affection for the children. I 'ave no wish for things like this . . . things that go on and on. I explain to you before, Katherine, that I 'ave not the respect for these things. It is not the music of my life to 'ave these things. And for you, Katherine, it would not do. It is not for you, the *faux ménage*. Ah, no! and even the *faux ménage* with the *rôdeur*, it will not work. It is impossible that it will work. So you must go back to your husband. And one day, it is possible, we will meet again, the two of us and we will remember this thing or"—he shrugged—"or we will not . . . and it will not matter. *Tant pis!* It will be a thing that 'appened . . . like Fegel, just a thing that 'appened."

"But it has meant something to you, hasn't it?" she asked softly. "It hasn't just been a . . . a moment of unimportance, of some trivial——"

"Ah, stop, please! Katherine, it 'as meant very much . . . ah, yes, more than I can say. But you 'ave a beautiful thing you do not pull it to pieces in your 'ands, eh? You 'ave the sunshine bottled in the old mill, where we were, you do not wish to tear down the stones to build a wall around yourself? I think, Katherine"—his strange, soft laugh, as in-turned and as secret as a private dream, throbbed for a moment in the darkness, and she had the quick thought that if she were able to see him the golden flesh at his neck would be palpitating like the throat of a singing bird— "I think you do not understand me very well, after all, eh?"

"Yes, I do. I asked the question because I wanted to know, that's all. That was why I asked if you wanted me to go away with you. Because I wanted to know that, too. But I wouldn't go away with you. You know that, don't you? I want to go back to my husband, to David. I haven't wanted anything else. Well, it isn't even going back, really . . . because I haven't ever been away from him, I don't think. If he wants me to go back . . ." Her soft voice trailed into silence.

"Ah, 'e will want, of course. You are a good woman, Katherine . . . a true woman. Yes, 'e will want."

"Good? True?" She stared down into the sighing darkness of the sea. "And weak, too," she murmured. "And faithless, and deceitful, and selfish."

"You are a true woman," he insisted softly. "It is the privilege for my 'appiness that you are this way. It is very infrequent that *le rôdeur* he encounters the true woman." He fell into silence for a time, and then, "I would like very much to kiss you now, Katherine," he said reflectively. "Yes, very much. And I can kiss you now and nothing else will 'appen."

"Yes," she whispered, and moved towards him.

He kissed her very gently, and for a moment his fingers stroked softly down her hair and her cheek, and then he lifted his face and said, "*Au revoir.*"

She did not reply.

It was a long time, in fact, before either of them spoke, and then it was Mouliet who said in a quiet voice, "Your 'usband is coming for you now. 'E is looking for you. I see 'im up there on the rise—there, where the light is on the cliff above the path."

She turned, and for a moment saw the tall, thin, slightly stooping figure silhouetted in the pool of light that spilt down from the yellow rocks. His shadow jerked for a moment on a boulder at the side of the path nearest the sea and skidded down the face of stone, and then was lost in the blackness.

"If you like," said Mouliet, "I will wait 'ere with you until 'e comes. I am not afraid to 'ave the talk with 'im if this——"

"No," she said gently. "It wouldn't help. I think it's best for you to go. I'd rather see him alone. I'd rather be here by myself when he comes."

"Yes," he said. "It is best, I think."

She could hear him moving off, the dry crunching of the weeds and prickles beneath his bare feet, the scattering whisper of the flints, a pebble rolling—tiny sounds emptying into darkness.

When David came she was sitting where he had left her, still staring down into the sibilant stirring of the dark sea.

"Hallo, Kate," he said quietly. "Mark told me where I'd find you. I've come to fetch you."

"Yes," she whispered. She looked up at the tall, shadowy figure standing on the path, and she tried to form some words but the tears that filled her eyes seemed to flood chokingly into her throat, and she could not shape the thing that she had to say.

"Come on, darling," he said gently. "Don't say anything. Don't try. Just come back with me, that's all. You don't have to say anything, darling . . . you don't have to say anything at all. Just let me take you home."

9

` THE JOURNEYS

"WELL!" said Mark, mopping his forehead with the crimson handkerchief he had bought at a waterfront shop. "One way and another it's been quite a morning!" He folded the handkerchief into four and began to dab with it at his beard.

The white stern of the island steamer was sliding away behind the rocky red headland, with a blue-and-white striped flag set square in the wind as if it was cut from painted cardboard. A thinning twang of radio music drifted back to them, then faded away under the slapping flurry of the disturbed water running towards them like an inverted V. It came right in to suck at the weedy harbour walls and all the coloured caïques kicked wildly at their moorings.

Mark patted at his damp beard and thought of the events of the morning. It had begun with the sad pilgrimage of Fegel's funeral winding up the rocky path to the little cemetery, where thin and silent cypresses stood like sentinels around the sun-washed walls. The tilted crosses on the ridge had looked like little white wedges set there for the sole purpose of fastening the blue of the sky to the deeper ultramarine of the sea. A sad, small cortège with nothing much to say . . . yet oddly peaceful in a way, an interlude of tranquillity, and a serene ending for a troubled man. David must have felt this too, perhaps felt it very deeply, for as they had left the graveyard together he had stopped on the crest of the ridge and looked out across the blue and silver glitter of the gulf, and, remembering China and that ancient geomancy of death and life that calls for the happy graves to lie between wind and water, he had murmured, "*Fengshui*—yes, he has that, at any rate." And then they had come down in silence to the bustle and confusion of the port.

And once again a sequence of happenings had rushed across, so that already the reality of Fegel's funeral had become blurred, faded, remote, its meaning lost in a maddened human activity, in a whirl of faces, a struggling dance of figures in progress, a bedlam of whistles, of bells, of clanging, of oiled wheels turning, of journeys beginning, of a ship sailing out, of shouting voices and the churn of water. And now even the ship was far away already, no more than a white speck in the deep Ægean blue, dwindling away, receding out of space and time, moving them off to their further destinies. For him, too, in another day or so. . . .

Mark sighed as he turned to Kate. "Funny to think they're gone," he said, and flicked his fingers. "Just like that. Gone!" He fumbled for his pipe. "It's quite possible we'll never see any one of them again."

"You'll have to see Janecek, won't you? If he's still working with you."

"I don't think he will be. Not when he gets back to Venice, among his own crowd. From that distance he'll see me as something pretty cheap-jack, pretty trumpery really. Well," he made a grimace, "it was always Suvora he was interested in, anyway. Not me so much. He could have made good use of Suvora." He lit his pipe and flicked the match away and said, "Kettering's the one I'm damned sorry for. Poor little devil!" He could still see him, red-faced and breathless among the jostling crowds and the spear-fishing guns and the underwater masks and the straw tourist hats, struggling with the baggage as he had always done, a fold of steamer tickets clenched between his teeth, his monocle dangling, all his revolutionary ardour staunched; following the cool command, the beckoning finger, the composed authority of his master . . . a miserable, flustered little figure too self-wounded and embarrassed even to make farewells.

"Yes, I'm sorry for him too," said Kate. "But it's his own choice, isn't it? I mean, it's what he wants."

"Is it? I don't know. Do we ever have our own choice really? Aren't we all slaves to the tyranny of some demand or other? Sometimes it's outside us, and visible and cruel, like Janecek. And sometimes it's there lurking inside us . . . part of ourselves really. But just as demanding. Just as terrible. Mixed up with so many other things that sometimes we don't know it's there at all until it jumps out and bites us. Listen to Mark Meredith, that old island philosopher!" he said, and grinned at her.

"Clothilde too?" Kate smiled. "Does she have a demon?"

"Well, if she hasn't one now I'm darned certain there'll come a day when she will have. Maybe not too far off in the future, either. In the meantime"—he paused to clear his throat—"she can make do with your friend Mouliet. Kate," he said with gentle seriousness, "you were lucky to get out of that, you know. Very lucky."

"What do you mean?"

"One day you, and the next day *au revoir* and off with dear Clothilde. The rosy pathway. The light fantastic. He'd have led *you* a dance!"

"*Le rôdeur,*" she said evenly. "That's all right."

"What do you mean, that's all right?"

"I mean it's the way he operates. It's his demon. It may even be a nicer one than ours. He wasn't a hypocrite. He didn't try to make it seem different from what it was."

"Oh, come now, Kate, do you think he'd have gone with her if Suvora hadn't paid her off, made the settlement, given her that apartment he kept for her on the Quai d'Orléans? Can't you see them both there, bouncing out of bed, looking across to Notre Dame, dashing over the river to the Boul' Mich' to show off their suntans?"

"I don't blame him. I don't blame him at all. She'll be part of his journey. That's what I said. *Le rôdeur.* He has a different music in his life. He told me that."

"That's only his line." Mark pursed his lips in disapproval.

"Perhaps. It's silly to look for reasons, though, because they're all tangled up together. The reason why Suvora sent Clothilde away is because he wants to marry Erica Barrington."

"He wants to *what!*"

"Oh, not yet, I think. He hasn't asked her. But he talked to Beth about it. He'll ask her to go cruising with him, I expect. They'd suit each other, I think, don't you? They seem to have both come to a point where they move in a sort of harmony with whatever surrounds them. At any rate, Beth approves—so I suppose that practically clinches it!" She looked across at him with a faint smile twitching her mouth. "Beth told him," she said, "that she was sick to death of people making messes, of *men* making messes, to be more explicit."

Mark grunted, and said, "Yes, well, that's something that remains to be seen, surely. *Cherchez la femme,* eh? It began with Eve, after all." He looked at her awkwardly, conscious that he was on difficult ground, fumbled with his pipe, then said, "Well, they've gone, anyway, so that's that. What do you want to do now?"

"I don't know," she said uncertainly. "What do you?"

"I want a drink," he said firmly. "Beer, I think. Unless you want to go up there with the others?" He offered her the alternative with some diffidence, and he was relieved when she shook her head quickly.

"No," she said. "Let them talk it out. We can leave them for a while. Come on. We'll go to that little tavern next to the sailmaker's loft, the place I took you to the night Mavro said you could have the house. Remember? We can still see the boat from there."

He nodded and stared across the sparkling jump of harbour waters to where the *Twelve Apostles* had moved out on a longer warp-line. There were several figures on the deck, and three dinghies alongside.

In the tavern two bare-footed fishermen were playing *tavli*. The scarred cat slept on the pile of discs beside the old phonograph with the long black horn painted with cupids and chrysanthemums. A drying octopus dangled from the rafters.

"Do you know, I'm really going to miss this!" There was a note of wistful surprise in Mark's voice as he looked around the shabby little room, listening to the chink of the beer bottles, the rattle of dice, the clatter of the pieces in the *tavli* box. "London won't be the same at all!"

"But you don't have to go, you know, Mark," she said. "Nothing has really changed. The house is there. The rent is paid. Or, if you'd rather, you can come and stay with us. You can go on with your play. That's what you came for. You don't have to go back just because he's gone."

"Ah, but I do, Kate. Not because of Janecek, though. Oh, no! His going would make me all the keener on staying. But that isn't the thing."

"What is the thing?"

"This place. Your island." He fingered his beard thoughtfully. "No, this is the nigger in the woodpile, Kate." He nodded to himself. "I like your island," he went on pensively. "I've grown very fond of it. I love that house up there. I do, you know. But the whole place simply scares me stiff! Scares the living daylights out of me! No, no, no—it's a very nice place, Silenos, but it just isn't for me. Not for me!" He shook his head firmly.

"But why?"

"I told you why. It scares me."

"Yes, but in what way?" she insisted.

"Well, too much light for one thing—too much glare, too much beauty, too much time. Almost indecent exposure, in a way. On the negative side, not enough cushions—it was you, remember, who spoke to me about

the cushions?—no air-locks, no neat little escape chambers, no tranquil-
izers. Far too many opportunities to come charging around a corner and
run slap-bang into yourself. Well, not even anything as simple as that.
Worse! To see right through yourself! Oh, no, that's not a nice thing,
Kate, not at my age, not at my time of life, to be able to see right through
yourself! All that straw stuffing showing! Or maybe even nothing there
at all—just an empty space between a bowler hat and a white collar, like
Wells's Invisible Man! Heavens! No, Kate . . . if I stayed here two more
months I'd never write another play in my life!"

She laughed softly. "You're only paraphrasing what I said to you," she
chided. "But you make it sound so . . . so dreadful." Her finger traced
along the crack in the deal table, circled a knothole, rubbed gently at the
roughness of the surrounding grain. "What about David?" she asked,
without raising her eyes. "What about him? Do you still think he should
run away from it too?"

"That's not for us to say, is it?" he said soberly. "That's up to him.
Although . . ." he broke off and turned his head away and stared out
through the narrow window—"no, I don't think he should," he said
quietly. "Not now. I think he's looked at himself. I think he's seen what
there is to see. I imagine he's past the point now of having to run away
from it. He's lucky, really." His eyes were sad as he watched the slow
swing of the masts against the sky. "Do you know," he went on reflectively, "it's exactly what he was trying to explain to me the day I
came . . . this business of crossing the line-of-no-return. In fact, he *hadn't*
crossed it then. He thought he had, but he hadn't. He has now, I think.
He's lucky." He turned to her with a careful solicitude. "Kate, it *is* all
right now with him, isn't it?" he asked anxiously.

"Yes. It's all right." Her finger traced the resinous smear of grain to
the edge of the table. "Thank you for what you did, Mark. It's all right
now. Really it is."

"And you?"

"Yes. Me too. It's all right."

"Kate!" Again he cleared his throat awkwardly. "Kate, I suppose this
will be just about our last chance to have a talk together . . . this sort
of talk, I mean. I . . . I just want you to know that I . . . well, that I
love him very much. Oh, I admit his failings, his weaknesses. He's
obstinate. He's a damned sight too self-absorbed. He operates according
to some twisty logic of his own. He's got some crazy ideas. But I do love

him, you see, and I want it to work for him. For you, too, of course. I love
you too, Kate. And I know you're both committed . . . not only to each
other, but to all this as well"—he gestured towards the open door—"but I
want it to work not because you're trapped in some sort of mutual self-
committal, but because . . . well . . ."—he waved his hands helplessly—
"well, you know what I'm trying to say, don't you?"

"You mean you're still worried about Achille?" she asked in a low
voice, her eyes still bent to the slow movement of her finger.

"Yes," Mark said gruffly.

"That's all right too," she said quietly. "David asked me if I wanted to
go and say good-bye to him, but I said I didn't . . . well, not in that way.
And that was true, Mark. I didn't want to. I'd said good-bye to him."
She was silent for a long interval, and then she looked up at him. "Mark,
why did it happen?" she said.

"What do you mean?" he countered awkwardly.

"Just that. Why? Up there at the cemetery this morning I was trying
to work it out. There you are, you see, it's sad again . . . standing there
beside the grave, with a bunch of rosemary in my hand to throw on to
poor Conrad's coffin, and not really thinking about *him* at all . . . just
thinking about myself and David and Achille and why . . ." Again she
was silent, and the finger which for a minute had been still began again
slowly to trace the darker convolutions in the wood.

"Now you're beginning to sound exactly like all the rest of them!" He
cut into her silence impatiently. "Looking for patterns in everything!
Explanations! Reasons! There's David talking about chain-reactions.
There's Suvora feeling guilty because he thinks he can be responsible for
these strange, flicking nervous charges that run from person to person.
For heaven's sake, Kate, there are other things that move us too! Things
we don't even begin to understand! Compulsions! The wash of other
currents that knock us this way and that! Accidents . . ."

"Yes." She nodded thoughtfully. "It *was* a compulsion . . . but you
see, Mark, it *wasn't* a thing I didn't understand. For a moment I understood it absolutely . . . it was something that shone so brightly, so clearly.
And now . . . I don't know any longer. I'm not sure . . ."

"As long as you're sure of yourself now, that's all."

"But I was sure of myself then. That didn't come into it, really." She
paused, searching in her thoughts for something of honesty that would be
valid to the case, but she found only a glimmer of the truth, and she
said, "You know, I think in all of us there is a part of ourselves that is

always lost . . . or unawakened perhaps. If we don't find it, or don't waken it—or don't have it awakened for us, rather—then I suppose we're always incomplete. It's as if we had some little secret chamber inside ourselves that sometimes is opened for us . . . by something or by somebody that is quite outside our experience. And when that is done we can close the chamber again and we're really the better for it." She stopped and lowered her eyes. She desperately wanted to be honest with him, but she knew that there was a point beyond which explanation to another was not possible. She was aware that Achille Mouliet no longer mattered, but equally she was aware that in some way he had enriched her life, rekindled it: she no more than sensed that the enrichment was a thing of such privacy that it could be symbolised not by her physical capitulation to his animality in the ruined mill—which, paradoxically, was the presumably moral aspect of the situation—but only in the spiritual sense of an uncommunicated belonging which had flowed between them on the night when they had swum together in the phosphorescent sea. The secret chamber had been opened, and looked into, and locked again—and she had gone back to David. And in some queer, inexplicable, disturbing way they were both the better for it. "I remember reading somewhere," she said musingly, "—it was a quotation, I think—that we live the first part of our lives with the dead, the second with the living, the last part with ourselves. I think if we've been allowed to look into that little private chamber of ourselves then we're better able to get through that last part."

"Yes, well that's getting into deep water, isn't it?" said Mark uncertainly. He was not at all sure that he had followed the drift of her observations. "So far as I'm concerned, of course, I'm entirely on old Bluebeard's side," he offered, making it quite clear that he had not followed. "Don't open doors you're not supposed to peek into. That's my motto. And, I should add, I don't believe in swimming out beyond my depth."

"You *have* to swim out beyond your depth," said Kate. "Or cross that line-of-no-return you were talking about. It's the same thing, isn't it? I suppose it is more dangerous, yes. But it's braver. And there isn't any other place where the freed spirit can live."

"Oh, Kate, you do exasperate me!" said Mark crossly. "You're becoming exactly like that damned husband of yours! Let's go and find the others, for God's sake!"

*   *   *

"One learns," said Suvora quietly. "One learns a lot of things—and some of them in a queer way."

He and David were seated side by side on the coping of the mole, their legs dangling over the harbour waters, their eyes only absently concerned with the activity aboard the *Twelve Apostles*.

"Only if one is prepared to, I suppose," said David.

"No, in spite of oneself, I think. From the accidents of impingement, too. From the unexpected. I've learnt a lot since I came to this island. From all of you. Important things, in a way. I think mostly I've learnt from him, though." His warm brown eyes looked out towards the pink-and-yellow caïque.

"Him? Andreas, you mean?"

"Yes. Do you know that even this morning, when I heard that he was going, I had half a mind to call and see Vlikos the banker about it."

"What for?"

"To make other arrangements. It would not have been at all difficult to have taken over the bank's underwriting of the cruise—to purchase the mortgage, as it were—and put the man and his boat under my own charter. An experimental cruise. Philanthropic, if you like."

"It isn't what *I* like. It's what *he* would like."

"Exactly. That is what I said—one learns." Suvora nodded slowly. "What do you think?" he asked after a time. "Can he make any sort of show of it with what he has? Being so shorthanded, I mean."

"With ten men?" David pursed his lips. "Well, who can say? But the point is, he does have to try, doesn't he? Pride comes into it. And there is always a chance, of course. I admit it doesn't seem much of a one, but still . . ." He shrugged. "He'll still get something out of it, though . . . something of self-respect, I suppose. After all, he is taking his boat to sea again. He's in command of his own fate. He's out of the harbour. He's making his voyage. He's free. There'll be that one moment when he steers her round the breakwater which they won't ever be able to take away from him. That's important, too. The moments of true belief aren't all that common."

"You have learnt a lot from him, too, haven't you?" Suvora glanced at him.

"Oh, yes." David nodded. "Oh, yes," he repeated the words softly. "That's what you said. One learns a lot of things." Strength, courage, acceptance, endurance—these were the eternal verities of a human dignity. And you had to build them with the materials that were at hand, because they could never be woven from the stuff of dreams: you had to make your journey with whatever crew, whatever provisions you could get. The importance was in the journey, in the sailing out and the sailing on, in the grip of your own hand on the tiller, in the line of that far horizon ruled on the retina of your own eyes. He could see now how deeply the sponge-boat captain had impressed his symbolism upon him, could understand that odd sense of communion he had always had for him. Yet Captain Andreas, within that secret, uncommunicative mind, must also have suffered his thoughts of fear and failure, even if he had not expressed them . . . must have seen his pride and his belief in himself shaken like a leaf in the wind. But the essence of fear and the essence of failure were not contained in the moment of true belief. They could not exist there. He recalled how one day he had thought of himself as Philoctetes, as the man left on Lemnos. Out of his despair and his self-pity it had seemed so valid then—the call to go back, to re-engage, and what was involved in it . . . the reasons behind the call, the validities as well as the falsities . . . the things that would have to be forgotten if one were to heed the call, the whole question of the values involved. The wound that would never heal set against the bow that could never fail. How complicated the story, and how challenging. Yet Captain Andreas would never see it this way at all. He would see it as something perfectly simple, because he didn't have symbols. To him, Philoctetes would go back simply because he was wanted, because there was a job for him to do. . . .

"Your wife is coming now," Suvora said quietly. "With your brother."

David nodded. He and Kate had built something. He could see that now. They had built something that was better than either of them had realised, and they had built it with the things that were to hand, here, now . . . with the materials available. All right, the talent of David Meredith might not be as great as he might wish it to be, nor his marriage as romantic, nor his island as idyllic . . . but he had brought off his own stand for the right to hold the tiller in his own hand, and, by God! this was something. This was something they could not take away from him, and would never take away from him. Since they were committed to the journey, then they would sail this way . . . and perhaps, as Erica Barrington had said, he would find what he was seeking and recognise it when he found it. And there was another thing she had said: "We have a sort of purpose that we have to try to fulfil."

The *Twelve Apostles*, which had seemed to poise for a moment with
the curved, upswinging prow static above the inverted pattern of the
suspended anchor, began slowly to move forward to the steady, throbbing
beat of the exhaust—"They're going," said Suvora, almost in an undertone—then turned a little away from them and began to cut a dark,
smooth arc across the still green of the harbour waters. A man on the fore-
deck was bent over the chains. Two men amidships were hauling in the
old automobile tires that were used as fenders. A small group of men
were clustered along the weather-cloth. At the stern there was only
Captain Andreas, a dark, stocky figure reaching forward to the engine
throttle, his thick legs straddling the tiller.

David knew that Kate had come up with them, and without looking
at her he reached for her hand and pulled her down to sit beside him.
They said nothing to each other as they watched the boat clear the caïque
moorings and straighten on its course, up to the end of the mole and
past the light-beacon, and Andreas had lifted his head high so that he
could see above the carved cap of the stempost.

"Perhaps we complicate ourselves too much," said Suvora softly. "Perhaps we do, you know."

David pressed his wife's hand, and turned to look at her, and he saw
that her eyes were wet and her lips trembling. It was a queer thing, he
reflected with a tightening dryness in his own throat, that this was
something he could never really know about her now—this quiet enclave
of her own, private and secret, which so long as he lived he might never
invade. And yet—he squeezed her hand more tightly—he knew that it
was also something that didn't matter any longer.

The *Twelve Apostles* made the last turn around the buoy, and its bow
was lifting and falling now in a slow, graceful dance to the run of the
clear gulf seas.

It was already almost past the slaughterhouse, where Costas the butcher
was too preoccupied with the leg-roping of a fawn-coloured steer to even
look at it; and the wake left by the boat had come in and slapped quick
waves around the base of the rock chute, where Dionysios had been
emptying the garbage brought down from the high houses in the pannier-
baskets of his donkeys. Normally the flurry of the waves would have
attracted the old man's attention, and he would have looked up to see
the cause of it. But he did not even notice the agitation of the waves
nor see the *Twelve Apostles* riding out to sea. For in his gnarled and

shaking fingers he clutched the five one-hundred-dollar bills which he
had found crumpled with some paper among the rubbish, and his eyes
were blinded by his tears, and his brain tried to grapple with the wonder
of this great good fortune that God had sent him.

THE END